HIGH PR
THE WIDE GAME

"Michael West proves himself to be a masterful storyteller, flawless in building momentum, and his skills in characterization match or even often surpass some of the most successful writers in the business. This is a first-rate novel, well edited and no holds barred. My jaw dropped, quite literally, at more than a handful of turning points in the story that I just didn't see coming, and I oftentimes couldn't put the book down. I know that's a pretty cliché phrase, but coming from me......well, that sort of intense preoccupation just doesn't occur too often. This is a work of first-rate terror and suspense, and for the seasoned reader sports a refreshingly original story methodology as a means to scare the wits out of you. This is his first novel, and I'll be watching the career of Michael West with sincere interest in his works to come. And I'll never look at corn fields the same way again."
~Nicholas Grabowsky, author of *Halloween 4: the Return of Michael Myers*, and *The Everborn*

"This thing is scary as hell! Creepy, creepy book."
~Cody Stark, *"Read This!" FOX-TV*

"Just when you think it will be predictable, BAM, it's not. Lots of twists and turns made this story stick and kept me turning the pages. If you like Koontz, then you will like this story too."
~Skullring.org

"4.5 out of 5...Don't open the cover unless you want to be sucked into a tornado of horror. Once you start in on this novel you won't be able to pull away...A believable, dark, nasty piece. Just remember the name Michael West because he has a future in the horror genre."
~**Brian Yount,** *Wicked Karnival Magazine*

"4.5 out of 5 stars...*The Wide Game* got me right in the fear center of my lizard brain."
~*Horror Web*

"*The Wide Game*...is a book written for horror movie fans. Michael West draws the reader in with a director's touch. With a deft hand, West creates wonderful characters who live and breathe on the page. It was easy for me to allow Michael to lure me into those terror filled rows and make me cringe at what might lurk there in the dark. Michael West has...undeniable potential to be an important voice in the realm of horror fiction."
~**Bob Freeman, author of** *Cairnwood Manor*

"Thrilling, exhilarating, fast-paced and ferocious, *The Wide Game* delivers the goods. It's *The Breakfast Club* meets *The Blair Witch Project*. It still haunts me!"
~**Marc Morriston,** *WTTV Indianapolis*

"I breezed through this book in no time. And I can't say enough about how real the relationship at the core of the story was. (Michael West is) definitely one to keep an eye on."
~**Maurice Broaddus, author of** *King Maker*

THE WIDE GAME

Michael West

Graveside Tales

THE WIDE GAME

Published by Graveside Tales

All rights reserved. No part of this book may be used or reproduced in any manner whatsoever without written permission except in the case of brief quotations embodied in critical articles and reviews. For information address:

Graveside Tales, P.O. Box
487 Lakeside, AZ 85929, USA
www.gravesidetales.com

This is a work of fiction. Names, characters, and incidents are used fictitiously, and any resemblance to actual persons, living or dead, or events is entirely coincidental.

Copyright © 2011 Michael West
www.bymichaelwest.com

Cover Art © 2011 Bob Freeman

"The Temptation of St. Anthony" engraving by Martin Schöngauer c. 1480-90

FIRST EDITION
ISBN: 978-0-9833141-0-3

For the Class of 1988,
This stroll down a dark and twisted memory lane.

ACKNOWLEDGMENTS

Thanks to: my family, especially my wife, Stephanie, for their never-ending love and support; Myrrym Davies, Dale Murphy, and the entire staff at Graveside Tales for making this possible; Bob Freeman for his always amazing artwork; Nikki Howard, Ericka Barker, and Meg Banta for their inspiration, and, most of all, their continued friendship; my pre-readers: Dione Ashwill, Sara Larson, David Lichty, Marc Morriston, Natalie Phillips, Ryan Tungate, and Chris Vygmont, for critiquing draft, after draft, after draft; all the Indiana Horror Writers; and, of course, my faithful readers everywhere.

And thanks to the following individuals for their guidance and their support, both personally and professionally: Julie Astrike, Clive Barker, Louise Bohmer, Maurice Broaddus, Gary A. Braunbeck, Tim Deal, Kitsie Duncan, Fran Friel, J.F. Gonzalez, Jerry Gordon, Bill Hardy, Kyle Johnson, Brian Keene, Michael Knost, Alethea Kontis, Debbie Kuhn, Michael Laimo, Tim Lebbon, Tom Moran, Kelli Owen, Rex Scott, Katrina Shobe, Jason Sizemore, Lucy Snyder, Brenda Taggart, Douglas F. Warrick, Wrath James White, Rhonda Wilson, Nora Withrow, and Brian Yount.

Quos deus vult perdere prius dementat:
Those whom a god wishes to destroy, he first drives insane.

THE WIDE GAME

PROLOGUE

Ten years had passed since the murders, and, like most who still made their home in Harmony, Father Andrew Chapman thought the nightmare was over.

The old priest stepped from his vestry into the evening dimness of Saint Anthony's Catholic Church, his mind preoccupied with far more recent sins. *The Harmony Herald* was tucked beneath his arm, filled to the brim with lurid tales of sex in the White House. He gave his pulpit a casual glance, pictured tomorrow morning's sermon, and sighed heavily. How in the hell was he supposed to stand up there and preach God's commandments when the leader of the free world had broken half of them?

He turned his attention to the rest of the building, wondering where the next catastrophe would choose to manifest. At sixty, the church was almost as old as its priest, and twice as temperamental. On Father Andrew's desk in the rectory, a repair list a mile long gathered dust. After all, Harmony was a small Indiana farming town, and there was only so much his parishioners could give. He shook his head and hoped tomorrow morning's masses would enjoy air conditioning, a roof that wasn't leaking, and a sound system that was in working order. It was a rare day when everything ran to spec.

Behind the altar, a bronze Jesus hung from His bronze cross, weeping bronze tears. Father Andrew genuflected before Him, then rose and gave the newspaper a final study. Just below Mr. Clinton's sexploits was an article on the local high school, on the Class of 1988 and their ten-year reunion. *God loves the small towns*, he thought as he turned away, a smile dawning on his weathered lips. Only in a one stoplight town like Harmony could a high school reunion and the President of the United States share ink on the same front page, unless of course the President had attended said high school.

The door to the vestibule blew open; humid August air flooded the tabernacle. Flames danced around the painted feet of a Madonna statue—candles parishioners had lit in remembrance of the dead.

Father Andrew whirled around and moved down the long center aisle toward the entrance. Heavy brass spindles formed door handles; he grabbed them and looked out into the night. No one looked back. *Must be a storm coming.* He started to pull the doors shut, then something near the threshold caught his eye.

A crow.

The bird laid on its back, staring up at the priest with eyes as glassy as sable marbles. Its beak hung open and mute, its wings unfurled and still. Someone had slashed up its belly; its newly freed entrails uncoiled onto the concrete steps below.

Damn vandals.

Last Good Friday, kids had marred St. Anthony's walls with spray-paint, scrawling red pentagrams and "666" across the pure white boards. The bastards even hurled a rock through a stained glass window depicting the Lord's Passion. Father Andrew ran an aged hand down his haggard face. There was a time, still sharp and bright in his memory, when the fear of God would have stopped young people from defiling sacred buildings, but that time had passed. Now God Almighty was something people thought they *might* believe in, and the

Devil? Well, there was *no* Devil. Didn't you know? He's an invention, a Judeo-Christian bogeyman, created to scare children into saying their prayers before bed. The concept of sin was outdated as well, something for a dead world. It didn't apply to the lives of modern men and women.

Over the years, Father Andrew had counseled couples seeking to be married in his church, and he often saw that the bride and groom had listed the same address under residence.

"You're living together," he would say with distaste.

"Sure we are," they would answer. "Is anything wrong with that?"

"Well...The Bible calls it fornication," Father Andrew would say to their surprise, then think: *And in the time of Our Lord, you'd be taken out in the street and stoned to death.*

Yes, Father Andrew was what the kids would call "Old School," and proud of it. A sin in the time of Christ was the same sin today; there was just a whole lot more of it to go around. There was a Devil, just as there was a Hell, just as there was a Heaven, and just as certainly as there was a one true God and His son, Jesus Christ. It was a package deal. If you believed in one, you had to accept the others.

"Amen," the old priest said aloud, then turned back toward the vestry, toward the broom and dustpan he kept there. His booming voice echoed through the empty house of worship, the same powerful voice that kept parishioners awake for his sermons. The breeze from the open door had blown out the candles, throwing much of the interior into darkness.

A blur of movement in the corner of the priest's eye; a dark shape rose swiftly from between the pews. The figure seized Father Andrew, curled its left arm around his chest, and held something up to his throat. He only saw it for an instant, but he knew it was a knife...a knife covered in blood. The attacker's hands were red and sleek with it.

"*Bless me, Father,*" a voice cried into his ear. It was so panicky, so shrill, he couldn't tell if it belonged to a man or a woman. "*Bless me, for I have sinned.*"

When he was in the seminary, Father Andrew would lay awake at night thinking about the sanctity of the confessional. What you were told in confession stayed in confession. End of story. If you slid the wooden panel back and saw Jack the Ripper or Charles Manson screaming murder, you tried to get them to turn themselves in, but you couldn't expose them—not to the police, not to the families of their victims, not to anyone at all. Although he had thought about this quite a bit in the forty years that followed, he'd never been confronted with a murderer, nor had he been held hostage at knifepoint.

You had to love St. Anthony's—every day held some new surprise.

"Please..." *My son? My child?* You? "...Put down the knife and we can talk about this."

"*I can't do that, Father.*" The bloodstained knife shook with each word. "*They're coming. They're coming for me and I need forgiveness.*"

The police? Father Andrew wondered, but before he could utter a word his captor screamed again.

"*I'm so sorry! Christ...Jesus...Please, Father, I need forgiveness for my sins!*"

"All right," he found himself saying. "Please, stay calm." He looked at the knife, at the blood. There was so much blood. "I'll hear your confession."

"Thank you, father," the figure muttered, a shaky voice choked by tears.

Now that it had lowered an octave, Father Andrew thought the voice sounded familiar, but he still couldn't say for sure who it was. He attempted to make the sign of the cross with his right hand, but his attacker's hold made it difficult.

"In the name of the Father, and of the Son, and of the Holy Spirit. Amen. May God, who brightens every heart, help you to know your sins and trust in His mercy." Father Andrew swallowed, his Adam's apple touching the wet edge of the blade. "What are the sins you wish to confess to God?"

"Father Andrew," the voice behind the knife said, "have you ever heard of the Wide Game?"

"Yes," the old priest replied. It was not a subject he wished to discuss, but he knew of it. Live any length of time in Harmony and you couldn't help but hear of it—hear what happened the last time a group of kids had played. What Father Andrew didn't know (and what his attacker had only just discovered) was that the game had not ended with the murders of ten years ago.

The game had not ended at all.

Part One:
Playing the Game

ONE

The fall of 1987 left a wound on Paul Rice's brain that would not heal. The memory of it would begin to fade, to permit some sense of normality to regrow, then something as innocent as a song on the radio would scrape the forming scab, allowing it to bleed into his thoughts once more. Though he was a man of twenty-seven, his pale blue eyes appeared older, and gray had banished much of the brown in his hair. He was tall, but had gained enough weight in the past decade that he was no longer a "bean pole," and, beneath his Planet Hollywood Indianapolis T-shirt, his back bore burn scars from the day he rolled his Mustang. He now drove a green '97 Jeep Cherokee, which he halted in front of his mother's house—the house where he grew up. His eyes drifted to the second story window, *his* window, and he found he was sweating.

He turned off the motor and swallowed. "We're here."

"Mamma's!" Christopher screamed from the back.

Paul looked in the rearview mirror. His son, asleep for much of the two-hour trip from Indianapolis to Harmony, was wide-awake now and clapping wildly in his car seat. At three, few things thrilled him more than a trip to Grandma's house.

Megan, the newest member of his family, still slumbered beneath the Baby Looney Tunes blanket of her own car seat. She had also been lulled to sleep by the motion of the Jeep, and she smiled into her fist. Paul often watched her, wondering what she dreamt. At two months old, she knew little of the world. He envied her.

"You ready?"

Paul turned his attention to the passenger's seat, to Mary, his wife. She wore overalls and a white, short-sleeved shirt that exposed her freckled arms. Her freshly permed hair formed a blonde mane around her tanned face, and even though her eyes—a deeper blue than his own—lay hidden behind sunglasses, Paul could still see the concern they held for him.

He nodded, emotion making him hoarse as he spoke. "Yeah. I'll grab Megan and the diaper bag."

As Paul opened the door, Mary reached over to lay her hand on his and squeeze it. He looked back at her, and she flashed him a grin. In reply, he offered her the best smile he could muster, and stepped from the Jeep into the muggy August afternoon. Paul tilted the handle on Megan's seat until he heard it click, then lifted it from the base. He slid the carrier over his arm, grabbed the diaper bag, and slammed the door before following Mary and Chris around to the concrete steps.

It was a large house. Cedar siding covered its walls and the shingled roof of the porch encircled it like a skirt. It had a full, unfinished basement, four large rooms on the first floor, four slightly smaller ones on the second, and an acre of lush green lawn that ended...ended at the corn.

Harmony was an island in a sea of corn. Christened by a handful of Catholic settlers in 1816, it was now home to thirteen thousand souls; men, women, and children, adrift between the shores of Indianapolis to the South and Chicago to the North. Weathered wooden barns and farmhouses made it reality, lining gravel and dirt roads that cut through the green fields like the veins of a leaf. The bustling downtown had Mahoney's

Marathon gas station to the east, and the limestone and marble of Town Hall to the west. Local businesses filled in the rest, and a stoplight swung in the wind halfway between. Nature baked it in summer, drowned it in spring and fall, and buried it beneath snow and ice in winter. But despite all of that, or because of it, the land thrived.

Paul had been to his mother's house the week Megan was born, a proud father showing off how well he could spawn, but the crop had been in its own infancy then. Now, as they used to say, the stalks were as high as an elephant's eye and a stone apart. They moved and swayed in the breeze, blades of grass in a giant's lawn, beckoning him to enter into their embrace.

All reports, in fact, predicted this to be the best crop of corn in ten years.

Mary's hand touched Paul's shoulder, a rubber band snapping him back into the world. "Your Mom's waiting."

Lynn Rice was on the porch, holding Chris in her arms. At fifty-four, she appeared younger than Paul—her hair jet black from a bottle, her skin smooth. When she smiled, however, furrows formed around her eyes, finally betraying a hint of her maturity.

Seeing her standing there, waiting for him, Paul flashed back to Duran Duran's *Strange Behavior '87* tour. He'd driven to Indianapolis with friends to see the concert. Afterward, Danny Fields suggested they run around downtown looking for the band's hotel room. That night, Paul wound up French kissing Deidra Perkins in the glass elevators of the Hyatt Regency, his first such kiss. That night, she became his girl. When Paul finally made it home at four in the morning, his mother waited on the porch in her robe, her face red with anger. He gave her a story about car trouble, and she had taken him at his word, but even her worst punishment would not have dampened the joy of that night.

"Paul," his mother said, hefting Chris higher in one arm, holding the other out to hug him.

"Hi, Mom."

When she pulled away, her eyes fell immediately to Megan. "Let me get a look at my girl. Oh...she's gotten so big."

His mother set Chris down on the step and took the carrier from Paul's arm. Lynn had no girls of her own, only Paul and his older brother Allen, and wanted a granddaughter. When Chris was born, she had all but given up hope of getting one from Paul. Then Megan came into the world—her dream finally fulfilled.

"Come on inside, I'll make you kids some dinner."

"We're eating at the reunion," Mary reminded her. "But I know Chris has to be starving. He only ate about half of his lunch."

"You didn't eat your lunch!" Lynn Rice gave her attention to her grandson, her voice changing to its I'm Talking To A Child tone. "What do you want for dinner?

Hot dogs or liver?"

Chris jumped up and down on the porch. "Hot dogs! Hot dogs!"

"Well, come on then."

Paul put his arm around his wife and they followed them inside, his Grandmother's grandfather clock greeting them as they entered. The huge brass pendulum still swung, waving each second into oblivion, its deranged ticking still clearly audible. Once, after a midnight screening of *The Rocky Horror Picture Show*, Paul took Deidra home to sleeping parents and they watched MTV, kissing and touching each other for hours. He could still remember speeding home, the sun rising over his shoulder, trying to enter the house without waking his mother, each swing of that grandfather clock pendulum a guillotine blade falling, each tick a small bomb going off.

A flowered border divided the walls of the entryway in half. Below the strip, they were painted blue; above, they were white and covered in pictures. Paul's own face stared back at him from behind some of the glass, others held his son, his brother, and then there were the black and white images of a stranger he had never met, his father who died in Vietnam.

"Chris," Paul called, pointing at the woman in a white, beaded wedding dress in one of the pictures. "Who's this?"

His son hurried over to look and a smile bloomed on his young face. "Mommy."

Paul nodded, smirking. "And who's this guy next to her?"

"That's you, Daddy."

"Six years ago this month," Mary recalled. "Can you believe I was ever that thin?"

"Can you believe *I* was ever that thin?"

They laughed together. For Paul, it was the first genuine laugh in days, and it felt good. He rubbed Chris's hair as they continued to follow his mother down the hall.

The kitchen lay at the back of the house. Lightly stained cabinets lined its walls, and its counters were mauve-colored, matching the flooring. In the center of the room stood an island with bar stools. Chris ran right up to one of the stools and climbed into it, making himself at home. His mother set Megan on top of the center island and reached for the knife block. A blade had once filled every slot, but now it sat half empty, its tenants lost and never replaced. She took a small steak knife, sliced open the hot dog package, then dug through her cabinets.

"Whatcha been up to, Paul?" his mother asked over the clatter.

"Not much. Just finished another Indiana commercial for the board of tourism."

"I saw one last night, durin' the news. I tell Mrs. Vogel they're yours when she asks about you. Always says she looks for your name every time she goes to the cinema, says she thought you'd be doin' the next *Star Wars* or somethin' by now."

"Me too," Paul snorted. On another day he might have smiled, knowing that people remembered him so fondly, but today the remark struck him like a slap—a reminder of his ambitions unfulfilled.

"This kid," she pointed at Paul but looked at Mary, "always had that video camera in his hand."

Mary smiled. "Still does."

"But this was back when they had regular sized tapes, not these Super 8 thingies you can hold in one palm. This camera had to go on your shoulder. You watch, Mary. Tonight, that's what they'll remember about him." She put a pot of water on the stove to boil. "Did you write that slogan, Paul?"

"The state came up with that one."

"'It's as close as your backyard.' What's that mean?"

He shrugged, not wanting to talk about his advertising business, not really wanting to talk at all. "It means don't go to Florida, or Las Vegas, or wherever else you want spend your money. Spend it here."

"You should use that Indiana Beach slogan in your ads: There's more than corn in Indiana. Something catchy. Something people know what it means."

Paul found an argument building in his throat and forced it down again. *Everyone knows what it means*! His eyes drifted to the field that filled the back window, and he thought to himself that there *was* more than corn, much more. Instead, he lowered his gaze to the kitchen table, to the red bound books that sat there. He knew immediately they were his yearbooks. "Oh, God mother... you didn't dig them out."

"I did. All four of them."

Mary lit up. "Let me see."

She hurried to the table, picked up his senior year, then flipped through the pages until she found his picture and squealed. "Look at your hair!"

"It was the eighties," he countered, then ran a hand through the finger-length cut he now sported. "It was the decade of big hair."

"God, you were starting to go gray even then."

She continued to turn the pages, rewinding his life.

Paul saw Danny Fields in his red and white Harmony High football jersey, holding Nancy Collins across his arms as if he were the monster in a 1950's movie poster. Danny smiled. Nancy laughed.

Paul could not help but remember the February night they all went to see *Nightmare on Elm Street 3* at the

Woodfield Cinema. Danny made his own Freddy Krueger costume, right down to finger-knives of silver-painted wood. When the lights went down, he put the costume on—yelling "Hey, Nancy" before chasing her around the theater. The audience screamed, then applauded, and Danny took his bows.

The next page showed the Harmony High Marching Rebels, performing at State Fair Band Day. One of the trumpet players was Mick Slatton. Paul recognized the glasses, glasses that magnified Mick's eyes until he looked like an anime character. Mick once shared the fact that, when John F. Kennedy said *"Ich bin ein Berliner"* to signify that he was one with the people of Berlin, the phrase actually translated to: "I am a jelly roll." The thought of it brought a smile to Paul's face even now.

A few pages later, Paul saw Sean Roche in the school pool, bleach-blonde hair hidden beneath a red bathing cap, brown eyes covered in goggles, with a fist held high in victory. Sean worked as an usher at the Woodfield, and, one day, he decided to conduct a little experiment.

"No one pays attention to ushers," Sean had said. To prove it, he'd tear tickets and, instead of "Thank you, enjoy the show," say "Fuck you, enjoy the show." The patrons never caught on. For two years, Paul saw every film that navigated its way to Harmony free of charge, thanks to Sean.

Robby Miller was the next member of Paul's old group to show himself. Mary turned to the "On the job..." photo spread, featuring students working outside of school, and there was Robby—strapping someone to a gurney at Harmony's volunteer fire station, the badge and light blue uniform shirt of an EMT clearly visible. If you asked him why he donated his time, Robby had been quick to point out that it looked good for college. This may or may not have been true; however Paul always felt Robby did it to feel important.

Once, after the "Glory of Love" Homecoming, Paul's mother asked how the dance was, and Robby told her they'd gotten laid. When Lynn Rice's face turned to horrified shock, Robby showed her the wreath of flowers around his neck. His mother had been less than amused.

Mary next found the Art Department spread and Paul saw Deidra. She stood in the Art Room, holding the painting of a VW Beetle that won her a Scholastic Gold Medal Award. Her eyes seemed to be looking right at Paul.

He held out his hand. "Can I see that?"

Mary handed him the yearbook, watching as he stared at it.

Deidra remained in the photograph as she remained in Paul's mind, her red hair cut at an angle: one side ended just below her right ear, the other hung past her left shoulder blade. As was often the case, she wore a white T-shirt (on the day of this photo, it was the Thompson Twins) and Chic jeans. Paul looked at her hazel eyes, her fair skin, the redness of her lips—lips that once professed her love for him.

The moment she walked into his freshman drama class, he felt an attraction to her. Initially, he found her to be edgy and unapproachable, but that changed when they took a directing class together.

Paul's assignment was to direct a scene from N. Richard Nash's *The Rainmaker*. He'd seen Deidra act enough scenes to know he wanted her for the character of Lizzie. In the movie version, the role belonged to Katharine Hepburn. He then had to choose his Starbuck, a sexy con man who promises rain for a dried-up town—Burt Lancaster in the same film. Paul decided to cast Tony Cleaves in the part. Tony was president of the Drama Club, and dating Deidra at the time. As a director, Paul thought the natural chemistry of a real-life couple would add authenticity to his project.

On the day the scene was to be presented, however, Tony was out sick. Paul was forced to act with Deidra, his character trying to convince her character she was pretty. At first, he'd been saying the words on the page, then something genuine happened: there was a tear in her eye. A single tear, but it caught the glow from the stage lights and sparkled as if it were a diamond. When he grabbed her and forced her to look in the stage mirror, it stopped being a scene. Paul was telling Deidra that she was pretty, that she could be more than what she thought she was.

"Say it," Paul urged, shocked by his own intensity.

"I'm...pretty," she said, and the single tear became a naturally flowing river.

As their classmates applauded, they hugged one another on an old couch someone had donated to the theater department. The feel of her head on his shoulder had been the greatest sensation of his life. At that moment, Paul knew he had feelings for her, feelings he could not act upon because she was dating Tony. Slowly, he forced himself to end the embrace, but Deidra would not let go. As they sat listening to critiques by Mrs. Vogel and the other students (the jury returning strongly in their favor), she held his hand. With everyone looking, she held his hand.

Acting was a weird form of intimacy, so it didn't surprise Paul in the least that this was the start of their friendship, not their romance. In the years that followed, Deidra felt close enough to Paul to come to him with her problems. He would offer his advice and his shoulder to cry on, and he could feel her affection for him grow. Many times—as they sat talking on the phone, at the movies, at a game—he'd wanted to be more to her than just a friend.

Finally, after the Duran Duran concert, he told her so.

She smiled and ran her fingers through his dark brown hair. "Do you know how long I've been wanting you to say that?" she asked him. "We sit talking about life, the universe, and everything, but whenever I'm close to you all I can do is wonder what it would be like—"

"—To kiss you."

She nodded, her face flush.

"Why haven't you said anything?" he asked.

She shrugged and lowered her eyes. "I wasn't sure how you felt. I kept waiting on you to make the first move."

And then he did make a move. He kissed her, in a glass elevator for all to see. At first it had been a mild kiss, but it quickly turned passionate, probing. After all the kisses that followed, it still burned in his memory, filling him with warmth. The memories continued to shower him, and, rather than bathe in them, Paul quickly turned the yearbook page.

The next layout was worse.

We Remember...
The Lost Members of the Class of 1988

When Paul saw the heading, he slammed the yearbook shut and tossed it across the kitchen.

Both Mary and his mother jumped. Startled expressions of fright melted instantly to worry; Mary rose from the chair to stand at his side, her hand on his back to comfort him. His mother walked over and retrieved the book from the floor. She turned it over in her hands, then placed it back on the table.

Paul looked at his feet, his hands shaking. He had not wanted this weekend to be about his pain. He tried to live his life. He spent his days doing what he loved—shooting tape, editing images together, creating order from chaos. He'd met Mary. Together, they had begun a wonderful family.

"Paul..." his mother started.

She did not know what went on in those cornfields. And even Mary, to whom he'd told nearly everything, had not *been there*. Neither could possibly comprehend it, truly grasp it, unless they'd been there.

His mother did not stop. "I know you feel guilt or something, but I just don't understand—"

"That's right, Mother. You don't fucking *understand!"* Paul looked at her, then Mary. When he spoke again, it was with deliberate control. "Sorry...I'm... I'm going to the living room for a minute."

Lynn Rice watched her son leave. "I've tried to help him," she said, then lowered her eyes to the pot. "I've never known what to say to him. Even when it happened, I didn't know what to say...what would help. I've prayed for him. I just wish he'd talk about it with someone."

"He talks to me." Mary moved to follow her husband. He stood in the entryway, his head against the wall. She walked up to him, stroked his graying hair. "Well, how'd it feel to tell your mother she doesn't know what the fuck she's talking about? I've always wanted to do it."

"I haven't," he said.

"Are you going to be all right?"

"I don't know." Paul regarded her with brimming eyes. "Those guys were my friends. And when I saw their pictures just now... I remembered the world I lived in. I remembered it all being taken away."

Mary brushed the hair from his sweaty brow. "I'm sorry."

Paul took her hand in his, brought it to his lips. "We don't have to stay long tonight."

Mary shrugged. "We can stay until it's over if you want."

"You won't know anyone and—"

"I'll know you. If *you* don't want to go to this, tell me and we can go see a movie tonight instead. We leave the second we walk in the door, if that's what *you* want to do."

He sensed a "but" coming.

Her eyes and voice turned serious. "But I don't want you not to go because of *me*. You'll only regret that later."

Paul kissed her fingers. "You're using your psych degree."

"And I'm not even charging you." She smiled, wrapped her arms around his waist. "I think it'll be fun just to be with you, to leave the kids at home for once. We can dance, we can eat our thirty dollars worth, and just enjoy ourselves. Just don't forget that you have to do the same for my reunion."

"Deal." He looked at her, gave a real—if slight—smile, and they kissed. "How 'bout I go upstairs and get ready, then I'll help Mom with the kids and you can get ready."

Mary nodded. There was more, but he would tell her when he was ready. She walked back down the hall into the kitchen.

Paul listened as she told his mother he was fine, then headed up the stairs to the room he'd once called his own. He found it just as he left it. His old desk was bare, but encyclopedias, dictionaries, and other reference materials filled the shelves above it. He'd tacked a collection of movie posters to the walls, and the textured white wallpaper remained riddled with holes. His eyes went to the door that hid his old closet and he moved with them.

The closet held an archive of his youth. Costumes—some from past Halloweens, others from his home movies—hung on hangers. Boxes marked "videos" sat on the floor. Paul opened one and found the raw footage to a college film. On the shelf above, more stacked boxes. Some were marked simply "Paul's stuff," others "School Papers." Whatever they contained no longer interested him, but his mother wouldn't throw any of his things away. Finally, he came upon an old Nike shoebox marked "Deidra" in his own handwriting.

Paul took the box from the shelf and backed away. Inside, he found everything just as he'd packed it years before. There were handmade valentine cards from Deidra, cards that said "HAPPY V.D.!" in bold black letters. And pictures. He sat down on the edge of his old bed and stared at a younger version of himself; dark brown hair, holding a grinning Deidra at the edge of Sean's pool, ready to drop her into the water. She laughed nervously, her arms around his neck, her legs kicking wildly in the air. The picture had been snapped just before Danny came up to give him a push, soaking both of them. Next, he saw a picture taken on the set of *Oliver!*—Paul in full costume as the uncle of Oliver Twist, his largest role; Deidra, who had been stage manager, smiling and cringing as he rubbed his face against her cheek, covering her in his make-up. Formal, posed pictures: homecoming, Senior Prom. Different clothes, the same smiles, the same promises. He then found a picture of his eighteenth birthday party. A patch of gray marred Paul's hair. He held his cake aloft, Deidra at his side. Neither of them smiled for the camera. Their faces were sad...haunted.

He rummaged through envelopes, dozens of them, catching flashes of her handwriting and not wanting to read any of them. Like dusty bullets, her words still had the power to wound him. She wrote to him for years. Notes. Letters. Postcards from family vacations. Her early correspondence, like their relationship, had been merely friendly, the first coming shortly after *The Rainmaker* incident, when it had been Deidra's turn to direct a scene...

Paul,

> *Many thanks for your critique of my project!*
> The Bad Seed *has always been one of my favorites, maybe because for a long time that's what my parents must have thought I was (I used to be a wild child, if you can believe that!). Your opinion really meant a lot. Sometimes people in that class can get so nit-picky, y'know? Especially Peterson! Whenever she speaks, I have to throw reins around my urge to kill! I don't care if she did do a fucking (sorry, does Language offend? I tend to dive into vulgarity from time to time—told you I was wild!) Burger Chef commercial when she was five! Anyway, thanks again!*
> *See you in class tomorrow!*
>
> Sincerely,
"Your Lizzie"
Deidra

Sometimes, her notes commented on the events of the day. The one that stuck out in Paul's mind was written in 1986, their sophomore year, on Wednesday, January 29th...

> *Paul,*
> *I cut through the library yesterday and saw a bunch of people gathered around an AV cart with the "Big TV" turned on. When they said "the space shuttle exploded," I couldn't believe it. I don't know why, but it just sounded impossible, y'know? —like a nightmare. Mrs. Berrett broke down and cried right in the middle of English class. She couldn't even teach. I've*

> *never seen a teacher cry before. My Mom was going on and on about this fire that killed some astronauts a long time ago. I didn't know anything about that, do you? This is gonna be one of those things like J.F.K. getting killed, or the Moon landing. We're always gonna remember where we were when we heard the news. Well, today the teachers* are *teaching, so I gotta go. Wish we still had a class together!*
>
>

Your friend,
Deidra

Still other notes shared things she had on her mind...

> *I'm glad you were at Sean's party. Once everyone started drinking, it was nice to have someone sober to talk to. If I'd gotten drunk my parents would have sent me to a convent (Well, fuck that, I don't drink anymore because I want to be in control of my own actions, thank you!). Either way, I'm glad you were there! Thanks again!*
>
>

Love,
Deidra

Once they started dating, however, her words turned into fine poetry...

> ♥*Hi, Love!*
> *Yesterday, when you walked into the room, it was like you'd walked onto a stage: the house lights appeared to dim and a spotlight seemed to come on, making you brighter than anyone else*

in the world. Y'know, I actually needed to catch my breath. I hope you don't think that's too sappy...

On the contrary, he'd found it incredible. He'd found Deidra incredible. Even now, if he closed his eyes, he could see her walking toward him. She was shorter, five-foot-six to his five-foot-ten. On the ring finger of her left hand, where a married woman would wear her diamond, she'd worn the false ruby of Paul's class ring—red yarn wrapped around the bottom to keep it from sliding. He could see her tuck her scarlet hair behind her ear and tilt her head up to offer him a kiss.

Paul opened his eyes and savagely swiped them with his knuckles, scraped away the forming tears as he looked back into the box. At last, he found the object of his search: a small golden charm on a chain, one side a smooth curve, the other a jagged zigzag. Etched into its surface was part of a heart, and imprisoned within the shape were words:

The
between
while we
one from
Genesis

Paul's fingers closed around the charm. Its chain trailed over his knuckles, and his eyes filled once more with tears, tears he'd told himself he would not shed. Why, after all these years, did she still have this power over him? Why, with all Paul had in life, did he keep a warm place for her within his chest?

He then saw a blue envelope, one with only "D.P." written where the return address should have been. He moved his fingers to it with hesitation, forced himself to...

...to look at Deidra with a troubled kind of tenderness—anticipation alive and tingling in his viscera, and, beneath it, something like guilt. He chalked up the latter to his Catholic upbringing. She lay on her bed with the script he'd written; her hazel eyes followed his words across the notebook pages. He'd been nervous about letting her read it, but even more nervous about this night alone with her.

Deidra's father was in California, opening a new plant for his pharmaceutical firm, and her mother had flown out to join him for a few days. It was a big thing for Deidra. She told Paul her parents had moved to Harmony because she'd fallen in with a bad crowd. Leaving her home alone meant, after three years, she had earned their trust once more.

She glanced up from her reading and smiled. "What?"

Paul realized he was staring and blushed. "Sorry."

When she looked back at his script, her eyes slid across two words, then rolled over and locked with his again. "I can't read with you looking at me like that."

She grinned at him. An angel's grin that brightened his dreams, so natural, so warm and tender, a grin made all the more special because she rarely revealed it. It was something of herself she showed only to her closest of friends...and to him.

Paul lowered his eyes to the camcorder in his lap. He'd been checking the footage he'd shot earlier this evening for the video yearbook. Harmony High's annual

Powderpuff Football Game. The girls dressed in red and white uniforms and played flag football. The regular varsity players did cheerleading routines in drag. "Again...sorry."

She tucked her hair behind her ear. "Can I ask you something?"

His eyes jerked up to her. "Sure."

She seemed a bit bewildered. "Why am I reading this?"

"You don't want to read—"

"It's just that..." She hesitated. "I mean we're finally alone and I don't wanna spend the whole night—"

"Reading my script, you already said."

Deidra looked at him with fondness, her voice soft. "You know I didn't mean it like that."

Paul shrugged. "It's just that I've been working on it for so long and I...I think it's finally ready. I need you to prove me right. Yours is the only opinion that matters to me."

"I'm honored." Paul could see the light burn brighter in her eyes as she spoke the words. She looked down at the notebook for a moment, then her face snapped back up and she laughed a bit. "But I still can't read with you watching me."

Paul held up his hand. "Pay no attention to the man behind the curtain." He put the eyepiece monitor of the camera over his eye. "I'll just be toiling over yearbook stuff."

Satisfied, Deidra began scanning his screenplay once more.

When he returned his attention to the camera, Paul saw an image of Danny Fields. The six-foot-tall, one hundred and seventy-five-pound running back—who averaged five and a half yards a carry and scored twenty-five touchdowns his junior year to win himself a full ride to Notre Dame—was doing cartwheels in a skirt.

Paul had to smile. One of the advantages of being the sole editor of the video yearbook: he could always find ways to sneak in footage of his friends. In fact, tomorrow, when the Class of 1988 played the Wide Game, Paul planned to chronicle the whole event with his camcorder, planned to splice a record of their adventure into this year's tape. It would be his way of immortalizing "the group."

The Wide Game had become the stuff of legend, Harmony's version of alligators in the sewer. Ask anyone, and, more often than not, they would tell you that they knew of a friend or relative who'd played before, knew of some "horrible thing" that had happened to them. But Paul's own brother, Allen, had been part of the group that played in 1984, and Allen's tale had been far from cautionary.

To participate, a player need only contribute five dollars and race through cornfields and woods to reach an old limestone quarry turned lake by heavy rain. The first one in the water won every dime, and, when *everyone* made it to the end, there was a day-long party. Tomorrow was Senior Skip Day, and most of Paul's classmates had decided to play. Danny said the prize was now a staggering one thousand dollars.

On the tape, Nancy Collins jumped up and down. She wore a red Powderpuff '87 T-shirt and sweats, her face streaked black under the eyes. In her hand she held a white #1 button trailing a blue ribbon. For the first time in four years, Red beat White.

Paul next saw Robby walk into the frame. He'd just come from a shift at Harmony's volunteer fire station and still wore his badge and uniform shirt. Deidra flashed him a polite smile. They dated the year before, went together to the Junior Prom. Paul had seen them in the video footage he edited for the 1986-87 yearbook. They looked happy, dancing together. Paul was no fool. He knew what happened after proms. And there were times, after they went to a movie or a football game with Robby and the others, when Paul wondered if the two had slept together.

He remembered working with Deidra on the *West Side Story* set in the school auditorium. She'd been painting the New York skyline while he glued individual Styrofoam "bricks" to a plywood wall. One afternoon, their conversation turned to sex, and Deidra had been open in her admission that she wasn't a virgin. Paul was fine with that. There were times when he felt as if he were the last remaining virgin in Harmony, and she'd told him it happened before she moved to town. This made the boy who deflowered her faceless, a stranger. Robby was another story. Paul saw him almost every day of the year. There were times when Paul wanted to ask her about it, but would instead banish the question from his thoughts, telling himself it was better he did not know.

He watched static wipe away Robby's image and cleared the thoughts from his mind. He aimed his camcorder at Deidra, watched her come into grainy focus in his black and white eyepiece monitor. Her creamy skin contrasted with the darkness of her hair, and her eyes sparkled in the lamplight. She looked up from her reading and into his lens; her face wore an enigmatic expression.

"What page?" he wanted to know.

"Twenty. They just ran over the zombie."

Paul turned the camera off and moved to sit beside her on the bed. "Do you like it?"

Deidra nodded. She handed the script over to him, letting go to cover his hands with her own. "The action was extreme."

He smiled, slid the notebook into his backpack at the foot of her bed. Perhaps tomorrow, if there was time, she could read more of it. "So you really thought it was good?"

"Oh yeah...I loved everything but the title. *Invasion of the Astro Zombies?*" She crinkled her nose.

"That was Sean's idea," he was quick to point out. "It's just a working title. I was actually thinking of calling it *In the Flesh.*"

She kissed him. "That's a Clive Barker title."

"Yeah, but who's gonna know?"

Deidra chuckled. "*Everyone* will know. What *I* wanna know is how you plan to film a head getting crushed under the car tires?"

"I make a head out of plaster bandages, fill it full of pig brains, then run over it with my Mustang."

Her nose crinkled again. "You're a sick puppy."

"Then why are you with me?"

"What can I say, it must be love." Deidra corralled her hair behind her ear again and moved in to kiss him; her fingers rose to his face, gently traced its contours. "In the spirit of sharing, I've got something I want to show you too."

"All right."

Deidra pulled a sketchbook out from under her bed and flipped it open. She paused, then offered it to him. "I just finished this tonight."

When Paul looked at the drawing, a startled expression crossed his face. There on the page, depicted in intricate, breathtaking detail, was his own profile. It appeared as if Deidra had individually drafted each hair on his head. She'd drawn him in an all-to-familiar pose: staring into the eyepiece of his camcorder, the Sony logo clearly visible.

"I don't think I got your nose quite right. I had to do most of it from memory so you wouldn't see."

"It's beautiful," Paul told her. Later he would think it odd that he used that word in connection with his own image, but no other adequately described what she had rendered.

Her hands found his face again; they turned it away from the sketch and to her lips. "You like?"

"I love," he said as their lips parted, then abruptly laughed, realizing he had nearly forgotten her surprise. He reached into his pocket and brought out a small package covered in rose-colored paper. "I have something else for you."

Her eyes instantly ignited with excitement. "Paul..."

"Open it."

Deidra took it from his hand and ripped through the wrapping to reveal a small, felt-covered jewelry store box. She rubbed her fingers across its surface, then flipped it open. A small golden charm on a chain rested on the satin pillow. It appeared broken, incomplete. Etched into its surface were curved lines and seemingly random words.

Paul reached into his shirt and pulled on the gold chain that hung around his neck. At the end of the chain twirled a mirror image of the charm in the box. Deidra held her present up to his necklace. The two charms fit together like a puzzle. The complete design formed two hearts, intertwined, and the saying inscribed in gold read, in its entirety:

> The Lord watch
> between me and thee
> while we are absent
> one from another.
> Genesis 31:49

"Some guys give the girl they love a promise ring," Paul told her as she stared at the two halves made whole, "but you've already got my class ring. So I thought this was a better way to show you how much you mean to me."

She traced the chain that hung around his neck. "You've had this on you all night?"

"I've had it on for a week. I kept waiting for some special moment to give you your half. Rumor has it tonight's going to be pretty special."

Deidra looked as if she might cry. She fastened her present around her neck, the golden half circle standing out against the white of her T-shirt. "I'll never take it off."

"I love you," Paul said.

She grinned, her chuckle clogged by tears of joy. "You are so getting lucky tonight."

He kissed her, then pulled away. "You know how much I want to be with you."

She nodded, moved in to kiss him again.

Paul stopped her. "But I want us to be together because that's what *you* want—because it feels right."

Deidra smiled. She turned out the light, striping the room with the moonlight that spilled through her blinds. "I do want it, and with you...everything feels right." As she spoke, Deidra leaned forward, brought her face within inches of his, her breath hot on his lips. "By the way, do you snore?"

"Do I...?"

"Snore. Do you?"

"No one's ever been there to say one way or another."

She smiled, her nose nearly brushed his, then she jerked back. "I just had a horrible thought."

Paul's heart skipped a beat. "What's wrong?"

"What if your mother calls Sean tonight?"

His mother had been told about Senior Skip Day tomorrow, was even going to call him in sick, and she knew about the Wide Game. But he had not confided in her that he was going home with Deidra after Powderpuff. Instead, he told her he would be sleeping at Sean's.

"All taken care of. Sean, Mick, and Danny are all staying at Mick's house tonight, because it sits right at the edge of the cornfields. Sean told his Mom that all the guys would be there."

She smiled. "Then when she calls Mick's?"

"You know Mick's Mom. She gets all of our names mixed up. She won't know which of us are there, and by that time the guys will all be asleep anyway. Mom won't want to wake her sleeping baby."

"You've got this all thought out. I never knew you were so deceitful."

Paul blushed in the dimness. "I did what I had to. I'd do anything for you."

Deidra raised an eyebrow at that. "Anything?"

They kissed. As it grew deeper, more passionate, Paul put the sketchbook on the floor and untucked Deidra's shirt. When he reached for the glorious curves of her breasts, she arched her back, allowed his shaking hands to fumble with the clasps of her bra. Paul pulled it off over her head with her shirt, then tossed the clothing aside, his lips traveling down her neck. The charm he'd given her sat on her left breast, he could see it rise and fall as she drew rapid breaths, a golden mirror that glowed with reflected moonlight. He threw off his own shirt and pressed himself against her; felt her warmth, her softness against his chest.

She placed her hand over his, guided it downward, positioned it on the belt buckle of her jeans. A moment later, his hand slid beneath the waistband of her panties, paused in her thick, coarse curls, then moved further south. Until now, this had been the climax of their intimacy; in his car, beneath an afghan as they watched videos in a darkened room—his mother or her parents mere feet away. Tonight, however, there were no parents...no limits.

Her voice was a hot whisper in his ear. "Did you bring it?"

Paul nodded and reached for his back pocket, his fingers glistening. His hardness pushed against his jeans, made them so tight that he could barely free his wallet.

He took the square Trojan packet from his billfold, held it out for her inspection, and hoped she could not see him shaking.

Deidra read the inscription beneath the Roman soldier's profile: "Ribbed for her pleasure. My, but you're the considerate one." She then slid from the bed, condom in hand, and moved to the stereo on the other side of her room.

Paul blinked, his length aching. "Whatcha doin'?"

"I've been thinking about this night all week." She found what looked like a blank Maxell tape and slid it into the player. "So I made us a tape of appropriate songs." She looked back at him and smiled. "Our own background score."

When Deidra hit the "play" button, her speakers broadcast the unmistakable beat of George Michael's "I Want Your Sex." She spun around and placed the condom wrapper between her teeth. Then, with deliberate slowness, she slid jeans and panties down long, muscular legs, revealing the triangular thatch of hair Paul had felt but never seen. Deidra kicked her clothes off into the corner, hiding the eyes of her Cabbage Patch Kids.

When Paul shed his remaining clothes, his movements were clumsy by comparison. He moved across the room, trying to dispel his own nervousness, his own feelings of inadequacy. Deidra was so beautiful, so funny, so...perfect. He opened his mouth to tell her this, but she placed a finger over his lips to hush him. He kissed it, his eyes drifting down her breasts and tracing the curves of her hips. She pushed on his chest, moved him back toward the frilly comforter that covered her bed. Paul did as she wished. At that moment, she could have asked anything of him and he would have done it with joy.

Deidra knelt before him. As Paul watched wide-eyed, she ripped open the Trojan wrapper with her teeth and placed the rolled condom between her lips. With mouth and hands, she slowly worked to unroll the prophylactic until he was sheathed in rubber.

Paul wanted to ask her where she had learned that little trick, but didn't. Deidra was far more experienced than he, more in control, and much more comfortable with her own sexuality. Once, she had gone so far as to call Paul from her tub while taking a bath. They had attempted phone sex that night, but Paul had felt very uncomfortable, concerned his mother would pick up the phone, hear them talking dicks and pussies, and have a coronary. Because of her experience, his greatest concern at that moment was that he might come too quickly. He didn't want that.

God, no.

The tape had transitioned from George Michael to Peter Gabriel's "In Your Eyes." And when Deidra looked up, Paul saw his own longing mirrored in *her* eyes. She climbed onto his lap, grabbed his head in her hands, and pulled him once more to her lips. Her tongue slipped into his mouth, playfully touched his own, stoking the fires within his flesh until he felt he would blister. Deidra burned with him; a film of sweat slicked her skin, flavoring her lips, her neck, her breasts.

Paul held her by her waist and drew her to him, let her feel how hard he was for her. She moved against him, glossing the rubber of the condom, breathing into him as she worked her hips. Paul uttered a low sound, a plea for her to end his starvation. Only then did she grasp him, sliding his length into her in a single motion.

No dream, no matter how vivid, could have prepared him for the sensation of moving within her body.

He grew lost in her warmth, in their glorious friction, the ecstasy of his orgasm building, demanding to be set free. He closed his eyes and tried to harness it; he turned his mind to his film, to the SATs next week, to the day that lay before them. In the midst of their passion, Paul thought about the Wide Game. Then, when he felt Deidra grip his shoulders like a vise, when he heard her moans mature to a guttural scream, he stopped thinking and surrendered his virginity to her in a burst of pleasure.

They collapsed onto the flowered bedspread, panted as the scent of their coupling hung in the air. Paul had heard the male orgasm compared to "three seconds in the arms of God." Nothing could have been truer.

They laid there in silence, Deidra's head on his chest.

She was the first to speak, "Your heart's beating so fast."

Paul ran his fingers through her hair, enjoying the feel of her naked form against him, feeling the palpitations within it. "So's yours."

"Did this change anything?"

Paul shook his head. "Doesn't change a thing, Deidra, except that I love you even more."

"Say my name again."

He gave her an odd look. "Deidra."

"I love the way you say it."

Paul smiled. It was the most wonderful thing he'd heard in his seventeen years. He thought of the countless nights that preceded this, leaving Deidra standing on her front porch, her kiss drying on his lips as he drove home, an emptiness gnawing at his chest from the inside, leaving him hollow. On those nights, Paul laid awake in his bed, mused about what she was doing, what she was thinking about, and then he took his length in his own hand until the empty ache was muffled by bitter pleasure. But the emptiness was never totally silenced. It remained his constant companion. Even when he and Deidra were together, he was always aware that, at the end of the night, they would be forced to go their separate ways. But now, as Deidra drifted off to sleep in his arms, he had at last found bliss.

Her tape played Starship's "Nothing's Gonna Stop Us Now."

Paul's brain grew quiet and he joined her in slumber.

TWO

Patrick Chance lifted his eyes to a cloudless September night. The moon was full, a bright orange light bulb with dark patches marring its surface, perhaps the fingerprints of the God or gods that hung it there. Stars spilled across the blackness, as if a vial of glitter had overturned. He spotted the Big Dipper and thought it amazing how the eye could organize shapes and patterns from such chaos.

Patrick returned his glance to the path before him, an earthen groove carved between tall cornstalks. The wind twisted his thick, raven hair into sculptures, then blew them down. Despite the brightness above, the rows remained dark, eerie.

This is a bad idea, he kept telling himself.

He'd always loved games, especially video games. Most days found him at Tony's Speedway Market, his hand on the controls of Centipede, Dig Dug, or Donkey Kong, listening to the cheesy music and sound effects as he racked up points. In fact, one day last June, his initials graced the top five spaces on all three machines. PCG. Patrick Chance the Great. But those victories were short lived. Every night at eleven, when Tony closed up shop and turned off the power, Patrick's achievements were erased. Winning the Wide Game would be different. Everyone would know. Everyone would remember. And it would be a victory no one could take away with the flip of a switch.

It would also be the only game he'd ever cheated to master.

Patrick was conscious of the tightly folded paper in his back pocket. He'd read it countless times, memorized each and every line until he could see the words hovering in the darkness ahead.

The object of the game is not to be seen.
If two players/teams DO see each other, they must exchange personal items.
These players/teams must then play the remainder of the game together.
If you think about deserting, remember the other player/team has your shit!
If you get to the quarry without them, they win and you lose.
The first one at the quarry gets the prize.
Tie Breaker: Without being seen, take items from players/groups you encounter.
If two players/teams arrive at the same time, the one with a personal artifact(s) taken from the other wins.

And then, at the bottom of the page...

Game begins at 9am.

"Do you even know where we're going?" he called out to Nick Lerner; the question was all but eaten by the roar of the wind and the rustle of the cornfields just north of Harmony.

Nick did not look back at his friend. He continued to light their way with his dad's Maglight. A white circle of illumination revealed living walls of corn on either side. Like a funhouse hallway, they seemed to be closing in. "Of course I know. My brother won the last Wide Game, remember."

"Did *he* cheat?"

At that, Nick stopped and turned his light on Patrick. "There wasn't a thousand dollar prize in '84, okay?" He lowered the flashlight and drew out a long breath; shadows played across his acne-scarred cheeks and swallowed his eye sockets whole. "Look, you wanna win, don'tcha?"

"You know I do."

"Well tomorrow these fields are gonna be crawling with people, people we'll have to share our winnings with if we bump into 'em. Do the math. I need four hundred and fifty dollars to buy Will Laymon's old car. It's a piece of shit, but it's a car, and it'll be bought and paid for."

"We're just gonna get caught," Patrick whined.

"Not as long as you keep your mouth shut."

And that was the reason Patrick was along for this ride. Insurance. Five hundred dollars to make sure no one ever found out about this false start. If he told now, he'd be just as guilty as Nick, and there would be hell to pay with the entire senior class.

"I'm no squealer."

"I know." A smile grew on Nick's face. The light caught the short hairs of his beard stubble, turned them white; because of his severe acne, Nick rarely shaved. He grabbed the hood of his gray sweatshirt, pulled it over his head, then slid his hand into the pocket of his jeans. It was getting colder. "Hey, if it helps, this is more of a challenge. Any pussy can find his way there in the light o' day."

They pressed on down the furrow.

"I heard some kid went nuts the last time they played this game," Patrick yelled over the hissing wind. "Chopped up a couple o' girls, then slit his own throat."

"First of all, that's bullshit," Nick said. "Second, you can't slit your own throat."

"You can too slit your own throat."

"It never happened."

"But a kid *did* go missing."

Nick nodded.

That much was fact.

Russell Veal. His parents told the Harmony Police he'd played the game, but the other kids claimed they never saw him. They went so far as to drag the quarry, but never found a body. The boy just vanished.

Patrick said nothing more. Nick's mind was made up, and he didn't want to dwell on the subject. He let his backpack hang loose from his shoulders, pulled his hands back into the sleeves of his leather jacket for some warmth.

The Maglight dimmed.

Nick stopped in his tracks; gawked at the dying light as if it were a favorite pet hit by a speeding car. "No... no...*no!*"

"Tell me you brought extra batteries."

"It's rechargeable. I must not have plugged it in long enough. *You* got a light?"

"*No!*" The word exploded from Patrick's lips in a misty cloud.

"Why not?"

"I didn't know we were doin' this. I thought I was just gonna sleep over, then we'd head out at nine like everybody else. What the hell were you thinking?"

"Lower your voice, will ya?" Nick looked around. "You're startin' to sound like my Dad."

"I what? I can't—" Patrick threw up his arms and laughed. "Do you know how much crap we've just walked into? We're in the middle of nowhere, in the middle of the night, and we have no way to see where we're going!"

Nick's hand was a shadow; it waved up and down. "Just shut up for a second." He glanced at the dead light, at the moon above, then said, "Look, we can still do this."

"Do you ever listen to anything I say?"

"This row is straight and the moon is bright..." He gave the Maglight a shake, made certain it was gone, then looked up and down the row; the whites of his eyes floated in a pool of darkness. "We're in the same shit if we go back or forward, right?"

"Then we should just stay right here," Patrick said certainly. "We've already got a jump on everybody else."

"You bring an alarm clock?"

"No."

"What happens if we oversleep and somebody finds us out here? Even if they don't figure out that we started last night, we're gonna have to share the prize."

"No," Patrick repeated. "We could fall down a ravine and break our legs, or step on a rattlesnake, or...shit. We can't do this, okay? This is totally insane and we can't do it."

"And you're gonna stop me how?"

"I'm not gonna stop you." He said as he knelt down and sat in the earthen groove. "But I'm not goin' with you."

Nick's eyes narrowed. "Fine. Sit there. Just keep your mouth shut and tomorrow I'll still give you your share."

"You're going alone?"

Nick turned into the darkness, his voice filled with ambition. "Looks like."

Patrick sat there a moment, listened as the *crunch...crunch* of Nick's steps grew faint, then looked up at the stars. He supposed he should go after his friend. If there *were* ravines, or rattlesnakes, or any number of other dangers, Nick may need Patrick's help. Besides, sitting in the middle of the corn—listening to the wind, and the rustle, and the bugs—was far less appealing than the prospect of moving on. Patrick sighed, rose to his feet, and began to jog.

Darkness surrounded him. He stretched out his arms until his fingers brushed against the leaves of the stalks, allowing him to run a straight line between the rows. In a few minutes, Patrick heard the *crunch...crunch* of Nick's footfalls once more and called out to him, "Wait up!"

"Pat?" It was Nick all right. "I was wondering when you'd—whuuu?"

The sound of loose dirt giving way, followed by a splash.

Patrick shook his head; Nick must have slid down a creek bed. "I told you there'd be ravines and stuff."

Around him, the field stilled as the wind withered to a gentle breeze. It was far too quiet, Patrick realized. There was no *splash...splash* as someone traipsed through water. No more *crunch...crunch* of shoes on dry earth. No sound of movement at all. He swallowed, then called out, "Nick?"

Silence.

As Patrick's eyes adjusted to the lack of light, his surroundings sharpened. He could see up the row, but he could not see Nick. He frowned.

"Nick?" he called again, his voice becoming shrill.

He heard a noise. It was a low sound, something close to a gargle.

Fear seeped into Patrick's body, woke the hairs on the back of his neck like an alarm and made them stretch. It swam straight to his heart and pumped into his veins, freezing his blood, making his entire body shudder. His jog faded to a walk, and his walk slowed until he took the path step after careful step.

He stopped.

Patrick's right foot felt nothing but air beneath it. The corn had been cleared from this place, and the ground fell away in a steep slope. Someone had dug a pit. No doubt about it. He teetered on the lip of the crater, unable to go forward, unwilling to go back, and squinted into the dimness.

Someone had driven wooden poles into the earthen floor of the pit and whittled them to sharp points. Nick had fallen backward onto these stakes; they protruded from his torso, from his right arm, his left leg, and from his neck. In the gloom, the skewers looked coated in oil. They were dark and...*shimmering*.

Patrick whispered his friend's name, the word growing faint and evaporating like the misty cloud that carried it. He knew Nick was dead, and yet this fact was totally impossible. He took a slow step back from the edge of the pit, ready to run screaming into the darkness and the corn, but he felt hands between his shoulder blades... pushing.

He fell onto the pointed stakes; the wood punched through his flesh and organs. *"Oh, Jesus!"* He managed to grab onto a nearby pole—used it to pull himself up, to roll onto his side. *"Uhhh...GOD!"*

With numb detachment, he looked down at his body, saw the dark spots on his ruined jacket grow larger and connect, saw his legs twitch and shake—dancing to some unheard beat.

Patrick's eyes rose once more to the stars and a silhouette moved in to block his view, a shape outlined by an orange halo of moonlight. The figure wore an open shirt or jacket that rose and fell on the swells of the wind, and there was something in its hand—something smooth and polished.

Patrick moved his blood-soaked lips. "Who...?"

The shape made no attempt to answer him. It moved quickly. Cold metal touched Patrick's forehead, the blade of a skate after an hour on an icy pond. It moved across his skin, left a searing wake of pain. Blood, warm and thick, flowed down into Patrick's eyes and ears, cascaded over his nose and into his open mouth, causing him to gag and cough away his final breaths.

With his last bit of strength, Patrick moved a lazy hand to his scalp; he felt the thick brush of his hair jerked away with a violent tug, felt the wet slush of flayed sinew, felt the hardness of bone, then felt nothing at all.

THREE

The night sky was obsidian glass, fractured by a white-hot fork of lightning. Wind moved violently through stalks of corn, tossing them about, sounding like the heavy breathing of an animal. Paul was in a field. He ran, and, though he had no recollection of how he got there, or why he now raced down this row, one thing was certain—he had to keep moving.

Light up ahead, a yellow-orange glow flickered through cracks in a wall of stalks. Paul broke through it and saw a bonfire. A figure dancing around the flames. A woman. Young, naked, her black hair hanging to her waist, her body painted in multi-colored streaks. In her hands, she carried a stick figure made of dried cornhusks. From her lips poured a song in a language he could not understand. Somehow, Paul knew she was a Miami Indian, just as he knew there was something making him run.

Paul put his hands on his knees and tried to catch his breath, his eyes still focused on the dancing girl. Finally, he found his voice: *"There's someone in the corn!"*

She took no notice of him. Instead, she finished her display and prostrated herself, depositing her "doll" on a woven swatch of cloth on the ground. The Miami girl mouthed a few words, then looked at the stranger who had flung himself into her midst. "The spirits call for their warriors."

"What's this about?" Paul begged.

The girl looked past him, into the corn. A crow landed on her shoulder, huge and black; its head cocked in Paul's direction as if he were some curiosity. The stalks exhaled a cold wind, snuffed the bonfire like a candle.

"*Mondamin* is here," said the Miami girl, her face bathed in orange moonglow.

Paul's eyes sprang open in panic.

Morning sunlight revealed the five members of Duran Duran. They stared back at him from the "Wild Boys" banner Deidra had tacked to her ceiling. The oddity of the dream melted into the fear that he had fallen asleep and not gone home, the fear that his mother would find his bed empty and have him castrated if she ever found him alive. As he looked around the room, however, this fear too evaporated. Senior Skip Day and the Wide Game registered, and—most important— Paul's mind found memories of Deidra: the feel of her body moving against his, the taste of her on his lips.

That had been no dream.

It happened.

The exquisite memories were replaced by the realization that she was gone. Paul tossed the sheet aside, put his feet onto the carpet, and saw his clothes lying in a heap. He slipped on his underwear, gave his scalp a healthy morning scratch, and moved out into the hallway. "Deidra?"

Her voice drifted up the stairs and he followed it.

She coughed. "I realize that, but I really am sick."

Paul walked into the kitchen and saw his love standing there, phone in hand, a handkerchief wrapped around the receiver. She was dressed in nothing but an oversized nightshirt and the broken half-circle charm he had given her. Her hair was a mess. Last evening's make-up still colored her pale, freckled face. She was beautiful.

"Thank you, Mrs. Elision... Ahuh... Ahuh... Goodbye." She hung the phone up, rubbed her hands down her face, and stared up at the ceiling.

"Having second thoughts?"

Deidra jumped.

Paul held up his hands in surrender. "Sorry."

"I was gonna slide back under the covers with you." Her voice held a touch of sadness. "I didn't want you to wake up and find me gone."

He put his hands on her shoulders. "What's wrong?"

She brought her own hands up to rub his fingers, her eyes on the phone on the wall. "All senior absences are unexcused today."

Over the years, everything that made Seniors special had slowly been taken away. Used to be, they got out of school a week earlier than the juniors and underclassmen. Now they went until the last day, same as everybody else. Used to be, seniors had their own locker area, The Commons, and any underclassman caught cutting through was dead meat. Now, the Guidance Office stood on the bones of that hollowed ground. Finally, there used to be a school sponsored Senior Skip Day. Now, they would be truant for observing it.

"You're worried your parents will find out?"

Deidra smiled joylessly. "I got up early this morning because I thought Mom might come home. It would be just like her to launch a surprise attack. I figured, if I saw her coming, I might..."

"Push me out the door?"

"The window."

"I see." He buried his forehead in her hair.

Deidra turned and wrapped her arms around his neck. "It's just that..." She reddened and her eyes dropped. "I made a lot of mistakes when I was...when we lived in Chicago. Now that everything's so right, I hate that I'm still paying for them."

Paul kissed her temple. "You're good with me."

She shook her head. "I don't deserve—"

"You deserve more."

Deidra kissed him, then jerked back. "Oh, shit, what time is it?"

Paul looked at his Swatch. There were no numbers, only neon hands on a brightly colored base. "Eight o'clock."

"Shit..." She broke away from him and ran toward the stairs. "I need a shower."

"Need some company?"

She looked at him, her mind searching for words behind her eyes.

Paul's face fell. "Didn't realize that was going to be a big stumper."

"I—you shouldn't—"

"Did I do something wrong?"

Sudden insight dawned on her face. "No, not at all. It's just that...this is gonna sound so lame after last night...I don't want you to see me like that, at least not yet."

"Lathered up?"

"You know what I mean." She moved her hands up her body.

"What—naked?"

"Yeah." Her face reddened again, as if it were trying to match her hair. "Hence the light being off last night."

"Oh." Paul couldn't believe what he was hearing. Even in the dimness of moonlight, her figure had been clearly visible. To him, it was flawless. "I don't understand. You've been—" He chose his words carefully. "—*naked* with someone before, haven't you?"

"Yeah." She looked at her toes. "But I didn't care how *they* saw me."

"Well, lights don't shine on what I see when I look at you."

She blinked. "Huh?"

"Your heart, Deidra."

"Oh." She rolled her eyes and giggled. "You are full of so much shit."

"Am I?"

Deidra smiled. "Look, how 'bout if we win the Wide Game—"

"*When* we win."

"*When* we win, we shower together before you leave."

At the words "before you leave," Paul felt emptiness try to gain a foothold within him and he squashed it. He was going to spend the entire day with the woman he loved, and nothing was going to spoil it. "Sounds great."

Deidra started to go up the stairs, then paused and turned to face him. "With Mom and Dad gone, it's been hard for me to sleep at night. The house has been just...every little creak, y'know?"

He nodded.

"But last night in your arms, I slept better than I have in my whole life." His face lit up and she blew him a kiss. "I'll save you some hot water."

Don't worry about it, Paul thought, still smiling as he walked back into the kitchen. He found the camcorder battery and charger next to his backpack on the counter, removed the fully charged battery, and tossed it in with the other two he'd packed for the day's events. For most, the weight of the camcorder would have been a burden, but Paul was accustomed to it. It was a part of him.

His eyes rose to the kitchen window. At the edge of Deidra's lawn, the cornfield waited, green stalks swaying in the breeze. Paul wondered morosely how far off the old quarry was, then questioned why he felt so odd. Bits of the dream crept back into his mind. Running. The crow. The naked Miami girl dancing around her bonfire.

"—get moving."

Paul turned his attention to the voice. Deidra wore a white INXS T-shirt and pink sweat pants, her savage hair curled and her make-up freshly applied. The smell of her perfume filled his nostrils, bringing memories of the previous night flooding back into his brain.

"Sorry?"

Deidra bent over, laced up her Nikes. "We're playing a game. What are they doing in your world?" When she looked up, her chuckle faded. "You okay?"

"I'm fine," he told her, then smiled, driving the nightmare back into the darkness of his subconscious where it belonged. "Just excited."

She replied with a satisfied nod.

He finished preparing the camcorder, then went off to ready himself for the Game.

FOUR

Harmony was what people in the city called a "hick town." Nothing to do but play basketball in your driveway, or maybe take in a movie that had been out for weeks before finally making its way to the Woodfield. Nothing to see but acres and acres of corn.

Robby Miller traipsed through this corn alone. He wore a green tank top, and his father's Army camouflage pants—which were loose and gathered around his legs like the folds of an accordion. His feet were clad in fire-resistant black boots; on his head, he wore a red Harmony Volunteer Fire Department ball cap.

Being with the Fire Department gave Robby a feeling of importance, as Paul had suspected, but, better than that, it made him privy to the town's secrets.

For example, Robby knew the black domes in Tony's Speedway Market, the ones supposed to hide surveillance cameras, were empty. He found this out during an inspection, when he pulled the domes down and found nothing but cinder block and metal rafters above the drop ceiling. Paul Rice had worked there for two years, and even he was ignorant of the ruse. But Robby knew.

He knew Mayor Perry beat his wife. Robby had seen her eyes bruised, her lips bloodied, her bones broken and in need of splinting. "She fell down the stairs," Perry would say, all business-like, or "She slipped on some spilled ice from the fridge." Mrs. Mayor never offered even a contradictory glance. She would sit there, crying, echoing her husband's words as if his arm were in her back making her lips move.

Everyone knew there had been a fire at the Woodfield Movie Palace back in the '50s, knew that a balcony full of people burned. Robby, however, knew the manager of the Woodfield liked to do the wild thang with the girl who sold the tickets. One night, Robby went along on a fire inspection, and he heard them in the business office—grunting, moaning, calling out to God. The manager was in his forties, and she, a sophomore at Stanley University, was just out of her teens. Sean Roche worked at the place as an usher, and he suspected something, but Robby *knew*.

Just as he knew sixteen-year-old Lisa Hayden didn't want to die, she only wanted her mother to *think* she wanted it. Robby had been on three calls to Lisa's house in the last year. She had turned the car engine on with the garage door closed, had taken an "overdose" of pills, and, last but not least, had slashed both her wrists. All of it was for her mother's benefit. The car had been turned on a few minutes before Lisa's mother was to return home from work, she had not taken *that many* pills, and the cuts on her wrist had not been deep enough, or in the right direction, to be life threatening. Lisa's mother thought these attempts were a cry for help. Robby knew.

He knew Sheriff Carter was a pervert. Once, they had been called out to his house and found him naked and handcuffed, *face down*, to the brass headboard of his bed. Carter's wife had lost the key to the restraints. She had been standing there, her face rosy with utter humiliation. And while she had taken time to cover her husband, she had not bothered to remove her strap-on. With great amusement, Robby had witnessed the latex dong waving back and forth beneath her robe as she moved.

He also knew Melissa Atwell smothered her baby boy while it slept and blamed it on crib death. Melissa had gotten pregnant last year, her senior year of high school. The father had been Bill Clouse, a friend of Danny Fields, and the quarterback of the Harmony High team. When ol' Billy went off to college and left her pregnant, Melissa made it known she wanted an abortion. But Harmony was a Catholic town, and her practicing parents forbid it. The baby was born, and it looked just like Billy—same hair, same eyes, same cocky half smile that looked cute on a newborn. And when the baby ended up dead, Robby had been one of the EMTs to answer the call. He'd gone up to Melissa and whispered into her ear, "Looks like you're free now." She'd said nothing, hadn't even raised a hand to slap him for the implied accusation, and, most important of all, she shed not one tear. And so he knew.

Robby thought only Father Andrew was more aware of Harmony's underbelly, and *he* was a priest. There was no way for him to have any fun with the knowledge. Robby could, however. Robby *did*.

Once, he had palmed a 3 Musketeers bar into his pocket at Tony's Speedway, looking up at the vacant black dome and smiling as he did it.

Another time, when he bought tickets to see *The Secret of My Success*, Robby asked the blonde in the box-office if the manager paid her well. She blinked and told him she did all right. "I hear you do more than all right," Robby said with a wink. He walked into the theater and left her behind the glass, face sinking and eyes wondering.

THE WIDE GAME

Boldest of all, when Sheriff Carter had pulled him over for speeding, Robby had come right out and asked him if he still let his wife fuck him up the ass. Carter's face had turned bright red with a cocktail of rage and embarrassment. At first, Robby wondered if the comment would earn him a night in a jail cell, but Carter had told him "Get the hell outta here" and Robby had driven on, free and clear.

When he told his friends at the fire station about this day, they told Robby even more interesting tidbits about the town. Well, not so much about Harmony itself... they were more about the cornfields around it, more about the Wide Game. Of course, they had told him the story of the Miami Indians—the tale he'd heard a million and *one* times by now. The braves would go out into the cornfields to play the Wide Game. Some would come back to the tribe as men and warriors, others never returned.

No one knew what happened to them.

Robby yawned, told them it was a bullshit story.

"That's what I used to think," his captain had told him. "But some strange shit has gone on over the years in those north fields."

He, and the other firemen and EMTs, then told Robby some new stories.

In September of 1946, a black family named Warner had moved to Harmony. At that time, there was a strong Ku Klux Klan presence in the town. One night, Klansmen broke into the Warner home and took Mr. Warner and his teenage son. The next day, they found them hanging from a tree at the edge of the northern fields, the ground beneath them muddy with their drained blood. A month later, Sam Fuller, the Grand

Dragon for the Realm of Indiana, fell into a threshing machine.

Some thought Warner's wife had pushed him, but she'd moved to Atlanta with her surviving son and daughter and had a truckload of alibis, so Fuller's death was ruled an accident.

In August of 1964, Peter Grant, Harmony's Baptist minister set fire to the north fields. When the fire department arrived to fight the blaze, he tried to stop them and had to be dragged from the scene in handcuffs. A few weeks later, he was found dead in his church, shot four times in the head.

Police questioned farmers who had lost their crops, but none were charged and no weapon or related evidence was ever found. To this day, the case remained unsolved...the identity of the killer a mystery.

In July of 1972, Marcia and Betsy Andrews, twin girls, were reported missing. Marcia found her way home the next morning, bloody, hungry, and confused. They found Betsy a few days later in the cornfield—what was left of her at any rate. The EMTs told Robby the coroner had ruled it an animal attack, but her body had been so ravaged identification of the beasts had been impossible. Dogs had been his best guess. Marcia remembered nothing of the time she and her sister were gone. The doctors thought the attack had been so traumatic that the memory had been blocked from her mind.

But they never found any dogs, and the blood had all come from Betsy. Marcia wasn't even scratched.

In October of 1980, EMTs had been called out to Route 6—a ten-mile stretch of dirt road running just north of town. Deputy Oates had found Cory Sparks wandering out of the corn, his pants covered in blood. Sparks owned a small farm that had been passed from father to son for generations. The town knew him to be a quiet, likable man who always had a kind word for everyone. When Oates tried to question him about what had happened, he took out a meat cleaver and claw hammer. The deputy drew his gun for protection, but Sparks had not attacked him. Instead, he turned the tools on himself, slashing and tearing at his own groin. Oats had to shoot him in the shoulder to stop him from killing himself. The EMTs told Robby that, when they arrived, Sparks was barely conscious from loss of blood, rambling about voices that knew his name.

They took him down to Indianapolis and locked him up, a permanent resident of the Central State Mental Hospital.

Finally, they told Robby the truth about Russell Veal. The kid had gone missing the day of the Wide Game, back in September of 1984, but it didn't end there. A month later, EMTs were called to the Veal home. It seemed Russell's mother, Sarah, had smashed the kitchen window and slashed her own wrists with the shards. Her husband told the police that his wife had called out Russell's name, then he heard the glass shatter.

Before she slipped into a coma at the hospital, and later died, Sarah Veal had said to her nurse: "His eyes are gone."

Robby chuckled to himself. At first he had not believed any of it, thinking the guys at the firehouse wanted to freak him out with all these little horror stories. He did some checking, however, and, from what he could find in old fire station logs, in newspapers at the local library, much of it *was* true. Robby, in turn, tried to freak Danny out by relaying the information to him.

"For God's sake, please don't tell that shit to anyone," Danny had told him. "Nobody's gonna play the damn game if you spook the shit out of 'em."

And so, Robby remained silent about the things he'd learned. Maybe he would share the tales at the quarry, when the game was over. *Yeah*, he thought with a smile. *I'll freak Nancy out, then watch her think about it when she has to walk back through these cornfields to get home.*

A power line divided the sky above the field. On it, two crows sat unnoticed. One spread its wings and pecked at its own black feathers. The other's head twitched; its eyes followed Robby as he continued down the row.

FIVE

It had been nine o'clock on the dot when Danny, Sean, and Mick started their hike into this crop, moving between the rows. With rain, the ground would have been a brown soup, pulling and sucking on their feet, slowing them down. The last few weeks had been dry, however, and, so far, they had made good time, plowing through the leaf-chocked furrows; every quick step brought with it a loud crunch.

But Mick could not hear these sounds. His ears were hidden beneath headphones, his Walkman blaring Orff's *Carmina Burana*. Sean and Danny had been talking sports, and, short of playing trumpet at the half time shows, Mick had little or no connection to the topic. He carried a black backpack, wore green shorts and a tie-dyed T-shirt; a Beatles logo across his chest, and, on the back, "I Get By With A Little Help From My Friends."

Harmony High was a beast with fangs, and it had been eating Mick alive for three years now. He walked the entrails of its halls, sat in the hostile belly of its classrooms, and Skip Williamson attacked him as if he were a bit of foreign matter rejected by the flesh. But sometimes, Danny was there to defend him.

Mick remembered a time when Skip had passed them in the halls, chains hanging from his black leather jacket, eyes narrowed in a Clint Eastwood squint; his brown, shoulder-length hair swung as he moved. Skip stuck out his arm, snagged the stack of textbooks in Mick's hands, then pulled them to the floor as he kept walking.

Mick bent down to pick his books off the rust-colored carpeting, silent resignation in his magnified eyes.

Danny would have none of it. He put a hand on Mick's shoulder and called after Skip. "Dickweed, get back here and pick these up."

Skip looked surprised. "You talkin' to me, Fields?"

"Yes."

The hallway became a clogged artery, everyone waiting to see how the scene would play out.

Skip looked around, then held out a hand. "This has nothin' to do with you."

"This is my friend," Danny nodded at Mick. "If you wanna mess with my friends, you wanna mess with me."

"I don't get you, Fields. Why does a guy like you hang out with *that*?"

Mick started to bend down again, and again Danny stopped him.

"Pick up the damn books, Skip."

Skip stood for a moment, looking at Danny's stone-faced expression. He hesitated, shifted his feet, then rushed down to the pile of textbooks. He threw the stack together and held it out to Mick, his eyes never leaving Danny's. "If you used a fucking locker, Slatton, maybe this wouldn't happen."

Shaking, Mick reached out and took the books back.

Skip threw up his hands. "We done here?"

Danny nodded. "Guess so."

Skip knew what would happen if the school delinquent and the school football hero got into a brawl. The fight would be broken up, the school delinquent would be handed a fat suspension, and, with all of his parents' "get out of jail free" cards used up, Skip would be shipped off to military school. So, on that day, with Danny at Mick's side, that had been the end of it.

But Danny couldn't be there every moment of every day.

When the teasing was heightened, when Mick was alone, the months that lay before graduation became serpent coils, smothering him, and he felt certain that he would die before he could escape. That's what today had become: an escape with his friends, a break in the day-to-day torment, and Mick welcomed it.

Danny ran a hand across the short-cropped lawn of his crew cut. "Need a break, Mickey?" he called back.

"Sure." Mick slid the headphones from his ears, heard the chirping of insects, the rustle of stalks moving against each other in the light breeze. He stopped and looked around. "Hey, how do we know we're heading in the right direction?"

Sean scratched at his arms. As captain of the swim team, he'd shaved them clean for speed in the water. Now, as the hair grew back, they itched terribly. "The quarry is north of town." He pointed up, a blue shaft of sky visible between the tassels above them. "The sun is to the right, so east is on the right, so we're walking north. When we hit the woods, we can tell by what side of the trees moss is growing on."

Mick smiled. "And what side of the tree means north?"

Sean thought for a moment, pointed one way, then another. He looked like the Scarecrow trying to give Dorothy directions to OZ. "I can't remember."

"Forget about the sun and moss. Check this out." Danny knelt on the ground, unslung his pack and opened it. He reached inside, pulled out a hunting knife, then freed it from its leather sheath. He held it up for their inspection, turned it over and over with pride. It was huge. The business end alone stretched eight inches in length, shiny steel, serrated down the backside like the jawbone of a dragon. The handle was black, textured, and grooved for fingers.

Sean nodded his approval. "Fuckin' A. Where'd you score that?"

"I bought it up in Michigan. Went fishing there with my Uncle over the summer."

"It's pretty cool," Mick admitted.

Danny unscrewed the butt of the knife, revealed a compass and, in the handle, a compartment that held toothpicks, a needle, and a small spool of thread. "Just like Rambo."

Sean snickered. "Yeah, I'd like to see you sew up your own arm like he did."

"I could, if I had too."

"You guys know that was just a movie right?" Mick adjusted his pack, his eyes focused on their own reflection in the blade. "Can I hold it?"

Danny shrugged and flipped the knife so that he now held it by the blade. When Mick wrapped tentative fingers around the handle, Danny surrendered it to him.

It was heavy, heavier than Mick thought it would be. He brought the blade up, as if stabbing an invisible man, and it caught some nearby leaves, sliced cleanly through them.

"Jesus!" Sean exclaimed. "It's a fuckin' Ginsu."

Mick smiled.

Maybe I could stab Skip in the chest and force somebody to give him a fucking heart.

And then Mick saw Skip standing there before him—eyes narrowed, brown hair whipping forward as he threw a punch. Mick brought the knife up again, and, in place of corn leaves, he saw Skip's fingers being severed. In Mick's mind, blood flew; Skip was on his knees, crying as he covered the bleeding stumps with his good hand.

Mick's smile grew.

Danny held out his hand for the knife's return. "All right, Mickey, the leaves are dead."

Mick blinked back to reality. He held the blade perpendicularly and Danny took it from him, returned it to the safety of its sheath. Mick watched him slide it back into the backpack.

Sean was ready to get moving again. "Okay, are we goin' north or not?"

Danny kept the compass off the knife handle. He held it in the palm of his hand; the needle pointed down the row in the direction they'd been hiking. "Right on the money."

They resumed their march. Mick slid his headphones back into place and followed. The choir sang in his ears while, in his mind, the dream Skip suffered further mutilation, made impotent by the blade of the knife. Without him, Harmony High was a monster with no teeth, no claws.

Neutered.

Harmless.

Mick sighed, knowing it would not last. The beast that was his high school would shed and replace its slain bullies like anaconda skin.

Over the sound of the music in his ears, however, Mick could hear a voice, a whisper as faint as a breeze blowing through his brain: *"Then again, maybe not."*

Six

Cindi Hawkins stopped in the middle of the row; her face held an expression close to horror. "I gotta pee."

Nancy Collins shrugged. "So go already."

"What if someone walks up on us?" Cindi danced from foot to foot. "Or, Jesus, your friend Paul with his video camera?"

Nancy grinned. "You think his life is so barren he'd want a tape of you pissing?"

Cindi blushed. "You never know."

"Oh, please!" Nancy shook her head and looked at the sky. "I'll stand watch. Just hurry up and go."

Cindi took a quick look around, then hurried off behind the green curtain the stalks provided.

After a moment of silence, Nancy could hear the sound of water striking the hard earth. She wondered if Cindi wet her pants as she took her squat and could not help but snicker.

Nancy ran a hand across her sweaty forehead, then dried it on her T-shirt; black letters across her breasts begged CHOOSE LIFE. She'd bought the shirt because she liked George Michael, because he'd worn it in a WHAM! video. Now, however, she only wore it around the house, when she needed something she wasn't afraid to get dirty. She'd come to realize that the saying made it sound as if she were some anti-abortion nutcase, but, in reality, she came down staunchly pro-choice.

Cindi screamed.

Nancy ran to the sound; her backpack bounced up and down on her spine. She pushed her way through the stalks, leaves brushing across her face, leaving strands of corn silk in her hair. Nancy tore into the row where Cindi had taken her restroom break, saw Cindi pull up her clothes as she scrambled to her feet. Had Nancy not been so concerned, she might have smiled at the wet spot on the back of Cindi's shorts and underwear.

"What happened?"

Cindi pointed to the foot of the stalks. There, across the row from the puddle she'd made in the dirt, a cloud of insects buzzed around a dead animal. It lay on its side, bloated, its eyes open and unseeing, its stiffened haunches jutting outward like the legs of an overturned table.

Nancy's face curdled and she backed away. "Sick!"

"Is it dead?"

"Extremely." Nancy looked around. "This whole cornfield and you decide to squat next to road kill?"

"I'm not morbid or anything!" Cindi adjusted her clothing; a black-and-white-striped, sleeveless top and ripped jeans shorts. Her outfit, and the style of her natural blonde hair, made her look like Debbie Gibson—fresh off the *Out of the Blue* album cover. "I was in such a hurry I didn't see it until I'd already started. I like looked over and saw it's beady rat eyes and those hug rat teeth...and I totally freaked."

"It's a possum, not a rat." Nancy began to chuckle. Once, at cheerleading practice, Cindi saw a flock of ducks land in a puddle behind the school and announced to everyone that she didn't know ducks could fly.

"I've always just seen them walking or swimming," she'd told them, "like penguins. Penguins don't fly, do they?"

You wondered if you should laugh or break down and weep.

Nancy waved the ripe air from her nose. "Didn't you *smell* it?"

"Like I said, I was in a hurry. Besides, my sinuses are acting up...and this whole field stinks like a barn."

"It's called *nature*."

"Sor-ree. I guess I'm outta the running for 'Miss Outdoors.'"

Nancy's chuckle faded, replaced by the sounds of hidden insects somewhere in the corn. Why had Nancy agreed to play this stupid game in the first place? She hated being hot, she hated being dirty, and, most of all, she hated bugs. And the cornfields had the latter in abundance. She could see leaves knitted together by spiderweb, could see black beetles as they moved across the green, and what she couldn't see...she could hear. The sound was all around them now—a high-pitched chirping, reminding her of the giant ants in that movie *Them*. Nancy wondered what was actually making the sound, then shivered.

Please, God, she thought, *let whatever those things are stay out there*.

Cindi grabbed up her backpack in one hand. "Let's just make steps."

Nancy nodded, followed Cindi back through the stalks, covering the ground in healthy strides. Had they come three miles? Four? Not far enough yet that they could slow their pace.

"Did you hear the forecast?" Cindi called back, her eyes on the blue path of sky above them. More light spilled into the row now, banishing the earlier gloom, bringing heat.

Nancy shook her head, wanting to conserve her breath for the long hike ahead. Cindi was a good friend, but, as her mother had said, she had the gift of gab. It seemed she had not stopped talking since they left Nancy's house at eight-thirty.

Eight-thirty.

Another part of this little game Nancy had not counted on was the extra time it had taken to walk from her house to the northern cornfields. She'd asked Deidra to join them, asked to stay at her house right on the edge of the crop, but Paul was already spending the night.

It was amazing how fast *that* relationship was moving. Before the Duran Duran show in July, they had never even gone on a date. Now, here it was September and they were already *doing it*.

Not that Nancy was all that virginal. She and Danny had been going out for almost a year now, and he had seen enough of her to know *her* blonde hair came from a bottle, but they had yet to go all the way. Instead, she kept him hungry, wanting more, serving him appetizers but never the main course. She was all too aware that a boy who got his fill quickly developed a taste for something new.

That didn't stop Danny from trying to wear down her resistance, however. In fact, she thought he liked the challenge. And, if he played his cards right, one night she might finally let him slide home. Nancy shook her head. Slide home. Why was something as beautiful as sex associated with such stupid metaphors?

She heard a rustling noise again.

Movement in the corn.

Nancy had been aware of it most of the morning, assigning it to the wind. The breeze had died down, however, and yet the sound remained strong. She looked around, but, like the bugs, the culprit remained invisible to her eyes.

"What's wrong?" Cindi asked.

"Shhhhhh." Nancy put a finger to her lips, then pointed to the right. "I think someone's over there."

"Oh, shit. Do you think they were watching me?"

Nancy rolled her eyes. "Would you get off this voyeur thing? If they find us, we're stuck with them."

"Did your boyfriend make these rules up himself?"

She glared at Cindi, her voice remaining a hoarse whisper. "*Shut...up.*"

Low voices filtered through the mesh of cornstalks, and though Nancy couldn't make out the words—distance, or the density of the corn, served to muffle them—they seemed familiar.

As she stood there, hunched over in the row, Nancy heard something faintly in her mind's ear. It was as if her thoughts feared being heard as well.

"*They're just about even with you,*" they whispered. "*If you can sneak up on them, you could try and take something. Then, if you both get to the quarry at the same time, you'll win.*"

It's not right, she countered.

"*No, but it's how you play the game.*"

"Wait here," Nancy told Cindi in a tone so hushed it was barely audible.

Cindi mouthed something like, "What are you doing?"

Nancy shrugged as she crossed over into the next row. She paused there for a moment, then crossed more of the rippled terrain that separated her from the voices. Then Nancy heard the beat of music—Axl Rose, singing from somewhere deeper in the corn. She shook her head. How did this group she was stalking hope to remain unnoticed when they were blasting "Welcome to the Jungle" to anyone within earshot?

She froze, troubled.

What if these people weren't playing the game? Nancy had heard of farmers growing crops of marijuana in cornfields, hiding the pot amid the stalks. These people—these *criminals*—wouldn't think her spying innocent. No. They would want the location of their weed to remain secret, wouldn't they?

She thought it over for a moment, then shook her head, frowning.

She didn't really believe those were pot farmers. What really bothered her was that she was about to become a criminal herself. Spin it anyway you like, Nancy was going to go up to someone and *take* their property.

The hushed tone within her skull urged her on. *"You're gonna give it back,"* it said. *"It's part of the game. You want to win, don't you?"*

She realized her inner voice made perfect sense. In spite of her misgivings, the thought she could return it at the end of the day, with a smile that said "no hard feelings," made the pill easier to swallow. It was all just part of the game.

Nancy pressed onward. A few moments later, she found herself one row away from her goal. She could see them, three forms sitting in the corn, smoking and passing around a bottle of something while they rested. They had a ghetto blaster with them. It sat on the ground, its speakers turned away from her, its bass cranked so that the soil vibrated with every lick of the guitars.

"You hear about that kid that killed himself listenin' to 'Suicide Solution'?" one of the boys asked. The voice sounded vaguely familiar, but Guns 'N' Roses overpowered it, distorted it somehow.

"That's bullshit," another boy answered. "Like Ozzy Osbourne can say 'kill yourself' and the kid's got no free fuckin' will. Nobody can tell you to do something and you just do it, like you're a goddam zombie. The kid made a choice to knock himself off and the parents are lookin' to blame Ozzy 'cause he's got money fallin' out his ass."

Nancy saw an open backpack; it sat at the foot of the cornstalks, next to the stereo, tempting her. She got down on her hands and knees, felt the music in her elbows as she crawled forward and leaned toward the pack. The stereo served to shield her below the covering of leaves, and the boys were not looking in her direction, but that could quickly change. She reached into the open bag; the teeth of the zipper rubbed across her knuckles. Her fingers found the pointed corner of a cassette case and grabbed hold. She slid it free of the canvas, the embossed Whitesnake logo shining beneath the plastic. The case suddenly fell open and the cassette began to slide. Her hand blurred out, grabbed it before it could crash into the bag. Slowly, she pushed the tape back into place and once more closed the plastic cage around it, her eyes flipping between her hands and the back of the boys' heads in the next row.

Nancy backed into the stalks, the tape clutched in her fingers. Her movement set the leaves into motion and her heart froze in her chest. Her eyes whipped up to the forms she knew but did not know, expecting to find their eyes on her, but they'd heard nothing of her actions. The commotion of the stalks was apparently imperceptible beneath the blare of Guns 'N' Roses.

Her crime complete, she retreated across the rows; hunched over, stealing backward glances to ensure she was not being pursued. Finally, with the voices and music growing distant behind her, and her heart thudding in her chest, she looked down at her prize. In her mind, Nancy saw the girl dancing on cars in the video for "Here I Go Again." *Boys*, she thought. *Show 'em tits and headlights and they'll buy anything.*

Nancy looked up and the green sword of a leaf struck her across the face. She brushed it aside, revealed Cindi's worried expression. Both girls jumped, then put fingers to their lips to hush each other.

"What'd you do?" Cindi wanted to know, her face somehow unsettled and anxious all at once.

Nancy held up Whitesnake, a satisfied grin blooming. "Our insurance."

Cindi's eyes drifted to the cassette, then whipped back up. "I'm so sure! You stole that?" She grew a grin of surprised disbelief. "Who are you and what have you done with Nancy Collins."

"I didn't steal it! I *borrowed* it."

Cindi rolled her eyes. "Whatever! I thought they'd caught you or some junk."

"Not me," Nancy smiled, tossed the tape into the air with one hand, then caught it with the other. "I'm too slick."

Still smiling, Cindi slid her backpack onto her shoulders. "Well let's go, *Slick*, before they find out you took their tape."

As Nancy followed, she tossed the cassette into her own pack—proud of herself. It was the first time she could remember not playing it safe...and it felt good.

SEVEN

"Did you dream last night?"

At the sound of his voice, Deidra turned to look at Paul, found his camcorder lens aimed at her. He was taping her now? Sweat soaked her, plastered her hair to her forehead. She was certain it was not a look she wanted preserved. She caught her breath and answered his query, "Yes."

"What did you dream?"

She smiled, flirting. "You want this on camera?"

Paul's voice became serious. "If it was about the Wide Game."

She waved a fly from her face, gave his lens an odd glance. "It wasn't."

"Okay." He stopped recording and lowered the camera, carried it by the handle above the deck. "What *was* it about?"

"I dreamed about you," she told him. Excluding herself, she'd dreamt about Paul more than anyone she'd ever known. He crept into her subconscious soon after they'd first met. In the beginning, he was someone who would just pop up—another bit of the dreamscape. Later, as they became closer, he moved from guest shot to supporting player. Now he was the leading man. And yet he wasn't the type of boy who would ordinarily nourish such dreams; he had no physique, no tan. His nose and ears belonged on a larger face, and the bow on this package was a crown of hair that rested on his head like a puffy, brown motorcycle helmet. Not at all like the boys she'd been attracted to in the past. But, unlike *those boys*, his eyes were dreamer's eyes—a million journeys being taken behind them—and he treated her with genuine care, affection, and respect.

Paul smiled. "What happened, if you don't mind me asking."

"I don't mind. It was prom time and I was dancing with Robby." Deidra saw Paul's smile quickly fade to a lame façade, and, knowing she'd said the wrong thing by mentioning an ex-boyfriend, she hurried on to the good part. "He left me alone and I was sitting there, in my rosy pink dress, with this huge *Gone With the Wind* skirt that cost my parents a fortune, and I just started crying. You magically appeared next to me and we talked."

"What did we talk about?" he asked, still cautious.

Deidra thought for a moment. She retained the images of dreams far longer than the words. Finally, she shrugged. "I'm sure you lavished me with a ton of praise."

"I never tell you anything that isn't true."

Deidra attempted a smile, wanting to believe him, but because of things she'd done in the past, she couldn't feel worthy of the compliment. She continued: "Anyway, we talked, and then we just got up and left. Don't ask me how we fit my dress into your Mustang, I don't know."

Paul chuckled, pushed away the leaves of a crooked stalk and wiped strands of corn silk from his black *Nightmare on Elm Street 3* T-shirt. "Then what happened?"

"I think you know what commonly happens after proms." She began walking backward, expecting to see him smiling at her, surprised he was not. "Did *you* dream?"

He nodded. "I dreamed I was running through the corn."

"Trying to win that shower?" she asked. She'd meant it to be cheerful, but Paul's face remained solemn. It frightened her a little.

"There was someone after me," he told her.

"Like who?"

"I couldn't see who it was. I just knew I had to keep running. I was scared...I mean I was *really* terrified." His voice held no levity. His cheeks had become ashen, and his hand gripped the handle of the camera until the knuckles turned white. "There was this Indian girl. She was dancing naked around a huge fire."

Deidra's concern vanished, struck dead by a bolt of irrational anger. She frowned at him, hurt beneath the frost of her gaze, her arms crossing her body. Paul had made love to her, then dreamed about other naked girls? When she spoke, her voice was bitter, reminding her of the "Old Deidra," the way she'd been before she moved to Harmony—depressed, confused, and always bitchy. "At least in my dream Robby had his clothes on."

Paul raised his eyebrow, her unanticipated flash of anger knocking him from his stride. "You know what he looks like naked?"

Deidra stopped walking. She didn't know what she expected him to say, but that certainly wasn't it. By the look on his face, she could tell he regretted the words, but it was now too late to take them back. She offered him an out: "You wanna hear about that?"

If he said "no," she would let it lie. Now that she was truly happy with someone, she was not eager to talk about her failed relationships. Robby had been but the latest pearl in a necklace of mistakes she had strung for herself over the years. Before the Duran Duran concert and Paul's kiss, she had started to wonder if it had grown long enough to hang herself.

Paul did not say "no," but she could tell he wanted to. He hesitated, then shifted his weight as his lips formed the words, "I think I need to hear it."

Deidra's frown deepened. "We dated. We went to prom. We fucked. He decided he wanted to fuck other people. I decided he should go fuck himself."

His face was slack and pale. "I see."

"I mistook sex for love, and it wasn't the first time." She sighed, knowing her admission was bruising him. It was painful for her as well. "Now you think I'm some huge slut, right?"

"Oh, please."

Deidra lowered her eyes, found Paul's ring on her finger and watched the golden half-charm rise and fall on her own breasts. "Then I need to hear something from you."

"Anything."

"Is this..." She waved her hand between them as if trying to clear the air. "...just about sex?—or do you really love me?"

She did not look at Paul, but she could tell the question shocked him.

A moment of uncomfortable silence stretched out, then Paul spoke with great tenderness. "I watched you walk into the auditorium—day one freshman year—and I loved you, and every day after that, I loved you a little bit more."

Deidra blinked; the motion squeezed a tear from her eye. "And I love you."

Paul moved to her, took her chin in his hand and lifted her eyes to meet his. The words came slowly to his lips. "I knew you weren't a virgin when we started seeing each other, and I don't care about your past. Really, I don't. Robby bothers me because I know him, and I just...I worry about being compared."

"Oh." Deidra shook her head. "Paul, last night was *beautiful*. Being your first—"

"My only."

She smiled at that. "You can't even imagine how much that turns me on, how special it makes me feel—how special *you* make me feel. More special than I've ever felt before, and that scares me more than any nightmare."

"Why should that scare you? You *are* special."

She shook her head again. "If you truly think that—"

"I *know* that."

"Then *know* that you're the one I love—the one I want."

"Okay," he promised her. "I'm sorry I asked you about Robby. It was none of my business."

"You're right, it wasn't," she told him, then her face softened, the "Old Deidra" melting away like ice. Harboring grudges came naturally to her, especially against herself, but she couldn't be unhappy with Paul; his nature prevented it. She kissed him. "I never want us to have any secrets from each other. If something is bothering you, tell me. If you keep it inside, we'll never get past it."

Paul nodded, tried to smile. "All right."

Deidra grabbed onto the straps of her pack and resumed her walk, pulled ahead of him in the row, deliberation in her stride. "Back to this Indian girl. What happened?"

"She said '*Mondamin* is here,' then I woke up."

"*Mondamin*?" Deidra asked, startled.

"Yes. Do you know what it means?"

She looked over her shoulder at him. "Okay, you know how much I hate history?"

He nodded impatiently.

"Well, I spent two whole weeks researching a report on the Miami Indians of Indiana. I must have checked out a half dozen books, everything the library had on their culture, their religion, everything. I'd read 'em and copy down whatever I thought looked good or interesting, then I put it all together so it made sense. I got an 'A.' Dad was impressed. It's still hanging on the fridge, I think. You must have seen it there."

"I didn't," he insisted. "I'd never heard the word until the dream."

"*Mondamin* isn't a word you just pull out of thin air," she said, not really believing him. Dreams were funny things. She would fantasize events, then awaken to find she'd left the TV on—programs on the screen prompting her. Paul may not remember reading that bit from her report, but the subconscious never really forgets. It's the ultimate pack rat—saving bits of junk in every available corner until it's needed to win Trivial Pursuit, or as an element in a dream. "It's the Miami word for Corn Spirit."

"Corn Spirit?" He slid the camcorder back onto his shoulder, zoomed in on her as she spoke.

"Yeah. It's part of this legend..." She looked at the lens and smiled. "Do you want me to start over?"

"No, but go on."

Deidra nodded, then looked at the sky, tried to draw the information from the depths of her own memory. "Umm...there was a time when there was no corn in Indiana. The Miami Indians hunted quail, and deer, and...bear, I think. Well, all of that got scarce and they needed a new kind of food to feed their families. The chiefs called for this big meeting and they decided to send their braves out into the wilderness to look for something that would always feed their people."

"When was this?"

"You're asking me about historical dates?" she asked with a grin. "It didn't really happen, Paul. It's a legend...like the headless horseman, or that guy slitting his own throat in '84."

He nodded. "Go on."

"So anyway, all the men of the tribe went out into the woods and searched. They searched the fields, the streams, the valleys and plains, but they couldn't find anything to feed their families. They were starting to give up, but one night, they sat around their campfire and prayed." Deidra lifted her hands skyward, acted it out for the camera, her voice deepening. "'Great Spirit,' they said, 'can you send us food so the people can live.' And then all of these crows appeared out of nowhere. It was the largest flock they'd ever seen. One of the crows spoke to the men—"

"The crow spoke?" Paul twitched.

"Did I say this was a legend? Anyway, a snake spoke to Eve."

"Sorry. I'll edit all this out, just start that last bit again."

Deidra resumed her story; amazed she remembered so many of the details. "One of the crows spoke to the men and said: 'You must fight one another. Those who are killed shall then be buried here...in the soil where you fought.' Well, nobody wanted to fight, but the crows told them they had to. They said the 'Great Spirit' wanted them to."

"And did they?"

"Oh yeah. They killed each other while the birds watched, then the survivors buried the dead. As soon as they'd finished, this grass popped out of the ground. It grew...and grew..." She grabbed a nearby stalk, yanked an ear from it. "...and then these ears of corn grew. The men ate 'em and knew their prayers had been answered. They gathered up a bunch of ears and took 'em back to the tribe. 'This is corn,' they said, 'from the Corn Spirit. Many of our warriors died that you might live.'"

"So death brings corn?"

Deidra let loose a shocked little giggle. "I guess it does."

Paul stopped recording and quickened his pace, moved up to her. He held out his hand, and she took it. "You wanna be the lead in my zombie movie?"

She blinked, her heart fluttering. "Are you seriously asking, or are you just asking because I'm your girlfriend?"

"Both. I want you to be a part of it. You've acted in school plays—"

Deidra chuckled. "I've been villagers and nuns. I mainly paint the sets."

"The point is I know you can act, and I think you'd be great."

"Thank you." She felt warmth flood her entire body. "And I think your movie's gonna be great."

"You haven't read the whole thing yet."

"I know, but I can still tell."

Paul smirked. "Thank *you*."

They moved on down the row. Deidra figured they must have covered close to five miles—about half way. As she held Paul's hand, she felt good about winning it all. In fact, she felt as if she'd already won.

EIGHT

"Three pages?"

"*Exactly* three pages. She doesn't want any more. She won't read any less."

Peter Sumners rolled his eyes. Their Senior English teacher thought she was doing them a favor. She knew that their absence on Skip Day would be unexcused, so, rather than giving a test they couldn't make up, she assigned a written paper on William Shakespeare—due Monday. "And how much of our grade and future lives are riding on this?"

Tom Little wiped his face on his T-shirt; the peeling decal on his chest proclaimed: "I didn't invent sin, I'm just perfecting it." He turned to Peter and smiled. "Let's just say, if you screw it up, you'll get another chance to screw it up next year."

"Thanks."

"The pleasure's entirely mine."

Their packs hung heavy on their backs as they continued between long, empty rows of corn. Both boys played the Wide Game with detachment, neither in much of a hurry, but neither dawdling. For them, this was no great adventure, and neither really held any hope of being crowned a champion. This was something to do, nothing more and nothing less. They couldn't sit at school; the classrooms would be empty, and their classmates would label them as deserters. Nor could they sit idle at home, watching MTV or playing Tetris while the rest of the senior class held the party of the decade. And so, reluctantly, they had paid their five dollars and they walked.

Peter's mother was nervous about him playing, and his father, a man of few words, had even fewer for him lately. He thought they were being overprotective. There was no way Peter could know what had happened when they had played their own game. He didn't know a boy had done unspeakable things to Peter's mother in the fields, didn't know that, before it was over, she had pleaded with him to do even more. His father knew. His father had been that boy. The utter disbelief of their own depravity kept his parents together. By raising the son they made that day, the only child his mother's scarred innards would ever allow, each hoped to one day atone for it, perhaps even forget it. Peter knew none of this, however, and his parents would not have told him if he'd asked.

Peter suddenly cocked his head, listening. "What was that?"

Tom looked back. "What was what?"

"Listen."

A rustle in the corn behind them, a slight sound, so quiet Peter might have imagined it. Then he heard the unmistakable *crunch...crunch* of footsteps in the dry earth. He froze in his tracks, his heart fluttering. "Someone's there."

Tom's mouth fell open, then he whispered: "Whata we do?"

"We don't have to do anything," Peter murmured. There was no sense in running. Running would create noise and draw unwanted attention. He crouched on the ground and motioned for Tom to do the same. "If we're quiet, they'll pass us by."

Only a few yards away, something set the stalks in motion. As the boys sank low to the ground, as they tried to find sanctuary in the retreating shadows, a figure took shape; backlit, a dark shadow blighting the green. Slowly, it resolved into distinct colors and details: a boy with dark hair and light skin, and, as he grew closer still, they saw it was Jimmy Grant.

Peter shook his head, his body tensing. He knew Jimmy, and he didn't much care for him. Jimmy liked to do annoying voices, liked to *sing*. Peter remembered riding the bus to grade school, sitting one seat up from him as he sang *"Oh Solo Mio!"* over, and over, and over at the top of his lungs. It had almost been enough to drive Peter to insanity then, and there was no way in Hell they were going to get stuck playing the game together now.

Tom sat in the dirt, his eyes closed, muttering something under his breath. Peter couldn't tell if it was a prayer or some kind of mantra, and he didn't much care which. All Peter asked was that his friend stay quiet.

Peter looked up into the corn, watched as Jimmy walked by. The boy moved quickly, and Peter could not help but wonder what Jimmy Grant would do with a thousand dollars if he were lucky enough to win it.

Singing lessons, I hope.

Jimmy departed just as he had appeared, a dark shape fading into the leaves.

When the rustle of stalks grew faint, Tom opened his eyes to look around. "Is he gone?"

Peter nodded. "Yeah...but let's sit here 'til he's *way* gone."

Tom wiped the dew of sweat from his face and exhaled. "That was way intense!"

"Yeah." Peter cringed. "Anybody but that guy."

"You don't like him?"

"He does these voices, and these bad jokes...I mean *really* bad."

The boys snickered, and, when they were sure Jimmy was gone, they rose to their feet and dusted themselves off. They were about to move on down the row when the stalks behind them were flung apart.

Peter and Tom jumped, both spinning around to look into Jimmy's smiling face.

"Gotcha," he said.

NINE

The compass led Danny, Sean, and Mick between the rows, led them toward the woods and the quarry beyond. High above, the sun baked the field and bathed them in sweat. Danny took a sip from his canteen and imagined the cool waters that awaited them when they finally reached the lake.

"I wonder how it went last night with Paul and Deidra," Sean said to no one in particular.

Danny shrugged. He didn't know what the situation was, but it was not his place to know. They were among his closest friends, and, from what he could tell, they made each other happy. That was all that mattered to him.

"She's his first," Sean continued. "From what I hear, she's been a lot of people's first."

"I can't fuckin' believe you," Danny said. Harmony High was the world's largest game of telephone. Someone would tell someone else a partial truth before first period, but, by day's end, utter fiction was being taken as gospel. "Like you fuckin' know."

Sean got defensive. "I know she slept with Robby."

There wasn't much Danny could say in response to that. Robby had made no secret of it, and Deidra, for her part, never offered anything to the contrary. If someone heard something wrong on the "telephone," they spoke up to correct it, and quick. She never did. "You still shouldn't talk that way about our friend."

"Paul's our friend too," Sean said. "I just hope he doesn't end up getting screwed in more ways than one.

Whenever he and Deidra are together now it's always 'I love you' and 'I love you more.' Who acts like that?"

Danny shrugged. "They're in love. You were talkin' about firsts, I think it's the first time either of them has really loved somebody."

"Still," Sean said with a look of disgust, "it makes me sick. I mean, they've only been dating for a few months. I think it's a little early for them to be pickin' out china."

"They've been dating for years," Mick threw in. Danny was surprised at how well the little guy was keeping up. Then again, Mick had lived through Band Camp. Practice every morning, break for lunch, march all afternoon, break for dinner, have a mock performance at night. It was like boot camp for nerds, not that Danny would ever say that to Mick. "They just didn't call it that until July."

Sean looked back at him, confused. "What?"

"Whenever they were together, I could always tell they were in love."

Sean chuckled. "Like you're some kinda expert."

Mick smiled. "You didn't need to be Dr. Ruth to see it. It was in the way they acted around each other, the way they talked to each other, the way they *wrote* to each other. But I don't think *they* saw it until last summer."

Danny nodded and pointed back at Mick with his thumb. "Exactly. I'm glad I'm not the only one that thought that."

At parties over the years, Paul and Deidra had always sought each other out. Danny would look over and see them sitting together, talking and laughing for hours. Sometimes, he heard bits of their conversations—

usually about movies, music, and stagecraft—but when their talk became personal, he always turned a deaf ear, feeling it was none of his concern. They were so comfortable with one another. When they got together, something switched on in their eyes like a light. The timing had just never been right for them to act on their feelings. Now that they had been able to connect, it was as if they were making up for lost time, in love with finally being able to say they were in love.

Danny smiled. "Paul's one romantic son of a bitch, I gotta give him that."

"Did he give you candy and flowers?" Mick asked with a grin; the sun hit his eyeglasses, caused them to reflect the corn.

"*No*. Get this, he picks Deidra up, okay, and tells her he's made reservations at this romantic restaurant. Well, of course she doesn't believe him, 'cause there's nothin' in town but fast food, sports bars, and truck stops."

Sean pointed his nose skyward. "I've always found Emma's Feedbag to be four stars."

"Here, here," Mick added with a faux British accent.

"You clowns couldn't find four stars if you were on the Hollywood Walk of Fame."

Sean shook his head. "Oooh, burn."

"Anyway," Danny continued, "Paul drives her back to his house, says he forgot his wallet or some shit. He's got the basement all decorated, I'm talkin' candles burning, lace table cloth and flowers on the table, fine china and silverware, and menus...the fucker made menus."

"Cool," Mick commented, impressed.

Sean nodded in agreement. "What was on the menu?"

"I don't know," Danny told them. "He bought two fancy microwave dinners from the Speedway, then he had her order first. Whichever one she picked, he ate the other one. Then his mother serves them like a waitress and then...ho...then he plays this mix tape he made for her, and they spend the rest of the evening dancing and making out."

Sean smiled. "Nice."

"Tell me about it. Of course Deidra calls Nancy up and starts goin' on and on about the whole thing. So then Nancy's on my back for weeks: *Did you hear what Paul did for Deidra? Why can't you do something romantic like Paul?*"

Mick laughed.

Danny shot him an indignant glance. "Shut up. It ain't funny."

"So what'd you do?" Sean asked.

"I got her some flowers and some nice bubble bath."

"Bubble bath?"

"*Yes*. It wasn't Mr. Bubble. It smelled like violets or some shit."

Mick laughed again, and this time Sean joined in.

Danny just nodded, his lips tightening until they were nearly white. "Just wait 'til you morons get girls. Then you'll see what I'm talkin' about. It's not all kisses and coppin' feels. It's fuckin' work bein' in a relationship."

"Did you just use the word relationship?" Sean cracked through his laughter.

"Poor baby," Mick managed.

Danny stopped, still nodding. Mick had never had a girlfriend, and Sean had never kept one long enough to be considered part of a couple. Danny had been dating

Nancy for a year. In the minds of their friends, and the whole school for that matter, they were now Dannyandnancy, as if it were one name and not two, just as Paul and Deidra were now Paulanddeidra, inextricably connected. Even after a breakup, the name stuck and you would catch yourself saying it before you remembered it was now Paulanddeidra, not Robbyanddeidra. When Mick and Sean lost their identities and became part of a couple, their laughing would stop.

"I gotta go piss," Danny told them; he dropped his pack to the ground and walked off into the green.

Mick took the opportunity to get off his feet. He slowly made his way to the ground, his joints popping as he moved. The tape in his Walkman had run out a while back, so he took a moment to find a suitable replacement. The *Notorious* cassette was at the top of the pile in his backpack. He slid it into the deck, looking at the field as he did so.

Skip was out here somewhere.

The thought made him grow cold despite the heat. Without thinking, he let his eyes drift to Danny's pack on the ground in front of him. The knife was there. He remembered holding it, the texture of the grip, the weight, the comforting heft of it as it slashed through the leaves.

When he tore his gaze from the pack and returned it to the corn, he saw Skip Williamson standing there. He wore torn white jeans with the symbol for anarchy drawn across the leg in black marker. The leather jacket he wore in the halls of Harmony High was absent, revealing a sweat-stained shirt that clung to his broad-shouldered, muscular torso. The shirt was made to look like the label to a can of Raid, the slogan altered to read "A.I.D.S. Kills Fags Dead."

Skip looked at Mick with disbelief, his shoulder-length hair dark and clumpy with sweat, his face glistening. He rolled his eyes at the sky. "Fu-uh-ck!"

For a second, Mick thought he was daydreaming, then he looked over at Sean for confirmation. When he saw his friend's alarmed expression, Mick's face drained of all color and he nearly shit his pants. He turned his eyes back to Skip, his lips moving to form a single, faint word: "Go."

Williamson looked momentarily confused, then his lips twisted into a sneer, a Billy Idol grin that held a malicious kind of joy. He grabbed Mick by the collar, hoisted him to his feet.

Sean's glance moved nervously from Skip, to Mick, off into the field, then back to Skip. "Leave him alone!"

Skip jerked his head, his gray eyes wide and manic. "Wanna make me?"

Sean stared at them, his mind reaching back to grade school, back to the jungle gym of their youth. In those days, "Skip" had been a friendly boy named Josh Williamson. They'd all played together at recess, pretended to be Godzilla, Gamera, and Rodan; they climbed that metal frame as if it were the tallest skyscraper in Tokyo, screeching and roaring before they broke character and laughed. But something had happened during the summer between 8th grade and their freshman year. Josh Williamson became "Skip." He traded sweaters and corduroys for leather and heavy metal band T-shirts; started smoking, then started smoking pot. Some thought he'd snapped, that some "other personality" had taken over and possessed him.

But Sean thought that the boy had made a conscious decision; if Josh wasn't going to get the attention he wanted through grades or sports, "Skip" would get it through fear and intimidation.

Skip made a fist, but before he could deliver the punch, Danny bolted from the corn. The football player grabbed Skip's shirt and tossed him to the ground where he landed in a cloud of dust.

"You better save that hand," Danny said. "After graduation, you're gonna need it to pump my gas."

"The Powderpuff King." Skip's eyes jerked up to meet Danny's stare, his mouth a thin line. Fields had been awarded the title at last night's game, the result of student voting. The way Skip said it, however, you would have thought it was a dubious distinction. "I should have known the Nerd would never go out without his Jock for protection. Isn't that what the coaches teach you, Fields?—wear your *jock* for *protection*?"

"Call us whatever you want, fucker," Danny told him. "It won't change the fact that you're a loser, and it won't stop us from kicking your ass."

"Three against one?" Skip's face flushed. "Go ahead. I'll let everyone know what kind of shits you assholes really are."

Danny shook his head. "I told you before: when you mess with him, you mess with me. That means *just* me."

A hint of the Billy Idol sneer returned to Williamson's lips. There were no teachers here to break up a scuffle, no threat of expulsion. It was just the two of them, face to face in the corn. He liked his chances. "Go for it."

Danny held up his hand and waved his fingers, beckoning Skip to throw a punch. "You first."

Sean and Mick watched, their mouths open, wordless and dry as Skip rose to his feet. In a fair fight, Danny had the advantage of size, but Skip could be mean, not just everyday callous mean, but *crazy* mean. Freshman year, Skip had found a kitten in his yard. He scooped it up, took it inside, and actually stuck it in a microwave. It might have been another lie of the "telephone," if not for the fact that he'd taken Polaroids of his crime. Skip had shown them to all of his pot-headed friends. Now they hung in his school locker, gory warnings for anyone that dared cross him. Against someone that depraved, Sean and Mick doubted any fight would be fair.

Skip danced like a prizefighter, his hands fisted. "I've been wanting a piece of you Fields."

"Yeah, I know which piece."

Skip's eyes thinned; he lunged forward. Danny backed away, caused him to stumble as his fist caught nothing but air. Whirling around, Skip threw a blind punch into Danny's bicep, wincing at the solid contact. Danny reached out, grabbed the collar of Skip's shirt, and pulled him back down to the dust.

Skip's gray eyes blazed. "We gonna fight or dance, *faggot*?"

"I don't know. You gonna put up a fight?"

Williamson scrambled back to his feet, lunged at him, off balance. Danny wrapped his muscular right arm around Skip's windpipe and pulled him upright. Williamson fought and scratched, he tried to grab a fistful Danny's hair, but he couldn't reach.

"You know as well as me I could bench press you without breakin' a sweat," Danny told him.

"Then why don't you?" Williamson managed. "You chickenshit?"

"Not my style. We're out here playin' a game, same as you. But you need to play by the rules."

"Just get the fuck offa me." Skip twisted in his grip, his shirt sliding up to reveal the pit of his belly button. He looked uncomfortable in the headlock, panicky. It was as if he actually believed Danny might crush his windpipe. He reached into his pocket and produced something shiny.

Danny released his grip on Williamson's throat. He grabbed the hand and squeezed it hard.

Skip's eyes widened and he cried out, "FUCK, LET GO! LET GO! LET GO!"

His voice was filled with agony

Danny's severe expression surrendered to an instinctive look of concern and he freed his captive.

Skip dropped what he had in his hand, his fingers cut and bleeding. The object landed on the ground with a heavy thud. It was a metal washer rimmed in tiny spears; a Japanese throwing star, a Ninja weapon. You could buy them, and swords too, at the cutlery store in the mall.

"Stupid shit." Danny kicked the throwing star to Sean, who pocketed it. He then backed away, watching Skip, trying to decipher a hint of his intentions. "You cut bad?"

"No!"

After a beat, Danny's face hardened. "Now that you've found us, you have to play the game *with* us."

Skip, for his part, licked his hand. "Bullshit."

"Hey, you could have hid in the corn until we walked away, but you had to be an asshole. Now you're stuck playin' with us."

"Look, I hate your fuckin' guts and you hate mine. Just forget you saw me and I'll leave you faggots alone."

"We've got your little Ninja star," Danny told him. "If you try and go on without us, you'll get disqualified and get shit."

Skip dropped his eyes. "So what, if we win, I gotta split the money with you fairies?"

"I keep my word," Danny told him. "If we win, I promise you'll get your equal share, same as the rest of us."

"This is bullshit," he protested.

"Yeah," Danny said, "but I've got the money and I say who wins and who loses."

Mick felt sick. "Does he have to play with us?"

Danny nodded. He didn't want to play with Skip either, but he had to set the example. If he didn't follow the rules, why should anyone else? Besides, the thought of Skip Williamson running around the field with weapons turned his stomach. It made sense to keep him in sight. "Those are the rules."

"You made the rules. You can bend 'em for—"

Danny shot Mick a hot glance and he shriveled from it, holding up his hand. "Your game."

"It's the Miami's game." Danny wondered why he said that, feeling the cold prickle of gooseflesh climb up his neck to roost in his scalp.

"I guess I don't have a fuckin' choice," Skip said at last, looking at his injured hand.

"Not really." Danny shifted his eyes to Mick again. "You got any Band-Aids?"

Mick nodded, slowly.

"Give 'em to Skip," Danny said, and, before Mick could raise his voice in protest, he added, "That way he has something of ours and he stops bleeding all over the fuckin' place."

Mick paused a moment, then reached into his pack and produced a metal tin of bandages. He took a few for himself before offering it to Skip. Williamson snatched it from Mick's hand and started covering the cuts in his own.

"Let's get going," Sean said, moving down the row.

Danny watched as Skip applied first aid, then turned his eyes once more to Mick. "You okay, Mickey?"

Mick nodded, his eyes avoiding Skip's glare. He began to walk away, sliding the headphones back over his ears as he moved.

Skip reached out and tapped them with his fingers. "Whatcha listening to, *Mickey*?"

"Duran Duran," Mick squeaked, his face still white as fresh Kleenex.

"*Duran Duran*," Skip mocked, then added: "Bunch o' queers."

"And what do you listen to, asswipe?" Danny asked as he picked his backpack off the dirt.

Skip tapped his chest with his fist. "I listen to Judas Priest."

"Ever been to one of their concerts?"

"Yeah."

"Did they have a huge video screen that showed naked women dancing?"

"No," Skip huffed.

"Well Duran Duran did," Danny said, "so shut up about the gay stuff and get moving."

The Billy Idol sneer dawned again on Skip's face and he began to walk. "Yes, your Majesty."

Danny turned away with hesitation, his stride quickening as they moved in the direction of the woods. Had he looked back, Danny would have seen Mick eyeing his backpack with great interest, but he didn't turn. He kept walking.

They all kept walking, kept playing the game in silence.

TEN

Cindi had not spoken since Nancy had stolen—
Borrowed!
—the cassette. As a result, they'd been making good time. The corn was still all around them, however, and Cindi wondered for the millionth time if she might be having more fun in school.

What Cindi lacked in actual intelligence, she more than made up for in social instinct. She knew how high school worked, and she was more than willing to use the system to get what she wanted. She'd become a cheerleader, had gotten herself elected to the student council, and was chosen as last year's homecoming queen. She had the right hair, the right clothes, the right body, but she was not so right as to be too ingenuine to pull it off. In the little cosmos that was Harmony High, she had become a star bright enough to pull others into her orbit. Girls wanted to be her. Guys wanted to be in her. But, like her father's precious lawn, popularity was something that required constant maintenance.

It was for the sake of this popularity that she was now walking her tight little ass off. Everyone who was anyone was playing. It was a necessary evil, like giving the smelly janitor an award for years of service so she could get her picture in the yearbook. And, if she wanted to get into a good school, to marry some doctor, lawyer, or stockbroker with aims of high political office, she needed to keep herself in the public eye.

She took a drink from her canteen, wiped the excess from her lips and shoved it back into her pack. When she returned her stare to the row ahead, she saw Robby Miller blocking their path. "Jesus!"

"Not quite, but thanks." The grin on Robby's face was meant to appear pleasant, but it was far too sly.

"What are you doing?" Nancy asked.

"Playing the game." He tossed her his volunteer fireman's badge.

Startled, she held out her hands to catch it.

Robby then held out his own hand. "You vixens have some things for me?"

Nancy reached into her pocket and produced the blue ribbon she'd won at last night's Powderpuff. "Here."

"Thank you." Robby took possession of it, then turned his attention to Cindi. "Your turn."

Cindi snorted and opened her backpack. She pulled out a laminated card and slapped it onto his palm.

He looked at it, disappointed. "Your video rental card?"

"It's personal," she huffed. "It's got my name on it. I'm not givin' you my panties or anything."

"Too bad."

She flipped him the bird.

"And where's *that* finger been, She Bop?"

Her face grew warm, mortification smoldering into hot anger. Freshman year, Cindi had discovered the joys of masturbation and made the mistake of telling *former* friend Amy Walsh, who then made it the talk of the school. The Cyndi Lauper song hit the airwaves around the same time, so some of the guys began calling her "She Bop." It was one of those awful nicknames that never seemed to die. Like a cancer, it would go into remission only to come back with a vengeance. "How 'bout I start calling you Jerk Off and see how *you* like it, prick?"

Robby shook his head. "I expected more diplomatic language from a member of the Student Council."

"I only use my *diplomatic language* with people I want something from," she told him. "And I *so* want nothing from you, so get lost."

Robby stroked his chin. "You see, that's where we have a problem." He held up her Video Shack card. "Rules are rules."

"Shit." Cindi looked ahead and saw where the road was leading. Her eyes narrowed and shot to Nancy. "We're stuck with him?"

Miss Goody-Two-Shoes Nancy shrugged. "It's the rules, Cin."

This only served to deepen Cindi's anger. These rules weren't from *on high*, for Christ's sake, they were from Danny Fields. And they were downright stupid rules at that. "This game totally sucks."

"You know," Robby said, looking Cindi up and down, "some people might say that hair and those short shorts make you look like a hooker. I wouldn't be one of them, though."

"Fuck you."

"Anytime."

"Okay, enough!" Nancy stepped in and held up her hands. "Cindi, just take a second to deal with him going with us." Cindi crossed her arms and glared at the corn as Nancy turned to Robby. "And you...just try not to deal with us at all."

Robby looked at Cindi, his hand sweeping the row. "After you."

"Oh no," Cindi insisted, smiling a sarcastic grin that did not even pretend to hide her anger. "After you."

He smiled, then turned and walked the furrow ahead of them, the fluorescent yellow stripe on his fireman's boots glowing as he moved.

"Lighten up," Nancy said as she pulled along side Cindi in the row. "It's just a game."

"It's a stupid game, totally stupid." She pulled on her shoulder straps, brought the pack slamming up against her back. "I feel sorry for those Miami Indian kids if this was like the only fun they had all year."

Robby reached into his own backpack and produced a small pink book. "You girls wanna hear some dramatic readings?"

"What is that?" Nancy asked.

He held the book up over his shoulder. The words "My Diary" set in gild across the front cover. "Oh, just Sandy Doan's innermost thoughts and feelings."

Nancy's eyes grew wide. "You took her diary?"

He nodded, pleased with himself. "I followed this group of girls for a bit until they sat down for a break, keeping in mind rule number one...not being seen. Then, keeping the tie breaker in mind, I found this open bag and—"

"That is so not cool!"

Cindi snickered. "This from 'Slick?'"

"That was somebody's music. You can hear music on the radio. A diary is somebody's thoughts. You don't just walk up and take—"

"I want to kiss Danny Fields so badly," Robby read, his voice cracking as it attempted femininity.

Nancy blinked. *"What?"*

He pointed to the page, grinning. "Right here in black...er, blue and white."

She hurried up to him, grabbed the book from his hands. Her eyes moved quickly across the scrawled thoughts and her face clouded over. "That bitch!"

As Nancy turned the page Cindi rolled her eyes. "Excuse me...could you be any more hippocratic?"

Robby laughed.

"What's so funny?" she asked.

"*Hypocrite*," he corrected. "Could you be more of a *hypocrite*? Hippocratic is the oath doctors take, She Bop."

"You are such an ass." Cindi offered him her scowl. "We may be stuck with you, Jerk Off, but you're stuck with us too. Either play nice or we start taking baby steps. By the time we get to the quarry, everyone will have come and gone."

Robby did not look at her, did not offer anything in reply. That was fine with her.

"'That idiot Cindi is so full of herself,'" Nancy read aloud. "'It's like she thinks she knows everything. Well her shit stinks just like everyone else's.'"

Cindi reached over and grabbed the diary from Nancy's hands. "That *bitch*!"

Robby and Nancy both laughed as she read on.

Tree branches stretched above the tasseled stalks ahead, reached up into blue sky. Win or lose, the game was almost at an end.

ELEVEN

40 INT. FARM HOUSE – NIGHT
    The CAMERA moves through the various rooms. We see that everyone is asleep except for David, who stands watch by the BAY WINDOW.

41 CU TAMMY'S EYES OPEN
    She looks at David.

42 INT. FARM HOUSE LIVING ROOM—NIGHT
    Tammy gets up and walks over to David.

>   DAVID
>   *Smiling.*
> Hi.

>   TAMMY
> What are you looking at?

>   DAVID
> Just looking at the stars.

>   TAMMY
> *Staring vacantly out the window.*
> The stars.

>   DAVID
> Sometimes, I wish I was up there. Away from all of this.

> TAMMY
> You want to be one with the stars?

David looks at her.

> DAVID
> *Snickering*
> I never thought of it that way, but...yeah. Maybe I do.

Tammy takes his hand.

> TAMMY
> Maybe I can help.

> DAVID
> And how's that?

> TAMMY
> Dance with me.

> DAVID
> There's no music.

> TAMMY
> Does there need to be?

David looks at her strangely.

Tammy leads him to the center of the room where they begin to sway back and forth as if dancing to a slow love song. We hear JERRY GOLDSMITH MUSIC—a creepy waltz—building.

She lays her head onto David's shoulder. After a moment, her head jerks up and she smiles. She OPENS HER MOUTH and CLOSES HER EYES as if she is going to kiss him.

David CLOSES HIS EYES, waiting.

SLIMY TENTACLES SHOOT FROM TAMMY'S OPEN MOUTH and WRAP AROUND DAVID'S HEAD. He cries out a MUFFLED SCREAM and struggles to break free of her grip. Her mouth OPENS WIDER than any human being's would, allowing the HEAD of a TOOTHY CREATURE to emerge from it.

Matt STIRS in his sleep, waking up to look at what is happening. He can't believe his eyes. He picks up his MACHETE and RUNS over to them. With ONE SWING, he SEVERS TAMMY'S HEAD from her body.

The body falls to the floor, lifeless.

Tammy's head still holds on to David's. MORE TENTACLES SHOOT from the stump of its neck. The scalp begins to split open like an eggshell as BAT WINGS emerge from it. The husk which once formed Tammy's beautiful face rips apart and slides to the ground with a SICK SPLAT, revealing the creature within.

Matt begins to HACK at the tentacles with his machete. The creature CRIES OUT, releases David, and takes flight.

"Jesus," Deidra muttered as she set Paul's script down in the straw between them. It was as if she wanted to keep him from coming any closer to her. "Where do you get this sick stuff? You're so nice."

Paul gave an uncertain laugh, not knowing how to answer the question he'd heard more times than he cared to remember. His mother, his teachers, his friends, and now even Deidra, they all seemed to want to psychoanalyze his inclination toward horrific images. It was as if they expected him to break into some sobbing confession, telling them he'd lived through some horrific experience that had forever marred his fragile brain. The truth be told, his life had been boring, spent entirely in the homes and fields of Harmony. The only horrors he'd ever witnessed came to his eyes via the television or movie screen. The twisted ideas, the truly *sick* concepts, were just sparks from the darkest recesses of his mind.

An English teacher once had his entire class take a Right/Left Brain Test. The way Paul understood it, the left side of the brain was responsible for logic, for reason and language, while the right side controlled creativity and emotion. Paul tested almost entirely Right Brain. It explained why he was flunking Algebra, why he had to agonize over every word when he wrote, why he visualized every sentence he read, and why he made films.

In fact, it was through the view screen of his camcorder that Paul had first seen the Hunton's barn.

The stalks had given way to a grassy plain where the wooden structure leaned on its axis like the tower in Pisa. Paint (had it been red?) had all but abandoned the boards, leaving them naked and weathered. Many planks had fallen from their roosts, creating cavities in the walls through which sunlight now streamed, allowing glimpses of the bales of straw stacked within.

Deidra suggested they go inside for a moment to rest. It was just after eleven, but the sun was already warming the rows. They had yet to take a break, and, as a result, felt confident they had a good lead on their friends.

Now, they lay in a pile of straw at the center of the barn, its sweet smell replacing the musty scent of the corn outside. Sunlight shone through the the Swiss cheese walls, throwing weird patterns on the floor, and chains hung down from pulleys in the rafters above; the breeze played with them, transformed them into strange wind chimes.

Deidra moved the pages of script, snuggled up to Paul in the straw, let the back of her head rest on his chest. Her eyes watched clouds drift past a hole in the ceiling, searching for shapes and patterns. "So, was Tammy an alien the whole time?"

"No." Paul watched her head rise and fall on his chest as he breathed, ran his fingers through the rosy locks of her hair. "It leapt into her when she cut off that zombie's head in the drug store."

"That's why she started acting so—"

"So *alien*?"

"Well, yeah." She smiled. "So I'm Tammy?"

"I'd like you to be."

"You wanna cut off my head?"

"It's a character, dear," he reminded her. "It'll be a shock to the audience, like Janet Leigh getting butchered in *Psycho*. No one will expect it."

"I sure as hell wasn't expecting it. I won't have to really spit out worms, will I?"

"Tentacles, and no," Paul promised. "It'll all be done with make-up effects. The worst part will be making a cast of your head."

She shot him a worried glance. "You mean like in that book you have?—Where they pour crap over the guy's face and stick straws up his nose so he can breath?"

"I can't afford any of that 'crap,' so it'll be plaster bandages...but you'll still need to stick straws up your nose."

"Something tells me I should have read this whole thing before I signed on," she grumbled. "What have you got against my head anyway?"

"Trust me," Paul told her, "after last night, I have no complaints about your head."

Deidra laughed. The full sound echoed through the barn's interior, and, when it faded, her voice turned thoughtful. "So what do you think it will really be like?"

"What?"

"The end of the world."

Paul shrugged, then smiled. "Zombies or no zombies, I'm gonna live in a mall."

Deidra snickered. "This is the apocalypse. There won't be any malls. There won't be anything." Her face grew grave. "The missiles launch, and thirty minutes later we're all shadows burned into the wall."

"You know we live in a target rich environment," he told her, still stroking her hair. "We've got Grissom Air

Force Base not too far away, Fort Ben in Indy, and then Chicago is probably a big bull's eye for the Russians."

"No big loss there," she breathed against his chest. "Anyway, it's better to be close to the Big Bang. That way we won't die slowly, with our hair and teeth falling out everywhere. We really will be burned to shadows."

Paul kissed her forehead. "It's all a little scary."

"Seriously, what would you do?"

"If I were with you, I'd hold you and wait for the end," he said without thinking. "And if we weren't together, I'd probably pray we'd be together when it was over."

"I'm not sure I want to be Catholic."

Paul's eyebrow rose. "Where did that come from?"

Deidra shrugged. "It's just something I've been thinking about, especially after the last couple of weeks."

"Let's see...Dan Rather walked off the set...Lorne Greene died..."

"The Pope."

"Oh, that."

Pope John Paul II had spent ten days in the United States. It was all his mother could talk about. The point of his mission, trying to repress dissent among American Catholics, seemed lost on her.

"He got as close as Detroit," Deidra said. "I'm surprised your mother didn't go see him."

"She wanted to. St. Anthony's was putting a group together. I think she just didn't trust leaving me alone for a few days."

Deidra laughed at the absurdity of that and Paul joined her. He was so straight-laced and dependable.

She had been close to being thrown out of her home, and yet her parents now trusted her with the responsibility.

She sighed. "I mean, for him to stand up there on his pulpit and say to all those Bishops that freedom of speech is 'incompatible with Catholicism.'" Her hands rose, becoming hooked, like claws. She then held out her fingers, tapping each of them as she listed other grievances. "Priests can't marry, women can't even *be* priests—"

"Do you wanna be a priest?"

Her eyes widened. "No. I told you, I don't know that I even wanna be Catholic. I mean, I believe in Jesus and all that junk, but the whole Pope thing just...I don't know. It's like he's such a total gynophobe."

"Guy-no-what?"

"Gynophobe. Afraid of women."

"Is that a real word or a Sniglet?"

She giggled. "I don't know. If it's not a real word it should be, and the Pope would definitely be one. It's like the whole Catholic Church is stuck in a fuckin' time warp. I mean Catholics don't even believe in birth control. Every time we have sex we have to have a kid? Forget that!"

"I'm pretty sure they frown on us having pre-marital sex at all," he chuckled. "And if you're really worried about my stance on birth control, I wore a condom last night, didn't I?"

She chuckled as well. "Okay. So you're saying you don't want to be Catholic either?"

There was a time when it had been true.

He'd been six or seven, and he knew that to be Catholic meant going to St. Anthony's Catholic Church.

He also knew that he wanted nothing to do with that place. It frightened him to the point of nightmares.

Paul would sit in the pews, looking up at the statue of Christ hanging on the cross, seeing His mouth hang open and His eyes turned up in agony. Worse still, in His torso Paul saw another face. The naval was a round, moaning mouth; the raised ribcage formed the high cheekbones of a skull, and the nipples were angry eyes. It was as if this God were screaming because something was *growing* out of Him.

Not to mention the golden-framed lithograph that hung above the entrance to the Church—Schongauer's "The Temptation of Saint Anthony." It depicted a bearded man surrounded by horrible monsters. The monsters pulled at his hair, at his clothes, at his flesh; monsters with claws, and beaks, and teeth. Some even had clubs.

Yes, as a small child, St. Anthony's was not a holy place.

It was the den of scary monsters.

Paul smiled a bit at the silliness of the memory and went on, "I'm just saying...the stuff against birth control, the no women priests...all that was made up by men. I still believe in God, in Jesus, in Mary, in the saints...all of that makes you Catholic, not the other stuff."

Deidra's head tilted on his chest, her eyes locked with his. "I just don't want anything to ever come between us, and I was wondering if you being Catholic, and me not wanting to be one anymore, would."

"If we decide to get married it might."

She looked away. "Oh."

Paul held her chin in his hand, tilted her eyes toward him again. "I mean to *the Church*. If we get married in the Church, I think you have to want to be Catholic, or at least want our kids to be."

"We can always elope."

"Yeah."

"Right after prom. Well, after after prom, anyway."

Paul grinned. "Whatever you say."

Deidra looked away from him again, her eyes focused off into the darkness. "We can move into one of those married dorms," she said after a brief silence, her breath hot on his chest as she spoke, "and I can star in all your college films."

"Sounds like paradise."

She offered him an evaluating glance. "It could be."

For a moment, he found himself in the future she described. Married. Living together at USC or UCLA, Deidra studying art and drawing storyboards for the films he was shooting for a grade. The vision brought a smile to his lips.

It was the response she'd hoped for. The evaluating stare became a beaming grin. "Just something to think about."

Paul kissed her forehead. "Being with you is just about all I do think about."

She held him tighter for a moment, then relaxed as she drifted off to sleep.

He ran his fingers lazily through her hair, stared up at the rafters of the barn without seeing them. Paul thought that this was the best day of his life.

TWELVE

Dale Brightman looked like the perfect specimen of a young man as he hiked the last mile toward the woods. He was an inch shy of six feet tall, possessed a healthy build, naturally even teeth that had never known brace or filling, skin clear of even the ghost of acne, and hair as golden as the corn that filled the husks around him.

Some would have gone so far as to call him beautiful.

The look in Dale's eyes was a serious one, one normally reserved for track meets. And why not? The Wide Game was a race after all, and he intended to win it. He'd won every race in Phys Ed—the dashes, the hurdles, had even run the mile in the shortest amount of time. When he joined the track team, however, he found it was one thing to be faster than any kid at Harmony High, but it was quite another to be faster than kids from South Bend or Peru. After his first fifty-yard dash, he'd stood there, his sides screaming, his legs numb from the workout, sure it must have been a pre-race nightmare, but it wasn't. Victory had been inches out of reach. Over and over, each of those fifty yards crossed his mind in detail. Had he started badly? No. Had he looked back? That was the deadly sin of running. You never looked back. And, of course, he hadn't. The truth of the matter was he had just not been fast enough. Fast enough to beat most of the other runners, sure, but not all. The coach, his parents, even his teammates had congratulated him on the effort, but the bottom line was that he lost. By one step, he lost.

Dale never wanted to experience that feeling again.

THE WIDE GAME

He trained, he drove himself to shave time off his runs, and the next time he raced...he won. A victory in the Wide Game would be just as sweet, something the school would talk about the rest of the year.

"There goes Dale Brightman," they would say. "He won the Wide Game, you know? Yeah, no one has ever made it to the old quarry faster."

He might even make the papers.

As he pushed the leaves from his path, Dale could not know how right he was.

He pressed onward, paced himself, and soon the row ended at the edge of a clearing. Dale stooped to catch his breath, but just for a moment. He had to keep going. He had to win.

Someone had been there recently. The ashes of a bonfire lay smoldering in the dirt, the wood made white by intense heat.

What happened here?

Around the cinder pile, something caught Dale's eye. He set his pack on the ground, stretching before he delved further into the clearing. Dolls. Cornhusk dolls had been placed on woven mats encircling the remains of the fire.

A large crow swooped over Dale's shoulder, its talons nearly touching his ear. Instinctively, his head sunk between his shoulders and his arm shot up to wave it away. The bird circled and dove in for a landing at the edge of the clearing. Its head jerked, turning its eyes in his direction.

"Shit," was all Dale could say as he gazed back at it, amazed.

Something moved in the corn.

It entered the clearing behind him.

Dale turned and the sun reflected off something metal, temporarily blinding him. A knife blade was then thrust deep into his left eye socket, forever robbing him of his sight. He opened his mouth to scream, but his attacker filled the orifice with corn leaves, muffling the cry. The blade was pulled free of his skull, and Dale fell backward onto the dead fire, a cloud of white ash blooming. His attacker fell upon him, and the knife invaded his chest cavity... again... and again... and again.

The crow cocked its head. Its mouth hung open as if shocked, its eyes watching blood gush from Dale's ravaged form, following the flow as it mixed with the embers and ash to create a dark sludge.

The corn swayed, and the wind that moved through the stalks made a sound like a crowd cheering.

THIRTEEN

Sean slid down a steep slope; his butt clearing the mantle of dead leaves, leaving a path of dark, rich soil. Below, a dead tree sank into the groundcover at the base of the ravine. Sean's sneaker punched into its rotting bark, halted his descent. He crawled between bare, moss-covered branches and joined the others in the dimness.

Skip rubbed at his face and hair, tried to rid himself of hitchhikers. "We'd be swimmin' now if we followed the fuckin' path."

"We'd also be stuck with more assholes like you," Mick said with surprising strength.

Skip glared at him, bits of the leaf bed still stuck to his sideburns. "This ain't *Revenge of the Nerds*, fuckhead. Let's see you act tough without Fields around."

"What is your deal?" Mick wanted to know. "Why do you hassle me so much?"

"Cause you're a fuckin' band queer."

"First of all, I'm not queer, and second, weren't *you* in band?"

Sean chuckled and he saw Skip's face soften a bit, looking for a moment like the Josh Williamson he remembered, but it was only for a moment.

"I quit in the eighth grade," Skip pointed out, then his sneer resurfaced. "And *I* played drums."

Sean chuckled louder in spite of himself. "Oh, what? —like there's no queer drummers?"

"Could you guys possibly make *more* noise?" Danny asked in a strained whisper.

Hot cornfields had yielded to the shade of this forest canopy, and their goal grew nearer with each step, but they had not been able to relax. They were not alone in this wilderness. There were voices, muffled by distance and foliage, but real...and closing in.

Sean's heart swam a four-hundred-meter race. As he crouched in the shadows of rotting branches, he fantasized they were Marines, caught behind enemy lines, surrounded by Russians, and trying to get home to the hot nurses they'd left behind. The plot brought a smile to his lips.

He'd given the military serious thought. When he saw *Top Gun* at the Woodfield, Sean wanted to fly jets and dogfight with Russians. Had he been of age back then, he would have eagerly signed his John Hancock on the recruiter's dotted line. Then came news from Beirut, a Marine barracks destroyed by terrorists' bombs, and the armed forces lost much of their allure. But now, in the safety of these Indiana woods, far from Kadhafi and Red Square, it was still fun to pretend.

From the South, a female voice, answered by a rumble of deep male laughter. They were close. Too close.

A stream of sweat flowed into Sean's eye and he wiped it away before it had a chance to burn. "Should we, you know, sneak up on 'em? We could take their shit and—"

"We'd have to backtrack to do it." Danny checked his compass, then pointed to the opposite wall of the ravine. No gentle slope there. It was a solid wall of limestone. "This ravine is running North-South. If we sprint down it, we should hit the quarry first and avoid 'em all together."

Sean nodded, glanced back at Mick and Skip. "Can you guys keep up?"

"Don't worry about me." A Marlboro jutted from Skip's mouth and he reached into his pocket for something to light it.

"Are you brain-dead?" Sean plucked the cigarette from between Skip's lips. "They'll smell it and know we're here, and besides that, we're up to our ankles in *dry leaves*."

Skip's eyes jerked open, surprised by the action, then narrowed to frustrated slits. "Jesus fuckin' Christ, I could've stayed home with my goddam Mom!"

Danny climbed out from beneath the dead wood and into the open ravine. He looked around, then motioned for the group to follow as he began to jog—his muscular body bent, his hands pulling his pack tight against his back.

Sean mimicked him, hearing the rustle of leaves and the clatter of loose rock beneath his feet as he moved. *When it rains, this gully must be like a river, water flowing right into the pit of the quarry.* The echo of the thought had barely faded from his brain when he saw the object of their quest.

At the end of the V-shaped ravine, olive drapes of foliage parted, revealed a hundred yards of flat, pale stone surrounding the excavation. Over the edge of limestone cliffs, Sean glimpsed the lake. It sparkled like emeralds in the sunlight, so calm and peaceful; Sean could not help but feel it was something untouched, something he and his friends would be the first to discover.

Danny slid down loose rock and dirt at the end of the clove. He staggered a moment, then stood bolt upright on the limestone, his fists thrusting skyward.

The rocks gave way beneath Sean's feet as well. He jumped, landed in a sustaining crouch, then leapt up to look around.

Stone faded to tall grass at the foot of the woods. Huge rock monoliths dotted the whole area, as if the pit had belched them out onto its lips. They were covered in spray paint—names, slogans, obscenities; the only sign human beings had ever been there. However, these writings were old, weathered. It appeared that Sean and Danny were totally alone.

They'd won.

"Yeah, baby!" Danny bellowed, his voice echoing across the chasm of the quarry.

"Number one!" Sean shouted, his heart beating a victory drum behind his ribs. After whispering for so long, it felt good to shout, to *win*. He gave Danny a high five.

Mick and Skip made their way out of the gully. Mick ran over to Sean and Danny, his hand held high for a triumphant slap. Skip looked happy, for once.

"I can't believe we actually did it," he said with a malice-free grin.

"You think people will complain that the guys running the game won?" Mick wanted to know.

"Fuck no," Danny balked. "When you're the best, who can argue."

Sean ran for the limestone cliffs. "I don't know about you guys, but I need a swim."

Along the way, he dropped his backpack, yanked off his shirt and removed his shoes. Sean looked over the stone ledge, prepared to dive into the refreshing waters below, but his eyes found two figures asleep on the rocks that lined the lake. "Shit."

When Danny pulled off his own shirt, he saw what Sean had seen. His victory smile faded, as if he'd just scored the winning touchdown only to have it erased by an asinine penalty. "You gotta be fuckin' kidding me."

By the time they reached the ledge, Mick and Skip were both in shorts. Mick looked at Sean and Danny, at the sleeping figures below, then back again. His mouth hung open in amazed disappointment. "Who the hell...?"

Sean shook his head. They were too far off to recognize, but one of them was definitely female. A black bikini showed off the curves of her figure.

"We should do a cannonball right next to 'em," Skip suggested.

Danny nodded. "Yeah."

FOURTEEN

Deidra and Paul won the Wide Game.

When they left the Hunton's barn, they felt as if they'd wasted too much time, but, as they surveyed the vacant quarry, the reality slowly sank in. They'd done it. They were the first. Paul cheered, then he set up his camera, grabbed Deidra around the waist, and they danced a victory jig.

Next, they'd gone for a swim. The water was cool, but far too deep for Deidra's liking; she hated not being able to touch bottom. And it wasn't long before Danny, Sean, and the others arrived to find them sunning themselves like sea lions on the rocks.

"What's shakin'," Paul called up to them, a broad smile on his face.

They won over a thousand dollars, and, upon their return to Deidra's house, she made good on her promise to shower with him. She loved sharing new experiences with Paul...teaching him things. By the time they turned off the water, an hour had passed and she had barely been able to walk—but that had more to do with the hike than the sex.

On Monday, they went back to Harmony High.

When Deidra entered a portfolio in the Scholastic Arts competition, her paintings earned her a truckload of golden keys and medals. She applied to schools Paul showed interest in, and received a full scholarship—the University of Southern California's school of Commercial Design.

They didn't elope after prom. Instead, they spent the night in a Dollar Inn off of I-74 and the following day at

King's Island amusement park in Ohio. At the top of a mock Eiffel Tower, overlooking the entire park, Paul got down on one knee and gave her a diamond engagement ring.

Deidra said yes, of course.

They graduated in May of 1988. The next month, much to the dismay of Paul's mother, they rented a U-Haul carrier, attached it to Deidra's Beetle, and drove out to California. Along the way, they stopped in Las Vegas. Deidra Perkins became Deidra Rice in the Graceland Wedding Chapel, an Elvis impersonator singing "Can't Help Falling In Love" as Paul kissed his bride.

They both attended college at USC. Of course, Paul enrolled in the film program, and Deidra cashed in her scholarship, studying commercial art and design. In her spare time, she did some conceptual work for the *Blade Runner*-inspired epic her husband filmed his senior year. The movie was so good, in fact, that George Lucas asked Paul to direct second unit on a third *Indiana Jones* movie.After that, Paul received directorial job offers non-stop. He finally signed on to helm a sweeping Civil War drama. His work was brilliant, earning a two-million-dollar paycheck and *eleven* Academy Award nominations, including one for Best Picture and another for Paul as Best Director.

On that cool March evening, Steven Spielberg opened the envelope and named Paul Rice as the winner. He stood, dumbfounded, then hugged Deidra. His hands were shaking as badly as they had the night they'd made love for the first time. He walked up to the podium and accepted the golden statue into those shaking hands. At the microphone, having not prepared a speech, he became flustered before finding his wife in the audience and smiling down at her.

"This is for you, honey," Paul told the world. "You're my inspiration."

The cameras were on Deidra as she mouthed, "I love you." She stood there, her hair up, held in place by a jeweled clip, a diamond necklace around her neck. Rivers of joyful tears flowed over her cheeks, and her Vera Wang gown was the color of...

Blood.

Deidra was covered in blood.

She tried to find its source, ran her hands up her body until her fingers disappeared into a gash in her throat. Horrified, she jerked her hands away, getting them caught in her necklace...a necklace that was no longer diamonds but a small golden charm. The crowd of movie stars seated around her melted away and stalks of corn grew to fill the void. She looked back to the podium where Paul had been standing.

A huge crow sat perched on the microphone, staring back at her.

"*Mondamin* is here," the crow told her in Paul's voice.

Deidra awoke to find herself stretched out in a pile of sweet-smelling straw, the dim interior of the Hunton's barn all around her. Her hands were on her throat, but there was no slit to be found there, only smooth, tight, youthful skin and the thin metal of the charm Paul had given her. She slid her hands up to her lips, wiped away a drop of drool that had formed in the corner of her mouth, then slid her fingers over her nose to her eyes and rubbed them.

THE WIDE GAME

They hadn't won the Wide Game, at least not yet. Prom and graduation were still months off, and marriage and Oscars loomed even further over the horizon.

When she said she dreamed of Paul more than anyone but herself, it was no exaggeration, but Deidra had never had a dream nose-dive into nightmare like that before.

I shouldn't have read his script before going to sleep.

Deidra scanned the barn for her Starbuck. He leaned against the doorframe, the Sony camcorder on his shoulder, his body made silhouette by the bright light from outside. She got to her feet—her brain sloshed within her skull, still trying to surface from the pool of unconsciousness—and walked over to him, placed her hand on his shoulder.

Paul jumped at her touch, jerked his face away from the eyepiece of his camera, horror flaring in his eyes like flashbulbs igniting.

"Boo." Deidra's voice was husky, still awakening.

"I thought you were asleep."

"Your script gave me nightmares."

He smiled. "There's no greater compliment for a horror writer than that."

Deidra was about to ask him what he'd been taping, but the words died in her throat when she saw the birds. Crows. Dozens of them. They covered the large John Deere farm tractor at the edge of the cornfield in a black, fluttering dust jacket.

When she spoke, her voice was shaky, dream images still clawing at her mind. "Hitchcock eat your fucking heart out."

"You took the words right out of my mouth."

"I've hung around you too long."

He smiled, bent down to kiss her forehead. "No, not long enough."

Deidra exhaled and shook her head, her heart fluttering in her chest. How did he do it? With a glance, Paul could make her feel beautiful. With a word, he could make any moment special. She pressed her forehead against his neck and cheek, felt his beard play reveille, and hugged him tightly. "God, I love you."

Paul took his eyes away from the camera again. "What?"

He looks drained, she thought, then wondered: *What did he dream?* "I said I got a bad case of lovin' you."

"I think it's contagious." Paul put the camera on the ground; he picked her up, spun her in the open doorway of the barn.

"Put me down," she squealed as the world moved around her. "Put me down before I hurl all over you!"

Laughing, he spun her over to the pile of straw and fell backward into its embrace. Deidra landed on his chest, her head still riding the merry-go-round. Paul smiled up at her, a hole in the roof creating a golden spotlight on his face. He looked renewed; his eyes sparkled, and he reached up to pick errant bits of straw from her hair, flicking them into the surrounding pile.

She ran her thumb along his bottom lip, wanting to press her own lips against it. Slowly, he reached up, laid his hand on her clothed breast; his soft, playful touch turned seductive, and she did kiss him. The wind must have died, killing the clanging chains in the rafters. The only sounds were their frenzied respiration, the wet noise of their lips and tongues, and the rapid thud of Deidra's own heart deep within the canals of her ears.

With the sun heating them, and the straw billowing against their bodies, it was as if Paul had pressed "pause" on his camcorder and halted time.

She felt him tug at the elastic of her pants and lifted her hips. Her pink sweats and panties slid away in a burst of straw. He kissed her shin, then slid his lips along the inside of her thigh. *I'm so glad I shaved my legs this morning*, she thought, then: *He's never done this for anyone.* The realization made her tingle and she tugged at his hair, urged his mouth to the sensitive bulb of flesh that waited for him. He lay there a moment, studying the folds of moist anatomy, then finally touched it with his tongue. As he experimented on her, she could feel his nervous excitement and this added to her own pleasure. Before she became lost in ecstasy, she managed words: "You don't have another Trojan, do you?"

He paused, lifted his head. "Two more."

"*Two*." She giggled. "You're ambitious."

Paul flushed. "Never let it be said I'm not prepared."

"I don't think anything can prepare you for this," she teased.

They lay in the straw, its fragrance filling their nostrils as they became one. Deidra told herself she had never felt more comfortable than within Paul's arms, that every thrust drove him deeper and deeper into her heart, and with her climax came a kind of twinge—a realization that the moment was waning and would never come again. Her relationships all became pelvic sooner or later, then became nothing at all. She began to tremble and she held Paul tightly against her to quell her painful, empty ache.

He wiped a line of tears from her cheek. "What's wrong?"

"I love you."

"Okay..." he pressed, waiting for more.

"This is too wonderful," she told him. "I'm afraid things will change."

"They will." Paul stroked her hair. It was now wet with her perspiration. "They'll get better."

She managed to force a smile to her lips. No matter how desperately she wanted to believe him, there was still a part of her filled with doubt. Paul loved the "new and improved" Deidra, but he'd never met the previous model. She'd given him hints of it, told him bits and pieces of her life before Harmony, and he'd seen bursts of her anger —like tornadoes, they were short, destructive, and impossible to predict. But he'd never met her inner demons at full strength.

Deidra was not an alcoholic. An alcoholic needed liquor to get through their everyday life. She only drank at parties, but once she got started, she didn't stop until she was drunk. At thirteen, drunk at a friend's birthday party, she lost her virginity to a stranger in a closet. At fourteen, she'd been involved with a drugged-out boyfriend two years her senior, a boyfriend who'd threatened to kill himself, and her, if she ever left him. Then, the summer before her freshman year, she'd become so intoxicated she nearly died of alcohol poisoning.

This final incident had forced her family's move from Chicago to Harmony, an attempt to remove the "bad elements" and turn their sweet daughter around. Deidra always found it ironic that they picked a town where the bars outnumbered the traffic lights, but it worked. She made a conscious decision to start a new life.

The inner demons never fully left her, however.

There were times—when friends were drinking, when things were bad at school, when relationships were failing—that she could feel them banging on the inner wall of her skull, begging...no, *demanding* her to bring a bottle to her lips and let them out to play.

How could someone as flawless as Paul love someone so flawed?

Another tear grew heavy in her eye and rolled down her cheek, racing to catch up to the ones that had gone before it. The golden half-charm hung down from the chain around Paul's neck, winking in the spotlight of afternoon sun. She found its mate lying on her chest and held it up to complete the inscription. Deidra was certain of her love. That was enough for her to want to believe in his.

"You really like the charms?" Paul asked.

"I love 'em." She kissed his forehead. "We should get going." She let go of the necklaces, rolled onto her knees and wiped her leaking eyes as she pulled her sweatpants and underwear from the straw.

Outside, voyeur crows remained perched on the tractor. They watched the shapes in the straw dress, watched them grab up their backpacks, then took flight.

FIFTEEN

As Paul and Deidra traipsed through the woods, the distant sounds of a soiree grew louder in their ears. Trees along the trail formed a kind of Wide Game Museum. Initials were carved into the bark; some paired, imprisoned within hearts, others alone or beneath sayings like CLASS OF '79 ROCKS and GO REBELS! Gradually, as the forest thinned, the sights that met Paul's eyes were part picnic, part carnival.

People were everywhere.

Nancy, Cindi, and the rest of the cheerleading squad danced on the rocks. A huge ghetto blaster at their feet broadcast Yello's "Oh Yeah," dueling with another, distant stereo's speed metal guitar (Metallica, or perhaps Megadeath, it was all the same to Paul's ears). Someone managed to drag a rusted, red Radio Flyer wagon to the site, loaded down with a cooler full of Budweiser. Paul watched as Mark Peck shook one of the cans, popped it open, and doused Amy Hoffman. A volleyball net stood in the soft grass to the left, an enthusiastic game in progress. A line of kids in swimsuits, Sean and Danny among them, dove from a tall cliff into the quarry below. Close to the edge of the woods, a couple moved beneath an argyle blanket, a blanket that hid the sight of their sex but not the reality of it. They were far enough from the action not to be tripped over, but close enough for the act to be considered daring. And last, but not least, the smoke of burning pot wafted through the air; its sickening sweet odor filled Paul's nostrils and made him blink.

"This brings back memories," Deidra said.

Paul looked at her, watched her face tighten into an expression of distaste. "You all right?"

"Fine," she lied, then shook her head. "Ancient history. I don't want to bore you with the details."

"Bore me."

She wagged her head again, tried to shake off whatever it was that had hitched a ride on her brain, then she brought her eyes up to his. "Don't let me do anything stupid, okay?"

"Too late," Paul told her sarcastically. "You're dating me, remember?"

She smiled a little at that; not much of a smile, but it was a start. "How could I forget?"

He glanced around the festival, at one hedonistic display after another, then lifted the camera from his side. "I should get some footage of this."

"I know," she said. The late afternoon sun outlined her body and highlighted the curls of her hair, granting her the look of an angel. "Why don't I get with Nancy and the other girls? We can meet up when you're done."

There was still a little bit of sadness in her eyes. She started to walk away and Paul grabbed her by the arm to stop her. "You sure you're okay?"

Her smile widened a bit and she drew closer to him, brought her lips to his cheek. "I'm fine," she whispered in his ear. "Go do your thing." She withdrew to arm's length, then her fingers slid from his grasp. As she walked away, Deidra looked back over the cloud of curly hair on her shoulder. "Just don't be long?"

"I won't be."

Paul watched the ladylike sway of her perfect hips as she moved, then raised the camera to his eye. He caught a glimpse of some shirtless guys on a nearby slab of limestone, HARMONY SUCKS sprayed across the rock in red paint. They followed Deidra with their eyes, then looked back to Paul as if to say "how does this video geek end up with *her*?" Paul grinned and continued recording the festivities.

First, he took video of the quarry itself. The pit was much larger than he'd expected, the size of a small reservoir, a mile or more in diameter. It was not a perfect square, but that was the shape of the peg Paul would use to fill it if he had to. The walls were terraced, comprised of six-foot squares with thin ledges at the bottom of each indentation. *Probably the exact size of a scoop shovel*, he thought. Twenty feet down, they met a murky green lake, but he could not tell how far they descended below the waterline, or where the bottom, if any, might lay.

He panned the camera. All around the excavation site, topsoil had been scraped away. The field of naked limestone that remained was now covered in blankets and towels, teenaged sunbathers baking in the unseasonable heat.

Paul focused on these partygoers, and he noted that the caste system of Harmony High was still rigidly in effect.

He zoomed in on the stoners. They were at the foot of a large rock monolith, lost in a smoky haze. Skip Williamson stood like some kind of prophet while the others sat at his feet. If you were high, Paul supposed, even the things Skip had to say must sound interesting.

He next found the cheerleaders, dancing amid the so-called "Populars." Some wore swimsuits, towels tied around their waists like sarongs; others remained in the clothes they'd hiked in, and most had drinks in their hands, a variety of liquors and sodas. Paul knew some of them would go on to be successful in life; doctors, lawyers, builders and businessmen, maybe even a politician or an astronaut or two. For others, however, this was their time in the sun. In college, they would no longer be the big fish but rather bits of flotsam and jetsam that would drift toward their diplomas and the white collar, nine-to-five existences beyond.

Deidra danced beside Nancy, sipping Mountain Dew from a can. He zoomed in on her, watched her laugh. They'd actually spoken of marriage this morning, hadn't they?

That wasn't so crazy was it?

After all, Paul's parents had married just out of high school. Those were different times, however. There was a war raging, and a married man was less likely to be called upon than a single one. Not that this axiom had held true for his own father. Still...if you loved someone, really loved them...

Samantha Cooper bumped into him, knocked his thoughts from their orbit and back into the universe of the party. He turned, saw her take used sandwich wrappers and cans from the crowd, saw her put them in the black Hefty bag she carried.

"Excuse me," she told him.

"No problem." Paul eyed her actions. "Who roped you into being trash collector?"

Sam, as she was called, shrugged. "Nobody 'roped' me into doing it." She brushed the raven hair from her face and smiled. "Once a Girl Scout, always a Girl Scout, I guess. I'm not picking up everything, but I didn't want this place to look like a landfill when we left." She laughed. "I could just see some Miami Indian coming along and crying."

Paul laughed as well, then he taped some close-up shots of the picnickers—eating, resting, playing cards, just talking. He'd never been to Central Park, but the view reminded him of footage he'd seen of that famous lawn. Greg Snider even threw a Frisbee to his dog.

Now that he had establishing shots and B-roll footage, Paul approached people with his camera, asked questions he'd thought up weeks before. His voice was low; the voice of Serious Interviewer, ambassador of the video yearbook. "Tell me about your Wide Game experience."

"Oh, man!" Jeff Laski put his arm around Beth Pollak. They sat on one of the flat, raised rocks that dotted the area. He drank Schnapps while she read a copy of Stephen King's *The Stand*. "There was one point, when we were in the cornfield, and it sounded like there were people all around us."

Beth looked up from her worn paperback. Paul could not help but notice the book's cover painting—on one side, a man's face, on the other, the head of a crow. They shared a single painted eye, and it glowed a deep, evil red. "And then you cheated."

"Did not."

"Did too."

"How did I cheat?"

"We saw those guys walk by and you just said to be quiet," she told him. "We were supposed to join up with 'em."

"Only if they saw us," he reminded her. "They didn't."

"That doesn't matter..." She looked at Paul through the lens. "Does it?"

"You only have to join up with someone if you see each other," Paul told her. "If you see them, and they don't see you, you don't have to join up with them."

Jeff nudged her. "See. I've never cheated on anything in my life."

"That state capitals test," Beth reminded him.

He rolled his eyes. "Nothing important though. I mean, as long as you know New York, New York—"

Beth giggled.

Jeff flushed and rolled his eyes. "Whatever. Anyway, I didn't cheat on this game."

"So you found the rules confusing?"

Jeff shook his head. "No."

Beth shrugged. "I guess I didn't understand that one rule."

"Did you actually take anything from anybody?" Paul asked Joy Montgomery, zooming in for a close up. She sat on a blanket with Christina Hill, eating Doritos.

"No," she said with a snicker. "I was too chicken. Christina's a master thief, though."

Paul panned over to her. "What'd you take?"

Christina covered her mouth. She had just filled it with Taco-flavored chips before her name was brought up. Her head bobbed as she finished chewing, then she responded, "I took John Maybee's watch."

"How'd you manage that?" Paul asked with a smile.

The girls looked at each other and laughed. A volleyball from the nearby game hit Joy in the back of the head. She picked it up and threw it back at the players, her lips never relaxing from their smile.

Finally, Christina was composed enough to speak again. "He ran into us and didn't want to stay, said we'd slow him down too much or something. So I go up to him and act like I'm Marilyn Monroe." Her voice became soft and breathy. "'I'm so sorry I can't walk with you, Johnny.' I got him so turned on that he didn't even notice I'd taken off his watch and shoved it in my pocket."

"Did anybody take something from you?" Paul asked Kirk Bachman.

He laid on a towel in his neon yellow swim trunks. Whatever tanning lotion he'd lathered in smelled strongly of coconuts. "Somebody took one of my fuckin' shoes."

Paul tried not to laugh. "How'd that happen?"

"I had a rock in it, so I took it off to shake it out, then I had to take a piss, so I just dropped it on the ground. When I finished, I turned around and it was gone. I had to walk the rest of the way in my socks. I don't know who did it, but when I find the fucker, here or on the way back home, I'm gonna fuck up his shit." He addressed the camera directly, his eyes hidden beneath black sunglasses. "You hear that? I'm gonna fuck your shit up!"

"Did you have fun?" was Paul's next question.

Peter Sumners pointed to Jimmy Grant as they sat laughing near the edge of the crowd. "I used to hate this guy...he drove me crazy!"

Jimmy nodded. "We got stuck together—"

"And we find out we like the same movies—"

"The same music."

Peter smiled. "Yeah. If it hadn't been for the game, I'd have always remembered him as the kid who drove me crazy singin' opera on the school bus."

"So who won the game?" Paul asked everyone he interviewed.

Jeff Laski had looked at Beth Pollak, then they both shook their heads.

"It wasn't us," Jeff said.

Beth looked around. "There were a lot of people here already when we got here."

Joy and Christina laughed again. "Not us," they said in unison.

"If you find out," Christina said, "let us know."

Kirk Bachman continued looking in the camera as he answered, "If it was the fucker who took my shoe, your ass is grass buddy. That's all I got to say. Your ass is fuckin' Turf Builder!"

"I think we were the very last ones here," Jimmy said.

Peter nodded in agreement. "Yeah, but, even if I didn't win, today was worth five bucks, man. I've had a blast."

Despite the fact that no one seemed to know the winner's name, they were very aware of a rumor about Skip Williamson and Danny Fields. Something had happened between them during the game and everyone seemed eager to pass what they knew about it to Paul.

"Skip said he and his friends are gonna gang up and kick Danny's ass on the way back," Jeff Laski told him.

"Williamson jumps out at Fields on the trail," Kirk said, relaying what he'd heard; he held his fist out in front of him, "and he pulls out this sword, man, and he says, 'I'm gonna mess you up, fucker...'"

"Tell Danny to be careful?" Joy begged.

"He is *so* hot," Christina said. "And that Skip, what's his childhood trauma anyway?"

As he heard the "Skip's gonna ambush Danny" rumor repeated again and again, Paul grew more and more worried. He decided his next interview should be with Sean and Danny. He could find out what really happened with Williamson and finally get the identity of the winner on tape.

"Hey, Paul!"

Mick bounded toward him, an open can of Bud in his hand. His face looked burnt beneath his bangs and his glasses reflected Morse code flashes of sunlight. Paul turned the camera in his direction and waved.

"How long you been here?" Mick asked.

"About an hour. Is this a raid waiting to happen, or what?"

Mick nodded, then took another sip from his can, wincing against the taste. "It won't get Harmony into Zagat's guide of fun spots, but I'm actually having a good time." He motioned to Paul with his can. "You?"

"Oh yeah," Paul said, then asked, "What's this I keep hearing about Skip?"

Mick upended his beer and killed it. "He ended up hiking with us the last few miles."

"*Williamson?*"

"The one and only." As he spoke, Mick pushed on the bridge of his glasses and scratched his earlobe. It was normally a quick nervous mannerism, but alcohol made it more conspicuous.

"How'd that happen?"

Mick shrugged. He tried collapsing the empty can in his hands, then placed it on the ground and smashed it beneath his shoe with an audible, hollow pop. "He found us in the corn and tried to mess me up, but Danny..."

"Was there a sword?" Paul asked, concerned and excited in equal measure.

"No. They threw some punches, Skip tried to pull one of those Ninja stars, but Danny took care of him." Mick looked around. "Where's Deidra?"

"With Nancy. So who won?"

"Chesterson and O'Riley."

"You're kidding?"

"I kid you not."

Danyell Chesterson and Monica O'Riley—along with Nancy, Cindi, and Kristie Lowe—formed the Varsity Cheerleading Squad. Paul swung the camera over to the rock, to the place where he'd seen them dancing with Deidra. He zoomed in on Danyell and Monica. Dark hair billowed around their pixelated faces like the foliage of Dr. Seuss trees. Paul lowered his voice and spoke loud enough for the microphone to register. "And the winners celebrate their victory."

"I'm beginning to think knowing Nancy is a good luck charm."

Paul took the camera from his eye and looked back at Mick. "How so?"

Mick shrugged, trying to find the bridge of his glasses with his hand. "Danny's her boyfriend, and he won Powderpuff King, and those two are like her best friends-"

"After us," Paul interjected.

Mick shook his head. "Women have women for best friends."

Paul cocked his eyebrow. "That's a bit sexist, don't you think?"

"It's true. Does Deidra tell you about her periods?"

"Well, sometimes," Paul said, shocked.

Mick gave a dismissive wave with his right hand. "Well...you're *Paul*."

"You're plastered."

This brought a nervous chuckle. "Yeah...yeah, you know I am." He held his index finger and thumb out in the air as if he held something invisible. "This is your brain on drugs."

"And this is your brain with bacon and toast." Paul turned off the camera, concerned. "How many beers have you had, man?"

"Just the one," Mick admitted, "but I think this pot fog is giving me a headache."

Paul put a hand on his friend's shoulder. "Let's go over and watch Sean and Danny dive."

"Sure."

They walked toward an outcropping of limestone turned diving platform. Billy Idol sang "Mony Mony" from the cheerleaders' stereo, the crowd chanting "Hey! Hey what! Get laid! Get fucked!" at the customary times. Paul watched Deidra try to keep up with the cheerleaders' moves and he chuckled. She saw him laugh and flipped him the bird.

"Paul!" Danny stood in line behind Robby and Sean, water dripping off his huge physique. "Hey, man, I thought we'd lost you."

Tiny rivers raced over Sean's abs. "How'd it go last night?"

Paul blushed a bit. "I don't kiss and tell."

Sean grinned. "That good, huh?"

"Fantastic," Paul confessed, then he noticed that Robby had lowered his head, avoiding eye contact, and he felt a tinge of delight. *Jealous much?* "So how much did the girls win?"

"A fuckin' fortune." Danny motioned to the crowd. "Over a thousand bucks."

"I picked the wrong two cheerleaders," Robby chuckled. "I ended up with Nancy and Cindi just before we got to the woods. Those two would not shut up. They talked the entire way. It's no wonder we lost. Everyone could hear us coming."

Paul nodded inattentively, his eyes locked with Danny's. "What happened with Skip?"

Danny looked to Mick, then back at Paul. "He tried to start somethin'. Nothing I couldn't handle."

"It was like a Schwarzenegger flick, man," Sean chimed in, his scalp visible through the wet spikes of his crew cut. "They start brawlin', Skip tries to go all Ninja, and Danny gets him in this killer headlock. I thought he was gonna pop Skip's head like a fuckin' zit."

Danny smiled. "He ended up playin' nice. When his stoner friends stumbled outta the woods, he went off somewhere with them."

Robby shook his head. "Man, that guy...If he ever gets in a wreck, and what little brains he has are flowing out his ears, he better hope I'm not the first on the scene."

"That's a terrible thing to say," Paul told him.

"Yeah," Robby admitted with enthusiasm. "The world would be better off without him, and you know it."

The line moved. Sean took his position on the rock and Paul raised the camcorder. He would need to change batteries soon, but he thought he might have enough to tape one dive.

Robby cupped his hands around his mouth like a megaphone. "Now diving... diving...for gold...gold...in the Korean Olympics, Sean Roche...Roche."

Sean took a bow and turned to face the water. He pulled in a deep breath, then jumped from the rocky platform—completing a mid-air tumble before piercing the water with minimal splash. The knot of spectators clapped as Sean kicked his way to the surface, spitting water and smiling up at them.

"How deep is it?" Paul called down, hoping his battery held out for the answer.

"I think I knocked skulls with one of the Chinese divers," Sean shouted in reply, then he did the backstroke toward shore, toward a spot where terraced limestone made awkward steps. He emerged from the water and thrust his fists in the air. "Top that, Fields!"

Danny stepped into position, thought for a moment, then backed up and ran for the ledge. He leapt into the air, pulled his legs up until his chin met his knees, and struck the water ass first, soaking Sean in the enormous spray. The crowd erupted into a mix of laughter and applause. Danny's smiling face broke the dark surface and his eyes found Sean at the water's edge. "How was that?"

Sean shook his head. "The Russian judge gave you a zero."

Danny swam to the side. "Fuckin' communist."

If the steps were not natural, then they'd been fashioned by giants. As he climbed, Danny thought even Larry Bird would have to stretch to stride them.

Nancy waited for him at the summit. "I need to talk to you."

Danny looked at her, his eyes quietly suspicious. "Okay."

Sean excused himself. "See you back at the cliff."

Danny nodded, wiped runnels of water from his forehead, then gave Nancy his full attention. "What's up?"

She looked around, then pulled the Whitesnake cassette from her shorts' pocket. "I stole this," she whispered, "for the game."

Danny smirked. "Good for you."

"I don't know who I took it from, so how do I get it back to its owner?"

His smirk became a full-fledged grin. "It's a tape, sweetheart, not a puppy." He pointed to the limestone plateau where she'd been dancing. "Why don't you put it in your stereo and see who accuses you of stealing it."

Nancy's head jerked forward, her eyes wide. "You don't have some kind of lost and found or something?"

He shrugged, then his arm swept the throng. "I didn't expect this to turn into fuckin' Woodstock." Then he added, "Just keep it."

"It's not mine," she huffed.

"Then, first thing Monday, turn it into the lost and found at school."

She considered that with contrite eyes, turning the tape over in her hand.

Danny sighed. "If you knew this was gonna bother you so much, why'd you play the damn game?"

"I've never been a big risk-taker," she told him.

He nodded.

"And it hit me...I'll be a college co-ed next year." Nancy's head snapped up, her bangs swayed back and forth. "Maybe I don't wanna play it safe anymore.

Maybe I wanna...get in touch with my inner reform school chick, stop being Daddy's well behaved little girlie-girl."

Danny's jaw dropped.

She giggled. "That hard to imagine, huh?"

He shrugged. "Just surprised, that's all."

"Not half as surprised as I am." She walked up to Danny, wrapped her arms around his wet torso, and kissed his chest. "Maybe tonight I could even...I mean, *we* could even..."

Danny peeled her from him. "Don't."

Nancy's smile faltered. "Don't you want to?"

"You don't know how much I want to. I just don't want to take advantage of this 'evil twin' phase of yours."

"Tea parties with Mr. Stuffy the bear were a phase." She drew closer to him again and he offered little resistance. "Behold me growing up, taking chances." She saw the odd look in his eyes. "What, that makes me some kind of sociopath or something?"

He chuckled. "Just wondering if this sudden urge to 'grow up' has something to do with Sandy Doan wanting to jump me."

"Okay, first thing...I only read the relevant parts—what she has tattooed on her butt is between her and God—and second...who brings their diary, their *intimate secrets*, on the Wide Game? She was asking to have a guy like Robby take it."

"So am I as good a kisser as she thinks I am?"

"You're better." Nancy tilted her head up toward his lips, and, after they kissed, she gave his back a slap. "And she better never find that out."

He smiled. "I'm all yours."

The sound of screams rose above the cacophony around them.

Danny's head whipped around and he saw people run for the cliffs. Robby and Mick stood there, looking into the water with slack jaws and shocked eyes. Mick held Paul's camera. Skip Williamson stood with them; his eyes were just as startled, but his lips curled up in a malicious grin. Before Danny could ask what had happened, a voice rose above the chatter of on-lookers.

"Sean Roche fell and hit the rocks," it said.

SIXTEEN

Sean felt hands on his arm, felt them *push*, then his feet slipped and the rocky outcropping abandoned them, left them to the mercy of air and gravity. The limestone cliffs spun past his eyes in a blur. It felt as if someone threw a brick at his shoulder blade, at his ankle, and his eyes slammed shut against the pain—bright showers of sparks igniting in the darkness. The next sensation to shatter his senses was the slap of the water across his chest, a slap so violent it forced the breath from his lungs and consciousness from his brain.

Paul handed his camcorder to Mick, shed his backpack, and dove off the cliff. Sean's hand sank into green murk; Paul latched onto it, pulled him to the surface. There was a loud splash, and, when Paul looked over, he saw Danny at his side. They worked together without a word; hoisted Sean onto their shoulders, and swam for the water's edge. Danny climbed out first, then reached down and pulled Sean from Paul's grasp.

"Is he breathing?" Paul wanted to know, watching bright streams of blood chart courses down Sean's back.

Either Danny didn't hear the question, or he just didn't take time to answer it. Instead, he rushed the summit of the cliff and the knot of spectators loosened to let him pass. "Robby!" He carefully set Sean on the ground and checked the crowd. "Where the fuck are you, man!"

Robby pushed his way onto the scene, took it all in. The first thing he noticed was Sean's right foot. It looked like a rag doll's foot; limp and flat against the ground, part of him and yet disconnected. Next, he saw the blood. It ran across the rock from beneath Sean's shoulder. He knelt beside his friend, checked for a pulse, for respiration, and was relieved to find both. With great care, Robby rolled Sean onto his side; thick threads of blood evacuated an open puncture wound in his back.

A castrating fear came over Robby, and he struggled to keep it from surfacing on his face. "Get me some fuckin' towels... shirts... anything!" His voice rose to a shrill whistle. "We need to stop this bleeding!"

A flowered beach towel hung near Danny's head. He grabbed it, handed it to Robby. Robby wadded it into a ball and shoved it hard against the breach.

Paul pushed his way through the crowd. His clothes clung to him, and water poured down into his squishing shoes. "Is he gonna be all right?"

Danny locked panicky eyes with him. "What the hell happened?"

"I'm not sure." He repeated his question for Robby, "Is he gonna be all right?"

"*I don't know*," Robby shouted, thinking of a million things they had done wrong so far. Had this been an ambulance run, they would have snapped a C-collar around Sean's neck to immobilize it, carefully brought him up the cliff on a back board, then put him on a stretcher and hauled ass to Community Hospital. Instead, Danny had just picked him up like a bag of raked leaves and dragged him up the rocks. Robby looked at the towel, watched the fabric turn dark, and his EMT training washed over his brain like a splash of cold water. "Get some towels, jackets, anything I can use to cover him up. If we don't keep him warm, his body'll go into shock." Robby shot a glance to Sean's twisted foot. Something was broken in there...an ankle, maybe a femur. "I need some sticks...a couple of belts...I've gotta splint his leg."

Some in the ring of spectators appeared to shift their weight, others looked down at Robby with frozen glances.

"Now people, come on!"

A member of the swim team offered the letterman jacket from his backpack, wrapped it around Sean's torso. Annette Wilcher took her Strawberry Shortcake beach towel and draped it across Sean's long legs. A few other on-lookers left the circle and returned with some thick tree branches. Danny broke the limbs into lengths that suited Robby's needs. Three others yanked the belts from their shorts and held them out for Danny as he passed. He grabbed them up, handing everything to Robby.

"Hold this," Robby directed; he grabbed Danny's hand and pulled it to the wad of towel at Sean's back, "and press it against the wound as hard as you can."

Danny did as Robby said; his stomach sank at the sight of Sean's blood in the towel. Nancy knelt down behind him, placed her hand on his broad shoulder. He looked at her, his eyes, normally focused and alert, now care-worn.

"He's gonna be fine." Nancy looked as if she believed it. "Robby knows this stuff."

Danny nodded and turned his attention back to the towel, pressed it hard against his friend's back. He had faith in Robby, but this was bad. Sean needed a hospital, and they were a long way from anything resembling that.

Robby took the sticks and belts, then moved to Sean's injured leg and pulled back the beach towel. He grasped the separated foot and turned it; audible snaps drew disgusted, worried reactions from the on-lookers. Robby's eyes found Annette Wilcher again. "I need you to hold his foot while I splint it."

She nodded, looking green, then knelt down and reached around Robby's grip.

When he was sure she had hold, Robby pulled away. He slid the belts under Sean's leg, placed two of the thickest sticks on either side, then pulled them tight, temporarily keeping the broken bones together. When the last belt was fastened, Robby looked up at Annette. "You can let go now."

She moved away, eager to do so.

The crowd began to drift. Entire groups gathered up their belongings to leave. Some looked concerned, others upset that their day of fun had come to such a screeching halt.

Deidra pushed her way through the spectators that remained. She found Paul and threw her arms around his neck; relief washed worry from her face with sudden tears. "They told me you fell."

"Sean fell." Paul patted her on the back. "I dove in after him."

She pulled away, wiped a tear from her eye as she looked down, transferring her concern. "Jesus."

Mick was behind her with Paul's camcorder and backpack. "How is he?"

Paul shrugged, then he took back the Sony and switched it from camera to playback. He looked into the viewfinder, watched the action in reverse as he searched through the tape. Finally, he saw Sean swim backward, saw him go underwater after his first dive. Paul hit stop, then let it play.

A rush of blurred images ended with a huge, threatening eyeball that filled the monitor. A quick zoom out revealed Skip Williamson. He went after Mick, his face twisted, his mouth moving in a stream of curses. Paul had not packed his earpiece, so his mind supplied the title cards to this silent film.

Williamson said that he could have won the game if not saddled with a queer like Mick.

Mick countered that it was Skip's own fault for being an asshole.

This led to a shoving match.

Paul shook his head, upset with his own unsteady camerawork. It looked as if he'd been dancing with it. This was not far from the truth. He had to dodge being knocked over by Mick and hit by Skip.

An icon flashed in the lower right-hand corner of the screen, a battery with a line through it, but Paul took little notice of it.

Sean burst into the frame, came between the combatants. Skip asked him about his Ninja star. Sean said he didn't have it on him. Skip threw him aside, then pushed Mick again. The blurred rush that followed ended on Sean as his body hit the water.

Static ate the image. The camcorder sucked the last drop of juice from the battery and shut down.

Paul looked at Mick. "Did you see anyone touch Sean after Skip?"

Mick shook his head. "He pushed Sean, then me, then everyone screamed."

Deidra's eyes rose to the camcorder. "Skip did this to Sean?"

"Looks like it."

A smile pulled at Mick's lips. "You got it on tape?"

Paul nodded.

Danny's face tightened. He looked at the towel again, saw that the bleeding had slowed, and turned to Nancy. "Hold this."

Nancy pressed the wad to Sean's wound with one hand, and grabbed Danny's muscular calf with the other. "What are you gonna do?"

Danny pulled free of her grasp. He stood, made a fist at his side. "I'm gonna kill that son of a bitch." He marched toward the limestone monolith. "Williamson!"

It was the bell at the start of a boxing match. The dissolving ring of spectators stopped in their tracks. Their focus shifted from Sean's plight to what they perceived as a title bout.

"Williamson!"

The other stoners looked at Danny, their eyes glazed and red, but Skip continued to look at the ground. Danny stomped toward him, slapped a joint from his fingertips and pushed him back against the limestone wall, PORK SUCKS FAT ONES sprayed in blue above Skip's head. Their principal's last name was Polk, but his weight had led the students to brand him Pork.

"Microwavin' little animals lost its edge?" Danny asked. "Now you wanna get your kicks from killin' kids?"

"What the fuck are you talkin' about, Fields?" Skip presented his best poker face, but inside he was sweating. Skip was a bully. He scared animals and people who were smaller or frailer than he, scared them with the threat that he could, that he *would* harm them. Skip had no power over Danny, however, and that fact drove him insane with rage. "I've had it, fucker! Stop hassling me and get the fuck outta my way."

"Or what?"

"Or you're goin' down."

"I'm impressed." Danny took a step closer to him. "You actually said that with a straight face."

Skip's mouth pulled into a sneer. "You asked for it."

Kenny Dorr and Mack Coyne jumped on Danny's back; Dorr's arms wrapped around his neck and Coyne punched his right side. Some of the spectators screamed, others chanted Danny's name—as if he were Hulk Hogan, and this was a tag-team cage match with Roddy Piper.

Paul handed his camcorder to Mick and took a step toward the action.

Deidra grabbed his arm to pull him back. "Are you insane? They'll kill you."

Paul shook free of her grip, but it became clear that his friend needed no help.

With his right hand, Danny grabbed a fistful of Coyne's greasy hair, with his left, Dorr's wrist. In what appeared to be a single, violent motion, he pulled both boys from his body and threw them onto the ground. Coyne landed on limestone, howling in pain. Dorr landed in the grass, leapt back to his feet, and charged. Danny brought his foot up hard, as if he were kicking an extra point, and the tip of his shoe speared Dorr's crotch. The scream that followed rivaled any Jamie Lee Curtis ever uttered on film. Both boys went down for the count, leaving Williamson to face Danny alone.

Skip launched a right hook aimed at Danny's chin. Danny ducked and stepped back into the grass. Skip stumbled, turned to fling up another jab. Danny grabbed the hand, pinned it against Skip Williamson's back, and pushed him down into the grass.

"You threw Sean off the cliff!" Danny told him; he pushed the point of his knee into Skip's spine and yanked his arm up to his shoulder blades. "He might die now because of you!"

Skip clawed at the grass and clenched his teeth against the pain. "I fuckin' hate you!"

"That's really easy, isn't it? Don't have to feel guilty, or sorry. You feel this?" Danny dug his knee in deeper.

"It was an accident," Skip screamed into the grass. The pain in his arm and back was unbearable. "I swear! I didn't mean to do it!"

"And I'll be sure to tell Sheriff Carter that when you help us get Sean back."

"Game's over, Fields. Get one of your nerdy friends to do it!"

"Sorry to inconvenience you." Danny pressed more of his weight into Skip. God help him, he wanted to cause the son of a bitch pain. Skip gnashed his teeth together and squirmed beneath Danny as he spoke. "But you've been caught on tape. Run now and Sean dies...the sheriff gets to watch you push him. Whatcha think he'll give your performance?—Thumbs up or thumbs down?"

The ramifications struck Skip's brain like a bullet. "What if I help you and he dies anyway?"

"That depends on how much you piss me off between now and then." Danny jerked Skip's arm upward. "So you'd better be real fuckin' *nice*."

Skip uttered a pitiful groan.

There was a voice in Danny's brain; it urged him to pull the arm up until it broke like Sean's leg, but Danny let more rational thoughts prevail and got off Skip's back.

Skip staggered to his feet. He looked at Dorr and Coyne. Neither of them made eye contact; they grabbed up their belongs and faded into the crowd, abandoning him.

Slowly, the spectators turned away. Some looked back at Robby Miller's heroics with Sean, others resumed their packing, and still others began the long walk home. No one paid any attention to *Skip*. Unlike his loss in the corn, this had been too public a defeat. Skip rubbed his arm, feeling his power at Harmony High evaporate.

"What do I need to do?" he asked, his voice meek.

Danny gave him a push toward Sean. "Let's go see."

Sean was still breathing, still unconscious, still covered in the letter jacket and Strawberry Shortcake towel. Robby had removed Nancy from direct pressure duty and she stood behind him, her eyes on Danny, visibly relieved. Mick, Deidra, and Paul regarded Skip with cruel, unforgiving glares.

Skip did not see them; his eyes were focused squarely on the ground.

"Skip's gonna help us," Danny said. "What do we need to do?"

"We need to make a stretcher," Robby told them. "We need two long poles and... Shit, I don't know, more towels. I need to tie the towels to the poles so we can all grab on and carry Sean outta here."

Danny nodded. "You got it."

"People are starting to leave," Deidra pointed out. "How many are we gonna need to carry him?"

"Six people should do it. Two at his head, two at his feet, and two to pick up the slack in the middle." Robby looked around. "Danny, me, *Skip*, Mick, Paul..."

"And me," she volunteered.

Robby nodded. "And you makes six."

"I can carry our packs and junk to help you guys out," Nancy offered.

"What about me?" It was Cindi.

"You don't have to come," Nancy told her. "You can hike back with Danyell and Monica."

She shook her head. "All my stuff's at your house."

"Fine," Nancy said. "Help me carry crap."

Deidra looked around. Sean's accident had been a pail of water on the Senior Class's fall bonfire. By the time they manufactured a stretcher for Sean, their little group could very well be walking back alone. "We should tell people to call for help when they get home."

"Good idea," Robby admitted. "Could you do that?"

She nodded. "Anything specific you want me to tell 'em?"

"Tell 'em to call 911, tell 'em to say we need a Lifeline helicopter out here. The dispatcher will take it from there."

"You got it." Deidra gave Paul's hand a loving squeeze, then pulled away.

"I'll help you," Nancy said. "The more people we ask, the better our chances someone will actually do it."

As the girls went to relay the message to anyone who would listen, Robby looked at his watch. It was 4:30. Night would chase the sun from the sky by six or seven, and this morning, without the burden of an injured body, it had taken nearly four hours to walk the distance to the quarry.

Robby hoped someone would reach home sooner, hoped they would make that 911 call, hoped help would come and shorten their hike. He did not relish the thought of walking back in the dark, in the inevitable cold that would accompany it.

Not at all.

PART TWO: MASTERS OF THE GAME

SEVENTEEN

The forest arched over the group, surrounded them like an ancient cathedral. Trees grew in straight lines, columns erected according to the blueprint of some great, unseen architect. Their roots lay buried beneath the ruins of some former temple; toppled trunks so elderly they had seen Miami tribes in their abundance, some ancient enough to remember when Man was but a fantasy God toyed with in the corner of His mind. Now, they lay moldering, their rotting skins covered in minor forests of mushroom umbrellas and swelling puffballs.

A dirt path wended its way through the undergrowth. The group took it slowly, like pall bearers, and Sean rocked back and forth with their every step; Danny and Skip supported his head, Robby and Mick held up his feet, and Paul and Deidra kept his torso aloft. Nancy and Cindi followed behind the make-shift stretcher, loaded down with backpacks and Paul's camcorder.

Mick adjusted his grip on the wooden frame, then looked down at his friend, his eyes lingering on the immobilized leg and the blood-soaked towel at Sean's shoulder. "Is he in pain?"

"He's unconscious," Robby said.

"But what happens when he wakes up?"

Robby shrugged. "He'll be in a shitload of pain."

"Can we give him something?" Danny asked.

Robby did not look up from the path. "Like what?"

"Tylenol or something," Danny said angrily.

At that, Robby grew angry himself. "Do you have a fuckin' Tylenol?"

"I have some Midol," Cindi offered.

"That's great." Robby flashed a humorless grin. "When Sean gets his first period, I'll call you."

"She's just trying to help," Nancy told him.

No one talked for a while after that, but the walk was far from quiet. Wind moved through laden branches, created a sound like a raging river, and the night insects stirred to life; their twittering rose until it was almost deafening, then fell suddenly silent. Together, the sounds became a woodland symphony, not a joyous tune, but a dirge. Within weeks, the forest would be stripped naked and left to die beneath a shroud of snow.

Deidra looked up into the eddies of wind-blown leaves. "The Miami thought these woods were full of spirits. They thought this place was so haunted that for five hundred years it's been one of their laws not to come in here."

Paul got off-step, the tip of his shoe catching Skip's heel.

"Watch it, fucker," Skip warned.

Paul blinked. "Sorry."

He thought Deidra might go on to relay the story she'd told him earlier, thought she might mention the crows and the corn. Instead, she left the thread dangling.

Robby picked it up. "Let me tell you some *real* scary stories."

Paul lowered his eyes. He saw a pair of bleached antlers sticking up from the seedbed of moss and leaves, as if a deer were submerged beneath it, waiting for them to pass.

Robby told them what he'd learned about the northern fields at the fire station. Danny gave him a dirty look, but that didn't stop him. He told them about the Warner lynching and the grand dragon's death in

'46, about the Baptist minister's act of arson in '64, and about the Andrews twins in '72.

Nancy grabbed Cindi's arm as if she needed protection. "Okay, I'm officially freaked out."

Skip smiled and jumped in with a tale of his own. "My uncle knew this guy back in high school in '72. He was driving down Route 6, around midnight, when he saw this little girl—maybe twelve—in his headlights, just walking along the edge of the cornfield at the side of the road. Well, it's late and it's cold, and this guy my uncle knew wonders what she's doing out so late, so he slows down to ask if she's all right."

Paul had heard this story before. He looked around, saw Nancy hold Cindi's arm a bit tighter and Danny stare at the path ahead as if he could not care less. Mick, Robby, and Deidra watched the back of Skip's head with great interest.

"The girl opens his back door and slides into the seat." Skip removed his right hand from the poles of the litter, flexed his fingers, then returned it. "She thanks him for the ride and he asks her what she's doing out so late. She tells him she went for a walk and got lost in the field, said her parents were gonna be worried about her. My uncle's friend says she must be cold and gives her his letterman jacket. He was a wrestler or something. Anyway, the girl puts the jacket on and gives him directions to her house. On the way there he passes by Townson Cemetery and has to slow down—you know, where the road gets all twisted, like a snake? Anyway, he turns to ask the girl if he's got his directions right and the girl isn't there. She's just fuckin' gone."

"Where'd she go?" Nancy asked as if she really didn't want to know.

"See, it was late, and this guy had a curfew, so he just goes on home. But, the next day, he goes to the little girl's house."

"Because..?" Paul asked, knowing the answer.

"Because he wanted his jacket back," Skip said. "Anyway, he goes to the house and knocks on the door. When it opens, he sees the little girl and asks her for his jacket. She gets all freaked and calls for her mom. The mother comes to the door and she's a total wreck. She asks my uncle's friend what he wants and he tells her the whole story. The woman says that it's not possible, that the little girl was home all night. My uncle's friend says he's not makin' this crap up, says Betsy has his jacket."

"How'd he know her name was Betsy?" Deidra asked.

Paul smiled. Skip screwed up the telling of the tale and she'd caught it.

"She told him when she got in his car. Anyway, the mother freaks out, tells my uncle's friend she doesn't know what he's trying to pull but he'd better get the fuck off their property. This guy is totally confused, so he asks what's wrong. That's when the mother tells him Betsy was Marcia's twin sister, tells him they buried her three months ago."

"That's enough, Skip," Cindi said with a taut voice. Nancy was strangling the blood from her arm.

"But that's not the kicker," Skip told them. "For some reason, after he leaves the house, he drives out to Townson Cemetery. He find's the little girl's headstone, the one that says she died in July, and sitting on the muddy grave, neatly folded, is my uncle's friend's letterman jacket."

Robby's eyes rolled over. "My cousin told me that when I was twelve, but he said it happened to a friend of his in Griffith. It didn't have anything to do with the Andrews twins or the cornfield."

Skip sneered at him, a sardonic glaze over his eyes. "Like your stories were any fuckin' better."

"Mine weren't stories," Robby insisted. "I'm not—" He caught sight of the trees and his train of thought derailed. "Jesus."

Paul looked up; he half-expected to see Mr. Warner swinging from a branch, white eyes bulging from his black face, eyes that burned with fear and rage. Instead, he saw a flock of birds. Crows. Hundreds of crows. The trees were black with them. His stomach and bladder felt slack.

Deidra was unnerved as well. "It's like they're following us."

Robby chuckled at that. "That's a sign of good luck...in Haiti."

Skip's lip twisted to a grin. "At least they're not vultures."

Danny flashed him a horrified glare, then gave his eyes back to the path. They needed to keep moving, to get Sean some help.

Cindi froze. "They're not gonna...attack us, are they?"

Aggravated, Nancy pulled her along until she began walking again. It was getting dark and Nancy did not want to be in the woods at night. "Birds don't attack people."

Robby saw his opportunity. "Sure they do." He took one hand from the litter and pointed to his face. "They go for your eyes and peck 'em out."

Cindi regarded him with mistrust. One of the crows cawed; she jumped. "Shit!"

"All day, when I've seen these birds looking at us, it made me think of this old movie I saw on Sammy Terry," Paul told them. Sammy Terry hosted late night horror movies on Channel 4. He was just an old man in a Halloween robe, a silly rubber spider named George as his sidekick, but he had the creepiest voice; every introduction promised a truly horrifying experience. The movies that followed, however, were usually schlock. "*The Beast With A Million Eyes*. Ever see it?"

"No," Danny said.

"The creature was this cheesy-looking thing. Some stage hand made it by covering a coffee pot with eyes."

Robby smirked. "Sounds like one of *your* movies, Rice."

"See, the studio said 'the picture's called *The Beast With A Million Eyes*, so we need to see a monster with a million eyes.'"

Deidra chuckled. "Makes sense."

Paul kept his eyes on the flock, but her words brought a smile to his lips. "In the script, the 'million eyes' were the eyes of birds. The creature was seeing everything through their eyes. I've done the same thing in my space zombie script. These creatures crawl inside people and turn them into zombies-"

"Stop it," Nancy said with no inflection.

"—but they're really all part of the same creature, like cells in a body, and, at the end of the movie, we see this huge brain with teeth and tentacles that knows everything and sees everything."

Deidra feigned upset. "Thanks for ruining it for me!"

"Sorry." Paul looked at her, still smiling. "But you're already dead, remember."

Nancy found anger to give her words weight. "I said stop it!" Everyone's eyes found hers, saw how uncomfortable the stories, and now the birds, had made her.

Danny shook his head. "Hop off this horror express, guys. Your bullshit's scaring the ladies."

"I'm tellin' you it's not bullshit," Robby contended.

"You're lumping these things all together, things that could really have happened, and trying to say that they mean something."

"You don't think they do?"

Danny shook his head again. "If you throw darts at a map, you're gonna find every town's had its share of strange stuff. Like the bumper sticker says, shit happens. It's not ghosts or ancient Indian burial grounds or any of that Sammy Terry crap. It's just this fucked up world bein' fucked up."

"What about these crows?" Paul asked. "You gotta admit *this* is weird."

"Weird, sure, but there's nothing supernatural about a flock of birds."

Cindi looked at the birds and they looked right back at her. "Well, it's not *natural*."

"Isn't there a special name for a flock of crows?" Deidra asked. "You know, like a gaggle of geese or a pod of whales?"

"I've always just heard them called a flock," Mick told her.

"No," Paul corrected, "I think they do have another name...something ominous..." It was on the tip of his tongue, but for the life of him, he couldn't remember it.

"I can't believe you people are such pussies!" Skip suddenly flailed his free arm outward; his mouth and eyes open wide as he let loose a scream.

In the trees, the crows did not move a muscle.

On the ground, everyone but Danny jumped. His eyes flew to Skip, shock and anger brawling within his gaze. "What the fuck are you doin'?"

Skip didn't answer. He dipped down to snatch a small rock off the ground. As he moved, the litter tilted and Sean's head lolled to the right.

Robby leaned over, grabbed the pole with his right hand and tried to pull it level. "Christ!"

Skip stood up, drew back his hand and threw it forward as if pitching a baseball. The rock flew into the crow-laden branches, struck one of the birds squarely in its black chest. It fell to the ground with a thud, its legs pointed out; its wings spread wide open. It looked as if it were trying to make a snow angel in the dirt path.

"Bull's eye!" Skip smiled and kicked the dead bird from the trail as he walked by. "Just a fuckin' crow."

Mick looked at the carcass, then to Williamson. He shook his head. "You're a fucking asshole."

Cindi's eyes were still in the trees. "Why didn't the rest of 'em fly away?"

Paul looked up. The flock had not moved. They should have scattered the instant Skip lobbed the stone, instead they held fast to their perches.

Skip's lips parted slowly and froze that way, at a loss to explain it.

"Maybe they're asleep," Robby proposed.

Cindi didn't buy it. "Their eyes are open."

Had she not been so unnerved, Nancy might have laughed, but her words to Cindi were humorless. "Birds don't have eyelids."

"They're asleep," Robby said confidently.

Mick squinted through his thick lenses. "I don't think so."

"Why not?"

"Because birds *do* have eyelids, and crows have two sets of them, an outer one, just like you and me, and an inner one—a thin membrane that covers their eyes when they sleep." Mick pointed toward the trees. "I haven't seen them use either one."

They emerged from the woods on the other side, carried Sean out onto a strip of tall grass. Stalks of corn stood before them, a green wall that stretched to the horizon in either direction. The red glow of sunset peeked between ribbons of dark clouds overhead, as if a huge claw had scratched a black sky and left it to bleed.

Paul noticed the difference in sound almost immediately. The music of the woods dulled, replaced by the soft noise of corn tassels brushing one another in the breeze. It seemed expectant, like whispers in the dark before a surprise party.

Danny's eyes found a dark spot in the green barrier; a place where the stalks lay bent and broken, pushed outward by contestants eager to win the Wide Game. He pointed to it. "I guess we go this way."

"Are you sure?" Paul asked. Two hundred people had entered the field from various points. If they picked the wrong path to follow, they could carry Sean further from the help he needed.

"I'll check." Danny reached into his pocket and produced a small compass. He looked at the needle, tilted the base so it covered the "N." The path clearly led southeast. "Yeah, this is the way."

"Let me see that." Skip snatched the compass from Danny's hand, stared at the metal threads that encircled the base. "You get this outta Cracker Jacks?"

Danny grabbed it back from him. "It's off the handle of my hunting knife."

Nancy looked to the sky, saw the sun slip toward the horizon like a match to water. She shuddered. "Anyone bother to bring a flashlight?"

Paul motioned to her. "Let me see my pack."

Nancy took a step forward, Cindi released the death grip on her arm and carried the black nylon knapsack to him.

With his free hand, Paul unzipped it and reached inside. He felt the laminated Trapper Keeper that held his script, felt the plastic camera battery (which he removed and slid beneath his chin), and felt a smooth metal surface that had to be his canteen. Finally, his fingers found the object of their quest; he removed a small, square spotlight from the pack, a long, black cord trailing over his hand like a tail.

He looked at Deidra. "I'm gonna need to let go for a minute."

She nodded. "Go 'head."

Paul released his grip and the litter dipped toward him. He zipped up his pack, used the new battery to power up the camera, then slid the spotlight into place. With its cord plugged into the proper jack, the light ignited.

Skip shielded his eyes. "Hey!"

Paul ignored him; he walked the camera around the stretcher and handed it to Danny. "This should do it."

Danny was impressed. "You came ready."

"Never let it be said he's not prepared," Deidra said with a smile.

Paul blushed, halted a grin before it captured his lips. He started to walk back to his post, but Danny held out the camera to stop him.

"Thanks."

He shrugged. "No sweat."

Danny smiled, then aimed the light into the darkened cornfield and found the path they'd made earlier in the day. When Paul took up his slack, they started in.

EIGHTEEN

Fingers closed across the sky, dark clouds, they blocked out the setting sun, forced night upon the field like a coffin lid slamming shut. Wind, so refreshing in the afternoon heat, turned frigid as a snowman's breath. And with the darkness and the cold came a fog, thick and white. It descended upon the stalks like a weary ghost lying down for a nap. The camcorder's spotlight bobbed and danced up the row, a glowing apparition on wisps of phantom hair. Crickets ended their conversation with the other denizens of the field, leaving only the whispering tassels and the crunch of the group's footfalls to break the silence.

Mick's glasses became as fogged as their surroundings. He removed them with his free hand, rubbed them across his shirt, his eyes narrow. When he replaced them, however, he still saw the world as a blur of light and shadow. "I can't see a thing."

Skip muttered something under his breath and Danny offered him a hostile warning with his eyes.

Mick took no notice of the exchange. "Can we stop for a minute?"

Cindi, who'd been quiet since the birds, perked up. "I could *totally* use a break."

Robby nodded in agreement. "I have to check Sean's wounds and vitals anyway."

"Fine." The worry was still clear on Danny's face, which glistened in the warmth of the spotlight. "But just for a minute."

They lowered the stretcher. When Sean was safely on the ground, Danny wiped the sweat from his forehead. Mick rubbed both sides of his eyeglass lenses with his shirt. Skip lit a Marlboro; the flame from his match turned pearly fog into hot, hellish smoke swirling around his head. Paul rubbed his shoulder and Deidra went to him, kneading his muscles with her slender fingers. He winced, but not because she hurt him. Her hands were like ice.

"Should I stop?" she asked.

"No."

She nodded, continued to work at the tight cords beneath his skin. "How far do you think we've come?"

"Hard to say." Paul looked up, tried to see stars through the lacy mesh of fog and found none. He closed his eyes, his body rocking back and forth with each pull and rub of her fingers. "We're moving pretty quick, considering. How you holding up?"

"Fine." She paused her massage. "Just worried about Sean."

Paul opened his eyes and found Danny, watched as the strength they'd always admired flickered within him like a flame fighting for life—anxiety threatening to extinguish it. Danny and Sean's friendship predated "the group." If the unthinkable happened...if Sean *died*... Danny could be inconsolable.

Danny watched as Robby found a pulse and timed it, watched him check the bleeding—which appeared to have all but stopped, then adjust the tightness of the splint. "How is he?"

Robby's body jerked, Danny's voice a gunshot blast in his ear. "He's stable, for now."

"Anyone need a drink or something?" Nancy walked around the litter, paid out backpacks.

Paul took his. "Thanks."

Deidra placed a hand on Nancy's shoulder, scanned her eyes. "You okay?"

Nancy shrugged, trying to grin as she handed Deidra her pack. She went to Danny's side, gave him his bag, then ran her hand across his crew cut and down his cheek. He took her hand in his and offered a grateful smile. They exchanged no words, and yet Paul saw an understanding between them. She looked around. "This fog's creepy, don't you think?"

"It is spooky." Cindi shivered. "I mean, after all those crows and everything."

Mick put his glasses back on. "It's perfectly natural." He spoke with conviction, but his magnified eyes were hardly persuasive. "The ground is warm from the heat of the day, and the air has gotten colder. One plus one equals two."

"Everybody ready to get moving?" Danny asked.

"Give us a full minute, would ya?" Robby reached into his backpack. "I need at least a *sip* of water."

Danny nodded.

Paul dug into his own pack, produced a denim jacket with a NO MORAL MAJORITY button pinned just above the left breast pocket. He slid it on and the night air stopped cutting so deeply. When he looked up, Paul was aware that everyone looked at him with envious eyes. With the warm forecast, they'd packed no jackets of their own. He was about to offer his to the group in shifts when he noticed Skip was not among them. "Where's Williamson?"

They looked to the spot where Skip had been standing, then whipped their glances into the surrounding mist. Long leaves protruded from it, fingers clawing their way through a blanket of gauze, but there was no sign of him. He'd simply vanished.

"Son of a..." Danny's hand clinched into a fist. He turned the spotlight of the camera on the milky wall of fog and marched toward it.

Nancy slid into his path. "Before you go all Captain Caveman on us, I feel I should remind you of something."

"What?"

"You warned Skip what would happen if he bolted. He didn't listen or he doesn't care. Either way, when we get back, you show Sheriff Carter the tape. I'll take his spot." She pointed at Sean's litter, then looked to Cindi. "Cin can carry my share of the bags, right?"

"Sure," Cindi huffed. "I'm *so* the bag lady."

"You really want him out there stalking us?" Danny sidestepped her. "I want him where I can see him."

Paul took a following stride. "Count me in for the insanity."

Deidra tugged at him. "Danny can handle this."

"I'll be right back." As Paul pried himself from her grasp, he realized *Friday the 13th* characters said the same thing before a stroll in the woods. He stole a backward glance as he moved into the haze, watched the chalky curtains close over Deidra and make her shadow.

Danny was on the move, the haloed spotlight at his side keeping him visible in the churning soup.

"What's the plan?" Paul asked.

A long leaf smacked Danny across the face. He angrily pushed it aside and raised the light, tried to find broken stalks or some other sign to point them in the right direction. "We find Skip, tackle him, and drag him back."

"And me without my shoulder pads."

"You know, Deidra's right. I can do this on my own." "Never doubted it." Paul nodded at the Sony in Danny's hand. "I'm just here to protect my camera."

There was a snap, followed by a crunch. Someone was moving to their left. Danny swung the camcorder's light around. Nearby cornstalks turned white in its glare and those beyond its reach appeared dark as prison bars.

Paul cupped his hands around his mouth. "*Skip!*"

No response.

Danny ran in the direction of the sounds, the spotlight bobbed madly across the fog in front of him.

After a moment's deliberation, Paul followed. "*Wait up!*"

As big as he was, Danny Fields was quick. It was one of the talents that won him his scholarship. He could find a hole in a defensive line and sprint like the Road Runner. Now his muscular legs carried him into the murk, plowing through cornstalks the way he plowed through linemen. Then, without warning, he stopped.

Something stood in the row. It loomed from the haze like a specter; tall, and dark—its arms outstretched.

Unable to halt his own run, Paul thumped against the form. He stood there for an instant; his eyes bulged from their sockets, then his mouth let out a wail. When he pushed himself away from the shadow, Paul got caught up in his own feet and fell back into Danny. They landed in a heap, panting, nearby laughter filling their ears.

"I wish you faggots could see yourselves!" Skip howled as he walked from the corn.

Paul looked up at the shadowy form he'd collided with. It was a huge cross with a figure attached to it. He thought he was at the foot of a large crucifix, wondered why that thought scared him, then realized it must be a scarecrow.

A muffled roar came from beneath him, "*Get offa me.*"

Blood rushed to Paul's face; he rose to his feet, allowed his friend up.

Danny whirled on Skip, punched him hard in the mouth to stop his laughter.

Before he could deliver a second blow, Paul grabbed Danny's arm just below his elbow. "You tryin' to kill him?"

"No," Danny said. He jerked free and spun around. For a moment, Paul thought he might have a punch for him as well, but he didn't. Danny normally left his unchecked aggression on the football field. There was nothing ordinary about these circumstances, however, and he had taken in more than his fill of Skip. "Smashing his face in should be enough for me."

Skip rubbed his split lip. "Bastard!"

"You'd know."

Paul asked flatly, "What were you trying to do, Skip?"

"I was takin' a shit. Then, I see you two crash into that scarecrow like a couple of dumbfucks."

Robby materialized from the haze like some elemental phantom. Concern glowed in his eyes and his voice wavered from its normal firmness. "You guys still among the living?"

Paul looked at him, surprise diving into fear for Deidra. "Tell me you didn't leave the girls alone back there?"

"Mick's with 'em. We heard screaming and laughing, so they had me follow the sounds to see what was going on. I gotta admit, I thought I'd find Skip doin' a slice and dice on your asses!"

"Your friends at the fire station really got you spooked, Miller." Danny flexed his fist, then dusted himself off. "Skip, retard that he is, just thought it would be funny to see us bump into a fuckin' scarecrow."

The imperious tint returned to Robby's words. "That's why I didn't go with you guys." He picked the camcorder up off the ground where Danny left it. "I knew it was a set up."

Paul brushed the dirt from his own clothing, and felt something warm and sticky on his jacket. He grimaced and held out his hand, tried to see what it was that he'd touched. Fluid glistened on his fingers, nearly black in the chalky gloom. He swallowed hard. "Robby, let me see the camera."

"Christ, Rice, can't you go two seconds without—"

"*Let me see it!*"

Robby handed him the Sony and he aimed the spotlight at his fingers. They were covered in rosy syrup. *Transmission fluid*, his mind offered, remembering a puddle that had formed on his gravel drive, a puddle that grew until he'd saved enough money to get his Mustang fixed. But this wasn't transmission fluid. Paul's stomach sank and he aimed the camera at the scarecrow. When the light hit it, his lungs emptied like punctured tires, leaving him vacant and cold. "Oh, sweet mother of God..."

Paul's first instinct had been right, a man had been crucified. Lengths of rusted chain lashed his body to the wooden cross. Corncobs jutted from his hollowed-out eye sockets, and his mouth hung open, a scream forever choked by corn leaves. Paul thought the boy wore a tie-dyed shirt, then he saw the letters—

HARMONY HIGH TRACK AND FIELD, barely visible beneath reddish-brown splotches and streaks.

—and he realized the shirt was covered in a slop of congealing blood.

Hey, Paul, his mind began, *you bumped into that thing. How does it feel to have part of that guy stuck to your jacket?*

Paul's stomach heaved. He dropped the camera to the ground, wished he'd never asked for it, and fell on all fours. What little he'd eaten that day came back up noisily, violently spilling across his lips and onto the ground.

Danny grabbed hold of the camera, placed the spotlight back on the Scarecrow Man, on the ruined track uniform he wore and the golden hair that blew in the breeze. "Jesus Christ...it's Dale Brightman."

"Shit," Skip whispered, unaware he was even speaking.

Paul rose to his knees, his eyes clamped shut, his throat blazing. "Our father who art in heaven—"

"Who could have done *that*?" Danny asked.

Paul's head rode the teacups at Disney World. He thought he might faint, but fought the urge. If he lost consciousness now, the others might go on without him and he would wake up at the foot of the cross, the Scarecrow Man looking down at him with bloody, corncob eyes. If that happened, Paul would go stark raving mad.

"—Thy kingdom come, Thy will be done—"

"Who could have done that?" Danny repeated as Paul went on with his prayer.

Robby took the camcorder from him, illuminated details of Dale's body with the spotlight. Dark slits, maybe three inches long, covered his entire torso. They had to be knife wounds. A broken rib jutted from his chest, pulled out as the blade was withdrawn for another strike. Robby had never seen a sight remotely similar. Whoever had done this was a real-life psycho.

"He's been stabbed," he announced with a steady voice that belied his own nausea.

"Where's your knife, Fields?" Skip asked unexpectedly, contumely.

Danny whirled and gave Williamson a hard push. "What'd you ask me?"

"You said that compass of yours came off a knife. Where's your fuckin' knife?"

"It's in my pack."

"Show me."

"I don't have to show you shit on a stick. You're the one with a history of violence." Danny motioned into the fog, toward where the others stood waiting. "Maybe you did Dale this morning and came out here now to check on your handiwork. What'd you use, a Samurai sword? More of your Ninja toys?"

"That's crap and you know it."

"What happened to your leather jacket?"

"My what?" Something close to fear danced in Skip's eyes, but his face remained indifferent.

"Your jacket. You never take it off, but you weren't wearing it when you caught up with us in the field. Did you get blood on it when you were stabbing him?"

"Screw that." Skip held up his hand, flashed fingers as he spoke. "Number one, I beat dorks...I beat *your* dork. Fine, guilty as charged. Two, what happened with

Sean was a total accident, okay. And fact number three is that I didn't wear my jacket because it was fuckin' hot out and not because I stabbed someone. My little throwing stars wouldn't do *that*, and I don't own a knife."

"Sure."

"I'm still waiting to see your knife, though. Did you get blood on *that*?"

With jerky, angry movements, Danny slid the pack from his back. His scornful eyes locked with Skip's as he unzipped the bag with harsh, broken strokes and reached inside. His hand dug through the contents, created a muffled clatter.

Paul's head stepped off the ride. He took a Kleenex from his pocket and blew into it, then wiped the spittle from his lips before tossing it into the murk. With a trembling hand, he beckoned the camera from Robby and aimed its light at Danny's pack. He could hear the familiar sound of tape being moved within and saw the red record light blazing in the dark below the eyepiece monitor. How long had it been on?

Long enough to record all the disturbing details of the Scarecrow Man.

Confusion sprouted in Danny's eyes and grew across his face. He tilted the pack into the light and continued to rummage, his movements becoming harried and frantic. After a moment, he turned the bag upside down, dropped the contents onto the dirt and raked his fingers through the multicolored pile. He reminded Paul of a child just home from Trick-or-Treating, emptying his pillowcase and searching for a favorite bit of candy.

He mumbled something to himself, then said, "It's gone."

Skip backed up into the fog. "That's what I thought,"

Danny grabbed his arm to stop him and Skip shook free of the grip.

Before Danny could do or say anything, Robby broke in. "What do we tell the others?"

"Nothing." Danny knelt down and shoved items back into his pack. "You've got the girls scared shitless as it is with all your bullshit."

Robby pointed back at what was left of Dale Brightman. *"This isn't bullshit."*

Danny was on his feet again. "Lower your fuckin' voice."

"We need to tell 'em something," Paul said, still looking through his eyepiece.

Danny looked at the blinking red record light and his face flared. "Quit wasting the battery," he said. "We'll need the light." He grabbed the lens, trying to jerk it away.

"I don't think you get it." Paul backed off, his face still pressed against the rubber square of the eyepiece, his naked eye shut. "A kid is dead, killed with a *knife*. Your knife is gone. For all we know, the killer is still out here with us and the more I get on tape as evidence, the better it will be for you."

"Yeah, okay," Danny said, matter-of-fact, as if Paul had just offered him a soda. Sean and Mick had seen the knife, and, even though they wouldn't mean to hurt his case, they'd be obligated to tell the sheriff as much. A dead boy, killed with a knife. A living boy who had a knife, then didn't. While nobody was looking, the prosecution would theorize, he'd gone off into the corn, killed Dale, then ditched the murder weapon. People had been executed with less. He could see the headlines now: *Football Hero Kills Track Star*. It was bad.

Paul watched these thoughts play across Danny's face. "Look," he told him. "I know there's no way in hell you did this."

Skip lit another Marlboro; the smoke drifted off to merge with the fog. "There's no way in hell I did this either, Rice."

Paul glared at him, tried to control his own temper. He too was having difficulty. "*Anybody* could have done it, just like anybody could have taken Danny's knife. That was one of the objects of the game, right? Take somebody's stuff without them knowing it." He turned the camera once more to Danny. "I only want to help you if I can, and this is the only way I know how. Please, let me do it."

Danny pushed a hand up his face and through his hair. He looked back at the crucified silhouette. "We should take him down from there, cover him up."

"Whoa...bad idea," Robby urged, looking around as if he expected something to jump out at him. "Tampering with evidence, blah blah blah... Look, can we just *go*?"

"We can't just leave him like..." Danny glanced at the shadow cross, not really wanting to see it again. "...*that*."

Smoke plumed from Skip's mouth and nose as if a bomb had gone off in his brain. "I'm sure as hell not touchin' it."

He tried to push past Danny. Danny grabbed him by the shirt and threw him back against Dale and the cross. It shuddered, the chains rattled and slapped against the wood, Dale's head rocked back and forth. A leaf, clotted with blood, was dislodged from his mouth. It fell onto Skip's shoulder and he brushed it away as if it were a poisonous tarantula, jerking forward and arching his back out in disgust.

"*It* is Dale Brightman." Danny stood in his face and Skip tilted his head to the side as if he were afraid of being kissed. "And now that you've touched *him*, help us get him down."

Robby held his head in his hands. "What the fuck are you doin', Danny? You're contaminating a *crime scene*!"

Danny did not look at him. "We're not leaving Dale like this. Paul can take video of...how he looks."

"Robby already did," Paul told him. "The camera's been recording this whole time."

He went on as if he hadn't heard, "That's what the cops would do anyway. They'd take pictures, then they'd take him down."

"What about the girls, and Sean?" Paul asked, thinking of Deidra in the darkness and fog, tacking Sean's name to the question for persuasion. "Any second now, they're gonna wonder why Robby isn't back yet and come lookin' for us all."

Danny nodded. "Robby, go back and tell 'em we're fine. I sure as hell don't want 'em to see this. We'll take him down quick. With three of us, it shouldn't take long. But we're not saying anything about what's happened until we get the girls back home safe."

With reluctance, they agreed.

Robby walked back into the mist toward Deidra while they took Dale Brightman from the cross. Paul used his jacket as a shroud. The night air was chilly against his naked arms, but the denim had been covered in blood. He set the camera on the ground, a rock lifting it to the proper angle to give them light and record the event. Later, if necessary, the police could see what they had done, could know they had taken the time and the care to do it. No murderer (or murderer*s*) that brutal would show such respect.

When it was finished, they followed the trail of broken stalks back through the fog. It occurred to Paul that a quiet had consumed everything—the voices of insects, the whispering of stalks, even the dry crunch of rocks and dirt at their feet. The entire world seemed void of sound. It made him grow even colder and he shuddered.

The gray vapor darkened and swirled as Deidra burst into the oasis of light they carried with them. There was fret behind her eyes and she pressed against Paul, filled his nose with the scent of her perfume. He welcomed her warmth and the taste of her kiss, wishing they were back in the safety of her bed, wishing they'd never left it.

"What happened out there?" she asked.

Paul shrugged. "We tripped over each other in the dark and Skip thought it was a riot."

"Where's your jacket?"

"I lost it. Didn't want to take time to look for it in the fog."

Deidra studied his face, his eyes. "What's going on?"

"Nothing."

She frowned, pushed her lips against his ear. "I thought we weren't going to keep secrets from each other?"

Paul looked over her shoulder. "I'm not keeping it from *you*."

She turned, saw Nancy and Cindi shiver in the light from the camcorder, then gave her attention back to him.

He pointed to his camera and whispered, "Later."

"How bad is it?"

"Bad," he said, then kissed her earlobe.

"Everyone all right?" Danny asked. All things considered, his voice sounded strong and steady.

Nancy shivered. "*No.*"

"Excuse me, why don't you guys just get over it already" Cindi said, "'Cause I'm really tired of this mindfuck you're all pulling."

Robby, who'd been giving Sean's vitals and wounds a thorough inspection when they arrived, looked up at her and smiled. Unlike Danny, however, his voice seemed shaky, his smile uneasy. "Could you possibly be more vague, She Bop?"

"If you call me She Bop one more time, I'm gonna beat your head in."

Paul could see the hurt in her eyes and wondered is she knew how visible it was. Then again, maybe she wasn't trying to hide it at all. Maybe she had it there for Robby to notice.

She pointed over her shoulder with her thumb. "Let me guess. You're clueless about the laughing and voices we heard back there."

Robby's face went slack and he shot a glance up to Danny.

"Back where?" The steadiness in Danny's voice flickered a bit.

Cindi swept the mist with her arm, more than a little pissed off. "I don't know. You take the camera...

thingimibob and leave us standing here in the dark, and the cold, and the—"

Nancy broke in, "Oh, stop being such a wimp, would you?" She looked at Danny, visibly tense. "We heard you guys screaming and laughing out there in front of us, and, as soon as Robby left to check on you, we heard voices and laughing *behind* us. I thought Skip was running from you guys or something..." She pointed in the direction of Dale's body and the cross. "...but then you came from over there."

While everyone else was staring at one another and the mist, Skip walked over to his backpack and removed his silver canteen. He drank deeply, then spewed the liquid into the fog, coughing. He brought the canteen over to the camcorder lamp, pouring its contents through the beam of light in a scarlet stream. "What the fuck?"

Cindi turned up her nose. "Gnarly!"

Mick readjusted his glasses on his nose, smiling at Skip's misfortune. "Fruit juice go bad?"

"Cold water," Skip said. "Now it's fuckin' warm and...*red*!"

"It's been in your backpack all day," Mick laughed uneasily. "And your canteen's probably full of rust or something."

This reasoning made sense. Rust had tinted the water red and a day in the sun had warmed it. It really did make sense. And yet, as he watched the thick, backlit stream flow from the canteen, all Paul could think was... *blood*. His mind quickly shook that grotesque thought off, however. It was impossible.

Skip finished pouring the—
BLOOD!

—tainted water onto the ground and threw the flask down beside it. Whatever the liquid actually was, now that it had been in his canteen, he wanted nothing to do with either, just as Paul had wanted nothing to do with the jacket the Scarecrow Man had touched.

"Let's just get moving." Danny told the group, anxious to get Sean to help, even more anxious to be out of the cornfield.

Deidra's hand moved to Paul's shoulder, gripping it lightly. She said nothing, just studied him with curious eyes, but he could tell she saw the fear in him. He offered her a lame grin, then slowly moved to take up his position on the stretcher.

Together, they moved into the haze.

NINETEEN

Nancy whirled around, stared into the darkening fog behind them. "What was that?"

"What was what?" Robby asked.

"I keep hearing things."

The comment was ripe for one of Robby's comebacks. Instead, he turned pale. "What kinds of things?"

"Like whispering or something. And then it sounds like someone's moving in the corn. I hear these footsteps, like one right after the other."

"I heard 'em too," Cindi told them; she now held Nancy as tightly as Nancy had been holding her. "You guys, something is definitely out here with us right now."

"It's just animals or somethin'," Danny said. "As long as you can't see them, they probably can't see you either."

And then Deidra *did* see something. It registered in the tail of her eye, a flutter in the misty air, like the lazy flap of large wings.

Crow's wings?

Dark patches stained the sheet of fog; silhouettes, large enough to be classmates, but hunched over, their movements in some way unnatural. When Deidra jerked her head in their direction, she found nothing but haze. There was no doubt that they were real, however.

She still felt their eyes upon her.

"What is it?" Paul asked.

"People." The word hung in the air like the mist that surrounded her.

One by one, the others looked at Deidra, then in the direction of her gaze.

Danny squinted. "Where are they?"

She gave a slight nod toward the thickening mist. "Out there."

"How many?" Paul wanted to know.

Deidra shrugged. "Two, I think."

"Friends of yours?" Danny asked Skip.

Was that actually fear Deidra heard in his voice? Danny...*afraid*? She gripped the stretcher's wooden frame, her knuckles white as the haze.

"Could be." Skip squinted, tried and see something through the gauze. "We'd planned to fuck you up good on the way back, and they were just gonna do it for fun before, to help me out. After you used his balls for punting practice, Dorr's gonna wanna get some payback for himself now."

Deidra's gaze shifted to Paul, appraised his face for some clue as to what was happening. She'd learned its language over the years; the look in his eye, his coloring, the pout or turn of his lips, the way his ears turned red when he was angry, embarrassed, or horny. There were times when she could decipher an entire story before he uttered a word. In the dimness, however, his wide eyes shimmered like drowned stars and his face spoke an alien tongue. The closest translation she could find was panic.

What did you see out there?

They crept between the rows. A few more hours and they would be clear of these cornfields, on a road, or in one of their own backyards. Deidra also clung to the hope that someone called 911, that help was on the way, hope that the blades of a Lifeline helicopter would fan off this mist and carry them up, up, and away to safety. After that, Paul could fill her in on what really happened.

She looked back into the haze, her hand still clutching the stretcher's wooden frame. Once again, she felt the distant watchers, stares that fused contempt with utter amusement. Coyne and Dorr, waiting out there in the darkness, looking for the right moment to pay Danny back in full for the embarrassment they'd suffered at the quarry. And if they were high, or...

Drunk. You can say it.

...or *drunk*, who knows what they might be capable of. Drugs, drink, and temper were not a pleasant cocktail.

You were famous for it.

Yes. She had been.

Deidra lowered her head, watched her shoes rise and fall in the blackness like plunging pistons, watched the breath puff from her lips and nostrils in tiny frozen clouds. But if it were Coyne and Dorr out there, why would *Skip* be nervous? They were his friends, after all. What could he possibly have to fear from them?

Unless he's worried it's not *them.*

The flapping wings. She didn't like that blur of motion, tried to tell herself she'd only imagined it, but she knew she hadn't. Her heart was a pain in her chest. Her whole body ached in anticipation of something. What it was she did not know, but she could sense its coming in the misty air.

Do you know how ridiculous you sound? So you saw some flapping wings? Big fucking whoop! You've been seeing these crows all day, right? Well, those guys were standing out there and a crow flew by them. End of story.

"So what do we do?" Robby asked, and Deidra nearly screamed at the sound of his voice.

Danny continued to look into the depths of the fog. "We keep going."

Deidra nodded, tried on a relieved grin. *Sure we keep going. Sure. 'Cause it's Dorr and Coyne out there. Danny's not scared of them. After all, he kicked their asses single-handedly, didn't he?* Her body shuddered against the chill of the night air. Why was it so cold? She hadn't heard anything about it being this cold tonight.

"HEY ASSHOLES!"

Deidra's entire body jerked as if she'd stepped on a live wire. She saw Danny, Skip and Paul whip their heads around and followed their example.

Cindi flipped her blonde mane into Nancy's face as she yelled into the mist. "YOU'RE A COUPLE O' WASTED, INBRED FREAKS. YOU KNOW THAT?"

"*What's wrong with you?*" Every muscle in Robby's neck tightened, turning down the volume he wanted to project. "*You trying to get us all killed?*"

Paul flashed him a look of disapproval.

Robby didn't see it, but Deidra did. Her fingers bore down on the wooden pole and her nails bit into its bark. She glanced back into the gray veil. Who did the guys think it was out there?

"Get bent," Cindi told Robby, then bellowed more taunts into the darkness. "GO BACK TO FUCKIN' YOUR PIGS, BANJO BOYS!"

"*Shut up, you stupid bitch!*" Skip screamed through clenched teeth, but his voice was far too strained to be threatening.

"What did you say?" Cindi gave him her patented icy stare. At least she had stopped yelling at—

The shadows with the flapping wings?

—whoever was watching them. Skip ignored her, but Cindi pressed him. "What did you just say to me?"

"I told you to shut the fuck up!"

"You called me a bitch."

"No, I called you a *stupid* bitch, and the more you keep jackin' your jaw, the more you prove me right!"

She sharpened her eyes. "If you weren't holding that stretcher—"

Deidra held up her free hand, every muscle in her back and arm a tight band of rubber. "Cin, just do what he says and shut your mouth for once!" She looked at Skip, then Paul, then her eyes flew to Danny. "You're all totally freaked, and I wanna know why. We all need to know why. Right now."

"No you don't," Danny assured her.

Nancy spoke up, nearly groaning the words, "Danny... what's going on?"

He looked at her. There were smudges of dirt on her pale cheeks. He could see the confusion in her eyes, could tell she was close to tears, and was suddenly embarrassed he'd kept their find a secret. The girls were in this mess with the rest of them, they should know. "We found a body."

"A body?" Cindi repeated with skepticism.

Nancy's fingers rose to cover her mouth. "Jesus."

"Let's just get the fuck outta here," Skip whispered, watching the fog with a kind of captivated fear. "Why are we standin' here talkin' about this shit?"

Deidra looked to Paul. "Who was it?"

He came close to revealing all they had seen in a panicky glut; the Scarecrow Man on his wooden cross with his corncob eyes and mouth full of blood-soaked leaves, how part of him had been smeared onto Paul's own jacket, but he wanted to spare her those horrors. He'd hoped to spare her any horror at all. "Dale Brightman. He was dead."

By dead, Deidra knew Paul really meant *killed*. "*You trying to get us all* killed?" Robby told Cindi. Killed. The word echoed through the caverns of her mind, became louder and louder until she thought her head might just do a *Scanners*. The ringing soon faded, however, and the word itself changed, became *murdered*. Dale Brightman had been murdered by what—*who*ever was out there watching them now.

"You guys are still trying to scare us, right?" The pilot light in Cindi's eyes flickered as she scanned the boys' faces, then, as she saw they were telling the truth, it went out all together. She said nothing. For the first time since Deidra had known her, Cindi was completely speechless.

Nancy blinked a single tear onto her cheek. "Who would kill Dale?"

Before anyone could venture a guess, Sean stirred in the stretcher. His eyes sprang open and his body tensed. He rolled back and forth in the towel slings and screamed, crazy howling shrieks that exploded from his throat in long, echoing waves. He sounded like an inmate from an asylum.

"What's wrong with him?" Danny asked, the words all but lost beneath the swells of Sean's cries.

"It must be the pain." Robby's voice was calm, but his eyes were huge and horrified. Sean's leg was immobilized and the bleeding in his shoulder had stopped hours ago. His vitals had been good...steady. There would naturally be some pain, but there was no reason for this display of agony. Unless...unless Robby had missed something; a broken hip or rib, a nerve pinched between the shards of two obliterated vertebrae...something... *anything* that would make Sean scream like that.

"Put the fucker down," Skip urged. "I'm about to drop his ass!"

They quickly lowered the stretcher to the ground, moved away from Sean as if he were some bomb about to explode. In fact, it looked as if he might do just that. Breath poured out of him in a white geyser, like a reactor venting steam, and his skin had gone from pale to a rosy pink. The latter might have been a trick of the camcorder light, but Deidra didn't think it was. It was as if he were burning inside.

Sean suddenly stopped rocking. He arched his back until he nearly stood on his head—a drill one of Deidra's ex-boyfriends was forced to do for wrestling practice—and then he cried out in a terror, "*Mondamin!*"

Paul looked at Deidra; his wide, shocked eyes confirming that she hadn't just imagined it. She thought Paul had simply seen the term in her report. This might have been the case, but Sean had never read it. Had never even been in her kitchen to see it hung on the fridge, her grade drawn like the scarlet letter in the upper margin. How did he know that word? How *could* he know it?

Sean continued to roll around on the towels, shrieking at the top of his lungs, "Mondamin *is here! Here!* Mondamin *is here!*"

Deidra covered her ears with her hands and looked away. There, in the haze, she saw a ghostly gray shadow. Though she could make out few details, she knew it wasn't Dorr or Coyne; it wasn't even human. It was twisted... slumped... she could see the dim, diffused light from the camcorder shimmer on its skin—its *moving*, pulsating skin—and its bony arms paddled the misty air. It looked like something from a surrealist's painting, Bosch or Giger came most easily to her mind, and it *did* have wings, not crow's wings as she had first thought, but huge, membranous *bat* wings.

No, she told herself. *I'm not seeing this. This...This is not real.*

Deidra sensed that the thing knew it had been seen, that it was in fact looking straight back at her. Beneath the weight of its stare, she felt her own skin rise and migrate across her body, leaving cold in its wake. Her hands moved to cup her mouth and she screamed into them. Her cries joined with Sean's, forming one loud symphony of terror as she backed away, watching the creature retreat into the fog as if it were her own tangled reflection in a fun house mirror.

Not REAL!

What happened next happened fast.

Paul wheeled at the sound of Deidra's screams, caught her as she stumbled and fell backward into his embrace. He felt the sobs course through her body like ripples on a lake, smelled the sour musk of frightened sweat overpower her perfume. He started to ask her what was wrong, but before he could even part his lips, the air filled with the sound of rustling feathers.

NOT...REAL!

The crows exploded from the milky void and the world became nothing but flapping wings, sharp talons, and beaks. To Deidra's eyes, it appeared as if they had stumbled into Hell's aviary. She felt hands on her shoulders, pushing.

It was Paul.

"*Get down!*" he told her.

Deidra dropped to the cold earth, Paul hugging her back. She tilted her head to the side, her hands over her ears, and tried to see what was happening. Later, she would curse herself for not closing her eyes, for not shutting it out entirely, but her curiosity had the better hand, and, once the violence started, it was impossible to look away.

The black column of birds headed directly for Sean as if trained to do so. The first one landed on his shoulder. It looked at his cheek a moment, then plunged into it with its beak. Another perched on his face and curled its talons around his bottom lip. Deidra saw red spurts of blood from the corners of Sean's screaming mouth as the crow tore the flesh from his jaw. The bird beat his ears with its wings, and its head bobbed up and down, pecking out his eyes. Another crow settled on his chest, another on his leg, and then Sean was covered in an undulating blanket of black feathers.

Deidra could watch no more. She turned away and saw Mick reach into his backpack, saw him pull out a knife. It was the largest blade she'd ever seen, like something a gladiator might take into the arena—one side smooth metal, the other serrated. What was Mick doing with a knife?—Mick of all people?

Her frantic mind tugged at her hands, pulled them down over her eyes, blocking out the horrors around her.

Just close your eyes, dear, it said, trying to calm her. *Close your eyes and it will all go away.*

This was just another nightmare, she realized. Only there could a flock of ravenous crows exist, only there could Mick wield a knife. It was all very comforting.

Any second now, she told herself, *I'll wake up safe in Paul's arms. We'll still have the entire day ahead of us, untouched. This time, I won't get up and make that phone call. I'm fucking unexcused anyway! This time, I'll stay in bed and screw Paul until his balls are bruised and I can't even think about walking. So what if Mom comes walking in! So fucking what! Everything will be fine; everything will be just peachy keen!*

But she knew she was wrong.

This was no dream, no nightmare.

This was as real as it fucking gets.

TWENTY

Everyone dove for the ground when the crows came, everyone but Danny Fields.

He'd never been a Boy Scout, but the term had been used on him before. Once he'd found a wallet at the State Fair and turned it in to security without so much as a glance inside. What did he care if there was money in it? There could have been a million dollars. None of it was his. In the dead of winter, he frequently saw stalled cars, cars that slid from the road into drainage ditches, and he never thought twice about stopping. He would offer the driver a jump from his battery, even a ride home if needed. One of the joys of having four-wheel drive was that you could get just about anywhere in Harmony, even in a foot or two of snow. He'd never shied away from helping strangers, and he sure as hell wasn't going to start now, not when his best friend was in terrible pain, in the throes of some gut-turning torture. Helping Sean was the only thought on Danny's mind.

He sprinted forward, covering his face with his muscular arms, once more employing the quickness that had earned him his scholarship. Danny crashed into a wall, not of opposing linemen but of crows. There were hundreds of them, perhaps thousands, each one a foot in height, with a wing span well over twice that. The weight and velocity of the flock knocked the wind from Danny's lungs and sent him tumbling, holes in his forearms where the fowl had pecked him. He smeared the rivulets of blood with his fingers, his eyes astonished and pissed-off all at once.

When he looked up, Danny saw the birds perch on Sean. He hopped to his feet, got two steps before Robby rose up and blocked his path.

"*Forget it, he's* gone!" Robby cried, trying to make himself heard over the chirping and cawing of the hellish flock. His was no longer the face of superior confidence, it was the face of a man scared shitless in an Irwin Allen disaster. His words were just as cliché, but when Danny looked back at Sean he could think of none better to describe the scene.

Sean *was* gone.

A fluttering black mound of feathers and beaks covered him utterly. His rocking, arching spasms faded and his arms stopped their wild flailing. Even his screams, muted beneath the volume of the flock, had ceased. It was as if David Copperfield had performed an act of teleportation. Any moment now, with a snap of fingers, the flock would fly back into the fog, revealing no wires, no mirrors, and no Sean. And yet, as the crows flapped about, Danny could still see *something* beneath them, blurred and unclear through the flurry and commotion, a nearly indescribable form. It could have been anyone. But it wasn't.

"Sean," Danny whispered. Robby pushed on his chest, tried to force him back, but his feet were set and he stared at the crows for a long, motionless second. He could taste his own fear as it rose up the back of his throat and stung his gullet.

Red fountains welled up, stained the flawless sable blanket. One of the crows hopped from the flock and onto the ground, its feathers covered in a crimson slick; matted, stuck together, useless. It twitched its head and flapped its wings, flung bloody droplets in every direction as it tried to take flight. From its beak, a length of small intestine hung like a huge red earthworm, snaked its way beneath the down cover and into Sean's open abdomen.

They're eating him, Danny's mind screamed. *What the fuck is that?*

When several birds took to the air, something rolled out from under the flapping mound. Sean's head. The connective tissues had been pecked away, orphaning his skull from the rest of his body. It rolled over twice, then came to a stop, the naked point of its chin in the air. The eyes were now gaping craters gathering blood, the ears ragged banners, the nose a ridge of pitted tissue. Fleshy curtains of lip had been ripped away, leaving polished teeth in a naked, glistening jawbone.

"No," Danny said, not noticing the tears that rolled from his eyes. "Jesus, Mary, no."

His feet moved now as Robby continued to push, but Danny was unaware of it. He was being carried away from the man-eating crows, away from the red bird with the huge worm in its beak, away from the rolling skull that had been his best friend, and, most importantly, away from the edge of insanity.

For that, Danny was grateful.

A moment later, he ran blindly into the haze, his legs pumping as if he were returning the ball for a touchdown. But this was no game, not anymore. He ran for his life, and he wasn't alone.

Paul laid on top of Deidra, pushed her flat against the ground. He glanced at the flock, saw Sean's gut droop from the beak of a crow, and felt his stomach crawl.

What's a flock of crows called?

He closed his eyes and screamed into Deidra's ear. "We're gonna get outta this! I want you to get on your knees and—"

"I can't move."

"Yes, you can. We're gonna crawl out from under these birds—"

"I can't!"

"*You have to!* You're gonna crawl out from under these birds, then you're gonna take off running! I'll be with you the whole time, I swear!" He opened his eyes, looked around to make certain the path was clear. "Ready?"

"*No.*"

Paul ignored her. If he waited for her to say yes, the crows might feather nests with their innards. "One... Two..." He shot a glance left, then right, as if they were about to cross the street. The way was still clear. "Three!"

Paul slid off Deidra's back onto his knees, pulled her up off the dirt. He crawled forward, tugged on the back of her shirt as he moved. After a few moments, she pulled even with him and was about to pass him by.

The video camera sat on the ground in front of them. Paul reached out and grabbed it, pointed its light away from the bloody scene behind them, illuminated the fog ahead. The way still seemed clear.

Now, with some distance between them and the attacking crows, Paul felt they could safely make their run. He staggered to his feet, pulled Deidra up with him. "*Run*, Deidra! *Run!*"

She shook her head. "Paul, I'm scared. I saw it out there! *I saw it!*"

"I'm scared too," he told her. It was the truth. "Grab my shirt and hold on, it's gonna be okay." He didn't know if he believed that last part. Something inside him wondered if anything could ever be okay again. But it was enough to get her moving. Deidra grabbed hold of the back of his shirt and they bolted into the mist, the spotlight from the camcorder lighting their way.

Paul heard something behind them; it plowed a path through the corn like a tractor, gaining momentum as it closed in on them. Some voyeuristic urge made him want to see it, made him jerk his head around, made him look into the fog.

There were shapes there, just beyond the reach of his camcorder light. He saw them shift in the murk, but they had no real definition. His eyes flitted from one stain in the haze to the next. They could be anything, anything at all. Part of his mind told him that he didn't want to see what they were, that he was better off not knowing. This part was joined by a screaming voice in his cranium, a voice that told him to watch where he was going and to run like hell.

He listened.

When Paul looked forward again, figures rushed into the light and he nearly screamed. Deidra did.

One of the figures put a hand up to its face. "Who's that?"

Robby's voice.

"Paul and Deidra." Paul lowered his light a bit so as not to blind his friend.

The second figure was Danny. He waved them toward a structure ahead. "This way!"

Paul couldn't tell what the building was. Its dark turrets loomed from the fog like the battlements of a

Scottish castle. He followed Danny and Robby toward it, his pace quickening now that his legs had a goal, a finish line they had to cross. And, as he drew closer, Paul saw that the towers were grain elevators; red paint had flaked away, patches of naked metal shining in the spotlight. There were four towers, rust-encrusted ladders ran up their sides, metal domes capped them like miners' helmets, and between them stood a building that was more shed than barn. Paul fixed his eyes on the doors that marked its entrance, hauling Deidra by her arm.

"Come on!" he cried, thinking: *We've got to get inside. It'll be safe inside. The birds and whatever's chasing us, whatever it is that killed Dale can't get us inside. Inside. Inside. Inside. Inside.*

In a moment they were all at the door. Danny threw it wide open and shouted, "Everybody in!"

Paul held them back. "Hold on a second."

The interior was dark and cold. There could be something waiting for them.

The Beast!

Something that sent the crows...

The million eyes!

...like a fluttering, black snowplow to push them here...to herd them to the slaughter.

The Beast With A Million Eyes!

This morning, it would have been a crazy notion. Now, it didn't seem insane at all.

Paul took a step into the shed, swept the interior with the camcorder spotlight. A lawnmower sat next to the door, an Indian head logo smiling up at him from its Tecumseh engine. The walls were rotting wooden boards covered in tools; shovels, pitchforks, and rakes.

Two windows looked out from the back wall, their glass panes opaque with grime. There were tracks in the mud floor, the perfect imprints of burdened tire treads. Whoever owned this shed, whoever owned the grain in the surrounding silos, had taken a load and gone for the night.

They were alone.

Strange how the thought of being alone with Deidra had filled him with so much joy twenty-four short hours ago. Now, the same idea chilled him to the bone.

Paul pulled her by the arm. "It's clear."

"I saw it," she told him. "*I saw it!*"

Paul fought to keep the screams in his own mind from reaching his lips. "It" was such a vague term. Had she seen blood spurt between black feathers?—Seen Sean's guts spill from the birds' beaks?—Or had she seen the dark shapes chase after them, herd them? He'd seen it all. Too much of it. If they were going to get out of this alive, they had to stay calm.

Danny strained to push the door closed. "A little light!"

Paul aimed his spotlight at the entrance. A wooden plank had been screwed into the door and a wooden "U" jutted from the frame. Danny spun the board until the "U" grabbed it, barring the door shut. He then stepped back into the shed, stared pacing like a caged animal.

"This *thing*... in the fog," Deidra went on. "*I saw it!*"

Paul turned the spotlight on Deidra, saw her tremble, and moved to hold her. "It's okay."

"Oh God!" Her eyes were the widest he'd ever seen them. "I think it knew I saw it!"

"Deidra, what—?"

"It had wings and...it looked at me!"

Paul grabbed the sides of her head and tilted her face toward his. "*Deidra!*"

She blinked at him and her eyes began to focus. "I saw it," she repeated, her voice soft as a whisper, watery lines drawn down her cheeks.

Paul spoke slowly and distinctly. "What did you see?"

Through tears Deidra said, "*Mondamin.*"

They shared a quiet moment, stared into each other's faces, then Deidra brought her hands to her mouth and moaned into them. Paul held her tightly to him, rubbed her back, and felt the sobs surge through her. She was so cold.

"What the hell does that mean?" Robby asked with angry confusion.

Paul continued to run his hand across Deidra's back as she cried into his shoulder. "It's a Miami Indian word for 'corn spirit.'"

"There's a word for corn spirit?"

Paul didn't respond. He looked down at the camera. "I'm gonna power down the camcorder," he announced, "Turn off the light."

Deidra shook her head. "No!"

"There could be a killer out there right now," he said. "And even if there isn't, we still have to worry about those crows. If they see the light coming from under the door or through the windows, they'll know we're in here. Besides, if I *don't* do it, the battery's gonna be dead and we won't have light when we need it."

She shuddered in his arms. "I can't be here in the dark. I won't be able to see."

"Sean was afraid of the dark," Danny blurted.

Paul and Robby's eyes snapped to him.

"He had to go to the basement when the tornadoes went through in '79. The power goes out and he's down in the dark listening to the thing go right by his house..."

This was it. The meltdown Paul feared would happen if Sean died, and this was not the time or place for it. There was still a long way to go. "Danny, I'm sorry about Sean. He was one of my best friends too, but right now we gotta get outta this damn field."

Danny's reflective eyes hardened in the dimness. "What was his favorite color?"

"What?"

"You were such good buds. What was Sean's favorite color?"

Paul shrugged. "I don't—"

"It was red. Did he like McDonald's or Burger King better?"

Robby tried to step in. "Danny, what the fuck—?"

"You two may have been his friends, but you didn't *know* him. A few hours ago...Jesus... *hours*..." His eyes traveled to another place and time for a moment then snapped back into the reality of the shed. "We were playin' a game, laughin' about who was getting what from what girl and what pranks we were gonna pull on the last day of school. I've known him since kindergarten. Twelve years, man. He's been there practically my entire fuckin' life and now he's...now he's *dead*. He's never gonna drink another beer, never gonna graduate—"

Deidra's face lifted from Paul's shoulder. "Sean's dead?"

Paul nodded helplessly in reply.

Her lip quivered and she shook her head. "Did Mick kill him?"

"No." Paul couldn't hide his confusion. "Why would you think that?"

Deidra answered through tears, "Because Mick had a knife."

Crows launched into the womb of light, and Mick's first impulse was to fall onto the dusty earth and cower in a fetal position. Then, he saw his backpack and remembered Danny's knife. With it, Mick could slice the crows as he sliced the corn leaves. This impulse gained strength, sprang forward to devour the first, and he reached out for the blade.

Mick rose up, left arm thrown over his face, knife erect in his right hand, and the birds surged around him in a fast-flowing torrent of feathers. Their heads and bodies thudded against him like beanbags hurled by a pitching machine, nearly pushing him off balance. There were *so many* of them.

Where did they all come from?

Talons scratched Mick's face, drew three lines of blood and scraped his glasses from their perch. It seemed to happen in slow motion. The thick lenses grew larger, the wire frames came into view, and then they tumbled end over end into a blurry haze. He didn't hear them shatter, the flock was too loud in his ears, but, broke or not, there was no way he could stop to retrieve them. He was prisoner to the living current of crows.

I'm like Velma in Scooby-Doo! he thought with an odd mix of amusement and horror. *I can't see!*

It was the last thing he allowed himself to think.

Mick slashed at the fluttering, squawking crows. The knife did its work well. Bodies came apart like jigsaw puzzles of feathers and flesh; wings flew off by themselves, heads corkscrewed to the ground, disembodied beaks mouthed the words to the surviving flock's shrill song. He bisected one of the birds, a red line of blood stretching out, tethering the pieces together; it flew back into Mick's face, painted a stripe of war paint across his cheeks and the bridge of his nose. His eyes slammed shut and his face contorted in disgust. He felt his stomach and privates twirl, fighting the urge to vomit as he hacked and slashed a path through the pecking congregation.

And still the river of birds flowed undaunted.

"*Danny!*" he called. If asked about the knife, Mick would simply say he took it as part of the game. Danny had been none the wiser, and, while Skip hiked with them, Mick felt protected.

"*Paul?*"

He heard the words echo through the caverns of his skull, but there was no way anyone else could hear them over the insane clamor of the birds.

The knife in Mick's hand resembled an Indian totem, painted red and covered in black feathers, but the blade remained sharp. He pushed forward, slashed blindly, and the ground became littered in plumed anatomy.

They're thinning out.

Mick jumped at the sound of the voice in his mind. He peered beneath his scratched and pecked arm, watched the fog fade from white, to gray, to charcoal. His first thought was that the crows had smashed the light, then that the battery on Paul's camcorder had gone dead. When he finally cleared the black cloud of feathers, however, he realized the light had not grown dark but distant.

Someone had taken off with the camera.

Mick broke into a clumsy sprint, the mist on his skin like cold rain, his heart throbbing in time with his feet. He had to strain to see the light now, and, a moment later, it disappeared into the fog.

He was alone, lost in shadow.

Mick froze in his tracks. Feathers fell from the knife and he bent over, hands on his knees, his labored breaths coming in puffs of white smoke. He looked around, wondered what he should do, then shot upright.

There, in the distance, another light.

At first, it was as small and as dim as the glow of a lightning bug. Then it came closer, swinging back and forth like a lantern on a rope. Above the light were three pale, glowing faces made fuzzy by Mick's naked eyes. Despite the cold, he began to sweat. No one in their group had brought a flashlight, and Paul's camcorder spot just ran off in the opposite direction.

A familiar voice called out, "Hello! Can anybody hear me?"

It sounded like Mr. Cupello—teacher, head of the Harmony High Music Department, and leader of the Marching Rebels. A long, loud sigh escaped Mick's lips and became a nervous chuckle of relief. He waved his arms in the thick air.

"Over here!"

The glowing faces jerked in Mick's direction and the light below them swung faster. Soon, they were within a few feet of him. Blurry or not, he knew that it *was* Mr. Cupello. The man looked like Groucho Marx, black-framed eyeglasses firmly anchored to a bulbous nose, and, below that, a bushy black mustache. His hair was slicked back to form a dark skullcap, and he wore the same suit he'd worn to all of their performances. Although there was no way to see the pattern of the man's tie without glasses, Mick was certain it would be musical notes.

The other faces had to belong to Sheriff Carter and Deputy Oates. Mick could tell both were in full uniform, their badges shining smudges in the aura of the flashlight. Their faces were glowing blobs to Mick, and there was no way for him to know what expressions they held.

Mr. Cupello shined his flashlight beam in Mick's unfocussed eyes. "Mr. Slatton, is that you?"

Mick suddenly realized he must look like a kid from *The Lord of the Flies*, covered from head to toe in dirt, gore, and feathers; he still held the knife. "Yes, sir."

One of the uniformed blurs spoke. "What the hell happened to you, son?"

It *was* Sheriff Carter.

Mick pointed off into the fog. "Sean Roche got hurt diving into the old quarry—"

Carter held up an indistinct blob for a hand. "We know all that. The whole town knows about it by now. We've had kids calling the station for hours. As soon as we figured out it wasn't some senior prank, we started lookin' for you kids."

Thank God, Mick thought. Deidra's plan worked. The others *had* called for help. Now they would all be safe. They would all be going home.

Suddenly, he remembered what Danny had said about Dale Brightman. "Sheriff, somebody's been killed out here."

Carter nodded. "We found the bodies."

Bodies? Plural?

The third blur spoke up. "It's Skip Williamson."

Mick's heart raced again, his hand squeezed the slick handle of the knife.

"We've got a warrant for his arrest." It was Deputy Oates. "He's a dangerous son of a bitch. We've got orders to shoot him on sight."

Carter nodded the smudge that was his head. "Killin' Skip'd make us heroes all right."

Mick blinked, wiped blood and feathers from his face with the back of his hand, and tried to focus. He wanted to see their expressions. Their voices were serious, but they had to be joking. Police didn't still give "shoot to kill" orders, did they?

For Skip they would, his tired mind was convinced. *It'd be self-defense.*

The Oates blur nodded at Mick as if he'd heard the boy's thoughts. "This town'd be better off without Williamson, that's for damn sure."

The shape that was Mr. Cupello nodded at the policemen, then turned back to Mick. "You've been through a lot, haven't you, Mr. Slatton?"

"Yes, sir."

"Well, it's almost over now."

And then, filtered through his corrupt vision, Mick saw Mr. Cupello smile. It would be the same smile he'd flash when no one missed a note, full of joy, confidence, and pride. Mick could not help but smile back.

The sheriff spoke up again, "We'll get the others and bring them back here so the helicopter can pick us all up." The black blots of his eyes went to Mick. "Will you be okay here alone for a few minutes?"

Mick nodded. *It's over*, he kept thinking. *It's all over.*

"I'll be fine," he said. "But Sean's in real bad shape."

"Don't you worry about your friend," Carter told him. "We're here now."

Mick drew in a relieved breath. *Thank God. Thank God.*

"Just don't go wandering off," Oates warned. "We wouldn't want you getting lost in this damned fog."

And with that, the hazy figures moved off in the direction Mick pointed out to them, became one with the rest of Mick's foggy surroundings, and he was alone again. The fear had faded from him, however. Soon they would be out of this mist, out of these cornfields, and away from the crows. Better still, Skip would no longer be a part of his life.

Skip Williamson would be dead or in prison.

Deidra's eyes darted across the walls of the shed. It looked as if they'd somehow come loose from their moorings and now rolled around in their sockets.

She's in shock, Paul realized. *She's confused. After all, why would Mick have a knife? If anybody had a knife it'd be...Skip.*

Skip. Now that made sense. Skip kills Dale, hangs him in some mockery of a crucifix, then throws away his blood-soaked jacket before meeting up with Danny and the others, just like Danny said. Then tonight, when he realized they were close to the scene of his crime, Skip retrieved the murder weapon.

Elementary, my dear Deidra. Elementary.

Danny went to the door and opened it, allowed eddies of razor-fine haze to swirl into the shed.

"What the hell are you doin', Fields?" Robby asked in an explosive cloud of breath.

"Nancy's still out there," he answered with surprising calm.

"So are the crows." Robby crossed his arms over his chest for warmth. "So's whoever killed Dale."

Deidra's eyes floated over to him. "*Mondamin*'s out there."

"Give me a fuckin' break, Deidra."

"Give *her* a fuckin' break," Paul said.

"Great." Robby looked at the tin roof and shook his head. "That's just beautiful. I can't believe we're having a serious conversation about Miami mojo bullshit!"

"You're the medic." Paul nodded at Deidra. "Can't you see she's in shock?"

Folded canvas drop cloths sat stacked on the floor behind the lawnmower. Robby snatched one up, flicked it open, and handed it to Paul. "Wrap this around her. It'll keep her warm."

"Thanks." Paul wrapped the canvas around Deidra, then held the camcorder out for Danny. "If you're going, you'd better take the light."

"I'll try and make it fast."

Paul shrugged. "Just bring back our friends."

Robby jumped up and down in the dirt, rubbing his arms. "Since I'll freeze my nads off just standin' here, I'll go with you."

Danny gave him a slight nod.

"We can't stay here alone in the dark," Deidra moaned, her gaze drifting.

Paul held her chin in his hand, forced her to look at him. "Do you trust me?"

Tears sloshed over the rims of her eyes. "Yes."

"I'm gonna be right here with you. Nothing's going to happen. I won't let anything hurt you."

She nodded in his hand.

Paul ushered her over to the corner of the shed. There were cardboard boxes there, each containing two large bottles of weed killer according to the stencil on the side. Paul placed his hand on one and pressed down, made certain the box was full and would hold their weight, then he sat Deidra down and knelt in front of her.

"I'm gonna lock the door behind these guys so nothing can get in, then I'll be right back."

She nodded, still trembling beneath the blanket.

Paul backed away from Deidra with great reluctance, counting how many steps it took to get to the door so that he could find his way back to her in the dark. One...two...three...four...five...and six.

Robby rubbed his arms and hopped. "You could've offered me the jacket, Rice."

Paul gave him a harsh glance. "It had Dale's blood on it."

"Blood I can handle," Robby replied. "This cold sucks."

"Sorry." Paul turned his attention to Danny. "Good luck."

Danny nodded, his eyes still on the fog; he gave Paul a rough pat on the shoulder. "We'll be right back."

"Just don't bring the crows back with you."

Robby stepped outside. "If you get bored, you can start us a fire."

"I'll just take our shelter apart for the wood."

At that, they both chuckled uneasily.

In one quick motion, Paul pushed the door closed, swung the latch shut, and turned to face Deidra. When people talked about coming darkness, he'd always heard them say it fell. It wasn't like that at all. Paul watched as it filled the interior of the shed like an oil spill, flooded over the tire tracks and lawnmower, washed across the walls and ceiling before it finally swept the boxes and doused Deidra's shivering form in its cold, black embrace.

"Paul?" she called out, her voice shaky.

"I'm right here."

Paul took his first step.

One...

The darkness was total, absolute. There should have been moonlight, but the fog blotted it out, diffused it. Even if there had been no fog, the greasy windows would not have allowed light in.

Two...three...four...

A scraping sound, like someone dragged nails across the wall, followed by a loud clang of metal against metal.

Paul nearly lost control of his bladder. He froze in place and searched the dark, letting his eyes adjust to the gloom. There was a beat of silence and then Deidra called out for him.

"I'm okay," he whispered back.

"There's something in here with us."

"No, there's not."

The shed had been empty. He was sure of it. There had been four walls, a lawn mower and...

The tools on the wall.

Of course. The rake or the pitchfork had fallen from its peg and banged into the shovel. That's all it had been.

"Something just fell off the wall," he said aloud.

"What fell?"

"I don't know."

"*What fell?*"

There was real terror in her voice now.

"I don't know," he repeated calmly, trying to hide his own escalating fear, trying to remember what step he'd been on. Was it four?—Or was it five? If he said four and it had really been five, he'd just bump into the boxes a little early, but if he said five and it had really been four...he didn't want to reach out and feel nothing there.

Four...five...

Another sound; the pitter-patter of paws accompanied by the squeak of an animal. It could've been a mouse, a rat, or even a bat, something small that had hidden itself away from the Sony's light. If the state of affairs had been different, being locked in a totally dark room with *Ben* would have been a horrible thought. As things were, however, Paul felt great comfort in the fact that there was no knife-wielding bogeyman lurking in the shadows with them.

"It's just a mouse," he told Deidra.

"And that's supposed to make me feel better?"

"Doesn't it?"

"Yeah...a little."

Her voice was very close now.

Paul took another step, and, when he reached out, he felt the canvas blanket and Deidra beneath it. He moved quickly into its protective fold, and she hugged him so hard he thought one of his ribs might have broken.

"It's all right," he told her, trying to calm himself at the same time.

Paul pulled the canvas tight around them and Deidra rested her head on his shoulder. It felt good to have her body against his and the warmth they generated fought off the cold, at least for the time being.

"Are you scared?" she whispered with quivering lips.

Paul kissed her forehead. "Yes."

"Remember what you said this afternoon? About wanting to be together at the end?"

"This isn't the end," he assured her. "Just rest a minute. The birds will all be gone soon, and Danny'll find everybody safe and sound. Just rest."

"Paul...when I tell you I love you, you know I'm not just saying it right? You know I mean it?"

"I know," he said. "*I* mean it too."

As he sat with Deidra in the dark, Paul looked through the nothingness toward where he knew the door sat locked, thinking about Danny and Robby. He hoped they would find Mick and the girls, hoped they would all get home safe. Most of all, he hoped they would bring back the light.

The light abandoned Cindi, left her in a black world where the air was alive with feathers, claws, and beaks. Her fingers raked the soil, gathered it beneath her pink-painted nails as she tried to crawl away. Two of the birds became tangled in her hair; their talons pulled, sent bursts of pain across her scalp and squeezed tears from her eyes. She shrieked into the ground, pushed a cloud of vapor and loose dirt into the air around her face.

"*Let go!*" She reached up and slapped at the birds with her hands. "*Let go of me!*"

Cindi hooked her fingers around one of the birds and yanked it free, locks of her naturally blonde hair still clutched in its claws. The crow was soft, like a bag of mashed potatoes, and she realized she'd crushed it. She tossed it down, did the same to its fluttering twin, then resumed her crawl through the darkness.

This is what it's like to be blind.

Her hand darted to her eyes to make certain the crows hadn't plucked them from her skull. She still had them. Cindi screamed into the void, tried to be heard above the commotion of the birds, "*Nancy?*"

No answer.

"*Deidra?*"

The corn remained silent.

"*Come on, you guys, where are you?*"

Cindi managed to stand. She waved her arms around, made certain there were no more crows to grab at her hair, then ran into the fog.

"*Anybody? Come on, where'd you go?*"

She could see Robby and the other *guys* abandoning her, but not Nancy, not Deidra. They would have come to her aid. They wouldn't leave a girlfriend out here in the dark.

Maybe they're just being quiet. Maybe Sean's screaming is what made the birds attack. And here I am yelling my head off! I need to be quiet. Yeah, yeah, that's what it is. They're being quiet and they turned out the light so the crows will go away. As soon as the birds go away, we'll get out of this fucking cornfield. I swear to God, I'm never gonna even look at corn again! Not even Green Giant in a can!

Then something else occurred to her, something that made her shiver in the darkness. Before the crows came, Danny had been serious about Dale Brightman. Dale was dead. They'd found his *body*. Maybe whoever killed Dale had killed everybody else.

Some Fangoria-*loving dweeboid is out here trying to be Jason. He's killed them, one by one, until now there's just me. I'm like his next victim. I'm all alone.*

Except, she wasn't alone.

Cindi sensed movement in the fog. She wheeled around and saw...nothing, a blanket of charcoal covering a black abyss. And yet, she could not shake the unpleasant feeling of being surrounded by strangers—

By things!

—that faded in and out of the darkness. Cindi thought she sensed fingers graze her hair, and she let loose the reins of a scream.

The crows still screamed in Nancy's ears.

When the flock attacked, she ran as fast as her tired legs would allow. Now, she looked back over her shoulder, saw the cornrows disappear in a V shape behind her, saw the transparent mist become opaque and impenetrable to her eyes. How long had she been running? How *far*?

I'm lost, she thought. *I'm lost out here in this fog and they'll never find me. They won't even know where to look.*

Nancy retreated down the row, retraced her harried steps.

"Guys?" she called out, or at least, she thought she did; she could not hear the voice outside her own skull.

The crows' echo faded from her ears, from her *mind*, and the world seemed to have gone mute. All night, the steady background noise of insects had been absent. Now, even the faint rustle of corn leaves seemed less audible. She sat next to a huge rack of speakers at a Huey Lewis and the News concert last year. Afterward, her ears felt as if they were full of cotton and she had to yell to hear her own voice. She had that same feeling now. The birds had made her deaf.

"I'm out here!" she screamed. "Don't leave me behind, don't leave me—"

Something appeared out of the fog, a dark, towering silhouette; a crazy shape, like some abstract sculpture Deidra might craft for art class. It seemed to have an elongated trunk, but its arms and legs were too slight, its body far too bony for it to be an elephant. It had fingers, long sticks of charcoal dangling from shadow hands, and a hunched back outlined by a jagged length of naked spine.

It's a tree, an old, creepy tree. Nothing to freak out about. Nancy started to look away, but her eyes drifted back, questioning. *Why would a farmer leave a seven foot, gnarly lookin' tree smack dab in the middle of his field? How could he till around it?*

The night sounds roared to life, as if someone plugged them in, an earsplitting chorus of chirps, whistles, and twitters.

Nancy's entire body tensed.

On her leg, the sensation of tiny pinpricks across her naked skin, a million crawling legs. She looked down and saw a black, segmented coil, rapidly spiraling its way toward her crotch. A pair of antenna jutted from its round, bulbous head; they swayed up and down, beat out a rhythm on her shorts.

Nancy screamed, shook her leg violently, but the millipede clung fast and refused to let go. Finally, she reached down and curled her fingers around the loathsome insect; she found it hard and slimy, clamshells coated in Alfredo sauce. Nancy stripped the millipede from her limb and it writhed in her hands, its tiny claws, sharp as sewing needles, stabbing her palms until they bled. She flung the creature at the corn, then broke into a sloppy, staggering run.

Each step brought a hollow popping sound, as if she were dashing across a carpet of bubble pack. And, when she glanced down, Nancy saw the furrow had filled with cockroaches. They climbed up her sneakers, latched onto her socks, hissing and biting the naked skin above her ankle. She swat at them with her fists, smashed them into pulp, but more rose up to take their place and continue the attack.

Nancy screamed for her friends, for help, just screamed.

Spiderwebs hung across the row in a lacy curtain. She ran headlong into it, strands plastered to her face, to her bloodied arms and legs. She cringed, swiped at her body, pulling sticky, cotton candy clumps from her flesh.

The web's architect blocked Nancy's path, a brown spider the size of a man, eyes like a string of black pearls, all focused on her. Hairy legs radiated from its thorax, disappearing into the corn on either side of the row; they lifted the body, suspended it a foot above the dirt. Its dripping fangs rubbed together in anticipation, and then...it spoke. "Nancy!"

It crawled toward her.

Nancy shrieked so loudly she thought her throat would burst open. A football-shaped rock sat in the dirt at her feet; Nancy picked it up in both hands and brought it crashing down on the creature's furry head. She smashed it again, and again, and again...listening to the spider's bones snap, listening to the moist thud of rock against newly revealed anatomy.

Only later would it occur to Nancy that spiders had no bones.

Skip Williamson laid in the dirt, thinking of all the animals he'd killed.

There were squirrels too numerous to mention. He'd stake out a sniper position with his BB rifle, watching through his sight as they disappeared from branches in a red mist. Sometimes he took the carcasses and nailed them to fence posts, taking pleasure in the imagined disgust of passers by.

There was the calico, no more than a kitten, really. It wandered through his yard, lapped up water from a puddle. He'd offered it a slice of ham, coaxed it up to his back step, then he scooped it up—stroking its wet fur, hearing it meow and softly purr. The microwave had been a few steps away, and he took each one with excited glee. He'd heard animals would explode in there, but he wasn't sure he believed it. He put the kitten on the revolving glass plate and shut the door. He couldn't remember how long he'd set the timer for—a minute, maybe two—but he remembered the power setting was high. When the light came on, the kitten paced wildly, like a tiger in a circus cage, then its purr became a shrieking growl. It touched the pad of its foot to the window in the door, its claws scratching at the glass. Skip wondered how it must have felt. Could you feel your blood boil? Could you feel your organs cook inside your gut? The window fogged, and then he heard a loud pop. When he opened the door, Skip had a momentary urge to gag. That reflex was pushed aside by rising laughter. He'd snapped a few Polaroids, then cleaned it up as best he could before his Mom saw the mess.

Last, and most relevant to his current situation, was the crow. He'd lobbed the stone at it without a thought. He wanted to show those pussies there was nothing to fear. Now, however, he *was* afraid. As he watched the flock fly into the light, as he dove to the ground and felt the sting of claws and beaks on his back, Skip wondered if animals could seek revenge. But what could crows do? Sure they could peck, they could scratch, but they couldn't really—

A crow landed a foot away from him; a length of gristle dangled from its bloody beak.

His mouth went dry.

"Look..." Skip rose up on his hands and knees, eyeing the bird between the sweaty tails of hair draped across his face. "I'm sorry about your little friend, all right? Tell all your brothers and sisters I didn't mean to—"

The crow jerked its head and the glossy pulp in its beak flopped over. An eyeball stared sightlessly from the wet tangle of flesh, reflected light from the camcorder spot growing distant in its dead pupil, then disappearing all together.

Raw panic clawed at what remained of Skip's self-control, impelled him to leap up and run screaming into the dark like a madman. He fought the urge. After all, he reasoned, if he couldn't see the bird, maybe the bird couldn't see him either.

He became very still and closed his eyes, waiting for the crows to go away. Somehow, listening to the busy flock was worse than the visual. He heard their squawks, heard the flapping of their wings, the noise their beaks made as they pecked and sawed on bone, the wet ripping sound of Sean's musculature being torn away. Then, after what seemed like an eternity, he heard the birds take flight.

Skip opened his eyes; amazed he could now see details in the dimness.

Sean Roche lay a few feet to the left, recognizable only because of the stretcher they had made. A shadowy jungle gym of ribs rose from a mulch of feathers and torn flesh. Arm bones ran down the length of the carcass, and naked vertebrae ended in a ragged stump where a head should have been.

Skip looked away, but disbelief pulled his eyes back to the remains. A school of piranha might have done this, but not a flock of birds. Skip had lived in Indiana all his life, but he'd never seen, never even heard of a crow attack. Normally, they'd take flight as soon as they saw you coming.

"Christ," Skip said aloud, almost in the tone of a prayer. He managed to stand, his knees creaking audibly as he did so. *They'll come out here and kill* all *the crows now,* he thought, *just like they did rabid dogs and mosquitoes that carry disease. They'll—*

Sean's hand jerked; the ravaged fingers tensed and relaxed, some electrical shock working through them. Blood flowed from his body with sluggish deliberation, as if it were fleeing something, and then he sat up. His head was gone, but he sat up just the same. The organs that remained in his open chest slid onto his lap as a wet clump.

"No," Skip said aloud, his mind unwilling to accept the feed from his eyes. He was about to tell himself that he'd done too many drugs when the corpse stood; innards, connected by the remnants of muscle and tissue, unraveled onto the ground, forming a demented red carpet.

The dead thing took a step and retrieved its missing head; it slammed the skull down on its wriggling spine, then tested the connection. Where eyes had been, ruined sockets now cried streams of blood, but Skip felt the weight of its stare just the same. The jawbone opened and closed, and a sluggish, clogged voice broke the silence into grating shards of words. *"This is your fault, Skip!"*

"No, it was the crows."

The dead man shuffled toward him, herded him back toward the cornstalks. If he had any imagination at all, the very idea would have driven Skip insane. *"You pushed me, broke my leg so I couldn't walk!"*

The thing seemed to be walking fine now. It took a step, dragged the splinted mangle of bone and sinew forward, then took another step.

Skip thought, *If that thing could run, it'd be on me in a second...biting me, swallowing my flesh, turning me into a zombie too. I'll walk around yelling "Brains!*

Brains!" like a fucking gimp and they'll have to chop me into little bits just to get rid of me.

Terror shot through Skip's body like animal tranquilizer. It paralyzed him, made him unable to run away, forced him to stay and listen. At that moment Skip wanted there to be a God, and he wanted said God to get rid of the dead thing advancing on him.

But the thing did not go away. It stood there, a cancerous tail of organs between its legs, a bony finger pointed at Skip. "*You killed me!*"

"It was an accident!"

"*There are no accidents,*" the carrion teased. "*You think you're out here by accident?*"

At that point, Skip didn't know why he was out there at all.

"*You came out here to play the game. So let's play.*" What was left of Sean's face pulled upward, formed a shredded grin. "*I'll give you a running start.*"

Tentacles squirmed their way out of Sean, slithered from every wound and imperfection in his flesh. The corpse began to convulse, trembling and rocking as whatever had taken up residence within worked itself free. And then the tendrils seemed to boil away, evaporating into the mist. There was a moment when Skip had the sensation of something standing between them, something cold and horrible, then a light breeze whipped past him, blew through the sweaty locks of his hair, and it was gone.

The body fell forward, its arms outstretched, grabbing for Skip. When it hit the ground, it was still and thankfully mute.

Skip did not wait around to see if the thing would rise again. He turned and hurried across the rows. The stalks brushed against him, their leaves closing in to hide his path. He tried to remember which way he'd come, which way he'd been going, but the only thing his mind had to offer was an image of the half-eaten zombie reaching out for him. The thought made him run faster into the corn.

Someone stood in the row ahead. He slowed his pace, stepped cautiously forward, wondering if he should be walking toward the dark figure at all. When he got close enough to see who it was and what they had in their hand, he exhaled noisily.

"Oh...*fuck*!"

Mick turned and faced the bodiless voice from the mist. He blinked, saw the gray linen stain, saw the stain move forward. How he longed for his glasses.

"Who's there?" he asked.

"You know damn well who this is, now put down that knife!"

There was no mistaking that voice.

It was Skip.

Sheriff Carter said they'd found the bodies he'd left behind. Now he's come for you, Mick. You're next!

Mick shook his head, held the knife out in front of him like a cross to a vampire. "Stay away from me!"

"What the hell happened to you?" Skip pointed an indistinct finger at Mick's chest. "Whose blood is that?"

Reflex made Mick look down, then he jerked his eyes back up to Skip. He'd nearly fallen for the oldest trick there was. Mick chuckled. "Nice try."

Skip held out a shadowy hand. "Gimme the knife."

All the better to stab you with, Mickey, my dear.

Mick took a step back, Deputy Oates' words buzzing in his brain.

Skip took another step toward him, his voice filled with frustration. "Gimme the knife."

"Don't come any closer."

"What the fuck's goin' on with you? Where's everybody else?"

"If you didn't kill them, Sheriff Carter and Mr. Cupello are getting them right now."

"Sheriff Carter and...? They're out here?"

Mick nodded. "They've got orders to shoot you on sight."

"What the hell are you talkin' about?" Skip took another step forward, closed the distance between them. *"Gimme the fuckin' knife."*

Mick shook his head no.

Skip took a final step closer, reached out to take the knife away.

Mick ducked and lunged, sank all seven inches of the blade into Skip's chest, and a jet of blood caught him squarely in the face. Skip's jaw hung open, his wide eyes stunned, almost dreamy. Mick withdrew the blade and stabbed him again, struck something hard beneath the flesh, probably a rib. Skip gargled now, rosy drool streaming from his lips. Mick pulled the knife free and watched Skip fall to his knees.

You didn't expect this, did you? Mick found himself thinking. *Didn't expect me to ever stand up for myself without Danny around? Well how do you like this?*

He drew back the knife and gave a hard swipe, caught Skip's throat and ripped it open. A gigantic splash doused Mick and the surrounding corn in a shower of red rain. And, when Skip Williamson fell over onto his side, what was left of his cruel and miserable life drained into the dirt.

"Jesus Christ!"

Mick looked up, a bright spot of light blinding him. He raised a bloody hand to shield his eyes from it. *It must be Mr. Cupello and Sheriff Carter*, he thought, *coming back with Danny and the others in tow.*

"I got him!" Mick sang. "I got Williamson!"

Nancy smashed the spider's skull with her rock until she heard the voice call out from the corn.

"Oh...*fuck!*"

She looked up with a start, nearly dropped the oblong stone on her own foot. Skip Williamson stood one row over. In the dim, diffused light of the haze, she could tell he was horrified.

"What the fuck are you doin'?" he asked.

"I hate bugs!" Nancy threw the rock down, heard another crack and squish, then lifted the stone, ready to bring it down for another blow. "Goddamn spider!"

Skip rushed her; he grabbed her arms, squeezed her bloodstained wrists until they ached. "Crazy bitch!"

As the stone fell away, a thought was born from the folds of Nancy's mind, filling her brain with terrors. *He's gonna rape me! Right here in the dirt! Right next to this huge, squashed—*

Her eyes had trouble focusing in the fog, but they eventually let her in on the surprise.

At Nancy's feet lay the body of a teenage girl, her head a confusing mess of flesh, hair, and fractured bone—a pink slug of brains worming through the jagged opening in her skull and onto the dirt. The sight robbed Nancy's lungs of breath and drew her stomach up into her throat. She looked at her own hands. They were black in the darkness, gummy with blood and raw matter. Now, they shook uncontrollably, flung heavy droplets left and right.

You wanted to get in touch with "the inner reform school girl," her mind recalled. *How's it feel?*

Nancy took a long, frozen look at the remains, saw the black-and-white-striped, sleeveless top and the ripped jeans shorts they wore. In the mélange that once formed a head, a white banana clip lay cracked in a clot of hair, dotted with blood. Nancy's body tensed, then went limp in Skip's grip and he had to fight to keep her standing.

Cindi.

"No," Nancy croaked, her face contorting into a pallid expression of fear and hopelessness. She felt the knots that anchored her to reality slipping, threatening to set her mind adrift, and she asked the question that went through Skip's head as well, "Why?"

Robby didn't know why he recorded their movements through the corn. At first, he'd held the Sony camcorder on his shoulder because the higher angle provided better light. Later, he'd done it simply because it gave him something to do. He was chilled to the bone and, even though he hated to admit it, he was scared.

Danny called back to him.

"What was that?" Robby asked.

"I see something up ahead."

Robby's grip on the camcorder tightened at the word choice. Some*thing*, Danny said. Not some*one*. He fumbled with the Sony's viewfinder. Danny's back glowed in the spotlight, but the rest of the screen was a gray blur. He stopped and tilted his head away from the camera, looked directly into the mist with eyes unfiltered. But Robby couldn't see what Danny saw. He could only see the fog.

"Danny, I don't—"

"Hey!" Danny took off running and was swallowed by the thick haze.

Robby hesitated. He wanted to find shelter back in the shed, wait for dawn. In daylight, thoughts of crows that now had a taste for human flesh, of spirits and Indian curses, would be ridiculous, laughable. In the darkness and fog, however, the thoughts seemed all too possible.

All those damn stories have you scared of your own shadow. Yes, the crows attacking was weird, but it was probably some kind of rabies or fever that drove them to it. Nothing supernatural at work here. Nothing. There's no fucking corn spirit. You're gonna find everyone and get back home, and, come tomorrow, you'll have one hell of a story of your own to tell the guys at the station. It'll be a classic, right up there with the Andrews twins and Russell Veal.

Robby wished he were at the fire station now, drinking coffee, relaying the day's events from the safety of memory. He stood and listened to the deafening silence, the camcorder tilted on his shoulder. It was like being buried alive. He could almost feel the fog push in on him, urging him to chase after Danny, wanting him to—

Danny's voice wafted from the void. *"Gimme the fuckin' knife."*

THE WIDE GAME

Oh, my God! Robby's mind cried out. *He's found the killer! The guy who hung up Dale Brightman is out there in this soup with Danny and you're standing here like a fucking four-year-old afraid of the thing in his closet! What kind of a friend are you, anyway?*

Robby prepared himself. He'd run into the fog, come to Danny's aid, and take away the killer's knife. He'd be a Goddamn hero and then there would be nothing to fear. Nothing to fear. Nothing.

He ran.

Through the Sony's eyepiece, two silhouettes came into view; Robby recognized Danny's large physique, but it took him a minute to place the smaller, frailer figure. It was Mick Slatton without his Coke-bottle glasses, and in the grainy black and white monitor, it looked as if he'd bathed in Hershey's syrup. It also looked as if he'd just pulled a large hunting knife from Danny's chest.

Robby froze up, dislocated from the scene that played out before him, searching for an explanation for what he'd witnessed, a trick of the light, of the fog. *Deidra said Mick had a knife.* That was true, but she also said she'd seen a corn spirit. She'd been in shock. How was Robby supposed to know she'd been telling the truth?

Danny dropped to his knees, shook his head to and fro. His lips hung open, promised words, but delivered only blood. Mick sliced through the fog and the knife found Danny's throat. Gore leapt from the gash as Danny fell onto his side.

Mick's face appeared nothing short of triumphant.

The icy grip of paralysis shattered, allowing Robby's legs to bolt into a drunken, staggering run. "Jesus Christ!"

Mick covered his eyes with one glossy hand. "I got him!" he sang into the splash of camcorder light. "I got Williamson!"

Blood deserted Robby's face like water down a drain, left him a horrid albino-white. When he reached Danny's side, Robby saw almost immediately that his friend was dead. The left and right carotid arteries had been severed, Danny's strong heart pumping the life right out of his body.

"Robby?" Mick's voice echoed from a cave. "I thought you were Sheriff Carter or Mr. Cupello. They said..."

The rest was lost to Robby's ears. Denial, or perhaps his medical programming, prompted him to drop the camcorder and rip off his own shirt. Robby tore the fabric into ribbons, wadded it against Danny's chest and neck. He checked for a pulse, found none, and began chest compressions, but, after a few futile minutes, Robby stopped and wept.

"Why are you getting this upset about *him*?" Mick's puzzled voice still held more than a touch of glee. "I thought you said you'd just let him die."

Robby's head jerked up, his eyes angry slits, his fingers curling into fists.

"Besides," Mick squinted, tried to bring Robby's expression into focus. "They told me it was all right to kill him."

Robby punched Mick square in the face with enough force to knock him to the ground.

"Why'd you do that?"

The voice was Cindi's, but not Cindi's; a crackling gargle.

Nancy's head snapped up, her mind filled with irrational hope. *She's not dead! I hurt her, but I didn't kill her. We'll make a stretcher for her like we did for Sean and she'll be fine. Sure, she'll be pissed off, but she—*

The optimism died in her eyes when she saw what had spoken.

Cindi's body stirred; she pushed up onto her hands and knees. Her face no longer resembled anything human. It was a plastic Halloween mask someone had stepped on, crumpled and cracked.

"Come on." Skip pulled Nancy backward, a disturbing familiarity in his voice, as if he'd seen this kind of thing every day and it no longer shocked him.

"*Danny says 'Hello,*'" the Cindi-thing cooed, and then, worst of all, it *grinned*. "*He's dead, you know. Dead and rotting.*"

"Shut up." Nancy's voice had gone as pale as her cheeks, robbing it of any authority.

Cindi lifted a hand to her clotted hair and tossed it back over her shoulder, a piece of her scalp came up as she did so. "*He came to me when you wouldn't fuck him. Did he ever tell you that?*"

"Shut up."

"*He came to me and I sucked his cock better than you and I let him stick it in me, and he came and he came and he came.*"

"Shut up," Nancy kept saying, "shut up, shut up, *shut up!*"

She broke free of Skip's grip and picked up a nearby rock, only half the size of the boulder she'd used to smash in Cindi's skull. She clasped it in one hand, lobbed it at the smiling corpse that now tried to stand.

The creature snatched the stone from the air; its hideous grin widened. *"That a girl!"*

A fresh barrage of sobs bombarded Nancy. This wasn't happening. None of this was possible, none of it. Skip ran to her, tugged on her arm, tried to drag her away from the smiling dead thing. She stopped fighting him and allowed herself to be whisked away.

"Murderers go to Hell, Nancy," the broken Halloween mask said. *"We'll keep a place warm for you down there, me and Danny."*

Then, just before the swelling mist devoured it, the corpse disgorged something dark, the shadow of a shadow; it moved sinuously into the corn and was gone. Nancy thought she saw the body fall, become inert, but she wasn't sure, and there was no way she was going to go back and check.

Robby checked again for signs of life. His movements were slow, dreamlike, and it occurred to him that maybe, just maybe, this was all some nightmare; a horrible, fever-driven hallucination. How else could he explain it?

Danny was not only dead, but cold to the touch.

See, Robby told himself as he took his hand away. It would take a few hours for a body to get cold. Even in this God awful chill, it wouldn't happen immediately. *This has to be some terrible dream. What the hell did I eat before bed to invent this shit anyway?*

Robby stared up at Mick as if he were a stranger. The camcorder lamp lit a small, bright circle on his chest, a glowing hole where his heart should've been. He still held the bloody knife in his hand and something repulsive blazed in his squinted eyes.

What the hell have you done? sat in Robby's mouth, waiting to be spoken.

Instead, Mick told him, "Sheriff Carter and Mr. Cupello will be back in a minute. They'll have everyone with them and they'll explain."

"Explain what?"

"That they had orders, that Skip was a killer and they were going to shoot him on sight."

Robby reached over, grabbed Mick by his neck, and pulled his face to within inches of Danny's. "Get a good look!"

Danny's open eyes gazed up into the churning mist with great fascination. Blood ran cold from the corners of his mouth, staining his lips, forming a wide clown smile.

"Can you see now?"

Mick winced; the unpleasant look faded from his eyes, replaced by a bizarre kind of lost terror. His lips puckered and he whined, "Yes."

"Who is it then?"

"It was Skip."

"*Who is it now?*"

"*Danny!*" Mick shuddered in Robby's grasp. He dropped the knife, brought his hands up to his face, and screamed into them.

"Where'd you get the fuckin' knife?"

Mick continued to sob and Robby tightened his grip. "*Where?*"

"It's Danny's!" Mick coughed through his tears, then added, "Part of the game!"

At the sound of Mick's bawling, Robby let go and stepped away; he ran his hands through his own hair. He was shirtless and drenched in sweat, but only vaguely aware of the cold. His nose ran and he wiped it with the back of his numb hand. He heard not a breath of wind, not a chirp of insect, no noise at all to distract his mind; left alone with the realization that two of his best friends were dead, another of his friends was a murderer, and they still had miles to go.

Worse still, Robby could not shake the feeling that all of this, from Sean's "accident" to Danny's death, was somehow being...engineered. It was as if something wanted them to be isolated out here in the fog, as if something wanted them—

"*Robby.*"

At the sound of his name, Robby turned back to Mick, saw the boy still sobbing into the dirt. And Danny was—

"*Robby.*"

Danny was dead.

"Did you hear that?" Robby asked.

Mick turned his face to him, tears clearing paths through the blood and grime of his cheeks. "Hear what?"

"Somebody just said my name." Robby spun around in a circle, stared into the dark, misty columns of corn. "Who's there?"

The haze offered no reply.

Mick chuckled, his breath sputtering out in white puffs like automobile exhaust. "Now we're both going crazy."

Then Robby heard the rustle of something moving through the corn. The sound seemed distant at first, then very close. "Tell me you hear *that*," he said. "Please, tell me you hear it."

Mick stood, his face a medley of sadness and stark terror. "I hear it."

Whatever was out there was now no more than a few rows away and the ground beneath their feet shook with its footfalls. At any moment, Robby expected it to move from the mist to stand right in front of them, some gigantic unholy terror, and he thought his heart might detonate in his chest at the sight of it.

"We should go." Mick fell back. He'd picked the knife up again without realizing it, held it out toward the noise. "We should go *now*."

Robby nodded, scanning the fog. *It knows your name,* his mind told him. *It said your name!* His whole body shuddered and he took several clumsy steps back, nearly tripping over the camcorder. *The light*, he realized. *The light's leading it right to us.* He picked up the Sony and shut it down. The lamp faded, darkness swirling in from every direction.

After a moment, the sound seemed to move away from them, back into the blind depths of the cornfield. Robby offered no sigh of relief, however. He continued to back into the dark mist, afraid to turn on the spotlight, afraid it would turn and come back at them. In fact, that seemed likely.

Robby looked back over his shoulder, saw a silhouette in the haze a few feet behind him. He took another tipsy step back, placed a hand on the shape's shoulder and uttered a stern whisper. "Let's go, Mick."

"I'm way ahead of you," Mick told him.

The voice sounded distant and Robby felt coils knot in his gut. He turned to look at the dark splotch of shadow that stood behind him. "Mick?" he asked. "Where are you?"

"Over here."

Robby's hand instantly recoiled. His head whipped to the left and he turned on the camcorder spotlight with fumbling hands. Its round, glowing eye caught sight of Mick. The boy stood about two yards away, his form hazy in the churning fog even at that short distance, but he was there...*way over there*.

The light turned before Robby realized it, turned toward the shadow he'd been touching. And then he heard a voice. Danny's voice. Clotted and rasping, but Danny's voice just the same.

"*Hey, Robby,*" it croaked.

"No," Robby moaned back. He halted the arc of the spotlight. It wasn't Danny standing there. Danny was dead. And if it wasn't Danny, Robby had no interest in seeing what it really was. "Oh, Jesus..."

"*Got a candy bar?*" the shadow asked in Danny's wet voice. "*One of the ones you take from Tony's when you think nobody can see?*"

Behind Robby, Mick screamed; they were high screams, screams that tore and frayed before they ended. As loud as they were, however, Robby could still hear Danny's gargling speech.

"*Whatcha screamin' for Mickey? Oh, yeah...you fuckin' killed me. Don't sweat it. Accidents happen, don't they? Like Skip knockin' over your books. Oh, hey...what'll happen when Skip comes for you now? I'm not gonna be there anymore, am I? You're just shit outta luck little man.*"

Robby forced his feet to move, forced them backward into the mist. He held the light low, not wanting to even catch a glimpse of the thing in front of him, not knowing if his mind could hold itself together if it saw what was there to be seen.

"Will Sheriff Carter think this was an accident, Mick? Gosh, I don't know." The shadow moved forward in a jerky fashion, as if it were the world's largest marionette. *"They'll probably put you in jail, huh? Lots of Skip Williamsons in jail, Mickey. And they'll just love you. You'll have 'em lined up around the cell block waiting to stick it up your tight little ass."*

As the reality of his situation hit him, Mick's screams suddenly wilted into whimpers. He sounded like a dog just struck by a rolled up newspaper.

"Hell, Sheriff Carter might even stand around and watch. He loves it up the ass. Just ask Robby there. He'll tell you. The sheriff likes it way up in there."

Robby reached for the sniveling form behind him, caught Mick by the arm and pulled hard, using unknown strength to keep his voice level. "We're outta here."

Mick offered no resistance. He fell back to Robby's side and, a moment later, they both ran. From somewhere in the gray nothingness of mist behind them, they could hear the shadowy thing laughing at their retreat—a ghastly cackle, full of joy and pain, the sound a witch might make as she burned.

Deidra's eyes jerked open and she straightened beneath the canvas blanket. She'd had the sensation of falling into a pit. Something had been below her, laughing, waiting down in the darkness to receive her flesh. She'd felt cold metal at her throat, the blade of the knife she'd seen in Mick's hand, and she wanted to scream. Her eyes were now open, but she saw nothing of her surroundings and feared her dream wasn't over. She feared something would surface from this sea of ink at any moment and try to pull her under. It would put the knife to her throat and slice—

Paul's voice in her ear, "It's okay, babe. I'm right here."

She'd dozed off. How could she even think of closing her eyes after what she'd seen? That thing was out there. As crazy as it sounded, she knew it to be true.

Deidra lifted her hand in the darkness, found Paul's face and felt its contours beneath the bristly growth of his dawning beard. He was really there. She felt the heat of his chest and the comforting weight of his arms around her. Somehow, she felt protected. Secure. Deidra then felt the cold piece of metal from her dream, realized it was the charm that hung from Paul's neck, the separated twin of her own, and she relaxed a bit.

She wriggled her body against his for warmth. "Nancy and the others?"

"Not yet." She could feel his head tilt, feel his loving gaze fall to her. "You okay?"

"No."

He chuckled a bit at that. "Me neither."

"What time is it?"

She felt him shrug in the darkness. "Nine. Ten, maybe."

"People will have made it home by now."

"Yeah."

"They'll tell their parents...call 911."

"They will."

"When do you think they'll come?"

"I don't know," he told her patiently.

She understood she sounded like a child with all her questions. "I'm sorry. I know you're as much—"

"As much in the dark as you are?"

Deidra managed a chuckle herself. "Exactly."

And then they were no longer in the dark; a faint light bled into the dimness. Deidra's eyes shot to the doorway, saw its outline glow brightly on the opposite wall.

She rose to her feet. "Somebody's coming."

Paul got out from under the canvas and crossed the shed. When he was almost at the entrance, someone started pounding on the door. They pounded so hard, Deidra wondered if they might not be trying to break it down.

"Who is it?" Paul asked.

"Open the damn door!"

Robby.

Paul pushed up on the latch and threw it open. The fog was *so* thick. It poured through the doorway in a great cloud, as if it were being pumped into the shed. Robby ran out of the haze, drug someone behind him. It took her a few moments to realize it was Mick; the glasses were absent from his face and he was covered in blood, black feathers clotted to his skin. In his hand, he held the large knife she'd seen earlier. It too was bloody.

"Oh, my God," she whispered.

"Shut the door!" Robby panted, tried to catch his breath. "There's somethin' out there!"

Paul looked at him, concerned, then his eyes whirled into the mist. "Where's Danny?"

"*Just lock the Goddamn door!*"

"What the hell happened?" Paul asked as shut out the fog and latched the door. "Where's Danny?"

"He's dead," Mick blurted out. "Danny...he...see, he *was* Skip. They said Skip was the killer. They said it was all right to kill Skip. So, it's not my fault. It's not. He was Skip, and they... they told me Skip should die... They told me..." And then he fell to his knees on the floor of the shed, tears eating away at his words until they were idiot mumblings.

Paul's stunned gaze rose from Mick to Robby. "Danny?"

Robby's face was grievous and hesitant. He licked his lips as if to speak, then nodded instead.

"How?" Deidra wanted to know. She felt numb, as if all her blood had evaporated. It wasn't possible. Danny couldn't be dead. Not Danny.

The words came slowly to Robby's lips. "Mick accidentally stabbed him."

"Oh, Christ." A single tear spilled from each of her eyes, traveled to her chin. She sat back down on the boxes before she fell over.

"Mick said he saw Sheriff Carter out there," Robby told them. "Said he was looking for us." He paused a moment, then added, "I didn't see him."

"What *did* you see?" Deidra's throat was bone dry.

Robby looked down at the camera and handed it to Paul. "I might have recorded some of it. I don't know. I'm not gonna look and see. You can do that if you want."

Deidra's watering eyes flared and she spoke through clenched teeth. "Tell us what it was!"

Robby told them all that had happened, all that he'd seen, all that he'd heard.

And, by the time he finished with the telling, Deidra cried more for herself than for Danny.

Mondamin was here to claim them.

They were all going to die.

TWENTY-ONE

Skip and Nancy stopped to catch their breath. The stalks waved around them, angry at being sideswiped by the pair as they ran. After a moment, the cold caught up with them, making Nancy shiver.

"Come on." Skip tugged on her arm. "Our joints are gonna freeze up."

"I killed her!"

"Lower your fucking voice!"

Nancy looked at him and Skip saw the eyes of a lost child. "It was a spider. This... huge...ugly... How could I have even thought...?"

There was no point in trying to reason with her. She'd withdrawn to a place where nothing Skip said could reach her. There would be time for her to grieve at her leisure, time even to repent, if she was so inclined, but that time would come later, in a place far removed from here.

Skip tugged again at her arm, more insistent. "Now, come on."

Without warning, Nancy smacked him upside the head and pulled away.

"Bitch!" Skip moved a hand to his throbbing temple. "What the hell was that for? I'm the fucker who's tryin' to save your life!"

She glared at him. "This is all your fault."

"My...Why does everyone keep saying that? How is any of this shit my fault?"

"If you hadn't pushed Sean, we'd be home by now. If you hadn't thrown a rock at the crows, they would have left us alone."

He pointed at her. "And if *you* hadn't picked up a rock, Cindi'd still be alive."

At that, fresh tears flowed from Nancy's eyes and she turned her face away from him.

Skip hadn't meant it to sound so brutal, but it was the truth. When he pushed Sean, he had no idea the bastard would fall off a cliff. Nancy, on the other hand, picked up a rock and bashed in Cindi's skull. She could blame Skip all she wanted, but in the end, it was Nancy who'd have to answer for that one.

He held his hand out to her. "Come on, we need to get outta here."

She shook her head.

"Nancy, we don't have time for this bullshit!"

"I'm not going anywhere with *you*."

Skip heard a whisper, faint enough to be mistaken for a stray thought in his brain. "*Leave her*," it said.

That was exactly what he should do. She was a killer after all, and a crazy one at that. Giant spiders? What kind of an idiot did she take him for? Then again, hadn't he just watched a pair of corpses rise from the dead and speak?

"*You might be next*," the whisper suggested. "*She's killed once, after all. And she liked Cindi. She doesn't give a shit about you.*"

Skip nodded. That would be the kicker, wouldn't it? He'd drag her back to civilization, then she'd bash his brains in to thank him for his pains. He held up his hands and backed away from her.

"You know what? Fine, we're done playin' the fuckin' game anyway. I don't need to stick with you and I don't need your bony ass slowin' me down."

"What was that?" Nancy wanted to know.

"What was wh—?"

Laughter. It came from somewhere in the mist, the conspiratory giggle of two small girls at play. It swirled around them as if they were standing at the center of a whirlpool. Then it was inside their skulls, dancing around their brains in a psychotic game of ring-around-the-rosy.

"Stop it!" Nancy slapped her hands across her ears, her fingers curled around her hair. "*Leave us alone!*"

And then it was gone, marooning them in a vacuum void of all sound. Skip opened his mouth to speak, surprised to hear his own words. "You ready to come with me now?"

Nancy ran to him, sobbing.

"*Leave her*," the whisper urged again. The voice sounded deeper than it had before, and Skip now knew it was a visitor to his mind, not a resident.

No fuckin' way, he thought in reply, then took her by the arm and ran with her into the darkness.

Paul and Robby paced across the center of the work shed. Deidra still sat on the boxes in the corner, covered in the canvas blanket, her head resting on her knees. Mick lay frozen on the floor where he'd collapsed; only by watching the rise and fall of his chest could Paul tell he was still among the living. The camcorder was also on the floor, its lamp light casting odd shadows on the walls and ceiling.

"No power on earth is gonna get me to go out there again tonight," Robby insisted. "We stay here until morning, make a run for it when it's light. They can't hurt us in the daylight."

"I knew we could count on you to know just what to do," Paul told him with frustration. "See, here's my problem, we're talking about *demons* and you're still acting like Mr. Superior. For once in your life, why can't you admit you don't know shit about something?"

"Because..." Robby looked to Paul, equally frustrated. "Look, if we were sitting in the Woodfield right now, we'd both be yellin' at the screen." He cupped his hands around his mouth. "'Don't go out there you stupid shits!'"

"You're right, we would. But, for the record, this is *reality*. And call me crazy, but I'm thinking all of us together in this ten by twelve cube screams smorgasbord."

"They want us split up," Deidra interjected. She wiped the residue of old tears from her cheeks and lifted her face to them. "That's what the crows were for. They got us scattered, not knowing what to think or do. Whatever we decide, we need to stick together."

For a moment they stood silent, exchanging apprehensive glances, then Paul stated his position to Robby. "Look, we need to run like hell until we reach minimum safe distance, and we need to do it now. There can't be more than a couple of miles left before we hit some houses. Without the stretcher to carry, we should be able to make good time. Hopefully, we'll run into Nancy and Cindi along the way."

"And what happens if we run into something else?" Robby asked.

"I don't know," Paul admitted. "At least if we're *out there*, we have places to run."

Deidra nodded her agreement. "Seconded."

Robby scanned the tight confines of the shed, the truth in what Paul had said sinking in; he sighed. "What about Mickey?"

Paul knelt down with caution, afraid sudden movement might set Mick off. Mick appeared nearly catatonic, concentrating on the corner of the shed as if it held something of interest; tears and drool had managed to wash much of the gore from his face, and Paul noticed with more than a touch of nausea that he still held Danny's bloody knife in his shaking hand.

"Mick?" Paul reached out, patted his friend's shoulder. "We gotta go."

Mick blinked and his focus shifted to Paul's face, his lip trembling. "I really screwed up."

"It wasn't your fault, Mick."

"Then...you believe me?"

Paul paused, not knowing what to think and yet certain Mick would never have purposely hurt Danny. Mick loved Danny like a brother. "Yeah, I believe you."

"Thanks."

"Think you can—?"

"Let's go."

"We can wait a second if you need—"

"I wanna go home."

Paul nodded. "Sure."

He reached out for the camcorder, then moved to the door. Deidra dropped her canvas blanket and crossed the shed to stand at his side. Her eyes were fearful but trusting. He kissed her temple and looked to Robby.

"Ready?"

"No, but I'll deal with it." Robby helped Mick up off the dirt. "You lead and I'll pick up the rear."

"Fine." They watched with anticipation as Paul put his hand on the latch. "Run."

Everything happened in a blur. Paul flipped the latch; the fog flowed in, its cloudy arms curled around the group as if to welcome them back, and they ran. The shed became a dark shape behind them, sank rapidly into the void. Light from the camcorder bobbed and weaved on the swirling mist, revealing little of their surroundings. Countless monstrosities could be standing a yard away, they wouldn't know until it was too late.

A shrill scream came out of the fog.

Paul stopped suddenly; Deidra plowed into his backpack, and he whirled the light around. For a moment, he thought it might have been the cry of an animal, then he wondered if he might've imagined the sound. Before he could ask the others what they'd heard, it came again—louder, nearer, and definitely female.

Robby's rattled expression confirmed the shriek was a reality. "That was...what was that?"

Deidra took a step toward the scream and Paul pushed her back. She looked up at him, mystified. "It's Nancy or Cindi. Those things—"

"Are setting a trap. They're trying to separate us again." Paul motioned with his light. "Or they just want us all to go that way, want to steer us off the right path."

"What if you're wrong?"

He looked her squarely in the eye, tried to sound firm and persuasive. "I'm not."

She nodded, her eagerness to be home transcending her fear.

After a moment, they resumed the quickness of their original pace. They'd been walking for so long, the edge of the field couldn't be far. As his light swung across the mist, Paul caught a glimpse of something in the row ahead, blocking their path. He recognized the dark shape almost immediately.

It was one of the creatures from Schongauer's engraving, an illustrated monster that had traumatized him as a child.

Deidra's voice drifted in from somewhere distant. "What is it? What's the matter?"

Paul's hands trembled so badly he nearly dropped the camcorder. A kind of horrified awe stole over him and he was suddenly six years old again, sitting in his pew at St. Anthony's, his young heart screaming in his chest. He nearly lost his balance and fell back into Deidra, starting a domino effect that would have sent them all to the ground.

"Let's move!" Robby urged. "What are we waiting for?"

Paul didn't hear him, and, even if he had, he couldn't move; terror bolted his legs to the ground.

It's a trick, he told himself. *Just close your eyes. When you look again, this thing will be gone. Just a bad dream.*

Paul's eyes snapped shut, but the demon haunted his darkness. Ram's horns spiraled off its forehead. Bones extended from its back like the scaffold of wings; they flexed and moved, unaware of their nakedness, trying to produce flight. It reached out with its spindly claws, its jaws open to devour him, its eyes bottomless pools into which he could feel himself fall.

Paul shuddered and whipped his head around to look at Deidra. She wasn't there. In her place stood the nude Miami girl from his dream the night before; black tresses cascaded over her shoulders, covering her breasts as they plunged toward the curves of her hips. Colorful handprints and streaks adorned her skin. In her hands, she held a cornhusk doll; fire engulfed the figure's tiny head, the flames flickering like red hair caught in the wind.

"The spirits call for their warriors," she told him.

"No." Paul shook his head to and fro, the golden half-circle charm around his neck plastered to his skin by sweat. "You're not real."

"Paul?" Deidra grabbed hold of his chin to stop his head from wagging. "What's going on?"

"I saw this big...thing..."

Why hadn't he seen her there when he opened his eyes?

"Look behind me, tell me what you see."

Deidra craned her neck; afraid she would find the obscene creature she'd seen before the crows. At the limit of the camcorder light she thought she saw a faint shadow drift off, like a floating hole in the haze, nothing more. "It looks clear... whatever you saw, it's gone now."

"Thank God."

Robby gave him a petulant glance. "Let me lead! I've had to run the gauntlet through smoke-filled rooms and I won't be stopping every two seconds to—"

"No." Paul insisted with polite contempt. He wiped his face with his hand, as if ridding himself of his panicky sweat would rid him of his fear. "I'm fine."

"Then move your ass!"

Paul tugged Deidra's hand and started forward. How far was it to the edge of the field? He'd told Robby a mile or two. That sounded about right. How fast could they travel that distance? Four minutes for a mile kept popping up, but he dismissed that notion, irritated at his brain for mentioning it. Four minutes was world record speed, wasn't it? They were nowhere near that. Paul saw the shadow of a twisted stalk loom from the mist at the edge of his sight, looking too much like a bony claw. He flinched, but did not stop. He kept moving, kept leading them on toward—

A rush of movement ahead, a dark blur against the white smudge of fog.

Paul took a stumbling step back and Deidra screamed. In the darkness before them, another cry rose like an echo to the first. Paul speared the shapes with his camcorder light, stunned by what it revealed.

Nancy ran to them, threw her arms around Deidra's neck.

Paul noticed blood on her hands and his stomach rolled over. He turned his eyes back to the path, blinked, and saw Skip. Williamson's face and posture were tense, antagonistic, as if he were angry to see them.

"I'll be damned." Skip aimed his squint at Paul. "Thanks for runnin' off with the light, fucker."

"Everyone was running scared. You should be glad I thought to grab it at all."

"How do we know it's really him?" Mick asked, his voice frightened and sad.

Skip offered a short, surly chuckle. "What if I don't believe in you faggots, either?"

"They're real," Nancy sobbed. "They're really real."

"Is Cindi with you?" Deidra asked.

Nancy pulled away, her eyes drifting to her own hands. "She's...I..."

"We found her dead," Skip blurted out.

All eyes shot to him, none more surprised than Nancy's.

"Must have been the same guy that got Brightman," he continued. "She was all fucked up."

Mick held his hands over his head; his fingers clasped together, the bloody knife pressed flat against his skull. What the sheriff had said, it had obviously scared him into making a mistake with Danny. He didn't want to make the same mistake again, but, as it became clear this was no mirage, that Williamson stood in their midst, horror took hold.

Why is everyone standing here talking to Skip? He's the killer!

Finally, when it looked as if everyone would shake hands and just move on, Mick found the courage to speak. "Sheriff Carter said *you* killed Dale."

Skip glared at him with sullen eyes. "*What?*"

"I saw them. The sheriff, Deputy Oates, Mr. Cupello...they said—"

They were all staring at Mick. Even though he couldn't see their faces clearly, he could tell they were embarrassed for him. It was the same look they had when Skip knocked over his books. They felt anger toward Skip, sure they did, but they also felt sadness for Mick. *How pathetic*, those embarrassed looks said. *If only he could stand up for himself. If only he wasn't such a slab of Jell-O!*

"*I saw them,*" Mick cried out. "*They said they found bodies. They said* you *did it!*"

Skip took a step forward, pointing. "I don't know what your major malfunction is, Slatton, but I didn't kill anybody!"

Fresh tears came to Mick's eyes, blurring Skip's image even more. "*It's your fault Danny's dead!*"

Nancy's head whirled to Mick. "Danny's...?"

"You're fucked in the head, man. And I swear, you call me a killer one more time and I'll—"

"You'll what?" Mick lowered his hands to wipe away tears.

Skip saw the knife for the first time. Caught off guard, he held up his hands and took a step back. "Whoa."

"For years, you've made my life a living Hell." Mick moved forward, smiling a bit when he saw Skip take another backward step. "What?" He held the knife higher. "Now that I can defend myself you don't wanna wail on me? You're such a coward."

"Put the knife down, Mickey," Robby said. "If Sheriff Carter wants Skip, let's give him Skip."

"No." Mick savagely swiped his cheeks with the back of his hand, smeared the blood that remained there. "I want to hear Skip say he's a coward. I want to hear him say he's guilty."

As Mick and Skip stood staring at one another, Nancy heard a voice. It was as if the surface chatter of her brain had gone suddenly quiet, allowing her to hear the background music, a beautiful choir that sang to her as one melodic, *hypnotic* voice. It was the same voice that had urged Skip to leave her in the corn, but she couldn't know that. The only thing Nancy knew for certain was that it told her the truth.

"*If you don't mind me saying so, you're the one who's guilty,*" it said. "*But wouldn't it be better if it was Skip? Better for you, better for everyone.*"

THE WIDE GAME

She understood what the voice meant. If Skip had killed Cindi, the police would lock him up and throw a party. But, plausible as it was, he didn't do it. Nancy did. They would find out about it sooner or later. She should take responsibility now and—

"*Skip's the* only one *who knows it was you*," the whisper reminded her. "*The police think he killed Dale Brightman, they would believe he killed Cindi too.*"

This thought made her heart beat with guilty joy. Skip was the real reform school kid here. She could say he did it and they'd believe her. They'd think he...

No. She had to face facts. She was the one who picked up the rock.

"*The rock Skip knocked out of your hand? I'm sure his fingerprints got on it. You could say you tried to stop him. After all, you were her best friend. Why would you kill her? Skip can say he's innocent all he likes, no one's going to believe him over a homecoming queen.*"

She wanted to do it, but she was still filled with uncertainty. It wasn't right, after all. It wasn't—

"*Is it right for you to throw away your whole life? You're a good girl, Nancy, such a good girl. Is it right that you should spend the rest of your life in prison?*"

No, but—

"*Then, right now, just say it was Skip.*"

But—

"*No one will ever know it was you if you just—*"

Yes.

"—*say it!*"

Nancy suddenly opened her mouth and screamed. "*Skip killed Cindi! He killed her!*"

Skip's head jerked in her direction. He almost looked hurt. Everyone stared back at him with hateful expressions. "What? You can't actually believe..." But he could tell from their eyes that they did. He pointed to Nancy. "She's fuckin' possessed!"

Mick could not help but smile. He'd been suddenly vindicated. Skip *was* a killer, just as Sheriff Carter said he was. When they met up with the police they would—

"*Kill the fucker.*"

The alien voice was like a starter pistol being fired off in Mick's head.

He sprang at the blur in front of him, knowing that this time it *was* Skip, knowing he was not going to be fooled again. Never again. The knife was in his right hand, its serrated edge a row of glistening fangs.

"Little shit!" Skip managed. He dodged Mick's lunge, took a few staggering steps back, and the sticky blade sliced air, fanning his face and neck.

Mick nearly fell, but quickly regained his balance; he turned and thrust the knife upward.

Skip feinted, then grasped Mick's hand and squeezed, trying to get him to release the blade. Mick stepped down hard on Skip's foot and threw out his elbow, forcing Skip to let go and stumble back.

For a moment, Paul had the urge to grab Deidra and take off running into the mist. Let them kill each other. Maybe whatever was out there in the fog would be so enthralled by the bloodshed, it would forget all about them and they could get home. Then Paul remembered the story Deidra had told him, got control of his impulses, and shouted, "This is exactly what they want!"

Skip and Mick continued to circle one another. It reminded Paul of the rumble in *West Side Story*. Neither of them appeared to hear him.

"Look at me, Goddammit!" Paul turned to Deidra. "Tell 'em about the legend with the crows."

She nodded. "The Miami were out looking for—"

Skip shifted his eyes to her for only a moment, but it was enough time for Mick to dive forward and stick the knife into his chest. When the blade was withdrawn, blood spilled out to cover the "A.I.D.S Kills Fags Dead" logo, turning Skip's entire shirt bright red. Skip looked down at the leak he'd sprung, then covered it with his own hands like the little boy who stuck his finger in the dike; he rocked back and forth on his feet, then reached out to grab hold of Mick, his eyes glassy and stunned.

Robby ran forward as Skip fell, pushed Mick aside to get to him. He put his hand on top of Skip's, adding to the pressure, feeling the warm gush of fluid between his fingers. "No, no, come on..."

Paul rushed over with the camcorder lamp, tried to help Robby see. A tiny red light winked at him from the front of the eyepiece and Paul came to the dark realization that he might have inadvertently filmed a murder.

Skip Williamson was gone. The teenager who bled out in the dirt was named Josh, and Josh was scared. He gasped, his face woeful and confused. He looked around, then turned to Robby. "They're everywhere," he said whispered, and blood followed the words from his mouth, flowing thickly down his chin.

Robby knelt there, feeling everything twist inside his own gut. At his hands, the warm gush became a trickle, and the trickle tapered down to nothing. He looked into Williamson's eyes and thought he saw the life flicker out of them. Robby never thought he could feel anything for Skip, but, at that moment, he felt a parade of emotions march across the ridges of his mind; astonishment, followed closely by sympathy, guilt, fear, and ultimately rage. His hands curled into fists and he began to pound on Skip's chest.

Paul thought Robby had been infected by Mick's insanity; he reached out to him, grasped him by the shoulder and pulled him up. "Stop!"

Robby's face whirled around, his eyes filled with fury. "Don't you tell me to stop! He's seventeen, dammit! Same as you, same as me, same as Dale, and Cindi, and...and Danny! You don't die at seventeen. You haven't even lived at seventeen! This is all...it was just supposed to be a *fucking game!*"

"It stopped being a game a long time ago," Paul said, his face grim. "And if *you* wanna live past seventeen, we gotta go." He stepped away from Robby, offered Mick a harsh glare. "You just stay away from us!"

Mick looked up, amazed. "I did it for—"

"You did it because you *wanted* to." Paul pointed into the fog. "And they knew it. They knew it and they used it to get you to kill Danny too."

"Danny...?" Nancy's gaze shifted from Skip's dead face to Mick's live one, then fell to the knife still clutched in his hands, the knife that now dripped fresh blood. She leaned back in Deidra's embrace, the hand she'd been holding over her mouth slipping down to reveal an expression of agony. "*You...?*"

Paul's fingers folded and the nails dug into his palm. He had to stay focused. If he didn't, he felt that the things he'd seen—Schongauer's demon, the Miami girl, or whatever the hell they really were—might have their way with him as well. Paul walked over to Deidra, tugged at her, blood from his own hand smearing across her arm. "Come on."

Deidra nodded, pulled on Nancy's CHOOSE LIFE shirt. It had been white at nine o'clock that morning. Now it was filthy, streaked and splattered in red. "We're going."

Nancy's feet went with them, but her eyes remained squarely on Mick.

Robby stood and moved to follow, still looking down at Skip, wondering what he'd seen. Angels? Relatives who'd died before him, come now to show him the way? Robby hoped that's what it had been. The alternative was far too horrid to consider.

"You heard Nancy." Mick pointed to Skip's body with the knife. "He was a killer."

"You heard Paul." Robby gave Mick a hard push as he walked by. "How's it feel to be their bitch?"

"When we find the sheriff, he'll tell you. He'll know I did the right thing." Mick watched Robby and the others walk off into the mist, and, when the light faded, he chased after them. He was not going to be left in the dark again.

They walked together in silence, their minds too filled with thought to make room for words. Another twenty minutes went by, and the corn seemed to wilt into the haze. A huge, shadowy "T" materialized in their path, and Paul found himself suddenly reminded of *Sesame Street*.

Today's Wide Game has been brought to you by the letter "T."

Amazing what the brain chose to remember when the body was gripped by fear.

Paul thought it might be another corpse, someone else hung on a cross like Dale Brightman, hung like the statue of Christ in St. Anthony's church. Instead, as he peered along his spotlight beam, Paul found something else entirely. At first, he was puzzled, then recognition took hold and he could not hide his joyous smile. A rusted metal clothesline, four ropes extending from its crossbeam to disappear into the haze.

Deidra identified it in the same instant. "We're back!"

They burst forward, put every bit of energy they had left into a sprint. A building stood before them, partially hidden beneath fingers of mist. Nevertheless, Paul could tell it was a house and he pulled Deidra to him, kissed her as they ran.

"Never in my life did I ever think I'd be this happy to see Harmony!" Robby cried, a smile dawning on his lips as they approached the back step.

"Is it real?" Nancy asked. "Tell me it's real!"

Paul threw himself against the back door, pounded for someone to open it. No one answered; darkness filled every window. "Hey," Paul called out. "We need some help out here!"

"It's probably some old couple." Robby bent over, his hands on his knees as he tried to catch his breath. "Either...they're asleep, or they... they're too scared to open up."

"They can call the police then," Paul told him. "That's fine by me."

And then Paul had a terrifying thought. Fog still billowed all around them. What if this haze blanketed the entire town? What if the demons had stolen everyone else away and left them here alone, with no one to help and nowhere to go? At that, Paul pounded even harder, shook the entire doorframe; the idea that Harmony was now a ghost town making him shudder as he screamed, *"Please, let us in!"*

Deidra giggled, dug in the pockets of her pink sweatpants. "I just realized this is *my* house."

Paul stopped trying to break down the door and shined his lamp around in disbelief. Deidra was right. They'd arrived on the back threshold of the Perkins' home. He caught her laughter, leaned against the side of the house, his ribs aching. They'd come full circle.

Nancy laced her fingers through her hair. Robby shook his head. Both were smiling. When Paul glanced over at Mick, however, his own laughter dried up.

Mick's eyes had gone dull with a kind of stoned disbelief.

Paul didn't like that look...not at all. He felt his face tighten, like the grip of a man hanging onto a ledge for dear life, and when he peered down Mick's line of sight—when he saw what Mick saw—his grip deserted him and left him numb with horror.

A whole congress of unimaginable silhouettes stood at the edge of the yard, cloudy abominations that bulged, flapped, and slithered. Though Paul could not see them clearly through the fog, his mind filled in the details, showing him Schongauer's demons; living, breathing, and coming to get him.

Deidra announced she found her keys and Paul screamed.

Everyone turned their heads to look, first at Paul, then at the mist. Paul hoped he was hallucinating, that each of them would see nothing there but haze. The look of alarm that washed over their faces told him different. The demons were there, real, and approaching fast.

Paul pushed Deidra toward the door. "*Get inside!*"

She fumbled with the key ring, tried to put her Volkswagen key in the lock, then switched to the house key. The door swung wide and they ran past her into the darkened house. Deidra reached over for the light switch, flipped it up and down. The lights remained dark.

"Goddammit," she cursed, "they worked fine this morning!"

This morning.

God, how distant that felt now.

Paul slammed the back door closed behind them and locked the deadbolt. He tapped Deidra on the shoulder, pointed across the room to the kitchen wall. "See if the phone works!"

She nodded and ran to the telephone. When she put it to her ear and heard the dial tone, she sobbed with joy. Deidra dialed 911, dancing up and down as if she had to use the toilet. It rang.

Robby, Nancy, and Mick backed up into the breakfast nook. Mick still held Danny's hunting knife, which in the hands of a prosecutor would be labeled Exhibit A. Robby saw a metal baseball bat propped against the roll-top desk and he grabbed it with both hands, held it up like a club.

A voice on the telephone line, "911, what is the nature of your emergency?"

"Thank God," Deidra cried. "We're—"

Being attacked by monsters from the corn?

"There's someone trying to get into my house!"

The kitchen window darkened and shattered. Deidra looked over to see a clawed hand push its way into the room, then evaporate into a wispy gray tendril of mist. She screamed, dropped the phone from her ear and let it swing back and forth from its curly noose of rubber cord.

Paul backed away from the door, joined the rest of the group. "*Upstairs!*"

They retreated down the dark hallway toward the landing of the staircase. The steps were now carpeted in heavy mist. Robby looked up, saw the fog drift down from the clouded upstairs hall.

"I don't think we should go up there," he said.

A shadow slid across the floor, then grew up the wall of the hallway. It appeared to be human. "*Mick?*" it called, a hoarse imitation of Skip.

Paul's eyes shot to Robby. "I like it down here a whole lot less."

"*You proud of yourself, little man?*" The shadow grew larger on the wall, came closer. "*We'll see how proud you are roasting on a spit.*"

Robby moved onto the stairs with hesitation and Nancy gave him a hard shove. The others followed, ascending the steps quickly, their feet disturbing the fog, making splashes of vapor. When they reached the second floor, Deidra ushered them into her room. It was just as it had been that morning with the exception of the bed. Deidra had taken the time to make it up, probably while Paul had been showering. They backed away from the door, crammed themselves into the far corner.

Deidra put her head on Paul's shoulder, her hand clutching Freddy Krueger's visage on his shirt. His right hand rose to her hair, stroked it. His other hand held out the camcorder, swung the light between the window and the doorway. Their breaths came in short, heavy gasps that broke the overwhelming silence of the house.

Then, they heard another sound.

Footsteps.

Something climbed the stairs. Deidra and Nancy drew in loud, hissing breaths. Paul backed up another step, pushed Robby flat against the wall. Mick watched the doorway with wide, terror-stricken eyes.

A shadow oozed over the carpet, then hit the door and slithered its way up. Paul tried to think of something that would help them, but he could find nothing. In a moment it would be in the room with them, Skip Williamson's re-animated corpse or something far worse.

Without a moment's thought, Mick dropped the knife onto the carpet and snatched the steel bat from Robby's trembling hands. He moved away from the group, rushed the open door, and, when the thing in the hallway turned the corner, he lashed out. The steel club struck the figure in the head, knocked it against the wall where it collapsed onto a bed of Cabbage Patch Kids.

Mick approached the thing with caution, tightening his grip on the bat. He half expected whatever it was to jump up, like a movie maniac who would never die, but it didn't. It just laid there, spilling dark fluid, staining the stuffed dolls.

"I think it's dead," Mick whispered, adding to himself, *dead again.*

The mist made a hasty retreat from the room, as if someone had turned on a huge vacuum and sucked it all away. If this had been a movie, Paul would have taken the footage of the fog rolling in and run it in reverse.

When the air was clear, he aimed the camcorder spotlight at the thing Mick had brought down, and, in his ear, he heard Deidra scream.

Even with his blurred vision, Mick saw it too. The shadow he'd clubbed wore a brown skirt and matching sweater; one of her shoes lay on the floor, the other hung loosely from her stocking foot. She lay on her side, her face covered in a splash of reddish-brown hair and flowing blood. Mick took two drugged steps back and looked over at the corner where the others stood cowering.

"It was a devil," Mick told them, then his eyes found the camcorder lens and his head cocked lazily to the side.

Deidra's mind made a sudden identification and her screams turned to wild sobs. "Oh, God...*Mom!*"

It was just like her mother to cut her trip short, to come home in secret, hoping to find Deidra sleeping innocently in her bed, fearing she would catch her drunk and fornicating.

Surprise, Mom! Deidra thought with sickening horror as she lunged across the room. *Surprise!*

Gwen Perkins opened her eyes. They were clouded as the fog had been. Her lips moved soundlessly, as if to accuse her daughter of something.

Deidra bent down, cradled her mother in her arms, and was warmed by a free-flowing river of blood. "Somebody help me!"

Robby ran to her. He felt for a pulse and found something weak that barely passed for one. He knelt down, dug his knee into the puffy face of a Cabbage Patch doll. It smelled of baby powder.

"Don't let her die," Deidra moaned. "Please, not my...not my mommy."

"Shove some of these dolls under her head to elevate it," Robby instructed. "But be gentle, we don't want to hurt her more."

Deidra nodded, did as she was told.

Robby opened Gwen Perkins' button-up sweater, exposed her lacy bra, and administered CPR. He looked to Paul and Nancy. "Paul, take off your shirt and wad it against her head. *Be gentle.* She's gonna have a skull fracture. Nancy, go downstairs and see if the 911 operator is still on the line. If she is, tell her to send an ambulance."

"I can't go down there," Nancy said.

"*Go!*"

She shook her head, whipping it from side to side.

"I'll go," Paul said, handing his shirt to Deidra. There was no way he could get to Mrs. Perkins' wound with her in the way, and he sure as hell wasn't going to ask her to leave her mother's side. He took a step toward the door, then saw the walls of the room bathed in alternating red and blue light.

"Freeze!"

Everyone but Robby and Deidra spun in the direction of the order, saw Sheriff Carter in the doorway, the pistol in his hands pointed right at them. A moment later, a second figure appeared with a second pistol, and Mick looked down at the bat in his own hands.

"Drop it!" Deputy Oates commanded.

Mick let go of the bloodied club and it hit the carpet with a heavy thud. He raised his scarlet hands toward the ceiling in surrender, and the deputy wrenched them back behind his back and handcuffed them together.

"Let me see everyone else's hands," Carter barked.

Nancy and Paul did as they were told.

"You're gonna have to shoot me if you want to see my hands, Sheriff," Robby told him, breathing hard between chest compressions. "I'm not losing another one tonight."

Carter didn't shoot. Instead, he radioed for an ambulance. Five minutes later, one arrived and Deidra accompanied her mother out the front door.

Paul watched her leave, then reached over to Robby and placed a hand on his shoulder in a gesture of thanks. "Will she live?"

Robby said nothing; instead, for the first time Paul could remember, he saw his friend cry.

Deputy Oates walked Mick down to a cruiser, and Sheriff Carter moved to the three remaining teens. Paul tried to glean some insight into their situation from the lawman's sullen eyes and leathery face, but got nothing. Carter's stare lingered on Robby for a moment, however, and Paul guessed that they knew each other. Finally, the sheriff told them, "I'll need you all to come to the station."

TWENTY-TWO

"Let's go over this again," Carter said.

Paul held his face in his hands, stared at the green cinderblock walls. He didn't know if they were painted green, or if they just reflected the painfully bright light of the fluorescent fixture overhead. It didn't really matter. What mattered was that there were three other interrogation rooms just like this one down the hall and at this very moment Deputy Oates, the Assistant District Attorney, and God only knew who else were talking to Nancy, Robby, and Mick. What mattered was that the State Police had been called. What mattered was that Deidra was on the way to the hospital, her mother dead or dying, and he couldn't be with her. As the sheriff went on and on with one question after another, Paul wondered if he would ever be with her again.

"Sheriff, I've told you everything. You've got the videotape. What more can I add to that?"

"Just makin' sure all my ducks are in a row. You found Dale Brightman murdered, fuckin' crucified—you'll pardon my French."

"I hear worse in the halls at school."

This brought half a smile to the sheriff's face. Just half a smile. "I don't doubt that. So tell me what happened next?"

"I *told* them not to take him down," Robby said. "But Danny wouldn't listen."

Deputy Oates nodded, then held up his Styrofoam cup. "You want some water or anything?"

Robby shook his head. He wanted to know what was happening with the others, then he wanted to go home, bolt his window, lock his door, and try to go to sleep. But he knew it didn't matter what he wanted. He also knew sleep would come to him slowly tonight, if it came at all.

Oates took a drink. "Now, Mick Slatton. He wasn't with you at this point?"

"No. He was back with the girls."

"And Danny," Oates directed. "He went to find his knife?"

Robby nodded. "Right."

"But it was gone."

"Right."

Oates took another sip of water, wiped his lips on his uniform sleeve. "Did he have any idea when it went missing?"

"No," Robby said impatiently. "I mean, he thought he still had it. Why else would he want to show us?"

"But you stole that knife, didn't you?" Assistant District Attorney Goldman asked as he pulled the empty chair away from the table and sat down. His eyes never wavered from Mick Slatton's blubbering face.

"It was just part of the game." Mick wiped away the tears with one cuffed hand, dragging the other up to his face as well.

Goldman checked his notes. "This...*Wide* Game? Yes. Was killing Danny also part of the game?"

"*No!* It was an accident. He was one of my best friends. Look, I told you before, I thought he was—"

"You thought he was Josh Williamson?"

"Skip."

"Skip. Of course. And Dale Brightman?—Did you think he was Skip too?"

Mick looked at Goldman with red, bewildered eyes and shook his head back and forth.

"And who did you think *he* was?"

"I didn't even see—"

"What about Gwen Perkins?"

Gwen...? The confusion in Mick's face thawed to reveal horrified concern. *Deidra's mother. Oh, Jesus.* "How is she?" he asked.

"I'm told she's critical." Goldman showed Mick an odd, baffled expression. "Tell me, when you swung that bat, did you think she was Skip too?"

Mick's voice was almost too soft to be heard. "You wouldn't believe me if I told you what I thought."

"But I'm supposed to believe that Sheriff Carter and Deputy Oates told you there was an order to..." Goldman checked his notes again. "To 'shoot Skip Williamson on sight'?"

"That's what they told me," Mick insisted.

"Mr. Slatton, what would you say if I then told you Sheriff Carter and Deputy Oates saw you for the first time this evening when they arrived at the Perkins' home?"

"That's not...I *saw* them."

"Just like you *saw* Skip Williamson when you killed Danny Fields."

"It was an accident," Mick contended once more, his voice growing even more pale.

"An accident."

"Yes."

"These were all just accidents."

"*Yes.*"

"But when you finally got around to killing Williamson, *that* murder was on purpose, right?"

Mick lowered his head, saw the handcuffs gleam in the overhead light. "I'd really like to call my mother now. I get one phone call, don't I?"

Goldman nodded. "Yes, Mick, one call." He leaned across the table, his eyes focused, his face stern. "But first, let's talk about Cindi Hawkins."

"Cindi?" Nancy asked with nervous alarm.

"Yes." Deputy Alison Landau, the first woman ever to serve the Harmony Police Department, spoke in a soft and caring tone. Nancy was too unstrung to wonder if it was sincere. "Cindi Hawkins. You found her body?"

"Yeah. It was dark. At first I...do I have to talk about this?"

Landau folded her hands on the table, looked at them a moment, then lifted her eyes to Nancy. "It would really help us find who did this."

Well, her mind began, *that would be me.*

Then she heard the other voice again, like a stranger whispering to her brain, "*Mick killed Danny.*"

The thought of never seeing Danny again brought new tears.

Deputy Landau reached for the box of tissues on her side of the table and handed one to Nancy. "Do you need some water?"

"No." Nancy wiped away the grief. "Danny's...he's really dead, isn't he? Mick...*killed* him."

Landau nodded, placed her hand on Nancy's for comfort. "I know this is hard for you. If you want a few minutes alone, I can—"

"There was this rock," Nancy blurted out.

"A rock?"

"Yeah." Nancy felt her lips quiver as she spoke. She saw Cindi smile at her as they walked the school halls, the image burned away in a flash of light, replaced by the smashed face of a horrid dead thing, but this face too was smiling. Nancy's hands flew to her eyes and she began to shake. She stood bolt upright, fell back against the green cinderblock wall.

"What is it?" Deputy Landau rose from her chair. "What did you see?"

Nancy opened her mouth, ready to confess to everything—stealing the Whitesnake cassette, murdering Cindi, lying about Skip...

The choir was back. *"And they believed what you said about him, didn't they?"*

Yes. Everyone had believed her.

"Nancy?"

Her face jerked toward the voice, saw Landau's troubled stare.

"What happened out there?"

Nancy shook her head. How could she hope to make this woman understand what she herself could not grasp? How could she have done it? How could she have been so... so *evil?*

"You're not evil, Nancy," the voices sang to her inner ear. *"You were tricked."*

That's right, Nancy found herself thinking, remembering what Skip had said about her being possessed. It made perfect sense. Some controlling force in the mist had made her see things, had forced her to do things she wouldn't normally do. She swallowed, the thought calmed her, stifled the guilty pain that screamed in her gut. *Yeah, that's what happened. They made me do it, didn't they? They* made *me.*

"*You're a promising young lady,*" the choir observed. "*Why have your life taken away from you over something that wasn't even your fault?*"

But the police would find out she did it sooner or later. If she waited, it would be—

"*They'll never find out,*" the whisper promised. "*Mick's the real killer here. He's the one who killed Dale Brightman. He's the one who took Danny from you. And he killed Skip and Deidra's mother, too. You saw those, didn't you? They're ready to lock him up and throw away the key. What's one more?*"

"What happened?" Deputy Landau begged again.

Nancy's lips parted, began with the truth, "I saw Cindi on the ground..."

"*Why waste your whole life over this?*"

"Her head was..."

"*Just tell them it was Mick,*" the choir coaxed. "*What's one more?*"

"I...someone had..."

"*Tell them.*"

Deputy Landau put a hand on her shoulder, tried to comfort her as she probed. "Who was it, Nancy? Who did this to your friend?"

"It was Mick Slatton." Nancy wept, then, over and over again she lied, "He killed her."

"It's all right." Deputy Landau hugged her. "You're safe now. He won't hurt you or anybody else ever again, I promise."

With vision made blurry by tears, Nancy thought she saw motion in the shadows of the interrogation room.

She held the woman tighter and closed her eyes, wondering if she would ever be truly safe again.

The steel door to the holding cell slid along its track, closed with a loud *clank* that echoed down the hall. Mick looked around his new environment, saw a metal bunk covered in a sheet and tan blanket. There were little balls of lint all over the cover, and the sheet looked as if it had been stained by something and could never be washed completely clean. At that, Mick's eyes unconsciously traveled to his own hands; he rubbed his newly freed wrists, tried to iron out the handcuff grooves.

"You sure you don't wanna call your folks?" Deputy Oates asked from the opposite side of the metal bars.

Mick shook his head. "The sheriff, he said he would tell them I'm..."

And the words suddenly escaped him.

Oates nodded. "All right then." He started to walk away, then pointed to the olive-colored door at the end of the hall. "I'll be right out there if you change your mind. Why don't you get some sleep? I gotta turn the light out anyway."

Mick nodded, distracted.

The deputy turned and walked out the door, flicking the light switch off as promised. A square of moonglow covered the cell floor, dissected into diamonds of light by the wire mesh embedded in the glass. Mick backed up to his bunk, sat down on the mattress, and the chaos of thoughts froze solid in his brain.

The darkness shifted, and Mick heard a rustling, whispering sound.

Instinctively, he pulled his feet up off the floor. There was something in the cell with him, some awful thing from the cornfield that had just been itching for this opportunity. Mick was alone, defenseless.

Oh God, he thought, shaking. *What am I gonna do?*

A whisper seeped into his ear, "*God can't help you now.*"

He thought of the silhouette that had spoken with Danny's voice, warning him this would be his fate. Now it was in here with him, and, if he should fall asleep, it would shuffle out of the shadows and avenge itself, wrap its rotting hands around his throat and choke the life out of him. Worse yet, for an instant, Mick actual thought he would let it.

"Who's there?"

"*Good thing you did this now,*" the voice said, and Mick realized he was hearing it in his mind. "*Next month, you'd have been eighteen and they'd be warming up 'Old Sparky' for your ass right now.*"

Mick's eyes snapped shut and he began to moan. *I really have gone crazy.*

"*Now, you'll just get life.*"

"No," he whispered through puckered lips, his tear-soaked cheeks glittering in the moonlight. He forced himself to open his eyes, to look into the darkened corner of the cell, to make certain he was alone. He wondered what would happen if he walked across the space into the shadows? What was really waiting for him there?

"*A hundred Skip Williamsons waiting for you in prison, Mick. They'll never let you rest. They'll beat you. They'll rape you. No Graduation Day to save you. With a life sentence, this is one monster you won't be able to escape. And no Danny to help. You made sure of that, didn't you?"*

This is the voice of my conscience, Mick thought, terrified that he might hear it for the rest of his natural life. Mick shook his head violently, then ran for the bars and squeezed his face between them. The truth in what the voice had said became painfully clear. There was no way out of this situation, just as there was no way out of this cell. No way at all.

"*There is one way out,*" the voice he thought was his conscience told him. Actually, he'd come to notice that it wasn't a single voice but a whole medley of them, some high, some low, all speaking the same words at the same time. "*You could kill yourself.*"

He turned around, pressed his back flat against the bars, his eyes peered into the shadows, searched for the outline of something hideous. If he killed himself, the thing in the corner wouldn't get him. If he killed himself, the new beast of prison would not devour him; these new, as yet unseen bullies would not attack him. But, even if he wanted to do what the voice suggested, there was nothing here in the cell to—

"*You could make a noose with the bed sheet, hang yourself. You don't have to suffer.*"

Let your conscience be your guide.

Mick moved slowly away from the bars, but his eyes never left the dark corner of the cage. Did he hear breathing over there? He was almost certain he did. He grabbed hold of the sheet and tugged it off the mattress. This was something he'd seen in movies. He knew it could be done. His only question was, could *he* do it?

"*You can do it,*" the whispers assured him.

Mick twisted the sheet into a tight coil, his eyes playing Pong between the work of his sweaty hands and the dark corner where something stood watching, *breathing*. He then wrapped it around his neck and tied a tight knot, one that would not give under his weight. He moved his feet to the bars, climbed the wall as if it were a piece of playground equipment. Mick looped the sheet around the highest crossbar so that, when he jumped, his feet wouldn't strike the floor, and then he stopped. What if something went wrong? What if he ended up in a coma, or as a quadriplegic?

"*Do it*," the whispers urged.

He stood on the bars in contemplation. At least in a coma, the bullies could not harm him, and, worst-case scenario, if he were paralyzed, they'd have to put him in a special prison, wouldn't they? They couldn't stick vegetables in with the other inmates. Either way, it was better than the alternative.

"*End it.*"

He turned to face the darkened corner of the cell. He had to escape.

"I'm sorry," Mick mumbled.

"*Do it!*" the voice said, now insistent, almost panicky.

Mick closed his eyes and stepped off the bars. The makeshift noose grabbed his neck hard, stopped his fall, and his eyes sprang open in sudden alarm. He felt the horrible pressure at his throat, felt it push in on his windpipe, suffocating him.

The darkness in the corner of the cell was on the move; it oozed across the concrete floor like scummy oil headed for a drain. Mick had the sensation of something fluttering above his head, a trapped bat or...or a crow.

He was aware of hands at his chest, could feel icy fingers clasp his heart.

"*Thank you,*" the many voices made one told his drowsy mind, and then they laughed.

It was the same laugh that had been echoing through the corn.

The same laugh he would now hear for all eternity.

The next day, reporters asked why Mick Slatton wasn't under any kind of suicide watch, and Sheriff Carter had to admit he'd had a lapse in judgment. What Carter didn't tell them was that there had been a voice, a voice he remembered from his childhood, a voice from when he himself had played the Wide Game. That voice said the kid would never survive in prison. That voice said Carter should have shot the boy when he'd first seen him, covered in blood and holding fast to the bat. That voice said Mick Slatton would be better off dead. And so, when they found the boy hanging in his cell, Sheriff Carter—who loved it when his wife cuffed him to the bed and mounted him with a huge, black dildo—was secretly glad.

Several members of the press made mention of Russell Veal's disappearance four years before in their articles and newscasts. A few even noted that his mother, Sarah Veal, had killed herself shortly after. No one cited Cory Sparks' attempted suicide with a meat cleaver and claw hammer, however. And the fact that Marcia Andrews had jumped from a Chicago high rise a few years before—leaving a note to her dead sister, begging forgiveness— also seemed to go unreported. Robby Miller could have made the connection for them had he known all the details, but the relevance seemed to escape the general media all together.

In other news...

Gwen Perkins, Deidra's mother, slipped into a coma. Two days later, she too was dead. Following an autopsy, county coroner Art Campbell ruled her death a homicide, the result of massive head trauma. What Art neglected to put in his final report was the fact that he saw Gwen Perkins' corpse open its eyes and look at him as he made his first incision, that he saw the thing smile and heard its voice. Art later retired and moved to Florida. The nurse at the convalescent home where he died quoted him as saying "It knew I fucked the pretty ones" just before his heart stopped beating.

There was nothing supernatural about the videotape from Paul's Sony camcorder, but the images were gruesome to say the least. Recorded for evidence were what was left of Dale Brightman, crucified on a wooden cross, Mick Slatton stabbing Danny Fields and slitting his throat, Mick Slatton stabbing Skip Williamson, and finally Mick Slatton swinging a metal bat into Gwen Perkins' skull.

Based on the tape, the Harmony Police Department, the Indiana State Police, the FBI, and volunteers from town combed the northern cornfields and woods. After several days, however, the search yielded only a few abandoned backpacks. No bodies or murder weapons, other than Danny's knife and Deidra's baseball bat, were ever recovered.

Despite the lack of actual corpses, based on the video taped evidence, blood evidence from the bat and hunting knife, Mick's statement and the statements of the other witnesses, Danny Fields, Skip Williamson,

Cindi Hawkins, and Dale Brightman were all considered victims of homicide. Two other missing seniors, Patrick Chance and Nick Lerner, were presumed murdered as well. Mick's suicide was considered by the investigators to be an admission of guilt, and, because he was believed to be the sole perpetrator of the murders, the cases were quickly closed.

For the families of the victims, it was all over.

For those who survived, however, it had yet to end.

Part Three: Surviving the Game

TWENTY-THREE

If Deidra's art instructor asked her to paint the very picture of grief, it would be a self-portrait. Dark brown sweaters and slacks had replaced her bright T-shirts and jeans. The weight of her depression had moved across her face like a glacier, turned the fullness of her cheeks into sinkholes and raised dark ridges beneath her pale eyes. But the difference ran far deeper than a change in appearance; it went all the way to Deidra's core. Inside, she felt as dead as the world around her—naked, cold, smothered.

The sky was a solid gray slate as she wandered through snow-covered fields, her coat bundled around her, her hood up against the wind. Furrowed earth lay frozen beneath her boots, tiny yellowed stumps protruding from the ripples all that remained of the once tall crop of corn. As she looked across the terrain, saw drifted snow like waves on a milky sea, she could not help but think how beautiful it was and sank deeper into sorrow.

She wondered what she was doing out here, but knew the answer all too well.

It was Christmas Eve.

If she'd stayed in her room, listening to the Eurythmics sing "Winter Wonderland," or John Cougar Mellencamp belt out "I Saw Mommy Kissing Santa Claus," she would only cry. She hated crying. Especially when she was alone.

Deidra's mother laid in that casket; her hands crossed over her chest, dressed in her Sunday best and all the jewelry she loved in life. The morticians had done a horrible job with her face. It looked puffy, as if they'd stuffed her with cotton. Perhaps they had. Deidra touched her before they put her in the ground—told herself that it was just to say good-bye and not to make certain she was dead—even kissed her on the cheek. It was like kissing a mannequin.

Deidra tried to think of something else, of *anything* else, but all she could do was imagine how horrible tonight would be; just her and her father in the empty home they'd made a half-hearted attempt to decorate. Thanksgiving had been bad enough, but at least she had...

Paul.

Without him, Deidra didn't know how she would've coped these last few months. He'd been constantly at her side—comforting her, loving her, asking nothing in return. There were times she felt guilty for it, felt that she'd used him. After all, she'd been in the midst of supreme depression. Everything upset her and she couldn't imagine she was any fun to be around. Most of the time, however, she'd just been grateful for his love... for his touch.

At night, Paul snuck out of his house, pushed his car down his long, gravel drive until it could be started without waking his mother, and he came to her. How romantic it would have been if she had a trellis outside her window for him to climb. In reality, she had to watch for his arrival, had to creep downstairs to let him in, then usher him silently up to her room. Fear of being discovered sent her blood racing through her veins, letting her know that she was alive. Their lovemaking was tender, passionate, and all too brief—islands of happiness in her otherwise miserable life.

THE WIDE GAME

The game brought about a definite role reversal in their relationship. Before, Deidra had been so sure of herself and Paul had wanted her. Now, it was Paul's strength that kept her afloat; she clung to him as if he were her life preserver.

It worried her a bit.

She continued walking. The wind howled all around her, flung snow into her face like bits of frozen confetti. She didn't know what she expected to find out here. Answers, maybe. Answers to a dozen questions that buzzed around her mind like angry hornets, and most of them started with "why?"

Why us?
Why now?
Why did I live?
Why did my mother have to die?

And the thing that popped up after each and every query, as if it might be the only answer, was *Mondamin*.

Mondamin *is here*.

The Miami may have put a name to this evil, but they certainly didn't create it. She realized that now. It was here before them, hundreds, maybe thousands of years ago, and it was here now after most had up and left it behind by force or by choice. It would be here long after the Class of 1988, probably long after Harmony was a fossil under the brush of some future archeologist.

It was eternal.

Civilizations were just a tick on its clock.

And they were all just toys who'd wondered into its playroom.

God, how she wished they'd never played the damn game.

"*Deidra?*"

She wheeled around at the sound of her name on the wind, half expecting to see her mother walking toward her—her head caved in and whatever stuffing they'd used for the funeral spilling out, blowing in the breeze. She saw instead a gray silhouette wading through the snow. As it came closer, Deidra saw color bleed into the shape. The figure wore a red and black coat with a matching knit hat and gloves. She recognized the outfit as Paul's

"I thought I'd find you out here," he told her.

"Why?"

He shrugged. "Because I find myself coming out here."

"I just keep thinking, maybe I'll find them."

Paul looked at his own boots. "They never found Russell Veal."

Deidra looked up, saw flakes streak across the gray sky like a shower of comets. "Where do you think they took them?"

"I think...I think it's better if we don't think about it."

She pursed her lips, watched the snowy field drift around them. "I wonder if I'll still come out here in the summer when there's...when it's growing again."

"Soybeans."

She blinked. "Soybeans?"

"Every other year." His eyes squinted into the wind. "You can't grow corn every year. It takes all the life out of the soil."

She had to laugh at that. "It certainly does. It takes the life right out." Her laughter brought a horrified look to Paul's face, then dissolved into sobs.

He went to her, clutched her to him. "It's okay. I'm here. I won't let anything ever hurt you."

At that, her contorted face relaxed and she felt an incredible rush of relief. *Yes,* she thought. *Thank God for that. Thank God for Paul.*

She kissed his cold cheek with chapped lips, then pulled away and wiped at her eyes. "I'm sorry."

"You're fine."

"No," she chuckled. "I'm not even in the neighborhood of fine."

"Maybe this will help." Paul reached into the pocket of his coat, removed a folded piece of paper. He held it out to her and she took it.

"What's this?"

"Your Christmas present."

She looked at him with more than a bit of guilt. "We said we weren't—"

"I know."

"But I didn't—"

"I know. It's all right."

"Christmas isn't until tomorrow."

She started to return the paper, but Paul pushed it back to her, his lips moving slowly to a smile.

"You look like you need it now," he said.

Deidra unfolded the paper with gloved fingers and found a page torn from a catalog. Rings. Diamond engagement rings and bridal sets. Half a dozen were pictured, but a few had been circled in black marker. Deidra looked up at Paul, watched him lower to one knee. Her eyes followed him down, filled with tears that stung in the cold flow of the wind.

"I wanted to have the ring in my hand when I did this," he said. "But I didn't have enough money saved up yet, and...I don't know...you being the one who's gonna wear it...I thought you might like to help pick it out."

"Paul..." She didn't know what to say. A million thoughts raced through her brain, each trying to be the first to reach her lips. "This..."

He pressed a finger to her mouth and took her leather-bound hand in his own. The wind seemed to die down, allowing the snowflakes to spiral onto them like fairy dust, like something out of a storybook.

"I love you." Paul's eyelashes caught the falling snow. "We've literally been through Hell together. Now I want the rest of our lives to be Heaven. I want us to spend it together."

She looked at him, saw his devotion, and her dreams came back to blazing life, lighting the caverns of her mind, banishing all the creeping shadows. His love for her was real. It was *strong*. And, even though she wasn't worthy of it, she wanted it. She *needed* it.

"Deidra Perkins, will you marry me? Will you be my wife?"

"Yes," she said, unable to contain her joy. She hoped she didn't sound too eager.

"Yes?"

She nodded. "Yes."

Paul's face beamed. He rose up, grabbed her around the waist and lifted her; he spun her around, the snowflakes whipping by like stars at warp speed. And they laughed. For the first time in months, they laughed.

And, for a moment, even though they stood at the very center of the dead field of corn, Deidra forgot about the Wide Game.

THE WIDE GAME

The game was all Nancy Collins could think about, however.

She laid on her pink bedspread, alone in her darkened room, and watched Christmas bulbs outside her window alternate from red, to blue, to green, then back again. Her father spent much of the day stapling the strands to their roof, used the Craftsman staple gun she gave him last Fathers' Day. He'd waved at her through the window and she'd given him a lazy wave in reply.

She heard him downstairs now, talking to her mother in hushed tones. They talked about her. They could scream if they wanted to. She didn't care.

They talked about her in the halls at Harmony High, too, from behind locker doors and hands held over mouths for fear she might read lips and know the truth. When she walked into a classroom, everyone went quiet, quiet but for the whispers that haunted her mind in the absence of other sound.

"*They know what you did,*" the whispers said, over and over again.

Downstairs, presents sat beneath the tree, beneath the watchful eyes of the angel on the top branch, her stained glass halo backed by clear lights, a glow that seemed to fill the entire room. Nancy wondered if Danny had a halo now.

She wondered if Cindi had one.

The things that zombie told her had been lies. Nancy knew that. Danny would never have slept with Cindi. Never. And they weren't in Hell. They'd done nothing to deserve that.

"*They know what you did.*"

But murderers *did* go to hell.

The lights outside Nancy's window blinked red, and in that crimson glow she saw Cindi's skull yawn at her with jagged teeth, a pink tongue of brains sticking out at her, giving her a raspberry.

A lonely tear grew pregnant and took a plunge from her eye, fell to its death on the bedspread. She wasn't a murderer, not really. She hadn't meant to kill Cindi. They'd tricked her—the demons—so it didn't count.

"They know you did it."

Danny and Cindi might have joined the choir invisible, but their ghosts haunted every corner of Harmony.

In high school, a football star and a cheerleader were like the President and Vice President of the United States of America. Danny and Cindi's lockers had become shrines, covered in notes and makeshift crosses, flowers stuck through the cracks around the door. Counselors had been brought in to help students deal with grief, but they could perform no exorcism to rid Harmony High of the memories.

And every afternoon and weekend, when Nancy left school, things grew worse. In a small town like Harmony, there was nowhere Nancy could go, nowhere she could hide. She'd see the restaurants where they used to grab burgers, the park benches where they ate ice cream cones in the summer heat, and the teen shrine of the Woodfield Movie Palace had become an unbearable tomb.

"You could kill yourself," the voices whispered to her.

Yes, she could do that.

She'd thought a lot about it. And those thoughts further fueled the guilt that gnawed at her insides. If she'd confessed to what happened in the corn, if she'd asked for mercy or understanding, would Mick have made the same choice?

"*You could kill yourself.*"

The thought had some appeal.

Deidra tried to help Nancy cope, but let's face it, she barely got through the day herself, and at least she had Paul. At least he could hold *her*, wipe away the tears, love away the pain. If Danny were here, death might seem more repugnant.

"*You could be with Danny and end all this pain, all this suffering.*"

Yes.

In Nancy's favorite film, *Somewhere in Time*, Christopher Reeve went back in time, fell in love with Jane Seymour. When he returned the present, he could not find his way back to her, no matter how hard he tried. In the end, Reeve sat in his hotel, day after empty day, just wasted away until he died of starvation. He floated over his body, then moved toward a bright light. And who did he find in that light? Why, Miss Jane Seymour of course. Forever young and beautiful, she held out a hand to him, and, in death, they lived happily ever after.

It could be that way for her and Danny.

"*Do it.*"

There was just so much pain.

"*End it.*"

It would be better to just...

"*Do it.*"

...just do it.

Nancy reached under her pillow and pulled out the gray box-cutter she'd hidden there. She put her thumb on the ridges of the switch, pushed it forward, and the triangular razor rose from its burrow. There had been flecks of paint on the blade when she'd taken it from the drawer in her father's workbench, but she'd washed it clean. Nancy didn't want to get lead poisoning or anything.

"*Do it!*" the whispers urged again and she moved the cutter to her left arm.

Nancy hoped it wouldn't take long.

She touched the blade to her wrist and pressed. At first there was no give, but, with pressure, the metal popped easily into her flesh. The initial sting, and the burning sensation that followed, were nothing compared to the pain of these last few months, the pain that would be with her for the rest of her life. She slid the blade down her inner forearm, toward the bend of her elbow; the skin parted like an opening eye, tears of blood dampening her virgin's sheets. Nancy changed hands, cut her right arm in the same fashion, the open wound wept across her white pajama top as she worked, then she leaned back against her pillows.

The knife slipped from her hand, and she looked dreamily at the ceiling; light from the window divided it into four squares, squares that were blue, then red, then green... She saw a shadowy tree in that window, its branches spreading outward, and something touched her breast, something cold—a snowman, groping her.

Her groggy mind turned to Danny, wishing she'd not been such a prude, wishing she wasn't dying a virgin. She hoped there was a heaven, hoped Danny would be there waiting, hoped there would be sex.

She felt so *cold*.

Her thoughts turned next to the frozen darkness of the fog, turned to Cindi. She wondered if Cindi would be in Heaven as well, wondered if she would understand, wondered if she could forgive.

Of course she will, Nancy thought dizzily. *Heaven's all about the forgiveness.*

She grew numb. More dark trees bloomed in that red window; more icy hands felt her breasts, and, as she lost consciousness, the chorus of whispers sang to her.

"*Thank you*," they repeated again and again. "*Thank you.*"

And then it was just like the movie. She floated up, spun away from her body, watched as the open mouths in her forearms drooled all over her clean bedspread. She didn't look happy, however, and there was no bright light. In fact, everything seemed to dim, to grow darker and darker still. Where was Danny? He was supposed to meet her now, to reach out and hold her hand as Jane Seymour had done for Chris Reeve. There were hands here nevertheless, a whole congress of hands, they pulled her into the dark, into nothingness. Her earthly body drifted away, a reflection in a falling mirror; she looked so alone, so *cold*.

By the time she heard the laughter, however, Nancy felt quite warm.

TWENTY-FOUR

A red and white striped tassel hung from Deidra's finger, a gold 88 attached to the clasp that bound it together. She stroked it with her fingers as if it were a ponytail, then batted it with her hand, watched as it swung to and fro. The tassel was their only souvenir of graduation. Their caps and gowns had been rented and returned. The diploma they'd been handed on stage was a rolled up piece of blank parchment, a stage prop. The real diploma would be sent to them later through the mail. Pictures would be developed in time. The only immediate proof there was ever a ceremony at all was the tassel.

Paul kissed her forehead, held her to him beneath the crazy-quilted blanket. They lay naked in the back of his Mustang, parked off a deserted stretch of back road, the seats folded down into a bed. The hatchback hung open, granting them a panoramic view of the cosmos; a stuffed Roger Rabbit hung from the glass, suspended by suction cups in its hands and feet; its huge, painted eyes stared down at them with manic interest. Paul left the radio on, and Terence Trent D'arby's soulful "Sign Your Name" drifted from the speakers. "What are you thinking about?"

Deidra grabbed the tassel to halt its sway. "After Nancy killed herself, I dreamed she was graduating with us. That I was somehow able to stop her."

"You had no idea what she was thinking, what she was feeling. You had enough to deal with."

"And you see how well I'm dealing with that." She brought her hands to her face; the strings of the tassel soaked up forming tears.

Paul felt close to tears himself.

Tomorrow Deidra would be gone.

Anxious to leave the bad memories of Harmony behind him, Mr. Perkins had taken a full time position at his company's California facility. Deidra would join him, would attend school there in the fall. Paul, who could only afford a state school, enrolled at nearby Stanley University. Officially, they were still going to get married one day, still going to be together, but Nancy's suicide—coming right on the heels of the game and her mother's death—had hit Deidra especially hard. Paul felt her slipping away from him, withdrawing deeper and deeper into herself, and he knew this time apart wasn't going to help them at all.

"I still don't see why you have to go," he whispered.

"Because I want you so badly that it actually hurts me inside. Because I can't get through the day unless I know it's gonna end in your arms." She turned her face to him, reached up and ran her fingers through his hair, his hair that had been streaked gray overnight. "I was lost for so long, out of control. Weak. Then I took charge of my life and I...I found myself. Now, it feels like I've lost myself again. Sooner or later, I've got to get it back. I need to get away from this armpit of the universe and get out of this funk."

"And what if you can't? At least together we can talk about what we're feeling. We can help each other deal with it." He swallowed. "I'm just worried you'll get out there and get so depressed you'll think about—"

"Killing myself?"

Paul nodded.

"What makes you think I don't think about it now?" He looked at her, shocked and worried.

She continued, "You think that because you love me, you know everything that's going on inside my head? You don't. And I'm sure I don't know everything going on inside of you."

"I haven't been thinking about killing myself." He looked at the class ring on his finger. She'd given it back to him tonight, afraid she would lose it in the move. It felt alien on his finger and the skin beneath it had begun to itch. "I'd just screw it up and end up a vegetable or something."

"Then you have at least *thought* about it."

"Everyone's thought about it," he said through thinning lips. He didn't want to fight with her. Not tonight. He reached beneath the blankets, ran his hand over the curls of her pubic hair. "But I'm afraid you'll actually do it. Like Mick. Like Nancy. I don't want to lose you."

Deidra was quiet for a moment and he wondered what went on behind her eyes.

"I don't want to lose you either," she said at last, her voice soft and deliberate. "I'll write you, just like I did every day at school. We have the telephone. Nothing's really going to change between us. It might actually make us stronger. I hope it will. And I *will* come back."

"Do you..." He tilted his head onto her shoulder, watched the golden charm he'd given her rise and fall on her breast. At least she hadn't given that back to him. The saying would mean even more now. Now they would truly be "apart, one from another." "You still love me?"

"Always." She rubbed her hand down his back. "In my entire life, I've never loved anyone *but* you."

They made love again that night, not knowing it would be for the last time. Afterward, Paul drove her home, gave her a passionate, desperate kiss on her doorstep. *Don't leave me here*, the kiss said. *Don't leave me here alone*. When their lips parted, she gave him a quick peck on the forehead and turned away without a word.

She'd been in California a week when her first letter arrived.

Paul opened it with anxious hands, wanting to know she was all right, hoping against all hope that it said she was coming back to him. Her handwriting was sloppy as ever, but he didn't care. He read every word, then read it again. He looked at it daily, wished for the sound of her voice and did his best to imitate it in his mind...

> ♥*Hi, Love!*
> *We're on the freeway so this may get messy*
> *(I know, my handwriting is always messy)!*
> *I miss you so much! I started missing you the*
> *second you drove away. That's one reason I*
> *didn't turn and watch you go. Things are pretty*
> *boring out here. The air sure smells different,*
> *and there's mountains (I'll have to send you*
> *some pictures)! The colors are ugly, though. No*
> *green. Only yellow and brown.*
> *I guess I should be happy not to see any green*
> *fields, huh? On the plane I kept thinking of you*
> *and that song by Peter, Paul, and Mary kept*
> *running through my mind—"Leavin' On a Jet*
> *Plane." I keep asking myself if I've made the*

> *right decision. I think I have. I hope I have. I gotta go. I'm not used to the time difference yet. Ugh!*
> *I really do love you!*
>
> *Deidra*
Write back...

And he did write back, often putting multiple notes in the same envelope. She wrote him as well, although less often than he would have liked. Her letters repeatedly began with an apology...

> *Sorry it's been so long! I've written you so many letters that I haven't sent—it's ridiculous. I'm sorry. I love you so much. I'm realizing it more and more each day. I love your letters—they keep me alive. Today I got a letter from you and a card! I love the card. Yes! If you can mail yourself to me—DO IT! You know how most girls sit by the phone? I'm sitting by the mailbox...*

In September of 1988, about the time they officially became college freshman in their respective states, the tone of her correspondence changed and she wrote him a depressing little note...

> *Paul, I don't know what to do. I said once before that we should never have any secrets from one another, so let me get one thing straight—I love you. I really do. Now another—I want to go out with someone (just as friends).*
> *I think of you all the time—I still constantly dream about you. I just don't know what to do*

about us... I'm so lonely out here, but I'm scared to death of hurting you. Jesus! I don't deserve you (don't argue, DAMMIT! I don't). What are we going to do about us? I can't live with this. I can't live with myself thinking that I'm hurting you, but I'm so lonely. What am I supposed to do? God, please tell me...

When he wrote her a response, at first he was brutally honest about what he felt she should do. He wrote that she had said she would marry him, that it was her choice to go out there, and her own fault if she was lonely. Sure there were attractive girls on campus he could ask out if he wanted to, but he didn't, lonely as he was, because of the fact that they were in a *relationship*. If they were married, and he was off shooting a film in Thailand, he wouldn't be unfaithful and he would expect the same from her. *Why should this be any different?* She'd said she would marry him. *Why should it be any different?* He read the letter over and promptly crumpled it up. If he put a two-thousand-mile leash on her, what did that say about him? He trusted her, trusted their love. What harm would there be in two friends going to the movies? And so he said it would be good for them to see other people socially, to make certain that their love was really forever. He gave her permission to date.

She did.

Paul didn't.

He'd expected her to come back to him over Christmas break, but she didn't have enough money for the ticket. Paul had said he would try and send her some. That fell through, however, when Paul's mother wouldn't allow her to stay in their house.

Paul barely said a word to his mother that entire Christmas season.

They continued to write back and forth, to call each other on the phone, but Paul could feel her grow more distant. Her letters grew less frequent; her phone calls grew shorter. In April, he found a blue envelope in his mailbox, one with only "D.P." written where the return address should have been...

> *Paul,*
> *I don't know how to say this. This letter is so hard for me to write, and I'm so afraid you're going to hate me no matter what I say. Everything's so different out here. I wrote you that once before. It's more true now. I'm different. I know you can forgive me. I know you shouldn't. But I need you to know that in my own twisted, tortured way, my love for you is real and strong and true. We've always said we should be honest, well here goes...I'm not coming back to Indiana. God, this isn't fair. I wish we'd had more time together, before that...you know. But to come back there, to see you and Harmony...I can't do it. I'm weak. I'm sorry. I'm gonna try to have a life and for me Harmony is always going to be death. I hope you can have a good life too, and I hope you can forgive me. It's better this way Paul. You won't think that now, but I hope, one day, you will.*
>
> *Love always,*
Deidra

Three months later, Paul received an invitation to Deidra's wedding and Robby pulled him from the burning wreck of his Mustang.

TWENTY-FIVE

Paul didn't see much social life during his years at Stanley University. He worked hard on writing, directing, and editing short films. For his senior project, he created a science fiction video about a man who went back in time, tried to make right the mistake that robbed him of his true love. The faculty ate it up. Not only did he make the prestigious Dean's List, but Paul also had his film screened in the campus' largest auditorium.

There were occasional letters from a Deidra *Shusett*, but he threw them away unopened as soon as he saw the name. Paul wondered why she continued to write when he had yet to send her even a sentence in reply. There were times when he pictured her alone at a table in a dark house, wasting her time writing words his eyes would never see. Horrible as it might have been, the thought always brought a smile to his lips.

In April of 1992, Paul attended a pre-graduation party at Hannigan's Tavern. He'd been exhausted from his all-night editing sessions in the video production lab, but he'd made an appearance anyway, even had a few shots of some tropical concoction one of the guys sat in front of him, but he was still far from drunk. As in high school, he found it much more fun to watch the drunks than to join them.

There'd been one other sober soul in the pub that night.

Her name was Mary. She had curly blonde hair, pale blue eyes, and a lovely, innocent smile. She wore a thin pink sweater that hugged the curves of her breasts and a black skirt with matching stockings. He'd never seen legs more perfect in his entire life.

They spent the next five hours talking and laughing about everything. Mary was a nice Catholic girl, set to graduate the following month with a degree in Psychology. While she couldn't open an office and analyze rich housewives' sexual dreams, she could be a counselor at a school or halfway house. In fact, she had just such a position lined up at a facility in Indianapolis. Special needs children. Emotional handicaps, mostly. Kids who needed a shoulder to cry on and someone to listen.

They continued talking as Paul walked her home. Mary had a soft voice and an understanding ear. He could tell she'd be the best damn counselor the world had ever known. She also had an apartment on campus, and it just so happened her roommates had been gone for the weekend.

"May I kiss you?" Paul asked her at her door.

Mary had nodded, had closed her eyes as he touched his lips to hers. They somehow found their way inside to her couch where they made love as if it were their last night on earth.

Two weeks later, they were engaged.

On August twenty-second, 1992, they were married at St. Anthony's Catholic Church. Paul hadn't wanted to be married there, but Mary's family church had been built like an amphitheater, and all her life she'd dreamed of a long aisle, lined in candles and flowers, huge stained-glass windows on either side. That description fit St. Anthony's. So on that sunny Saturday afternoon, his bride-to-be walked down the aisle, walked right beneath the huge, golden-framed picture of

Schongauer's "The Temptation of St. Anthony," and they said their vows under the watchful eyes of demons.

Paul started as an editor for an Indianapolis video production company and quickly moved up the ranks. Soon he was writing and directing commercial spots and corporate training tapes. And, two years later, he'd started his own company.

Mary continued to work at the children's home. There were days she thought it was the greatest job in the world and there were nights she came home in tears. That was one of the reasons Paul had fallen in love with her. She cared about people. She cared deeply. It was on one of the crying nights, when he'd kissed away her tears, that they conceived their first child—a boy they named Christopher.

In 1995, Paul and Mary were doubly blessed with a new home and a new baby. They built their house in the suburbs, as far away from cornfields as was possible in Indiana, and the baby had been the most wonderful gift anyone had ever given him. Part of him, the part that still played the Wide Game the way some veterans still fought the Vietnam War, didn't feel he deserved such a wonderful child.

Paul's business continued to prosper and gain recognition. Mary continued to work at the group home, but on a part-time basis. Chris continued to grow and took up a lot of her time.

In 1997, Mary discovered she was pregnant again. It wasn't planned, but it wasn't unwelcome. Megan was born in June of 1998 to happy parents and an even happier grandmother. It was in fact the happiest time of Paul's life...until the phone call.

TWENTY-SIX

Paul had fallen out of the habit of picking up the phone at his mother's house years ago, probably about the same time he started calling it his mother's house and not his own. But on this warm June day, when they'd come to show Lynn Rice her new granddaughter, Paul happened to be standing next to the phone in the living room when it rang, and he instinctively answered it.

"Rice residence."

"Paul?" a woman's voice asked through the line.

"Yeah." With the phone still at his ear, he turned to look at Megan. She was on her back on her Looney Tunes blanket, waving her arms wildly while Paul's mother hovered over her with a camera. Mary sat on the couch with Chris in her lap, smiling down at Megan with loving eyes. Anyone who doubted the existence of love at first sight obviously wasn't a parent.

"Paul Rice?" asked the woman on the other end of the line.

"Yeah. Who's this, please?"

"You don't recognize the voice?"

It *did* sound familiar to his ears, but he couldn't place it. He was about to say as much when the caller answered her own question.

"It's Deidra."

The smile that had been blooming on Paul's face wilted to a dumfounded frown. A starter's pistol went off in his brain, sent his blood racing. He backed out of the room, drug the cord around the corner and into the hall.

"You still there?" she asked.

"Yeah."

"It's been a long time."

He nodded, realized she couldn't see it, then spoke. "Yeah. A long time."

"I hear you got married." She spoke softly, arranged her words with care.

"Yeah...yeah, I did." His eyes strayed to the wedding picture that hung on the wall, studying Mary's smiling face. His eyes slammed shut. "So how's your husband doing?"

"Actually, I'm divorced."

His heart stumbled, then got up and raced again. Why did that matter to him? What bearing could it have on his life now? "I'm sorry to hear that," he lied and tightened his grip on the telephone.

"Yeah," she said. Then, after a pause, "Now you've got me doing it."

"I'm sorry?" He stared at the wide gold band around the ring finger of his left hand.

A nervous snicker came across the line. "Nothing."

Then came a long silence on Deidra's end, and Paul had the urge to hang up.

"So, why'd you call?" he asked instead.

"Actually, I didn't think you'd be there. Robby said you moved out of Harmony."

Robby, he thought. *Why didn't you tell me she'd called you? Why didn't you tell me—?*

What? That she was divorced? What does it matter, Paul? What does it matter?

It didn't matter. Not at all.

"Just visiting," he told her.

"I was just calling to see if your mother knew if you were going to the reunion in August. Now I can just ask you."

Paul's head tilted toward the kitchen, his eyes found the field of growing corn out the back window. His heart worked so hard and so fast that he thought it might come apart beneath the strain. "Yeah. I'm going."

Did he hear her draw in a breath?

"Great," she said. "The three of us can talk."

Paul thought that she meant both of them and Mary, then reconsidered. The third person was Robby, of course—the remnants of the old group. The survivors. Who else could they talk to at the reunion?

Remember when I hit that home run?

How could I forget! You remember when the demons made us kill each other in the corn?

Ahhh, yes. Good times. Good fucking times.

"Sounds great," Paul said.

Another moment of silence, and he could not help but wonder what she looked like now, what she was thinking.

"Well," she said at last, "I guess I'll let you go."

"Okay."

"I'll see you at the reunion then."

"You will."

He stood there and waited for the silence to become the buzz of a dead line, then he clunked the receiver back down on its base and took a seat in the living room.

"Who was that?" his mother asked without looking up from Megan.

"Someone wanting confirmation that we were going to the reunion."

Mary did look up. "Are you okay? You're white as a sheet."

"Fine. My stomach's just bothering me. I'll...uh...be in the bathroom."

She watched him get up with skeptical eyes.

"I'll be fine. *Really.*"

Mary nodded, slowly returned her attention to Megan, and Paul headed for the stairs. He made his way up to his old room, crossed it to the closet, and retrieved the old Nike shoebox that contained his life with Deidra. He forced himself to open it, forced himself to find the blue envelope with no return address, the envelope that said "D.P." The letter inside showed no signs of yellowing, no aging of any kind. It was now as it had been when he first read it.

Paul sat down on the bed he'd once called his own. He closed his eyes, steeled himself before he looked at her handwriting. He read the first few lines...

> *I don't know how to say this. This letter is so hard for me to write, and I'm so afraid you're going to hate me no matter what I say...*

Then saw...

> *God, this isn't fair.*

And then his eyes shot to...

> *I hope you can forgive me.*

He didn't want to forgive her. He wanted to hate her. Why in the hell did she have to call him? Why now, when he'd tried to move on as she had done? Why did she pull at his brain...at his heart?

He wished now he hadn't decided to go to his...

"...reunion."

Paul blinked the dust from his eyes. How long had he been sitting there?—Deidra's old letter and his half of the golden charm clutched in his hands? He ran his fingers down his face and shoved the note back into the envelope.

"What was that?" he called out.

Mary's voice drifted up the stairs and through the closed door of his old room. "I said, if you don't hurry, we'll be late for the reunion."

No, he decided, *I don't want to be late.*

He closed the shoebox and realized the necklace was still wrapped around his hand. He'd been squeezing it so hard that the imprint of the chain was tattooed into his palm. He slid it absently into his pants pocket and tried to imagine what it would be like to see Deidra again.

Mary Rice sat at the brass make-up table in the guest bedroom of her mother-in-law's home, brushing her blonde hair. The repetitive motion of the strokes seemed to calm her nerves. Downstairs, she heard Paul and the children—her family, her *life*.

She'd talked her husband into going to this reunion. At the home where Mary worked, she looked into the eyes of children who'd seen their parents beaten, who'd seen them killed right in front of them, and she saw something hollow there, as if the flash of evil they'd witnessed had burned itself onto the negative of their souls. Sometimes, when she'd read the files of these same children, when she'd see the horrors they'd been through put into such neat and antiseptic print, it made her cry. It was the same with Paul.

He'd told her about this "Wide Game," how he'd seen his friends—people he'd known his entire life—kill each other out there in the cornfields. His words were always strained, as if he had to force them from his lips, and when she looked into his eyes, she saw the same blemish on *his* soul, the same hollowness. He'd seen evil. He'd seen horrors she couldn't even hope to understand. And, sometimes, she felt as if he were slipping away from her.

This reunion'll be good for him, she told herself. *It'll help him to deal with what happened. It'll help him move on.*

Then another voice in her head spoke up, *Move on with you or with* Deidra?

She paused her brushing.

Something turned in Mary's stomach. She sank into the seat cushion and her face tried on a strange, meditative look. She didn't like the fit and quickly shook it off, set the brush back on the table. Nerves. Just nerves.

Over the years, they'd talked about Deidra, this woman who'd broken Paul's heart, who still wrote to him, letters Paul pitched unread. A lot of emotion there, still raw despite the passage of time, and tonight, they would see one another again, face to face.

I trust my husband. Mary picked up her eyeliner, tried to maintain a steady hand as she mulled over these last six years with Paul. *We share a life, a* family. *All he shares with her is a memory.*

In the mirror, her face faded, gave way to her own memories, memories of Todd Denny. He'd been tall, ruggedly handsome, and auburn haired. She saw them dancing at their Senior Prom, Todd in a white tux with tails, Mary in a black gown with white trim, a corsage of tiny white orchid blossoms held to her wrist by elastic. She remembered taking that dress off, remembered Todd moving inside her darkness, remembered the pain of his entry melting into pleasurable friction.

We all have first loves, she told herself, her face swimming back into the mirror. *And we can never forget them. We* shouldn't *forget them. But they don't have to be our last love...or our deepest.*

Mary applied a coat of red to her lips, kissed a Kleenex, and stood. She looked in the full-length mirror attached to the back of the bedroom door, hoped it was of the funhouse variety and knew it wasn't. She was still too heavy in the gut and her breasts... her breasts were *huge*. She put her hands to them and gave them a jiggle in disgust.

Got milk?

Mary sighed, then smoothed out the rosy fabric.

Oh well, she thought. *It's as good as it's gonna get.*

She walked down the stairs and into the kitchen. Paul leaned on the center island, watched Chris eat Oreos with a smile on his face. She brought a fist to her red lips and coughed noisily into it. Paul turned to her, a surprised expression softening to genuine affection.

"Wow."

She did a twirl, her skirt pinwheeling. "I clean up good?"

"You clean up great." He moved to kiss her, then mouthed, "I love you."

Mary ran a hand through his still damp hair, feathering gray into what was left of the brown. "We'd better get going."

"Yeah."

She looked back at Chris eating cookies, his mouth somewhere in the chocolate debris on his face, and Megan rocking in her mother-in-law's arms, taking in her bottle of breast milk as if she'd been rescued from a desert.

"There's two more bottles in the fridge," Mary said. "And there's a can of ready-made formula in the diaper bag. If you're getting low on the milk, mix it in with the formula. She doesn't like to drink the ready-made straight."

"Bye Mommy." Chris waved. "Bye Daddy."

Paul returned the wave. "Bye kiddo."

"You be good for Grandma," Mary said.

"We'll be fine," Paul's mother told her. "You kids go and have fun."

Mary nodded and they made their way out the door to their waiting Jeep. She hoped they would have fun. She really hoped this would be a night to remember.

TWENTY-SEVEN

When he opened the door to Harmony High School's gymnasium, Paul thought he'd stepped back into his senior prom. Columns of red and white balloons tethered floor to ceiling. Red shrouds draped round tables, turned the holy hardwood terrain of the basketball team into a huge dining room. The basketball goals themselves had been raised until their backs were flush against the rafters; nets hung limp from their rims. The overhead lights were dark. Instead, candles flickered from centerpieces like tiny campfires, and people huddled around them, swapping stories. Huge speaker towers had been erected on either side of a DJ table—blasting The Pet Shop Boys' "It's a Sin"—and small spotlights blossomed from metal trees, flashed primary colors to the beat. Dancers moved in this rainbow-tinted gloom; guys wore suits and polo shirts instead of tuxedos and cummerbunds, but the women were dressed to the nines in sleek dresses and lacy gowns. A large banner stretched across the far wall—"WELCOME BACK CLASS OF 1988!"—and, much to his surprise, the scene coaxed a smile to Paul's lips.

"Hello!"

Paul turned his head toward the voice, saw a woman draped in a red satin dress with her hair pulled up into a braided sculpture on her head. She did not look familiar to him, and he wondered if he should know her. "Hi."

She sat behind an official-looking table. He walked over to her, saw a white tag stuck to the satin swell of her left bosom, HELLO MY NAME IS...printed in bold blue lettering, and beneath that, she'd written *Shelly*

Parker in black ink. *I don't even recognize her name,* Paul thought, and, for a moment, he wondered if this was the right reunion.

The woman smiled and pointed to the pre-made nametags that littered her table; all had the same blue HELLO MY NAME IS... and names in black ink as the one she wore herself. "Can I get you to find your names, please?"

Paul snickered. "I didn't realize there'd be tests."

The woman's smile remained constant. "Just this one."

Paul scanned the tags, saw names he knew and names that were less familiar. He found their tags and handed one to Mary. "Here's yours, dear,"

"Why, thank you," she told him.

He continued looking at the table until he found what he'd really been searching for: HELLO MY NAME IS...*Deidra Shusett (Perkins)*. She wasn't here. Not yet, anyway. Paul felt oddly relieved by that. He returned his attention to his wife, saw her use a pen to write something on her tag. "What are you doing?"

"Everyone who's walked by since we've been standing here looks at me like they wonder if they should know me. I thought this would save any confusion." She put down the pen, peeled off the backing, and pressed the tag to her breast. Beneath her name, she'd written: *wife to Paul, mother to Paul's children, and no we've never met.*

Paul chuckled. "Wanna grab a seat?"

"Sure."

There were plenty of empty seats scattered about, but the only truly empty table was near the far wall.

They made their way to it, awkwardly snaking around the other tables.

Mary looked at Paul as he pulled the chair out for her. "Nothing like taking the scenic route."

"I just wanted some privacy for us. It's been a while since we were alone."

He pulled out the chair next to her and sat down. Mary's face caught the light of the candle and seemed to glow with warmth. He could tell she didn't believe a word of it. Her glistening red lips curled into a grin. "You're going to have to talk to somebody sometime."

"I will," he assured her. "There's just nobody here yet that I *really* knew. As soon as Robby or someone else gets here, you won't be able to shut us up."

She examined his face for a moment, then said, "Okay."

Paul looked around until he saw a bar. "Want something to drink?"

"Diet whatever. Breast feeding."

"Right." He nodded and his eyes drifted to her chest; the HELLO MY NAME IS... sticker stared back at him. "Megan gets all the luck."

She smacked his arm lightly with her fingers. "My drink, sir."

Paul kissed her on the cheek, then rose from his chair. "Coming, Madame."

He made his way to the bar on the opposite side of the gym, a far cry from the punch bowl of prom. Well, not really. Someone always ended up spiking it with vodka or a home-stilled vintage of some kind. The air conditioning was on, Paul saw it move the balloons and streamers near the vents, but the gymnasium still felt muggy and warm. He reached up to loosen his tie and undo the top button of his shirt.

The kid behind the bar looked barely old enough to consume what he was serving. "Help you, sir?"

"Bud Light and a Diet..."

"Coke."

"Diet Coke."

"Comin' right up."

The kid reached under his bar and produced a short-necked bottle of beer. He opened it, let a wisp of cold mist drift up like smoke from a stack, then set it in front of Paul. Small glaciers melted down the sides of the brown glass. Before they were gone, Paul lifted the bottle to his head and rolled it across his sweaty brow. Why was it so hot?

"—the Wide Game."

Paul's heart iced up. His eyes jerked in the direction of the voice that had uttered those words, found two couples standing next to him at the bar. It took his mind a moment for recognition to kick in, but the men were Peter Sumners and Jimmy Grant. The women they were with were new to him.

"That's right," Peter laughed. He looked at his companion. "We all played this game senior year, a race through the cornfields. The rule was that you couldn't be seen. If you were seen, you got stuck with the guy that saw you. I was so pissed Jimmy found me 'cause I couldn't stand this guy."

Jimmy nodded as he drank. "Then we come to find out we had a lot in common. We ended up rooming together at Purdue."

"Ahh, the irony," Robby said at Paul's shoulder, making him jump.

Paul rolled his eyes. "*Jesus.*"

"Not quite, but thanks." Robby held a finger up to catch the bartender's attention. "Scotch on the rocks, barkeep."

"What do you mean 'Ahh, the irony'?"

"The game was the beginning of some friendships and the end of so many others." He turned to look back at the dance floor, his elbows on the bar. He wore a blue suit coat, matching slacks, and a white dress shirt. The tie around his neck had Homer Simpson asleep at his console, a donut falling from his drooling mouth. "Bitch Queen here yet?"

Paul took another drink from his beer. It was empty. He'd finished it off without even realizing it. "She's not the 'Bitch Queen'."

"However you wanna play it." His eyes scanned the gym a moment. "Did you know she hates Springsteen? Called him a no-talent hack. I think it's one reason I broke up with her. Anyone who worships Duran Duran over The Boss-"

Paul sang mockingly in a gravely voice, his neck straining.

"God, not you too."

"All I know is that if they can give Springsteen an Oscar, I gotta get one before I die."

Robby rolled his eyes. "I'm surrounded by idiots."

Paul regarded him seriously. "Nervous about seeing her again?"

"Me?"

"Yeah."

"Not really." He saw the skeptical look Paul gave him. "Hey, she *loved* you. I just got her off, and she could've been fakin' that."

Paul smirked. "Thanks for the reminder."

"Hey, what are friends for? You just need to remember she walked out on you."

"Thanks again."

The bartender brought Robby's Scotch and he lifted the drink to his lips. "Just tryin' to help."

"You can stop any time." He saw Mary's Diet Coke behind him on the bar. The ice had all but melted. He held up his empty beer. "Can I get another one of these?"

The kid behind the bar fetched him another Bud Light.

Robby took a sip of his drink and winced. "Woah! I was expecting them to water down their booze."

"We're not students anymore," Paul pointed out. "We can get drunk if we want to."

Robby eyed him strangely. "This from The Keymaster—designated driver and friend to party drinkers everywhere?"

"I like to indulge from time to time."

"The only time I've ever seen you touch the stuff was champagne at your own wedding."

Paul picked up Mary's Diet Coke without looking at him. "Wanna sit with us?"

"Who else *would* I sit with?"

They moved away from the bar, drinks in hand, weaving through a dozen tables and fragments of conversation.

"You look terrific—"

"—and I barely even recognized—"

"—your husband? How long have you been—"

"—vice president of an internet company. Aren't you—"

"—divorced. Then we got re-married. Then we got divorced again."

Mary sat just as he left her, staring out at the dance floor. There were two things Paul could never get her to do: bowl and dance. She was quick to agree to a slow dance, to spin in place with her head on his shoulder, but she was afraid to get out there and just move to the music. She'd said she was scared she'd look stupid, to which Paul would always ask her if she'd ever watched *him* dance.

"This music," she said when she saw him. "Pop Music" by M blared from the speakers. "It's like I'm at a skating party and I'm ten years old."

"A what?" Paul asked.

"A skating party. You know, roller-skating. The school had a night where everyone would go to the United Skates of America."

"There's no United Skates in Harmony." Paul held out her drink. "One Diet Coke, Ma'am."

She smiled as she took it from his hand. "Did you have to squeeze it yourself?"

He pointed to Robby. "You said I should talk to people."

"Hey, Robby."

Robby raised his glass. "Hello, Mrs. Rice."

Mary chuckled. "Oh, *please*. His mother is Mrs. Rice." She motioned across the table to the many empty chairs. "Have a seat."

"So who's that girl at the table taking names?" Paul wanted to know.

Robby laughed as he sat down. "Oh *her*. That, my friend, is the new English teacher."

"What happened to Mrs. Riley?"

"Retired."

"Polk still principal?"

"Oh yeah."

"I thought his heart would have given up on him by now." Paul said it as if he were afraid of being overheard. Old habits died hard.

"Somebody told me he's gonna have his stomach stapled."

Paul grimaced. "Maybe I should go buy stock in staples."

Robby coughed; he'd taken a drink from his Scotch and a burst of laughter caught him by surprise.

"You all right?" Paul asked, starting to get up.

"I'm fine," he said, still coughing as he tried to laugh. "I'm a trained medic. If worse comes to worse, I can give myself the Heimlich."

Mary laughed as well. She reached out, took Paul's hand in her own. He was glad she was with him. Very glad.

"So, they let you have the night off from the fire station?" she asked, turning the conversation from private Harmony High insights.

"Off from the fire station, yes. They're not gonna need me tonight, anyway."

"And why's that?"

"There won't be any big runs." He nursed his drink a bit more, then went on. "It's gotten to the point where I can usually sense when something's gonna happen. I call it my Spidey Sense."

Mary laughed. "Like the Incredible Spider-Man?"

"The Hulk's Incredible," he corrected. "Spider-Man's *Amazing*."

She rolled her eyes and giggled. "Whatever."

Robby's face fell. "Speak of the devil, my Spidey Sense just kicked in."

Paul shifted his weight, laughed. "And what danger lies ahead, oh *Amazing* One?"

"Deidra's coming."

"I know."

Robby nodded over Paul's shoulder. "No, I mean she's coming this way."

Paul turned, saw Deidra walking toward their table. When she saw his face she stopped. *She didn't know it was me*, he thought. *My back was to her. She saw Robby sitting here and decided to walk over, but she didn't know it was me until I turned around.* She only hesitated for a moment, but to Paul it seemed much longer. He let his eyes drink her in. She wore a red party dress, two thin straps over her shoulders to hold it up; the fabric—silk or satin, he couldn't tell by looking—gathered in smiling folds across her breasts, and the skirt barely kissed the tops of her knees. She looked taller than he remembered, then he saw her red stiletto heels. Her skin was pale as a white candle and her hair burned a bright red around her freckled face. She was thinner than he'd imagined, than he'd hoped. She looked fantastic.

Deidra weaved between the remaining tables that separated them and walked up to the back of an empty chair. Her pale eyes greeted Robby, skated past Mary, and landed squarely on Paul; her voice didn't seem the least bit shaky. "Hello there."

Paul felt his neck and face grow warm, remembering how he had looked in his mother's mirror before leaving. He looked older, by much more than ten years. He was about twenty pounds overweight and the gray in his hair had spread since he'd seen Deidra last, conquering much of the brown and vanquishing it. Worst of all, looking at her, he *felt* older.

He pointed to the woman in the chair next to him. "This is my wife, Mary."

"Nice to meet you," Mary told her pleasantly, going so far as to even offer up a welcoming grin.

"Nice to meet you," Deidra said, moving her eyes from Paul.

At least she's acknowledging her existence, he thought.

Her eyes whipped back, however, like two snapped rubber bands. They were almost jovial. "I wasn't sure you'd make it."

He tried to smile. "How could I pass up an open bar?"

Her cordial expression tottered a bit at that. He could almost see her sprockets turn, wondering: *Was he honestly trying to make a joke or was he throwing my past problems in my face?* To be honest, Paul didn't know which it had been. Not really. His eyes went to the glass of clear liquid in her hands and she said "Club soda," as if she felt the need to tell him she still wasn't drinking.

Deidra sat down, left a few empty chairs between them, and crossed her legs beneath the white tablecloth. Her right shoulder strap slipped from its perch and Paul could not help but look at her bare skin. Having not had much experience with women, Paul wondered how people who slept together could remain friendly afterward. It seemed an alien concept. Once you'd bared yourself to another person, weren't you always naked in their eyes? She raked the strap back into place with her fingers and looked at him in silence, as if she were not sure how to approach a conversation.

Paul could offer her no assistance. *It's like the first day of school all over again and we're total strangers. Whatever we shared, whatever closeness we had, seems to be part of some past life.*

"So how is everybody," she asked at last.

"Fine." Paul squeezed Mary's hand. "We just had a little girl about two months ago."

Deidra nodded and offered an unenthusiastic grin. "Congratulations." Her eyes shot to Mary for a moment. "To both of you."

"Thank you," Mary said.

"Our son's three now," Paul continued. "And on the twenty-second we'll have been married six years."

"Six years?"

"Six, yeah."

Deidra brushed a few rosy strands of hair from her face and tucked them behind her ear. She no longer sported the angle cut. Her hair had grown down past her shoulders. There was still a whisper of curl to it, but nothing like the perm she'd donned when he'd loved her. "So what's it like to be back in Harmony?"

"Some of us never left," Robby huffed.

Deidra looked over at him and Paul took the opportunity to draw in breath. "Sorry."

"No worries. The town's starting to take steps into the twentieth century. By the time we have our twenty-fifth reunion, it might actually be up to the '80s."

All of them chuckled at that, although Paul and Deidra's laughter was nervous at best.

Robby went on, "You know, for what I pay for my ranch home with full basement and DSS I couldn't even pay rent in Indy."

"DSS?" Paul chafed. "Where's my Superbowl Invite?"

Robby smiled. "Next year."

Deidra looked at Paul's wife with interest. "And what do you do, Mary?"

"I'm a counselor at a home for abused children."

"That's great." Deidra's voice was so low it barely registered above Kenny Loggins singing, "I'm all right, nobody worry 'bout me." She looked back at Paul. "You must be proud."

"I'm very happy," he told her.

"What about you, Deidra?" Robby asked. "We've shown you ours."

She looked at her glass. Paul thought she might be blushing, but it was probably the mood lighting. "Well, I went to school for graphic design, I married a man I went to school with." She looked at Mary. "We had no children." Then her eyes returned to Paul's. They were sad eyes, almost apologetic. "We had a house in San Diego with a pool and a maid who came in once a week to change the sheets and we started to drift apart. One day we woke up and realized we didn't have anything to talk about and so we did something *very* Californian: we talked to our lawyers and nullified our little marriage contract. Now the only contact I have with John is the check he sends me every month. I work for an advertising firm in Cincinnati now." She brought her drink to her full, red lips and sipped. "Just a hop, skip, and a jump away."

"Depends on how high you can hop and how far you can skip," Robby said.

"Well, at least we've all managed to move on after graduation," Deidra pointed out. "We've all become productive members of society. We haven't slit our wrists or hung ourselves."

Robby and Paul offered her dubious looks.

Mary didn't seem to notice.

"Not *yet* anyway." She pointed to Paul. "You two don't have to live with this guy."

"Aren't we the lucky ones," Deidra said with asperity, then took a drink.

Robby spoke up. If you dangled a loose thread of conversation in front of him, he had to pick it up. "Back in '87 there was this sixteen-year-old. Her name was Lisa." He drank from his half-empty glass of Scotch. "Lisa Hayden. She turned the car engine on with the garage door closed, took some pills, slashed both her wrists."

"At the same time?" Mary asked, uncomfortable with the direction the conversation had taken.

He chuckled humorlessly. "No. Different times. But see...she didn't really wanna die."

"Sounds like she had a death wish to me," Paul said.

"No. It was all so she could get her mother's attention...her mother's *love*."

"Did it work?" Deidra asked.

Robby blinked and looked up from his glass. "Sorry?"

"Did it *work*?"

"Sure. Sure it did. Her mother was a little distant, but she loved the girl. They got counseling. Became best buds. Best buds."

"Why don't I sense a 'and they lived happily ever after'?" Paul asked.

"A few months ago, she was back in town visiting Mommy Dearest and decides to listen to her little portable boom box while she took a bubble bath."

Mary brought her hand to her lips. Deidra lowered her eyes.

"Blew a transformer. The whole west side of Harmony was without power for a day."

Paul sipped his beer, his eyes on Robby. "Ahh, the irony."

Robby smiled. "Killing yourself without really killing yourself."

"What?" Paul looked at Robby's glass of Scotch. "How many of those have you had?"

"I'm serious. It's what I like to call throwing yourself on the 'foreseeable bullet.'"

"'The foreseeable bullet?'"

"Right," Robby nodded. "Say I'm Joe Depressed, and I want to be done with this sorry ass life. Do I slit my wrists? Hell no! I go run with the bulls. Now, it's *foreseeable* that the bulls could trample me. It's *foreseeable* they could gore my little dejected heart out. But, if it happens...is it really suicide? I didn't put a pistol in my mouth. I didn't swallow a handful of pills, or hang myself. In everybody's eyes, I was living life to the fullest." He took another drink. "Was it suicide for Lisa to bring her stereo into the bathroom? It was *foreseeable* it might fall in the tub, might kill her, but the death gets ruled an accident. An accident." He looked at Paul. "Driving your car at sixty-five miles an hour, jumping hills on Route Six might get you killed too."

Paul glared back at him. "So could running into burning buildings for a living."

Robby held his glass aloft in a toast. "Touché." He upended what was left of his Scotch until the ice cubes smacked his lips, then slammed the glass down on the table. "Either way, death isn't for certain, but it is *foreseeable*."

Paul looked at his own drink. "You can drop the sledge hammer, Oliver Stone. I get your message."

Robby stared at him a moment, then his eyes drifted to Mary's sad face. "Well, I've just brought this party to a screeching halt, huh?"

"I've worked with a lot of kids over the years that've attempted suicide," she told him. "They get so depressed they can't see any other way out, they can't see they have their whole life and so many choices ahead of them. But I think all of us have *thought* of suicide at one time or another. I know I remember getting depressed, thinking how I might do it."

Paul looked at her. "And how would you have done it?"

She shrugged. "Pills. Take a bunch of sleeping pills and wake up singing with the Heavenly Host."

"Suicides go to Hell," Deidra pointed out.

Paul's eyes whipped to her, surprised once again by her attitude.

Robby's grin grew wider. "Another reason why the 'foreseeable bullet' theory works so well. If it's not really a suicide, you can't really go to Hell."

"I don't know about any of that," Mary said. "But the point I was trying to make is that, when you're in high school, it all seems so serious. Every little thing has cosmic ramifications. Everything is life and death. It's only when you get some distance from it that you realize it wasn't really that way at all."

The three classmates looked at each other silently, memories waltzing across their faces. Mary looked at them; aware she had touched on something she shouldn't have. "Now I've hit the party brakes."

Deidra changed the subject. "I'm just dying to dance." Her eyes shot to Paul. "Would you mind?"

Paul's lips parted, so did Robby's, both struck dumb by the curve ball. Paul's eyes shifted sideways to Mary, tried to see the expression her face held, startled to find her smile.

Deidra forced herself to look at Mary. "Would you mind me dancing with your hubby?"

"Hell, no," Mary said with a cheerful laugh. "I don't like to dance anyway."

What is she thinking? Paul wondered, then thought, *This is her idea of therapy. Throw me into the lion's den and let me work out my problems. Damn her psych degree.*

Deidra's glance quickly reaffixed itself to Paul. "How 'bout it?"

He nodded nervously. "Sure."

Deidra rose from her chair, walked around the table to him, and held out her dainty hand. He stood up quickly, *too* quickly, then smiled at Mary and Robby as if to apologize for making an ass of himself. He took Deidra's hand and allowed her to lead him out onto the dance floor.

Mary sat at the table and watched them walk away, still uncomfortable with the situation, more uncomfortable now that she'd seen this other woman.

Until tonight, Deidra had just been someone Paul talked about in hushed tones, someone who'd hurt him deeply, someone who he still cared for, even if he wouldn't fess up to it. Now she had a face—a pale, beautiful face—and she had a body, a gorgeous figure with hips that had never borne the weight of children and a flat belly that had never been stretched.

We share a life, she reminded herself. *All he shares with Deidra is a memory.*

It had become her mantra over the last few days.

"You're a brave woman," Robby said.

Mary blinked and turned to look at him. "How so?"

She didn't feel very brave. At that moment, she felt quite the opposite.

"Don't you know who Deidra is?" he asked, shocked.

"Paul's first love," Mary said matter-of-factly. "We do talk, you know."

"And you're okay with them..." He moved his hands together, intertwining the fingers.

She laughed nervously. "What? They're going to throw off all their clothes on the dance floor?"

Robby shrugged and smiled at the absurdity of it. "Guess not."

Mary's eyes drifted back to Paul. He looked stiff as he tried to move to the beat. He looked uncomfortable with Deidra. *Good,* she could not help herself from thinking. Paul glanced back at her, gave a little wave, as if he'd read her mind and wanted her to know she had nothing to fear. She smiled and returned the gesture, then returned her eyes to Robby.

"The way I see it, I can either be a jealous bitch from Hell, or I can let them move past whatever it is that's still haunting them. Paul will be happier for it, and so will I."

Robby's face was aghast. "You're the Amazing One. Dump him, marry me."

At that, they both laughed.

On the dance floor, Paul and Deidra moved to Escape Club's "Wild Wild West." Deidra held her arms high above her head, her wrists almost touching one another. Her hips and torso swayed and snaked, the red silk of her dress hugging her form, her eyes shifting between Paul's face and the floor. Once he saw her panties clearly outlined beneath her thin skirt and looked away.

The song changed, became Peebo Brison's "If Ever You're In My Arms Again." Paul stopped moving. He looked at Deidra, tossed a glance to the DJ table, then turned to walk off the floor.

"Not so fast." Deidra wrapped her hand around his wrist to stop him. "We only danced to half a song."

"This one's too slow."

She stepped close to him, close enough that she had to tilt her face up to look at him. "You scared?"

"Scared?"

"Your wife said she wanted you to dance."

"I'm sure she'll—"

"—be fine with it." Deidra took his hand in hers and placed her other hand on his waist. "Just keep your hands off my ass."

Paul looked at the ceiling, let her lead. A mirrored ball hung from the rafters; it caught the spots, created a snowfall of light all around them as they moved. It reminded him painfully of the day he'd asked Deidra to marry him. The day she'd said "yes." When Deidra began to sing along with the words of the song, he came to the realization that everything had been orchestrated.

"You requested this, didn't you?"

A hint of her old smile, the one he'd once compared to that of an angel. "It's a little too maudlin, I know, but all the other ones I thought of requesting were even worse."

Paul didn't know what was on his face, he felt totally numb, but whatever it was caused her smile to falter and she lowered her head to avoid his gaze.

"I have to tell you something," she said to his shoes.

"No."

"You don't even know what it is."

"I have an idea, and I'm not gonna go down that road with you tonight." His voice was colder than he wanted it to be, but so be it. Part of him thought she deserved the cold shoulder. "You made your choice."

"Guess I deserve that." Her voice was soft, concentrated. She lifted her eyes to him again; they glistened in reflected light from the mirrored ball above. "But, right or wrong, I need to tell you this, and if I don't tell it to you now I'll never have the balls to even try again."

"Fine. Say what you need to say."

"I love you, Paul," she told him. "I never stopped... really, I never stopped. All I ever wanted from God was someone who loved me, really loved me...and He sent me you. God, how you loved me. You never lied to me, you kept all your promises...anything I wanted, you gave it to me without argument, without question. But I thought it was too perfect...I thought *you* were too perfect."

"Nobody's perfect, Deidra."

"You were too perfect for *me*. I wasn't...I wasn't worthy of your devotion." She sighed and looked at the ceiling, at the dancing circles of light that spun there. The muscles in her throat flexed and tightened; when her eyes found his again, they brimmed with tears. "At least, that's what I thought back then. So, what do *I* do? I do to you the same thing guys had done to me: I just walked away. I...I *hurt* you. I've tried to tell myself that...that those *things* split us up, that if we'd never played the game, if my mother hadn't been killed, we'd still be together. Married. But, you're right; it was my choice to leave. I screwed everything up. I know that, okay? I just want..." She tugged at the chain around her throat, pulled its full length from beneath the neckline of her blouse. A half circle of gold hung from its clasp, the same charm he'd given her before the Wide Game. It caught the lights of the dance floor and flirted with him. "I want to turn back the clock. I want everything to be like it was... *before* the game. I want it with all my heart, Paul." Her voice faltered. She let the charm fall to her breasts and looked back down at her feet. "The question is what do you want?"

Paul shook his head. "My wife is here."

"That's not an answer."

"What am I supposed to say, Deidra?"

"That you never stopped loving me, that there's a hole in your heart your wife can't fill."

Paul reached up, touched the broken gold disk, his thumb skating across the missing half of the Bible quote etched into its surface. He felt his own fragment of the charm burn a hole in his pocket, but he wasn't going to bring it out. He wasn't going to show her he'd kept it.

That would be admitting she was right. But there was truth to what Deidra said, even if he wouldn't acknowledge it openly. There was a dark pit in his heart—in his *soul*—not even Mary could light. For three years, he'd waited for Deidra to come to him, to say the exact same words in the exact same way, but she hadn't and now it was too late. He wanted to say this to her, to be honest about it, but the only words he could find were, "I'm sorry."

He let the charm fall back against Deidra's chest and backed away.

"Listen to me, Paul. Please! Would it kill you to listen?"

She grabbed his wrist, tried to halt his retreat, but this time he shook free of her and hurried from the dance floor. His forehead and neck throbbed in time with his heart and he loosened the tourniquet of his tie, tried to breath. He needed to get out of this humid gym, to get away.

The Men's restroom hadn't moved in the ten years he'd been gone. Paul threw the door open and rushed inside. It stank of old cigarette smoke and urine, just as he remembered. Several solitary men stood at the urinals, but they knew the "eyes forward" drill and did not turn to look at him. He moved past them to one of the stalls, pushed the swinging door closed behind him and saw that some aspiring artist had scrawled PORK SUCKS THE BIG ONE above the portrait of a huge penis on the back of it.

Ahhh, Paul thought in spite of the whirlwind in his skull, *the classics never die.*

He sat down on the toilet, let his head rest against the tiled wall behind him; the cool ceramic reverberated against his skull, muffled music from the gym. He covered his eyes with his hands and massaged his temples.

So what's the plan? Paul asked himself. *We just gonna sit here avoiding her and hope she goes home?*

Put like that, it suddenly didn't sound like much of a plan at all.

Someone opened the restroom door, allowed the dance music in, and Paul heard a sharp *click-clack* against the tiled floor, like someone walking in stiletto heels. One of the guys at the urinals hurriedly zip up, another cried, "Hey!" Paul knew what was happening, but when Deidra threw the stall door open, his body jerked in surprise just the same. She stood there, her face as red as her hair, burning with frustration, anger, and—he supposed—love.

"I just poured my heart out to you and you run and hide in a fuckin' bathroom like I gave you cooties at recess?"

One of the guys from the urinals hurried past her, eyed the deep-cut V of Deidra's naked back with a blend of amusement and annoyance, then glanced up Paul.

"This is a Men's room!" Paul told Deidra as if it were news, his face warm with embarrassment.

"Then what are you doing in here acting like a little boy?"

"What the hell do you want from me?"

"I just told you I still love you. You could show some fucking interest."

"You want me to go, 'Ahhhh...poor Deidra'?"

"No, I thought you'd want to tell me how you feel for once."

"*For once—?*"

"Ten years of letters and not even a fucking word. I bet if your Mom had Caller I.D. on her phone you wouldn't have answered my call either."

"Look, Deidra, it was no secret how I felt about you. I told you I loved you, that I wanted to spend the rest of my life loving you. You didn't want to hear it then and I'm sure as hell not going to give you the satisfaction of hearing it now."

"Because you feel guilty about your wife?"

"Because it's *over*."

"Really?"

"*Really*."

"I didn't think we were ever going keep secrets from one another."

"What are you talking about?"

She stepped into the stall with him. Paul thought she might close the door and climb onto his lap, press her body against his as she had their first time together. She wore a skirt after all. It would take no effort to slide her panties to one side. He could be inside her in a matter of seconds, moving in her warmth, the warmth a piece of him was cold without. As he thought all of this, he felt himself stir and he balled his hand into a fist, dug the nails into his palm to make the dirty sensations stop before there was no way for him to ever be clean again.

But Deidra didn't close the door. She tapped his chest with her finger, her face as stern as a teacher giving discipline. "Nothing will ever be over between us, not as long as you keep running from it."

"You're one to talk about running away, *bitch*," Paul shouted, his voice harsh, cruel, his hands still fisted and shaking. At that moment, he wanted so much to hate her. He wanted his hate to rise up and strike down any surviving love, any remaining lust. He wanted his anger to burn it all away. "I can't believe I even bothered to save your life."

"Fine." Her eyes, close to tears, became thin slivers. "Good-bye, Paul."

She turned away, started to sob, and, in that moment, the feelings he'd tried so desperately to kill called out to her, "Deidra?"

Her heels made loud clicks against the tile as she hurried across the room.

Paul stood up and moved after her in spite of himself. "I'm sorry, Deidra."

She didn't answer. She didn't look back.

"I said I'm sorry." He reached out for her shoulder as she opened the Men's Room door, turning her back to him. "Wait a second."

"You really think the Game is over?" Deidra said, her voice splintering, then she repeated, "Nothing's over as long as you run from it."

She shook off his hand and rushed through the doorway. Paul followed her out, watched her nearly stumble and fall between the tables, regain her balance, then almost run right into a couple and spill their drinks. She excused herself and moved quickly into the dimness of the gymnasium, melted into the crowd until she faded from his sight.

Paul stood in front of the Men's Room, his hands still clenched, throbbing from the pain of his fingernails digging in. *You really think the Game is over?* Her words had left him feeling afraid, sweating. *Nothing's over as long as you run from it.*

A hand slapped his shoulder and he nearly jumped clear of his skin.

It was Robby. "What's goin' on?"

"What are you doing?" Paul asked with irritated uneasiness.

"Relax, I'm not spyin' on you or anything. I can't believe how cool Mary is with you and Deidra dancin' together. If it were my wife—"

"You don't have a wife."

"But if I did, I can imagine she'd cut off my Johnson before she'd let me get close to one of my old fucks."

Same old Robby, Paul thought abruptly. *Charming as ever*.

Robby pointed to the Men's Room door with his thumb. "Anyway, I'm just here to take a piss." He looked around curiously. "Where is Deidra, anyway?"

"She left."

"You call her a cunt and tell her to stay outta your life?"

A cunt? Oh, thank God Paul never used that word. If it had been readily available to his brain he might have blurted it out in place of "bitch." "Bitch" was bad enough, but he thought he could at least apologize for that one. From what little he knew of women, calling Deidra a cunt would have been about the worst thing he possibly could have done.

"Something like that," Paul said, troubled.

"Good for you." Robby flashed a supportive—and maybe even a little surprised—smile, patted Paul on the back, then gave a quick look over his shoulder to the restroom and backed away. "Gotta go. See you back at the table?"

Paul nodded. "Sure. Yeah."

He walked back over to Mary. She sat alone, looking off into space in serene contemplation. Paul wondered what she thought about. *Probably wondering if you're going to come back to her or run off to Mexico for a quick divorce.* Now why would he think that? Mary had not shown even a twinkle of jealousy or worry. It was as if she knew him better than he knew himself, as if she were absolutely confident in his love for her.

"Hi, beautiful," he said as he took his seat. "What's a gorgeous woman like you doing all alone in this dive?"

She blinked and turned her eyes to him, blushing. "Watching my husband having a good time at his reunion." Her expression turned doubtful. "At least that's what I hope I was doing. Where's your girlfriend?"

Paul's mouth popped open and he found himself mute. He suddenly remembered his thoughts in the bathroom stall, when he believed Deidra might try and have him right then and there. Were they written on his face now for Mary to read?

"Hello?"

"She's not my girlfriend," he muttered. Then took a deep breath. "I don't even know if she's a friend."

Mary reached over to brush a few sweat-soaked strands of hair from his forehead. "What happened?"

"I said some things to her, hurtful things. They just popped right out of my stupid mouth."

"She still loves you," Mary said thoughtfully. Paul was surprised that it wasn't in the form of a question. "Your mother told me about the letters Deidra writes to you, the ones you have her throw away."

Paul went pale and held his head in his hands.

"She's never going to be able to get on with her life if she doesn't get to talk to you about this, if you don't *listen*."

Spoken like a true counselor, Paul thought, but he didn't say it.

"And, if *you* don't talk to her, you may not be able to get past it either."

Paul bit his lip. "What should I do, Doc?"

She reached out and took his hand into hers. "I think you know where she's going."

Paul nodded. After what she'd said, he was terrified he knew exactly where to find her.

"Then go after her," Mary whispered. "Find her and talk this thing out."

Paul shook his head. He finally knew what Mary wanted from him. For years, she'd known ghosts she could not see nor even hope to understand haunted him. And as long as he was caught up in the past, in Deidra, in the fucking game, he was only half a husband to her. Mary deserved so much more than that. Paul knew that, and, even if she would never openly say it to him, she knew it too. "God, I love you."

"I know you do," she said finally. "That's why it's okay for you to go."

"Hey, kids," Robby said as he walked up to the table. Paul rose. "Robby, do you think you could take Mary back to my Mom's house?"

"Oh-kay." His eyebrows gave a quizzical leap. "What gives?"

Paul did not reply. He bent down, gave Mary a soft kiss, told her again how much he loved her, then made his way to the door. In his heart, it was not love or even lust for Deidra that stirred and stretched.

MICHAEL WEST

It was fear.

TWENTY-EIGHT

A full moon watched over the northern fields like a glowing cyclopean eye. The rows of corn stretched outward—on, and on, and on. Endless. Green and ready for the harvest. Just being near the stalks at night brought on a dull, phobic feeling that lanced Paul's brain and made his throat pulse.

What am I doing out here? This is utterly ...

The word he searched for was 'crazy,' but his mind suddenly experienced a kind of aphasia and he was unable to even think it.

What's a flock of crows called?

He gave his head a shake and slid his sweaty hands into his pockets. His right hand found the broken half-charm resting on a coil of chain and the fangs of its jagged edge bit into his palm.

Jesus, get me through this night.

He stood next to the driver's side door of the Jeep for what seemed like a long time. The white clouds of gravel dust the Cherokee kicked off the road had settled and he could no longer hear the steady *drip...drip...drip* as condensation from the air conditioner struck engine parts on its way to the ground. He took a deep breath, then crossed the grassy slope that separated him from Deidra.

She was there, just as he knew she would be, standing at the edge of the field, the wind roaming through her blazing hair. Her fingers played with the chain around her neck, the charm blinking in the moonglow. A lightning bug buzzed by, illuminating her glistening cheek with its hazard beacon.

"Go away." She wiped at her face, glared at him, sorrow and rage dancing in the darkness of her eyes. "Just... just go."

He stopped his approach. In his pockets, his hands were shaking. He watched waves billow across the sea of corn, then lowered his head. His eyes burned and he fought to keep the scalding tears from boiling over.

"I'm sorry," he told her. "I didn't know what I was even saying until I'd said it. It's just that...this whole reunion has me thinking about the Goddamn game again. I can't ever seem to really stop thinking about it. I think I do, but I know it's always there in my brain." He hesitated to go on, looking over at Deidra to see if she was even hearing him. He couldn't tell. She looked out at the corn, watched the stalks bow gently to the wind. "We came so close to losing—"

"We *did* lose," Deidra blurted out. "We lost everything that matters."

"We survived."

"And what a great joy *surviving* has been."

Paul looked up at the moon. It was so full and bright, so...familiar. He sighed. "You gave me *Misery*."

"Excuse me?" She flashed him a look close to betrayal.

"February 14th, 1988. You gave me a hardcover copy of Stephen King's *Misery*."

She nodded, her face showed a hint of a smile. "I remember."

"Do you remember what you wrote inside?"

Deidra shook her head, but in her face he saw vague familiarity.

"'For Paul, my only friend, my only *love*, the one who's always there to listen to my fears and hold me until they go away. I'll love you forever.'"

She looked out at the corn. "Sounds like me."

"After you wrote me..."

"A Dear John letter." There was regret in Deidra's voice.

Paul nodded. "I took that book off the shelf and thought, 'She gave me *Misery*, how appropriate is that?'"

"Paul—"

"Let me finish." She nodded slowly and he went on, "The truth is...I kept telling myself that to help me try to get over you. But it didn't help. You hurt me so much, and I desperately *needed* to hate you. But I couldn't. Hard as I try, I *can't* hate you, Deidra. The time we spent together...it wasn't misery. Whenever I look back on my life, it's you I think about. Even with all the...with everything that happened, your love is a wonderful memory."

A long stretch of silence followed, broken only by the short symphonies of crickets, and then Deidra angrily swept her cheek with her fingers. "It was so stupid to think you'd drop everything for me."

He looked at her, his chest and throat aching as he spoke. "There's this part of me that wants to, this part where you still live, this part that will always love you." He swallowed. "But, like I said, that's all just a memory now."

Deidra looked at him. "I miss you. Every moment of every day for ten years." And then she returned her gaze to the swaying stalks. "You know what I keep thinking about?"

Paul shook his head.

She offered the tears on her cheek another angry swipe. "I keep thinking about Dickens' *Christmas Carol*." She chuckled huskily at that and returned her eyes to him. "You ever think about Hell?"

Paul's heart paused in his chest. When it resumed beating, its pace was quicker, as if it were running from something.

"I think Hell is something we make. We build it for ourselves, brick by brick."

"Deidra—"

"I keep thinking that maybe that's what this is, some demented *Christmas Carol*, with me as Scrooge. Those things are...they're showing me what Hell will be like, trying to get me to change my life or..." Paul could actually see the pain in her eyes. "...appreciate what I have. The last ten years without you...that's been my Hell."

A hot tear ran down his own cheek. "You wrote and asked me to forgive you."

"Just about a million times."

"I do forgive you, Deidra."

She looked at him again, and he saw the ache abandon her eyes to longing. "Right now, my heart is screaming for me to run over there and kiss you. My lips recall what it was like and my body remembers the feel of you. You ever hear stories about people loosing their foot...and they can still feel it there? All these years...I've felt you." She chuckled, but her tears strangled it until it sounded harsh and pained. "How pathetic am I? All these years...I'm still waiting for you to make the first move. But, you're never going to make it, are you?"

"Deidra, don't—"

"Don't love you? Been there, tried that."

He looked at his shoes, hands in his pockets, longing to hold her. "I just wanted...I forgive you. I don't hate you. But we'll never be just friends. We can't be."

She nodded. "I know."

He turned to walk back to his Jeep; the gentle slope to the road suddenly seemed like a mountain.

"Paul?" Deidra called from behind him. "Will you hold me?—Just to say good-bye?"

He stopped, swallowed hard. The request wasn't a shock. In fact, at the back of his mind, he'd wanted to be the one who'd made it. But it wasn't right. He felt too much like a cheater as it was, coming out here to be with her, even if he had Mary's blessing to do it, and to touch her now...seemed somehow *wrong*. Maybe he was just afraid it wouldn't stop with a farewell embrace. "I don't think that's a good idea."

"It's just a hug." She made steps toward him, her face solemn and trembling as she held out her arms. "Please."

Paul made no effort to stop her as she curled her arms around him. Her eyes fluttered closed, and, when she squeezed him, he removed his hands from the holsters of his pockets and placed them on her back. He smelled the sweet, floral scent of her hair; felt the cool rain of tears on his neck. His hands moved up and down her spine, felt the silk of her dress, felt that she wore no bra beneath it. At that moment, God help him, he wanted her. In his chest, his heart was being drawn and quartered, a section of it pulled to his love for Deidra, to his life with her that never was. Marriage. College in California. Walks along the beach. Redheaded children who'd inherited their mother's quick temper. It would be easy to get involved with her again, right now, here in the grass. Part of him begged for the chance. But a greater portion of his heart was pulled back to his wife, to his family. In the darkness behind his eyes, he saw Mary smiling on their wedding day. He remembered the births of his children, heard their laughter. The thoughts filled him with warmth, like coming home from the office on a snowy day. And then his heart stopped its tug-o'-war and swung wholly in Mary's direction. Walking away from Deidra now was the right choice, the *only* choice. He stiffened, halted the movement of his hands on her back. It was time he got back to his mother's house. It was time he went *home.*

Deidra pulled away from him, but not completely. It reminded him of the day they performed *The Rainmaker*. He'd forced himself to let go of her, and she hadn't been able to totally break contact. Her eyes searched his, then she asked, "If you had to make one wish, right now, what would it be?"

That I never met you sprang into his mind, but that wasn't the truth. He had a wish, had made it silently in his heart for a decade now. After a moment of contemplation, Paul finally gave it voice, "I wish we'd never played that fucking game, that we all lived happily ever after. Every one of us."

"That's been my one wish too." She smiled, stretched to softly kiss his cheek, then turned and moved back toward the cornfield.

Paul stood by his Jeep, hands moving back into the safety of their holsters, and watched her walk away. "Where are you going?"

She nodded at the corn. "Out there."

"*What for?*" he asked, his voice cracking.

"Remember what I said about this being *A Christmas Carol*? I'm tired of 'Christmas Yet to Come.' Maybe, if I walk out there...our wish will come true. This will all have been a nightmare...I'll wake up next to you...and I will never, *ever* let you go."

"Deidra...that's—"

"Crazy? Then it'll prove once and for all that I'm a total nutcase."

"I can't let you go out there."

She smirked. "Like you could stop me." She turned then, lifted her open hand to him, her fingers waving slightly. "Come with me."

The invitation took Paul by surprise. He wiped his sweaty face with his hand, like trying to pick up a spill with a wet paper towel. To walk into that field was insanity...and yet, he found himself wanting to go with her. He could feel something out there in the corn, something calling to him the way a flame beckons to a moth, calling him toward a place where the Game could finally end. He thought he actually took a step toward Deidra, toward the field, but he may only have imagined it.

"No," Paul said at last, shaking his head.

"Why not?"

"Why...?" *Because it's* foreseeable *that we'd get ourselves killed*, he wanted to say, but he suddenly thought Deidra already knew that. "I'm married," he told her. "I have children. I have a *life*."

"And I don't." The tone of her voice was odd.

"I didn't mean—"

"You're right. I don't have a life."

Her fingers played with the chain around her neck again, with the charm he'd given her. He knew what the tone in her voice was now. It was *understanding*. Understanding of what, however, he could not say.

"I was here earlier today," she told him. "I hiked out to that shed, the one where we hid that night. You remember?"

Paul nodded and his mouth went dry.

Deidra walked up to her car, reached inside the driver's side window to retrieve something, something tightly wrapped in newspaper. She turned the package over and over in her hands before moving back across the grassy incline, holding it out to him. "Here."

"What is it?" Paul slid his hands from his pockets; suddenly aware he still held his half of the charm. He clinched his fist around the golden half-circle to hide it, but it was too late.

Deidra saw the necklace and smiled, her glistening eyes locked with his. "You kept it. I knew you'd keep it. I just knew it."

"Here." Paul swallowed, took the package from her hands and tucked it under his arm. It was flat, whatever it was. He grabbed her by the wrist and put the charm into her open palm. "I don't need it."

"This isn't like the game, I didn't give you something of mine." Deidra's voice crackled, her eyes dropped to the charm, disappointment weighting the corners of her mouth. When her gaze returned to him, there was no doubt anymore about that look of understanding in her eyes. She knew something. "It's yours."

Paul took the package from under his arm and studied the newsprint. She'd used this morning's paper.

He could see a story about tonight's reunion staring back at him. After a moment he gave her a questioning look.

"Remember the night before the game?" she asked. "The night we made love for the first time?"

"Of course I do."

"You put your script into your backpack at the foot of my bed."

He nodded, not seeing where she was going but wanting her to get there quickly.

"The next morning, when I went downstairs to call the school, it was sitting on the kitchen counter."

Paul's stomach sank, but he didn't know why.

Deidra smiled as if she did know, then she wiped away the last of her tears. "After you open it, go home to your wife. If she still wants you, fine. If not, just know that *I* do."

The terror Paul felt was a white-hot poker in his gut. "What is it?" he repeated.

"Proof," she said with genuine gravity.

"Proof of what?"

Deidra pointed to the corn. "That the Game's not over, that they want us to go out there and finish it." She was silent for a moment, thinking it over, then she said, "I'm remembering things about that night. At first, I thought they were just nightmares, like all the ones I've had ever since the game, just patchwork ghosts sewn together from scraps of fantasy and discarded memories. But they're not. They're skeletons in the closet of my brain finally starting to rattle their bones. *Our* skeletons." She motioned toward him, then back to herself. "Yours and mine. Like it or not, Paul, we're a team. We belong together. You'll see. You'll see it and come with me."

Paul shook his head. "No. I won't."

Deidra closed her hand around his half of the charm and nodded at the package he held. "Then open it, Paul. Open it and go home to your wife. You know where to find me."

He watched her walk up to the wall of stalks, watched her part them with delicate hands, as through she were stepping through thick stage curtains to start her performance, or leaving the stage after her acting was done. In a moment, she was out of his sight and the aching loss in his chest seemed to dull to a manageable pain.

Paul looked at the package she'd given him, then up at the moon, the all too familiar moon, and wondered if he could hit it from here. He drew back his arm to fling her gift into the corn; halfway through the arc of his pitch, however, he stopped himself. He drew in a long breath and exhaled just as slowly.

"Damned if I do," he murmured, "and damned if I don't."

Hesitantly, Paul undid the tape and pulled open the newspaper. A butcher's knife. He recognized it as one that had been missing from his mother's knife block for over a decade. The blade caught the moonlight, gave him an evil wink.

Repulsed, he dropped the package. The pale reflection of Paul's own bloodshot eyes gazed up at him from the blade. A rusty film of dried blood covered much of the cutting surface, but he could remember a time when the metal was shiny and glazed over by fresh, bright gore, could remember touching it within his backpack and telling himself it was just his canteen.

His breath abandoned him. His blood rushed to his head, beat against the inside of his temples as if he were something it needed to escape; a burning building, a sinking ship. A chaos of whispers filled his ears, a wall of white sound that brought with it memories he'd locked away from everyone, including himself. Movement, a shadow, no more than a flutter really; it registered in the corner of his eye, moved toward him from the corn. Paul wanted to scream, could feel it bubble up the well of his throat, but what escaped his mouth was a husky rasp. He fell back against the Cherokee, slid down its side until he assumed a kind of fetal position on the ground, his gaze focused on the knife...on the blood.

His body may have left the dense fog of the cornfield ten years before, but his brains were only now clearing it. They hadn't played the Wide Game. They themselves had been played. He'd been a pawn on a chessboard, a toy soldier in a war fought for the amusement of obscene fates, and these murderous memories they'd hidden from him were their trump card finally played.

He closed his eyes and images flashed in the darkness, horrible slides illuminated by a flickering, piercing light within his brain. Faces. They washed over him in a sudden glut, as if a mighty dam erected in his mind had burst violently open, drowning him. Nick Lerner's face as he lay dying on the wooden spikes Paul and Deidra had buried in the ground. Patrick Chance's face as Paul cut into it with the butcher's knife and pulled away his scalp. Dale Brightman's face as the knife disappeared into his eye. Dale had found the cornhusk dolls, dolls Deidra made from her Miami Indian research. And, finally, Deidra's face, glistening in the bright sunlight as she helped him strap Dale to the wooden cross with chains they'd taken from the Hunton's barn. These moments were dream-like, surreal, and yet he knew they had not been created by his mind but *recorded* by it. They had happened. They had all happened.

Now Paul was certain that he wasn't alone. There were others out here with him, looking, laughing, descending.

Closer.

Closer.

Paul reached over and scooped the knife from the grass, held it out to ward off his attackers. As he looked around, the shadows leapt back, but their whispering remained in his ears.

"*You killed them,*" the unholy chorus sang. "*You killed those boys...*"

"You made me," Paul found himself saying, the words scalding his throat.

They laughed at his misery. "*Did we?*"

He lowered the knife, wished he'd died in those fields, in his car crash...wished he'd never been born at all. He didn't know if the demons had taken over his body as he slept, had forced his hands to do their will, or if he'd done it all on his own. It didn't really matter. Either way, it had been *his* hands that had killed.

"*End it,*" the demons urged.

Slowly Paul turned the knife on himself, its bloody point aimed at his heart.

"*Do it.*" The whispers were now insistent, demanding. "*Do it!...Do it!...Do it!...Do it!...Doit!Doit!Doit!Doit!Doit!Doit!Doit!Doit!Doit!Doit!*"

Paul closed his eyes, felt their icy hands rush in to hover over his chest, waiting for him to bury the knife in his flesh, waiting to claim his heart...his soul. That was the only way they could have him, the only way he could really be theirs. He saw Schongauer's engraving flash once more in his mind, saw the creatures all around St. Anthony, pulling at his skin, tearing at his flesh. In a moment, that would be Paul.

At last, Paul Rice found he was able to scream.

TWENTY-NINE

Somehow, he managed to get into his Jeep and drive.

He navigated the dark and winding roads without seeing them. The interior of the Cherokee seemed to dissolve around him and Paul found himself standing once more in the corn, his mother's butcher's knife still clutched in his hand.

The Miami girl stood next to him in the row, naked and streaked in color, her eyes dark pools into which he wanted to dive. She reached out and held his shaking hand, her voice insistent, "The spirits call out for their sacrifice."

And then she transformed; her skin grew dry, cracked, appeared more cornhusk than flesh. Her body split down the center, peeled back to reveal Deidra's nude form hidden within. Paul's mind accepted the vision with surprising ease, as if it had always suspected the deception. The look on Deidra's face wasn't one of fear, but the same odd look of understanding he'd seen before she'd given him the knife. And then she uttered something strange, something he'd never heard before, "*Mondamin* is here."

As if on cue, the demons took turns in his ear, reminding Paul how Patrick looked after Deidra pushed him onto the skewers, how the boy had screamed and called out. Paul remembered it clearly now. Patrick had cried for help, had called out for...

God.

In a moment of clarity, like a master chess player, Paul saw his escape move. He drove to St. Anthony's and bolted across the parking lot, looking up at the church as hope and terror danced in his heart, the knife—Deidra's "proof"—held in his fist. The demons told him it was best to just end it, best to turn the knife he'd used on so many others on himself, but he couldn't do that.

He *wouldn't* do it.

To do that would be to lose, to admit defeat.

Paul leapt up the steps and reached out for the large oak doors. A crow swooped down at him, stabbed his hand with its beak, drew tiny rivulets of blood. He slashed at the bird and it fell dead to the concrete, spilled its contents like an opened piñata. Paul looked around, waiting for the entire flock to swoop in and devour him utterly.

What's a flock of crows called?

And finally, his mind permitted an answer: *It's a* murder, *Paul. A* murder *of crows.* Murder!

He pushed open the doors and ran into St. Anthony's. A breeze blew past him, extinguished many of the candles, threw the chapel into partial darkness. Father Andrew stood at the altar. Paul looked down at the knife, saw it stained in fresh blood—the crow's blood, blood from his own wounded hand—and he hid between the dim pews. If the old priest saw the manic look in Paul's eyes, saw the wild gray mane of his hair and the blood on his knife, his salvation might run out the door.

That would ruin everything.

Father Andrew ran to the entrance, and Paul worried he might have run out without hearing his confession, then he heard the priest's shoes on the tiled center aisle, coming closer.

Confession is good for the soul.

"Amen," Father Andrew shouted, as if answering Paul's thoughts.

It occurred to Paul that Deidra had been right: he *was* still playing the Game. Only now, he was playing to win.

The truth shall set you free.

Father Andrew passed by him on the way to the altar, open newspaper still in one hand. Paul rose up, curled his left arm around the old priest's chest and held the knife—

The proof of his sins!

—up for the old priest to see.

"*Bless me, Father,*" Paul cried out into the holy man's ear, his voice panicky, shrill, almost like a woman screaming. "*Bless me, for I have sinned.*"

"Please..." Father Andrew muttered back. Paul heard fear in his voice as well. "...put down the knife and we can talk about this."

"*I can't do that, Father!*" Paul looked over his shoulder to the front door, to "The Temptation of St. Anthony" which hung framed above it. The creatures drawn there seemed to writhe, to howl—as if they knew the endgame was at hand and felt their prize slipping from their grasp. "*They're coming. They're coming for me and I need forgiveness.*" And then the slide show started in his mind once more, flickers of atrocity that brought fresh tears to his eyes. "*I'm so sorry! Christ, Jesus, please, Father, I need forgiveness for my sins!*"

"All right," Father Andrew said, his voice surprising tranquil. "Please, stay calm. I'll hear your confession."

Paul's sobs became grateful tears of joy. "Thank you, father."

"In the name of the Father, and of the Son, and of the Holy Spirit," the priest said, making the sign of the cross with his right hand. "Amen."

Amen.

"May God, who brightens every heart, help you to know your sins and trust in His mercy."

God didn't show me my sins, Father, Paul thought, *but He did bring me to you. He did show me how to end this, how to win.*

"What are the sins you wish to confess to God?"

"Father Andrew," Paul said, "have you ever heard of The Wide Game?"

He began his confession, telling the story from beginning to end, braiding his own tale with those of Robby, Mick, and the others to create the complete tapestry of what had happened. He kept nothing secret. Nothing. And, by the time he'd finished, Paul and Father Andrew sat facing one another in one of the pews.

"You're not making this up," Father Andrew said, breaking the uncomfortable silence that followed. Paul was surprised to find the words were not in the form of a question. The priest looked at a slow-spinning ceiling fan that hung down from the rafters. "I remember the fall of 1987. Quite a few young lives lost. Quite a few funerals held in this building." He nodded at the altar, where pictures of Danny and Cindi had been placed amid bushels of flowers. "You say there were... demons?"

Paul nodded, shocked to find that he actually felt better. "I know the Church has kind of distanced itself from—"

"*Society* has distanced itself from the thought of demons, Paul. The Church hasn't totally given up on the idea." Father Andrew turned to look at the drawing above the door. St. Anthony's torment at the hands of sketched devils. "And I certainly believe. I remember seeing the video you spoke of. It was on the news, wasn't it?"

"Yes."

"Mick Slatton stabbing the Fields boy. They were good friends, isn't that right?"

"Yeah." Paul nearly choked on the word, his eyes still hot with tears. "Danny was like Mick's big brother. He stuck up for him all the time—that day even."

"I remember hearing that at the time and thinking it odd. The more I thought about it, the more it disturbed me. I'm sure you remember how this town reacted to the news, to the *loss*. As a priest, I was expected to have something *inspirational* to say in the face of it. I'm afraid I had to rely heavily on Sacred Scripture. I could find no words of my own to explain it, nothing that would offer any kind of comfort, anyway." He drew in a breath and his eyes returned to Paul. "No, I don't have a problem believing the demonic aspects of your recollection. Rarely do we encounter them so directly in our lives—well, throughout history, really. But for people to do the things I saw to one another, and have heard about tonight... Maybe devilish tomfoolery is the best available explanation."

Paul cringed. "Father, *tomfoolery...?*"

"I'm sorry, Paul. I didn't mean to belittle this. I'm used to taking weighty issues of the supernatural and—" He glanced around at the empty pews. "—dumbing them down for the consumption of the masses." The old priest's sympathetic eyes found Paul's again. "Feeling better?—More in control?"

"Yes." Paul's face warmed and he started to rise from the pew. "I'm...I'm better. Thank you."

Father Andrew grabbed him by the wrist. "Where are you going?"

"I'm going to do what Deidra said I should do. I'm going home to my wife. I need to tell her everything I've told you before I forget again."

"I don't think that'll happen, do you?"

Paul shook his head and the tortured faces strobed for a moment in his eyes. They were his now, his for eternity.

Father Andrew now looked troubled. "And what then?"

Paul sighed. He should turn himself in; let them put him in jail, or perhaps an asylum. The tears flowed now, and he wiped at them with his hand, smeared blood across his face. "In the morning, I'll go to the police. I know you're not supposed to tell anyone what I've confessed, but if you could come with me I'd—"

"Here." Father Andrew took a handkerchief from his pocket and handed it to Paul. "Wipe your face and wrap that hand." The priest stood and moved toward the outer aisle, beckoning Paul to follow. "Walk with me."

Paul did as he was asked, wiped away the blood and bandaged his wound as he followed.

"If turning yourself in would result in justice, in peace for the families of your victims, I'd say you were doing the right thing. Hell, as a priest, I'd be obligated to talk you into it. If I couldn't convince you, I could always call the police myself and anonymously mention your name—the sanctity of the confessional preserved and my conscience clear." Father Andrew paused, took a still burning candle from a candelabrum and re-lit the blackened wicks around it. "But I fear justice is out of our grasp. I'm sure you'll remember Sheriff Carter was even forced to admit that. Had your friend Mick not killed himself, he'd be walking freely among us now." He cocked his head at Paul. "No bodies."

Paul remembered. As damning as his videotape had been, they never found a corpse in the field. And Deidra's mother...any lawyer worth his weight in salt could have gotten Mick manslaughter at worst.

"As for peace..." Father Andrew continued, "Coming forward now would bring them just the opposite, I'm afraid. This will throw a national spotlight onto their pain and this town will be torn apart all over again. I know one of the mothers, Paul. She barely survived the loss. Now, ten years later, I just don't think she can live through it again."

"I don't deserve to be let off the hook, Father."

Father Andrew put the candle back in its place. "What about your wife?"

Paul's stomach sank. "She—"

"You may in fact deserve the legal hassles, the loss of reputation, but your wife certainly doesn't, does she?"

Paul didn't know how to respond.

"She didn't choose to marry a murderer, Paul."

"She didn't *know*!"

"*You* didn't know. And you aren't a killer presently, are you?" Father Andrew raised a hand and placed it on Paul's shoulder. "God is constantly placing forks in the road we travel. We can travel down the easy path, or walk the more difficult trail. The choices we make define us, shape us into who we are."

Paul lowered his eyes. "I deserve—"

"You deserve nothing." The priest's sympathetic tone turned punitive. "You don't get to walk the easy path."

"Going to prison, never seeing my wife and children again...you call that *easy*?"

Father Andrew nodded. "Come forward with your guilt, let them strip away your name and give you a number, let them stick you in a cell and tell you where to walk and when to do this and that. They'll take away all those pesky choices, won't they? No. That's the easy way out, much more righteous than Mr. Slatton's way, of course, but you're still not facing who you are. You're just giving up."

"Then where's my penance?"

Father Andrew looked at him sternly. "You want penance, do you? Okay, how many Our Fathers and Hail Mary's should I tell you to recite? What would be enough to cover this?"

Paul's eyes widened, his mouth hung open as he tried to find the appropriate response to fill it. There wasn't one.

"Let me show you something." Father Andrew turned and walked to the altar, stared up at the bronze image of Christ.

Paul kept pace, confusion running through his mind. He couldn't believe what this priest was telling him.

"Not very accurate, our statuary."

Paul looked at the bronze figure, remembering his childhood aversion to it. "Yeah, I've heard that argument. He's too American looking. He should be—"

"He shouldn't even be recognizable as human. He wasn't just a naked man with blood on his forehead, on his hands and feet. By the time they put Him up there, in all likelihood, His back was shredded open to the bone. Many people didn't survive a Roman scourging, you know. That's why they called their 40 lashes '40 minus one'—they took one off in case the punisher lost count. That extra lash could be the one that did you in. Leather whips with glass and stone flung and drug across His back. Thirty-nine times, Paul. Blood loss alone would sometimes kill them."

Paul felt uncomfortable. Part of him wanted the beating the priest described. Part of him thought he deserved that and more. After what he'd done, it seemed only fitting. Then there was the six-year-old inside him; the one who'd seen this image of Christ as something horrible. That part of him now cried.

Father Andrew continued, "Our religion is based on the concept that we are incapable of making up for what we've done in God's eyes, so He made up for it Himself. He paid the price. By our pictures and statues you'd think that the price was merely a public and humiliating death, one of, say, starvation. For all the horror it would evoke, I still wish I had a more accurate vision of what He really looked like—right there at the altar for all to see. God, hung on a cross, body mutilated beyond all recognition."

Paul's new memories of Dale Brightman assaulted him. Stabbing him again, and again, and again as Deidra watched, then chaining him on the wooden cross—creating a mockery of what the priest had just described. Paul wiped at the tears that scalded his cheeks.

"He did it voluntarily, Paul. For all the power of Rome, no one made Him do it. They couldn't have; He was God. He died for us...not for Himself, but for us, for our sins. All sins. Your sins. Your murders, Paul."

Paul shook his head.

Father Andrew nodded at the bronze Christ. "We can't make up for our sins, so He did it for us...and it's *done*." He turned his attention back to Schongauer's engraving above the door. "I've often seen you look at that."

Paul nodded. "It makes me uncomfortable."

"That's what it's there for. It's above the door to remind you of your sins, the sins you bring here with you. I hope that people look at it and are all the more grateful when they look at this bronze Jesus here, this beautiful reminder of Christ. I hope they leave this building with His mercy, His peace."

They stood in silence for a moment.

Father Andrew sighed. "As far as your religious obligations, Paul, you've clearly repented. Now you can either accept the mercy of Christ...or not. That's your choice. That's it. No time in prison, no angry mob, no knife held at your neck will ever fix what you've done. You can't pay it back. You can't. You repent...and you accept."

Paul continued to look at the engraving over the door, but now he did not concentrate on the demons. Now he focused on St. Anthony's face, calm, almost serene. "I'm still not comfortable with this."

"And you shouldn't be. You should never be comfortable with what you've done, never let yourself excuse it, or try to shift the blame from yourself. Price paid or not, you'll always have to struggle with what you've done. Someday, you may even have to share it with others."

Paul swallowed. "Father, I'm scared. Knowing what I've done, what I was even capable of...how can I look at my wife again? How can I ever hold my children? Will I even see them the same way?"

"Look at me," Father Andrew instructed. "Do you have any urge to kill *me*?"

"*No.*"

The priest nodded. "No. You've repented. This doesn't define you. Understand, Paul, it's not even who you are anymore, and that's both a choice you make today, and it's because of the choices you've been making for the last decade. That's what repentance is, why it's different from just being sorry. It's seeing things as God sees them, in all their glory or ugliness, and adopting that perspective. When people are *sorry*, they say things like, 'I didn't mean to...' or 'I wish I hadn't...' When people have repented, they say 'I had no right... I had no excuse...' and they say the 'I can't believe I did that' in a wholly different way than do the merely apologetic. You've seen what you've done, who you've been, and opted to do and be something altogether different."

"But there has to be more..."

"Look up there, at the crucifix. See it as I've described it, as it *really* was—with the blood, and the torn flesh...see the agony of it...and you tell Him that's not enough for you. Tell Him that *you* need more."

Paul looked at the statue, his cheeks bathed in fresh tears, then lowered his eyes and slowly shook his head.

The priest's right hand rose and he placed it on Paul's head. "I absolve you in Christ's name. You've been forgiven much, Paul. Now do what Jesus said to those like you—love much. Not as payment, but just in response—to honor what He's done for you. In a sense, we all get off Scott-free upon entering Heaven. You're getting that now. React accordingly."

"What? Live a good life and try to earn it?"

"You can't earn this, Paul. You must honor it."

Paul continued to look at his shoes. He felt calmer, but there was no great sense of relief.

Father Andrew walked to the vestry and retrieved a broom, dustpan, and trash bag. He handed the dustpan to Paul. "Now, help me clean up the mess you've made on my steps."

Paul nodded. "Thank you, Father."

They swept the dead crow into the trash and the old priest left Paul alone. He stood in silence on the steps to St. Anthony's, looking out into the surrounding fields. The corn swayed gently in the moonlight and he walked across the asphalt parking lot to stand at the edge of the rows. After a moment's contemplation, he drew back his arm and flung the knife into the corn. This time he did not stop the arc of his pitch and he watched as the knife turned over and over, landing in the hidden depths of the field.

Like Deidra, once it entered the stalks, he would never see it again.

Paul turned away, walked back to where his Jeep sat parked, and drove off into the night.

THIRTY

No streetlights stood along the white rivers of gravel that cut through these northern fields. The road was dark beyond the Cherokee's headlights, and, to Paul, it looked as if the route were being created as the Jeep's approached. Ruts had been worn into the roads from the weight of vehicles, and pits filled with water after even the slightest rain. On either side, the corn swayed, whispering. The stalks were so tall they seemed to blot out the stars, turning the world dark.

Paul flipped on his brights in time to illuminate a small signpost that read Rural Route Six. He watched the sign go by the passenger's side window, turn red in his taillights, and his grip on the wheel tightened.

Route Six.

The road abruptly dipped, as if to give him confirmation that this was where he had his accident. This, he realized suddenly, was the first time he'd driven it since that night. His heart accelerated in his chest and his scarred back seemed to itch with the memory of its own creation.

June 1989. His freshman year at Stanley University had not been particularly enjoyable. He got so little enjoyment from anything since Deidra left him, even less since she wrote to say good-bye, but he'd tried to go on, tried to get through the daily chores of life.

He'd come home for the summer to find his job at Tony's Speedway Market waiting for him. It had been hot that year. He remembered that part clearly. Every day, around four in the afternoon, the skies had opened up and covered the town in a downpour—as if someone had picked up Harmony, Indiana and moved it to the tropics while everyone slept.

One afternoon, he'd come home from a day of bagging groceries and helping elderly ladies out to their cars—

Oh, no tips, ma'am. Customer Service is Tony's business.

—to find a letter from Deidra on the counter. It was the first one he'd received in months, and, as the daily rain fell against the window, he was showered in anxiety, the forces of hope and fear at war within his heart and brain. The envelope was fancy—marbled blue in color, with an edge that looked frayed, torn. He opened the letter only to find it wasn't a letter at all...

> *Mr. Benjamin Perkins*
> *requests the honor of your presence*
> *at the wedding of his daughter*
> *Deidra Jeanne Perkins*
> *&*
> *John Eric Shusett*

At the bottom of the invitation, written in Deidra's familiar scrawl, were the words: *I don't know if you can make it. But I'd really like to see you. Please come.*

How long Paul stood there looking down at the invitation he could not say. It was as if someone had slipped him the zombie drug from *The Serpent and the Rainbow*. He was alive, could actually feel the blood flowing through his veins and the pressure that pushed it along, but he was unable to move. At least he was standing. If he were lying down, they might think he'd died. He heard a voice seep into his consciousness...

"Paul?" His mother. She sounded frightened. "Paul, what is it?"

He didn't answer her. He couldn't form words. The drug. *Someone soaked this damn invitation in that zombie drug and now they'll put me in a coffin and let the worms have their way with me and I'll feel it because I'm still alive and I'll feel them burrow right through my heart and I can feel them now squirming around in there and it hurts, God, how it HURTS!*

"Paul?" She looked at what he had in his hand, took it from him to read it herself. Understanding seemed to come over her, and, worst of all, worse than anything she could have done at that moment, she looked relieved. *It's over,* that look said. *She'll be out of his life now. I never liked her. I never liked her for my son.* "Well, she must really value you as a friend if she wants you at her wedding."

Paul's paralysis broke. He backed away toward the door, then ran through the rain, ran to his Mustang. He stabbed the key into the ignition, slammed his foot down hard on the gas. His tires squealed, kicked up gravel as he raced onto these country roads. He had no idea where he was going, had no plan in mind. He only knew he couldn't stay in that house another second. Looking at that invitation was like watching water whirling into a drain, but it wasn't water slipping away, it was his future—all of his dreams, all of his hopes, all of his love spiraling down into darkness. And his mother was *happy* about it. From the look on her face he was surprised she hadn't done a little dance.

The Mustang sped along. How fast it had been going, Paul could not say. He hadn't been paying any attention. His mind hadn't even been in the car. All of his insides slipped down, sank into his right foot, gave it weight, gave the car speed.

He'd somehow made it to Route Six. The Mustang hit the crest of the first hill and went airborne, flung his guts and organs back up into place. The car landed with a violent thud and Paul's mind and body reunited. It hit the second hill and went airborne again. This time, when it landed he gave the steering wheel a panicky turn, sent it off the road and into the black cast-iron stove that seventy-year-old Alice Truman used for a mailbox. The stove sent him to the opposite side of the road. He went into the drainage ditch and the Mustang rolled over...the roof caved in...rolled twice...the windshield exploded into shards...rolled a third time...and then the world went black.

He awoke feeling strangely cold. It was June, tropical heat, and yet he'd been freezing. The Mustang lay upside down and Paul hung suspended from his seatbelt with blood in his face. He wiped it away with detached interest, then looked out his passenger's side window. The roof of the Mustang had folded like a tin can. Where the window had been, a pair of wrinkled, metal lips now curled into a smile full of jagged crystal teeth. His eyes turned lazily to his driver's side window. Corn grew down like green stalactites. He reached up and tried to find the latch to his seatbelt.

"*Paul.*" Not a single voice, but a choir...a group of voices singing his name.

He wiped a handful of fresh blood from his right eye and looked again through his window, swinging back and forth as if doing some acrobatic trick in a sling. He saw the shadows between the stalks move, uncoil—saw eyes like embers burning in the darkness.

The demons.

They were coming toward him.

Paul screamed; he reached up, tried to find the latch that would set him free. It should've been there, but he couldn't find it with his hands.

"*Thank you*," said the many voices speaking as one.

Fire. He heard the crackle of flames—just as it sounded on his sound effects tapes, like someone wadding paper into a microphone. Fluid had pooled below Paul on the floor—*the ceiling!*—of the Mustang. It might have been gasoline. He thought he remembered smelling gas. But if it had been gas, wouldn't the car have just blown up? Whatever it had been, it burned; tongues of red-hot fire licked his back, bathed it in heat, burned his shirt and the flesh beneath it.

Paul's screams grew louder. He saw activity in the corner of his eye, saw slithering scales, saw fluttering batwings. Sharp, yellow fangs smiled at him like the jagged glass of the passenger window and there were voices—voices calling out his name.

The creatures were all over the Mustang now. He heard them crawling across its exposed underbelly, heard them scratching at the metal, laughing, mewling in victory at the prize it held for them.

"*Thank you*," they told him again and again. "*Thank you*."

I'm in Hell, Paul remembered thinking. *I thought I'd won the Wide Game, but I lost...I've lost everything and the winners have come to collect.*

And then he was gone.

If it had been one of his movies, he would have used a slow fade to black. It was the language of film. Everything got fuzzy and the screen slowly grew dark.

The reality of it had been closer to a jump cut. He was in the car, the demons all around him, and then he wasn't. He was in an ambulance staring up at Robby. Robby looked frenzied. It reminded Paul of the day Sean fell. It reminded him of the Wide Game.

There was something strapped to Paul's face. An oxygen mask. It smelled funny and there was a horrible moment when Paul thought he might vomit.

"Paul, can you hear me?" Robby shouted at him. "Blink twice if you can hear me?"

Paul blinked twice.

Robby nodded. "You were in an accident. You've got a gash on your head and your back got cooked just a little."

He might have said more, but Paul had drifted back into unconsciousness. Later, Robby would tell Paul that he'd heard him screaming into the oxygen mask—things like, "I should've let them take the bitch" and, "I should've killed her in the shed when they asked me to." Paul remembered nothing of what he'd said; all he could remember was the pain.

That Paul's back had been "cooked just a little" had been a grand understatement. His back had been *barbecued*. For the rest of that long summer, Paul's mother had applied two different medicated ointments to it throughout the day and covered it in gauze. She hadn't said a word about the accident, hadn't discussed with him what had happened or punished him in any way. Perhaps she thought he'd suffered enough. Burns as severe as his had been never really healed, after all. They just stopped oozing and scarred over, leaving a lasting reminder.

In addition to his back, a sliver of glass from the windshield had found a new home in his scalp. It had taken a dozen or so stitches to close the gash left behind when the doctors removed it. Of course, it could have been worse. Robby told Paul that, if he hadn't been wearing his seatbelt, he would have been thrown out the windshield and the car would have rolled right on over him. If that had happened, all the king's horses and all the king's men would have scratched their heads and gone home. Game over.

Paul also might have burned alive in his car had Alice Truman not called Robby and the Harmony Fire Department to his aid. He'd called some weeks later to thank her. Insurance paid for her new cast-iron stove mailbox. Why she used a cast-iron stove to this day Paul still had to wonder.

He'd also thanked Robby for his help, told him what he'd seen that night, asked him if he believed it.

"If you want me to tell you you were so out of it you imagined the whole thing, I will," Robby said when he'd finished. "You might have just heard us working on your car to get you out."

"That's not a 'yes' or 'no' answer."

"After what we've been through, after what we've *seen*, I don't think I can give you one. All I can tell you is that, when we got there, you were alive but unconscious in a burning car, and you were alone."

Paul nodded and they were silent for a time.

"Look, Deidra was a fucking bitch for leaving," Robby blurted out at last. "And inviting you to her *wedding?* What the fuck is that? I think she was lookin' for you to pull a Dustin Hoffman and carry her off."

He'd probably been right.

Paul had taken his half of the golden char. around his neck and thrown it in the shoebox wh. kept Deidra's letters, notes, and cards. The wed. invitation was thrown away. His mother had tried to t. him he needed to send a gift, said to just ignore it was impolite, but there was nothing he could send. He'd already given her the greatest gift he had to give, and she obviously didn't want it.

That fall, Paul had gone back to Stanley University as if nothing had happened. But there were still times, when he caught a glimpse of his scars in the mirror, that the night he rolled his Mustang came to visit his memory. He'd think about the blood, about the flames. He'd think about a demon reaching through the broken driver's side window, touching his chest with its cold claws...forced to withdraw at the last possible moment in frustration.

A demon with dark, yellow-rimmed eyes that glowed like headlights in the rain.

Paul became aware of the water soaking his head and his eyes flew open like pulled blinds. *I've fallen asleep at the wheel*, he thought. *I've crashed again and now I'm wandering around in another rainstorm with a concussion.* He shuddered and rapidly blinked his eyes. A hot mist billowed all around him, obscured everything. *Oh, God,* his mind cried. *I'm in the fog! I'm in...*

Steam.

The water was hot. He looked up and saw a metal shower nozzle protruding from the haze like a Martian death ray, blasting him with heat. It wasn't a rain shower but a bathroom shower, and it was scalding.

Paul cringed and moved out from under the stream, groped through the haze, tried to find the handles that would turn off the water. He found them and began madly flipping, turning off the hot water and dousing himself in liquid ice before finally killing the spray entirely.

He looked at his naked body, his skin red from the hot shower. Next, he threw open the white plastic curtain and scanned the room. The mirror was a sheet of frosted glass. Blue-gray tile lined the walls. A brass sculpture of jumping dolphins sat on the marble sink, glistening with condensation. Above the toilet hung a wooden sign that read: *If You Dribble When You Piddle, Be A Sweetie And Wipe the Seatie*.

His mother's bathroom.

Paul chuckled. Frightened as he was, he had to laugh at the situation. He stepped from the bathtub and onto the linoleum, shivering at the drop in temperature. No towel had been laid out for him, only his clothing tossed on the floor. Still disoriented, he opened the cabinet under the sink. The towels were there, just as his mother had always kept them. He yanked one free, nearly toppling the whole stack, and dried himself. When he was no longer dripping, he wrapped the towel around his waist, scooped up his clothes, and opened the door.

The hallway was dark. With the exception of the gentle whir of air conditioning and the insane ticking of the grandfather clock downstairs, the house seemed totally quiet. Paul crept down the hall, saw a line of light painted beneath the door to the guest bedroom where he and Mary slept. He opened the door and walked in, trying to look normal, knowing that it wasn't possible under the circumstances.

Mary lay on the left side of the bed, he saw her crescent beneath the sheets, but he couldn't tell if she were sleeping. A light burned on the bedside table and the hands on the clock pointed to one. Had she stayed up waiting for him? She'd told him to go after Deidra, to talk to her, but had she been wondering if he might do more? Had she been worried, at least subconsciously, that he might not come back to her?

Paul had placed the bassinet next to his wife's side of the bed, and Megan now laid there in peaceful slumber, her mouth jerking into a smile then relaxing. God, how he longed to know what she thought. What joy filled her dreams?

Paul moved to the dresser, folded his damp clothes before going to the window. When he pulled the curtain back, he saw the Jeep in the glow of the porch light. The front was not smashed in. The fenders weren't dented. The tires weren't flat. The windshield seemed flawlessly in place. If he'd hit something on his way home, it didn't appear to have left its mark.

Robby had been right about Paul's car crash. He *had* wanted to die, just as Nancy had, just as Mick had. He'd tried to kill himself and *they* had come for him. Had Robby not dragged him free, not stopped him from dying...from committing suicide, they would have taken him straight to Hell and he would never have met Mary, would never have become a father to two beautiful children, would never have known what it meant to truly be alive.

Slowly, he turned to face his wife. He felt warm all over. Not from the heat of the shower. He felt warm because he was ashamed. "Mare? You up?"

"Yeah." She rolled over, propped her head in her hand. Her eyes were not accusing. Her face showed no anger or jealousy of any kind. He noticed she wore the Tweety Bird nightshirt he'd given her for Mothers' Day. "You okay?"

Paul nodded, then slid his hands across his wet hair and clasped them behind his neck, his thumbs touching the soft ridges of scarring on his back.

"You sure?"

"Yes."

She held out her arms to him. "Come here."

He dropped the towel and went to her, naked and scared. She held him in her arms and kissed his forehead. He laid his head on her breasts, the breasts that had nurtured his son and now kept his daughter happy and smiling into her fist at night. He heard the beating of her heart beneath them, muffled but steady, and, God only knew why, filled with love for him. They lay in silence for a while.

"You deserve so much better than me," Paul said at last.

"I don't want better," she whispered, then chuckled. "I don't know if that sounded right."

"If you wanted to leave me, I'd understand. I wouldn't blame you in the least."

"Did you sleep with her?" Mary's tone was businesslike. She knew the answer.

Paul's head jerked up, his eyes locked with hers. "*No.*"

"Did you talk things out, move past what happened?"

He thought of his conversation with Father Andrew, his *confession*, and the absolution he'd received afterward. "I think so. As past it as I'll ever get, I guess."

She smiled. "Then why would I want to leave you?"

"I don't know..." He felt his throat tighten. Tears ran freely from his eyes, soaking her nightshirt. "I've done things, before I met you, horrible, ugly things..."

Mary wiped the flowing tears from his cheek. "You've done nothing but show me tenderness and love since I've known you. I couldn't ask for a more loving husband, or a more caring father for my children. What's past is past, for both of us. You're my future and I don't want anything more than to love you."

And then she kissed him, deeply, passionately. She rolled onto him, and she did love him, gently, slowly. They bit their lips, muffled their sounds so as not to wake Megan from her dreaming. And when they had finished loving each other, Paul told Mary he loved her and she told him the same.

It's over at last, he thought, then drifted off to sleep with his wife held snugly in his arms.

EPILOGUE

The shadows in the bedroom seemed to writhe, to recoil. As Paul Rice slept his first good night's sleep in ten years, they slithered grudgingly from the corner, robbed of their victory. The shades oozed across the room, pausing a moment over Megan's bassinette and her innocent, slumbering form. She stopped smiling into her fist, squirmed, and flung her tiny arm out as if to fan a mosquito from her ear. The dark shapes retreated from the house, made their rounds through Harmony, hovering over all the other bassinettes, all the cribs, keeping their full count. The shadows smiled at the possibilities, the clean slates waiting for their mark, then they joined the darkness within the field of corn that swayed in the distance. There they would sulk and plan, waiting for their next opportunity to play.

MICHAEL WEST is a member of the Horror Writers Association and served as President of its local chapter, Indiana Horror Writers. He lives and works in the Indianapolis area with his wife, their two children, their bird, Rodan, and turtle, Gamera.

His children are convinced that spirits move through the woods near their home.

ALSO FROM GRAVESIDE TALES
SKULL FULL OF KISSES BY MICHAEL WEST
$12.95

Turn the page and enter a world of shadow, as Michael West brings together his most disturbing short stories—twisted tales of forbidden desires and ghoulish deeds, where nightmares manifest in the most mundane and unlikely of places...The basement of a Japanese restaurant, where a seductive creature promises comfort to a lonely hitman, if only he will set her free...A ruined city, where survivors of a natural disaster have become prey to something unnatural...An Indiana farmhouse, where a frightened child attempts to fool the Angel of Death...And the darkest regions of space, where a man fights to protect the woman he loves from invaders only he can see...

Ten reasons to lock your doors. Ten reasons to keep the lights on. Ten reasons why you may never sleep again.

Purchasable at GravesideBooks.com

ALSO FROM
GRAVESIDE TALES
HUFFER BY MICHAEL J. HULTQUIST $14.95

After huffing paint for too many years, Gus Gerring's life is thrown into turmoil when a Hawaiian-shirt clad entity he dubs "Satan" appears and imbues him with the power to see "evil" in other people, along with the choice to do something about it. But will knowing the evil deeds of his loved ones prove too much to take, even for Gus's chemical-ravaged mind? Especially when it comes to learning what his mother and her boyfriend had to do with his father's suicide, why his Uncle Ham is killing hookers down in Texas, or why the cops are beating a path to his door to get next week's lotto numbers. To Gus, it all seems like one horrible, huffing-induced nightmare. But is it?

Purchasable at GravesideBooks.com

ALSO FROM
GRAVESIDE TALES
THE BEAST WITHIN, EDITED BY MATT HULTS:
$16.95

Grab a silver bullet and prepare yourself for 20 tales of animalistic terror crafted by authors from around the world. Travel across the ages and go beyond the myth to discover the horrific secrets of the werebeasts. From ancient cultures to the high-tech future, nowhere is safe from the shape-shifting bloodlust of The Beast Within

Purchasable at GravesideBooks.com

ALSO FROM
GRAVESIDE TALES

HAWG BY STEVEN SHREWSBURY: $14.95

Blue collar tough Andrew White knows that in the rural community of Miller's Fork bad things are best left in the dark. He soon learns that monsters wear many shapes. In a populace rife with of vice and deception, something has broken loose ... something hidden and feral.

Purchasable at GravesideBooks.com

ALSO FROM
GRAVESIDE TALES

EVERDEAD BY RIO YOUERS: $14.95

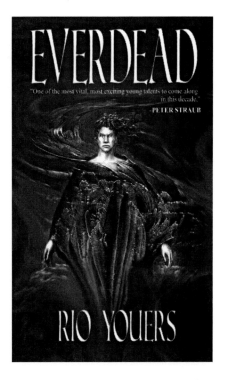

Toby Matthews has come to San Antonio to recover from a broken heart, and it seems that beautiful Cass Tait may be the cure. But as their relationship begins to bloom, they stumble upon an unspeakable darkness. They stare evil in the eye, they see its true heart, and know that only they can stop it. Before the sun goes down, they must decide whether to run …or whether to stand like heroes and fight.

Purchasable at GravesideBooks.com

ALSO FROM
GRAVESIDE TALES

FRIED! FAST FOOD, SLOW DEATHS:
EDITED BY COLLEEN MORRIS AND JOEL A. SUTHERLAND $14.95

23 stories of monsters, maniacs, murderers and milkshakes. Devour the tale of a band of hobos who crave human flesh. Chow down on the myth of an abandoned restaurant that serves as a gateway for lost and demented souls. Gorge yourself on the story of the veggie burger that turns human beings into human beans. Pig out on the account of the fast food joint that stands as humanity's last hope for survival in a zombie-infested world.

Purchasable at GravesideBooks.com

ALSO FROM
GRAVESIDE TALES

SIDESHOW P.I.: THE DEVIL'S GARDEN, BY NATHANIEL LAMBERT AND KEVIN SWEENEY: $12.95

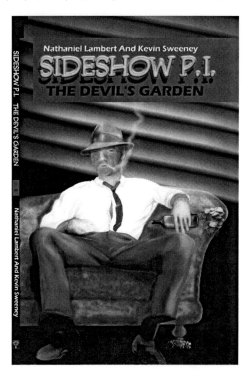

New Ramoth. A city covered in scar tissue, where survival of the fittest decides who's on top and crime is the only promotion system. Enter Eddie "Dog Boy" Gnash, ex-carnival freak turned private investigator. Now the bodies are piling up, and the fate of New Ramoth rests in the hands of this fur-covered freak—Eddie Gnash, Sideshow P.I.

Purchasable at GravesideBooks.com

ALSO FROM GRAVESIDE TALES

HARVEST HILL $16.95
31 TALES OF HALLOWEEN HORROR EDITED BY MICHAEL HULTQUIST AND DOUGLAS HUTCHESON.

Welcome to Harvest Hill, Tennessee: a seemingly idyllic community. But within the shadows of this restful town roams a centuries-old evil that rears itself in some awful form or influence every Halloween when the veil between worlds is thinnest. We offer a choice crop of truly disturbing accounts - large and small, stretching from the 1700s into the present day. If only the residents understood the unspeakable thing that has writhed and raged among them for ages, and keeps growing ... in HARVEST HILL.

Purchasable at GravesideBooks.com

ALSO FROM
GRAVESIDE TALES
CARNIVAL OF FEAR BY JG FAHERTY $15.95

The carnival is in town...
What was supposed to be an evening of fun and laughter for JD Cole and the other students of Whitebridge High turns into a never-ending night of terror. Trapped inside the Castle of Horrors by the demonic Proprietor, good friends and bitter rivals must band together to make it through the maze of torturous attractions, where fictional monsters come to life, eager to feast on human flesh. Vampires, zombies, werewolves, and aliens lurk around every corner as JD and his friends struggle from one room to the next, fighting for their sanity, fighting to survive, fighting to escape ... The Carnival of Fear.

Purchasable at GravesideBooks.com

ALSO FROM
GRAVESIDE TALES

DOPPELGÄNGER BY BYRON STARR: $14.95

James Taylor has always had strange dreams. Now a new terror has entered James's sleep, bringing with it visions of death and carnage. Visions of a beast that stalks human prey and slaughters without remorse. Visions that soon become a reality for the residents of Newton, Texas as the creature's victims are discovered. Like it or not, James knows it is up to him to act. Alone or with the help of local law enforcement, he plans to use his special talent to stop this monstrous Doppelgänger before it strikes again.

Purchasable at GravesideBooks.com

The Beast Within 2

Edited by Jennifer Brozek

Coming Soon